I0595533

James Thomas Fields

Favorite Authors;

A Companion Book of Prose and Poetry

James Thomas Fields

Favorite Authors;
A Companion Book of Prose and Poetry

ISBN/EAN: 9783337077280

Printed in Europe, USA, Canada, Australia, Japan

Cover: Foto ©Andreas Hilbeck / pixelio.de

More available books at **www.hansebooks.com**

Nathaniel Hawthorne.

Favorite Authors

A COMPANION-BOOK

OF

PROSE AND POETRY

"My Books, my best companions."

Fletcher

BOSTON

JAMES R. OSGOOD AND COMPANY,

LATE TICKNOR & FIELDS, AND FIELDS, OSGOOD, & CO.

1873

Entered according to Act of Congress, in the year 1860, by
TICKNOR AND FIELDS,
In the Clerk's Office of the District Court of the District of Massachusetts

UNIVERSITY PRESS:
WELCH, BIGELOW, AND COMPANY.
CAMBRIDGE.

CONTENTS.

A VIRTUOSO'S COLLECTION.

By NATHANIEL HAWTHORNE.

THE other day, having a leisure hour at my disposal, I stepped into a new museum, to which my notice was casually drawn by a small and unobtrusive sign: "To be seen here, a Virtuoso's Collection." Such was the simple yet not altogether unpromising announcement that turned my steps aside for a little while from the sunny sidewalk of our principal thoroughfare. Mounting a sombre staircase, I pushed open a door at its summit, and found myself in the presence of a person, who mentioned the moderate sum that would entitle me to admittance.

"Three shillings, Massachusetts tenor," said he. "No, I mean half a dollar, as you reckon in these days."

While searching my pocket for the coin, I glanced at the doorkeeper, the marked character and individuality of whose aspect encouraged me to expect something not quite in the ordinary way. He wore an old-fashioned great-coat, much faded, within which his meagre person was so completely enveloped, that the rest of his attire was undistinguishable. But his visage was remarkably wind-flushed, sunburnt, and weather-worn, and had a most unquiet, nervous, and apprehensive expression. It seemed as if this man had some all-important object in view, some point of deepest interest to be decided, some momentous question to ask, might he but hope for a reply. As it was evident, however, that I

1

could have nothing to do with his private affairs, I passed through an open doorway, which admitted me into the extensive hall of the museum.

Directly in front of the portal was the bronze statue of a youth with winged feet. He was represented in the act of flitting away from earth, yet wore such a look of earnest invitation that it impressed me like a summons to enter the hall

" It is the original statue of Opportunity, by the ancient sculptor Lysippus," said a gentleman who now approached me. " I place it at the entrance of my museum, because it is not at all times that one can gain admittance to such a collection."

The speaker was a middle-aged person, of whom it was not easy to determine whether he had spent his life as a scholar or as a man of action ; in truth, all outward and obvious peculiarities had been worn away by an extensive and promiscuous intercourse with the world. There was no mark about him of profession, individual habits, or scarcely of country ; although his dark complexion and high features, made me conjecture that he was a native of some southern clime of Europe. At all events, he was evidently the virtuoso in person.

" With your permission," said he, " as we have no descriptive catalogue, I will accompany you through the museum, and point out whatever may be most worthy of attention. In the first place, here is a choice collection of stuffed animals."

Nearest the door stood the outward semblance of a wolf, exquisitely prepared, it is true, and showing a very wolfish fierceness in the large glass eyes which were inserted into its wild and crafty head. Still it was merely the skin of a wolf, with nothing to distinguish it from other individuals of that unlovely breed.

" How does this animal deserve a place in your collection ?" inquired I.

"It is the wolf that devoured Little Red Riding Hood," answered the virtuoso; "and by his side — with a milder and more matronly look, as you perceive — stands the she-wolf that suckled Romulus and Remus."

"Ah, indeed!" exclaimed I. "And what lovely lamb is this with the snow-white fleece, which seems to be of as delicate a texture as innocence itself?"

"Methinks you have but carelessly read Spenser," replied my guide, "or you would at once recognize the 'milk-white lamb' which Una led. But I set no great value upon the lamb. The next specimen is better worth our notice."

"What!" cried I, "this strange animal, with the black head of an ox upon the body of a white horse? Were it possible to suppose it, I should say that this was Alexander's steed Bucephalus."

"The same," said the virtuoso. "And can you likewise give a name to the famous charger that stands beside him?"

Next to the renowned Bucephalus stood the mere skeleton of a horse, with the white bones peeping through his ill-conditioned hide; but, if my heart had not warmed towards that pitiful anatomy, I might as well have quitted the museum at once. Its rarities had not been collected with pain and toil from the four quarters of the earth, and from the depths of the sea, and from the palaces and sepulchres of ages, for those who could mistake this illustrious steed.

"It is Rosinante!" exclaimed I, with enthusiasm.

And so it proved. My admiration for the noble and gallant horse caused me to glance with less interest at the other animals, although many of them might have deserved the notice of Cuvier himself. There was the donkey which Peter Bell cudgelled so soundly, and a brother of the same species who had suffered a similar infliction from the ancient prophet Balaam. Some doubts were entertained, however, as to the authenticity of the latter beast. My guide pointed out the venerable Argus, that faithful dog of Ulysses, and

also another dog, (for so the skin bespoke it,) which, though
imperfectly preserved, **seemed once to** have had three heads.
It was Cerberus. I was considerably amused at detecting
in an obscure corner **the fox that became** so famous by the
loss of his tail. There were several stuffed cats, which, as a
dear **lover of that** comfortable **beast,** attracted my affectionate regards. **One was Dr.** Johnson's cat Hodge ; and in the
same **row stood** the favorite cats **of** Mahomet, Gray, **and**
Walter Scott, together with Puss in Boots, and a cat of very
noble aspect **who had** once been a deity of ancient Egypt.
Byron's **tame bear came next. I must not forget to mention**
the Erymanthean boar, **the** skin of St. George's dragon, and
that of the **serpent** Python ; and another skin with beautifully variegated hues, supposed **to have been** the garment
of the "spirited sly snake" which tempted **Eve.** Against
the walls were suspended the horns of **the stag that Shake-**
speare shot ; and **on** the floor lay the ponderous shell of the
tortoise which **fell upon the head** of Æschylus. In one **row,**
as natural as life, stood the sacred bull **Apis,** the "cow with
the crumpled **horn," and** a very wild-looking young heifer,
which I guessed to be **the cow that jumped** over **the moon.**
She was probably killed by **the** rapidity of her descent. **As**
I turned away, my eyes fell upon an indescribable monster,
which proved to be a griffin.

"I look in vain," observed I, "for the skin of **an** animal
which might well deserve the closest study of a naturalist, —
the winged horse **Pegasus."**

"He is not yet dead," replied **the virtuoso ;** "but he **is so**
hard ridden by many young **gentlemen of** the day that I
hope soon to add his skin **and skeleton to** my collection."

We now passed to the **next alcove of** the hall, in which
was a multitude **of** stuffed birds. **They were** very prettily
arranged, some upon **the branches of trees,** others brooding
upon nests, and others suspended by wires so artificially that
they seemed **in** the very act of flight. **Among them** was a

white dove, with a withered branch of olive-leaves in her mouth.

"Can this be the very dove," inquired I, "that brought the message of peace and hope to the tempest-beaten passengers of the ark?"

"Even so," said my companion.

"And this raven, I suppose," continued I, "is the same that fed Elijah in the wilderness."

"The raven? No," said the virtuoso; "it is a bird of modern date. He belonged to one Barnaby Rudge; and many people fancied that the Devil himself was disguised under his sable plumage. But poor Grip has drawn his last cork, and has been forced to 'say die' at last. This other raven, hardly less curious, is that in which the soul of King George I. revisited his lady love, the Duchess of Kendall."

My guide next pointed out Minerva's owl and the vulture that preyed upon the liver of Prometheus. There was likewise the sacred ibis of Egypt, and one of the Stymphalides which Hercules shot in his sixth labor. Shelley's skylark, Bryant's water-fowl, and a pigeon from the belfry of the Old South Church, preserved by N. P. Willis, were placed on the same perch. I could not but shudder on beholding Coleridge's albatross, transfixed with the Ancient Mariner's crossbow shaft. Beside this bird of awful poesy stood a gray goose of very ordinary aspect.

"Stuffed goose is no such rarity," observed I. "Why do you preserve such a specimen in your museum?"

"It is one of the flock whose cackling saved the Roman Capitol," answered the virtuoso. "Many geese have cackled and hissed both before and since; but none, like those, have clamored themselves into immortality."

There seemed to be little else that demanded notice in this department of the museum, unless we except Robinson Crusoe's parrot, a live phoenix, a footless bird of paradise, and a splendid peacock, supposed to be the same that once

contained the soul of Pythagoras. I therefore passed to the
next alcove, the shelves of which were covered with a miscellaneous collection of curiosities, such as are usually found
in similar establishments. One of the first things that took
my eye was a strange-looking cap, woven of some substance
that appeared to be neither woollen, cotton, nor linen.

"Is that a magician's cap?" I asked.

"No," replied the virtuoso; "it is merely Dr. Franklin's
cap of asbestos. But here is one which, perhaps, may suit
you better. It is the wishing-cap of Fortunatus. Will you
try it on?"

"By no means," answered I, putting it aside with my
hand. "The day of wild wishes is past with me. I desire
nothing that may not come in the ordinary course of Providence."

"Then probably," returned the virtuoso, "you will not be
tempted to rub this lamp?"

While speaking, he took from the shelf an antique brass
lamp, curiously wrought with embossed figures, but so covered with verdigris that the sculpture was almost eaten
away.

"It is a thousand years," said he, "since the genius of this
lamp constructed Aladdin's palace in a single night. But
he still retains his power; and the man who rubs Aladdin's
lamp has but to desire either a palace or a cottage."

"I might desire a cottage," replied I; "but I would have
it founded on sure and stable truth, not on dreams and fan-
tasies. I have learned to look for the real and true."

My guide next showed me Prospero's magic wand, broken
into three fragments by the hand of its mighty master. On
the same shelf lay the gold ring of ancient Gyges, which
enabled the wearer to walk invisible. On the other side of
the alcove was a tall looking-glass in a frame of ebony, but
veiled with a curtain of purple silk, through the rents of
which the gleam of the mirror was perceptible.

"This is Cornelius Agrippa's magic glass," observed the virtuoso. "Draw aside the curtain, and picture any human form within your mind, and it will be reflected in the mirror."

"It is enough if I can picture it within my mind," answered I. "Why should I wish it to be repeated in the mirror? But, indeed, these works of magic have grown wearisome to me. There are so many greater wonders in the world, to those who keep their eyes open and their sight undimmed by custom, that all the delusions of the old sorcerers seem flat and stale. Unless you can show me something really curious, I care not to look farther into your museum."

"Ah, well, then," said the virtuoso, composedly, "perhaps you may deem some of my antiquarian rarities deserving of a glance."

He pointed out the iron mask, now corroded with rust; and my heart grew sick at the sight of this dreadful relic, which had shut out a human being from sympathy with his race. There was nothing half so terrible in the axe that beheaded King Charles, nor in the dagger that slew Henry of Navarre, nor in the arrow that pierced the heart of William Rufus, — all of which were shown to me. Many of the articles derived their interest, such as it was, from having been formerly in the possession of royalty. For instance, here was Charlemagne's sheep-skin cloak, the flowing wig of Louis Quatorze, the spinning-wheel of Sardanapalus, and King Stephen's famous breeches which cost him but a crown. The heart of the Bloody Mary, with the word "Calais" worn into its diseased substance, was preserved in a bottle of spirits; and near it lay the golden case in which the queen of Gustavus Adolphus treasured up that hero's heart. Among these relics and heirlooms of kings I must not forget the long, hairy ears of Midas, and a piece of bread which had been changed to gold by the touch of that unlucky monarch. And as Grecian Helen was a queen, it may here be mentioned that I was permitted to take into my hand a lock of her golden hair and the bowl which a sculptor modelled from the curve of her perfect breast. Here, likewise, was the robe that smothered Agamemnon, Nero's fiddle, the Czar Peter's brandy-bottle, the crown of Semiramis, and Canute's sceptre which he extended over the sea. That my own land may not deem itself neglected, let me add that I was favored with a sight of the skull of King Philip, the famous Indian chief, whose head the Puritans smote off and exhibited upon a pole.

"Show me something else," said I to the virtuoso. "Kings are in such an artificial position, that people in the ordinary walks of life cannot feel an interest in their relics. If you could show me the straw hat of sweet little Nell, I would far rather see it than a king's golden crown."

"There it is," said my guide, pointing carelessly with his staff to the straw hat in question. "But, indeed, you are hard to please. Here are the seven-league boots. Will you try them on?"

"Our modern railroads have superseded their use," answered I; "and as to these cowhide boots, I could show you quite as curious a pair at the Transcendental community in Roxbury."

We next examined a collection of swords and other weapons, belonging to different epochs, but thrown together without much attempt at arrangement. Here was Arthur's sword Excalibar, and that of the Cid Campeador, and the sword of Brutus rusted with Cæsar's blood and his own, and the sword of Joan of Arc, and that of Horatius, and that with which Virginius slew his daughter, and the one which Dionysius suspended over the head of Damocles. Here also was Arria's sword, which she plunged into her own breast, in order to taste of death before her husband. The crooked blade of Saladin's cimeter next attracted my notice. I know not by what chance, but so it happened, that the sword of one of our militia-generals was suspended between Don Quixote's lance and the brown blade of Hudibras. My heart throbbed high at the sight of the helmet of Miltiades and the spear that was broken in the breast of Epaminondas. I recognized the shield of Achilles by its resemblance to the admirable cast in the possession of Professor Felton. Nothing in this apartment interested me more than Major Pitcairn's pistol, the discharge of which, at Lexington, began the war of the Revolution, and was reverberated in thunder around the land for seven long years. The bow of Ulysses, though unstrung for ages, was placed against the wall, together with a sheaf of Robin Hood's arrows and the rifle of Daniel Boone.

"Enough of weapons," said I, at length; "although I would gladly have seen the sacred shield which fell from heaven in the time of Numa. And surely you should obtain the sword which Washington unsheathed at Cambridge. But the collection does you much credit. Let us pass on."

In the next alcove we saw the golden thigh of Pythagoras, which had so divine a meaning; and, by one of the queer analogies to which the virtuoso seemed to be addicted, this ancient emblem lay on the same shelf with Peter Stuyvesant's wooden leg, that was fabled to be of silver. Here was a remnant of the Golden Fleece, and a sprig of yellow leaves that resembled the foliage of a frost-bitten elm, but was duly authenticated as a portion of the golden branch by which Æneas gained admittance to the realm of Pluto. Atalanta's golden apple and one of the apples of discord were wrapped in the napkin of gold which Rhampsinitus brought from Hades; and the whole were deposited in the golden vase of Bias, with its inscription: "To THE WISEST."

"And how did you obtain this vase?" said I to the virtuoso.

"It was given me long ago," replied he, with a scornful expression in his eye, "because I had learned to despise all things."

It had not escaped me that, though the virtuoso was evidently a man of high cultivation, yet he seemed to lack sympathy with the spiritual, the sublime, and the tender. Apart from the whim that had led him to devote so much time, pains, and expense to the collection of this museum, he impressed me as one of the hardest and coldest men of the world whom I had ever met.

"To despise all things!" repeated I. "This, at best, is the wisdom of the understanding. It is the creed of a man whose soul, whose better and diviner part, has never been awakened, or has died out of him."

"I did not think you were still so young," said the virtuoso. "Should you live to my years, you will acknowledge that the vase of Bias was not ill bestowed."

Without further discussion of the point, he directed my attention to other curiosities. I examined Cinderella's little glass slipper, and compared it with one of Diana's sandals, and with Fanny Elssler's shoe, which bore testimony to the muscular character of her illustrious foot. On the same shelf were Thomas the Rhymer's green velvet shoes, and the brazen shoe of Empedocles which was thrown out of Mount Ætna. Anacreon's drinking-cup was placed in apt juxtaposition with one of Tom Moore's wine-glasses and Circe's magic bowl. These were symbols of luxury and riot; but near them stood the cup whence Socrates drank his hemlock, and that which Sir Philip Sidney put from his death-parched lips to bestow the draught upon a dying soldier. Next appeared a cluster of tobacco-pipes, consisting of Sir Walter Raleigh's, the earliest on record, Dr. Parr's, Charles Lamb's, and the first calumet of peace which was ever smoked between a European and an Indian. Among other musical instruments, I noticed the lyre of Orpheus and those of Homer and Sappho, Dr. Franklin's famous whistle, the trumpet of Anthony Van Corlear, and the flute which Goldsmith played upon in his rambles through the French provinces. The staff of Peter the Hermit stood in a corner with that of good old Bishop Jewel, and one of ivory, which had belonged to Papirius, the Roman Senator. The ponderous club of Hercules was close at hand. The virtuoso showed me the chisel of Phidias, Claude's palette, and the brush of Apelles, observing that he intended to bestow the former either on Greenough, Crawford, or Powers, and the two latter upon Washington Allston. There was a small vase of oracular gas from Delphos, which I trust will be submitted to the scientific analysis of Professor Silliman. I was deeply moved on beholding a vial of the tears into which Niobe was dissolved; nor less so on learning that a shapeless fragment of salt was a relic of that victim of despondency and sinful regrets, Lot's wife. My companion appeared to set great value upon some Egyptian darkness in a blacking-jug. Several of the shelves were covered by a collection of coins, among which, however, I remember none but the Splendid Shilling, celebrated by Phillips, and a dollar's worth of the iron money of Lycurgus, weighing about fifty pounds.

Walking carelessly onward, I had nearly fallen over a huge bundle, like a pedler's pack, done up in sackcloth, and very securely strapped and corded.

"It is Christian's burden of sin," said the virtuoso.

"O, pray let us open it!" cried I. "For many a year I have longed to know its contents."

"Look into your own consciousness and memory," replied the virtuoso. "You will there find a list of whatever it contains."

As this was an undeniable truth, I threw a melancholy look at the burden and passed on. A collection of old garments, hanging on pegs, was worthy of some attention, especially the shirt of Nessus, Cæsar's mantle, Joseph's coat of many colors, the Vicar of Bray's cassock, Goldsmith's peach-bloom suit, a pair of President Jefferson's scarlet breeches, John Randolph's red-baize hunting-shirt, the drab small-clothes of the Stout Gentleman, and the rags of the "man all tattered and torn." George Fox's hat impressed me with deep reverence as a relic of perhaps **the truest** apostle that has appeared on earth for these eighteen hundred years. My eye was next **attracted** by an old pair of shears, which I should have taken for a memorial of some famous tailor, only that the virtuoso pledged his veracity that they were the identical scissors of Atropos. He also showed me a broken hour-glass **which** had been thrown aside by Father Time, together with the old gentleman's gray forelock, tastefully braided into a brooch. In the hour-glass was the handful of sand, the grains of which had numbered the years of the Cumæan sibyl. I think that it was in this alcove that I saw the inkstand which Luther threw at the **Devil, and** the **ring** which Essex, **while** under sentence of death, sent to Queen **Elizabeth.** And here was the blood-incrusted pen of **steel with which Faust** signed away his salvation.

The virtuoso now opened **the door of a** closet, and showed me a lamp burning, while three others stood unlighted by its side. One of the three was the lamp of Diogenes, another that of Guy Fawkes, and the third that which Hero set forth **to** the midnight breeze in the high tower of Abydos.

"See!" said the virtuoso, blowing with all his force at the **lighted lamp.**

The flame quivered and shrank away **from** his breath, but clung to the wick, and resumed its brilliancy as soon as **the** blast was exhausted.

"**It** is an undying lamp from the **tomb of** Charlemagne," observed my guide. "That flame was kindled a thousand years ago."

"How ridiculous **to** kindle **an** unnatural light in tombs!" exclaimed **I.** "We should **seek** to behold the dead in the light of heaven. **But what is the meaning of** this chafing-dish **of glowing coals?"**

"That," answered the virtuoso, "is the original fire which Prometheus stole from heaven. Look steadfastly into it, and you will discern another curiosity."

I gazed into that fire, — which, symbolically, was the origin of all that was bright and glorious in the soul of man, — and in the midst of it, behold, a little reptile, sporting with evident enjoyment of the fervid heat! It was a salamander.

"What a sacrilege!" cried I, with inexpressible disgust. "Can you find no better use for this ethereal fire than to cherish a loathsome reptile in it? Yet there are men who abuse the sacred fire of their own souls to as foul and guilty a purpose."

The virtuoso made no answer except by a dry laugh and an assurance that the salamander was the very same which Benvenuto Cellini had seen in his father's houschold fire. He then proceeded to show me other rarities; for this closet appeared to be the receptacle of what he considered most valuable in his collection.

"There," said he, "is the Great Carbuncle of the White Mountains."

I gazed with no little interest at this mighty gem, which it had been one of the wild projects of my youth to discover. Possibly it might have looked brighter to me in those days than now; at all events, it had not such brilliancy as to detain me long from the other articles of the museum. The virtuoso pointed out to me a crystalline stone which hung by a gold chain against the wall.

"That is the philosopher's stone," said he.

"And have you the elixir vitæ which generally accompanies it?" inquired I.

"Even so; this urn is filled with it," he replied. "A draught would refresh you. Here is Hebe's cup; will you quaff a health from it?"

My heart thrilled within me at the idea of such a reviving draught; for methought I had great need of it after travel ling so far on the dusty road of life. But I know not whether it were a peculiar glance in the virtuoso's eye, or the circumstance that this most precious liquid was contained in an antique sepulchral urn, that made me pause. Then came many a thought with which, in the calmer and better hours of life, I had strengthened myself to feel that Death is the very friend whom, in his due season, even the happiest mortal should be willing to embrace.

"No; I desire not an earthly immortality," said I. "Were man to live longer on the earth, the spiritual would die out of him. The spark of ethereal fire would be choked by the material, the sensual. There is a celestial something within us that requires, after a certain time, the atmosphere of heaven to preserve it from decay and ruin. I will have none of this liquid. You do well to keep it in a sepulchral urn; for it would produce death while bestowing the shadow of life."

"All this is unintelligible to me," responded my guide, with indifference. "Life — earthly life — is the only good. But you refuse the draught? Well, it is not likely to be offered twice within one man's experience. Probably you have griefs which you seek to forget in death. I can enable you to forget them in life. Will you take a draught of Lethe?"

As he spoke, the virtuoso took from the shelf a crystal vase containing a sable liquor, which caught no reflected image from the objects around.

"Not for the world!" exclaimed I, shrinking back. "I can spare none of my recollections, not even those of error or sorrow. They are all alike the food of my spirit. As well never to have lived as to lose them now."

Without further parley we passed to the next alcove, the shelves of which were burdened with ancient volumes and with those rolls of papyrus in which was treasured up the eldest wisdom of the earth. Perhaps the most valuable

work in the collection, to a bibliomaniac, was the Book of
Hermes. For my part, however, I would have given a
higher price for those six of the Sibyl's books which Tarquin
refused to purchase, and which the virtuoso informed me he
had himself found in the cave of Trophonius. Doubtless
these old volumes contain prophecies of the fate of Rome,
both as respects the decline and fall of her temporal empire
and the rise of her spiritual one. Not without value, likewise, was the work of Anaxagoras on Nature, hitherto sup
posed to be irrecoverably lost, and the missing treatises of
Longinus, by which modern criticism might profit, and those
books of Livy for which the classic student has so long sor-
rowed without hope. Among these precious tomes I observed
the original manuscript of the Koran, and also that of the
Mormon Bible in Joe Smith's authentic autograph. Alexander's copy of the Iliad was also there, enclosed in the
jewelled casket of Darius, still fragrant of the perfumes
which the Persian kept in it.

Opening an iron-clasped volume, bound in black leather, I
discovered it to be Cornelius Agrippa's book of magic; and
it was rendered still more interesting by the fact that many
flowers, ancient and modern, were pressed between its leaves.
Here was a rose from Eve's bridal bower, and all those red
and white roses which were plucked in the garden of the
Temple by the partisans of York and Lancaster. Here was
Halleck's Wild Rose of Alloway. Cowper had contributed
a Sensitive-Plant, and Wordsworth an Eglantine, and Burns
a Mountain Daisy, and Kirke White a Star of Bethlehem,
and Longfellow a Sprig of Fennel, with its yellow flowers.
James Russell Lowell had given a Pressed Flower, but fragrant still, which had been shadowed in the Rhine. There
was also a sprig from Southey's Holly-Tree. One of the
most beautiful specimens was a Fringed Gentian, which
had been plucked and preserved for immortality by Bryant.
From Jones Very, a poet whose voice is scarcely heard

among us by reason of its depth, there was a Windflower and a Columbine.

As I closed Cornelius Agrippa's magic volume, an old, mildewed letter fell upon the floor. It proved to be an autograph from the Flying Dutchman to his wife. I could linger no longer among books; for the afternoon was waning, and there was yet much to see. The bare mention of a few more curiosities must suffice. The immense skull of Polyphemus was recognizable by the cavernous hollow in the centre of the forehead where once had blazed the giant's single eye. The tub of Diogenes, Medea's caldron, and Psyche's vase of beauty were placed one within another. Pandora's box, without the lid, stood next, containing nothing but the girdle of Venus, which had been carelessly flung into it. A bundle of birch rods which had been used by Shenstone's schoolmistress were tied up with the Countess of Salisbury's garter. I know not which to value most, a roc's egg as big as an ordinary hogshead, or the shell of the egg which Columbus set upon its end. Perhaps the most delicate article in the whole museum was Queen Mab's chariot, which, to guard it from the touch of meddlesome fingers, was placed under a glass tumbler.

Several of the shelves were occupied by specimens of entomology. Feeling but little interest in the science, I noticed only Anacreon's grasshopper, and a humble-bee which had been presented to the virtuoso by Ralph Waldo Emerson.

In the part of the hall which we had now reached I observed a curtain, that descended from the ceiling to the floor in voluminous folds, of a depth, richness, and magnificence which I had never seen equalled. It was not to be doubted that this splendid though dark and solemn veil concealed a portion of the museum even richer in wonders than that through which I had already passed; but, on my attempting to grasp the edge of the curtain and draw it aside, it proved to be an illusive picture.

"You need not blush," remarked the virtuoso; "for that same curtain deceived Zeuxis. It is the celebrated painting of Parrhasius."

In a range with the curtain there were a number of other choice pictures by artists of ancient days. Here was the famous cluster of grapes by Zeuxis, so admirably depicted that it seemed as if the ripe juice were bursting forth. As to the picture of the old woman by the same illustrious painter, and which was so ludicrous that he himself died with laughing at it, I cannot say that it particularly moved my risibility. Ancient humor seems to have little power over modern muscles. Here, also, was the horse painted by Apelles, which living horses neighed at; his first portrait of Alexander the Great; and his last unfinished picture of Venus asleep. Each of these works of art, together with others by Parrhasius, Timanthes, Polygnotus, Apollodorus, Pausias, and Pamphilus, required more time and study than I could bestow for the adequate perception of their merits. I shall therefore leave them undescribed and uncriticised, nor attempt to settle the question of superiority between ancient and modern art.

For the same reason I shall pass lightly over the specimens of antique sculpture which this indefatigable and fortunate virtuoso had dug out of the dust of fallen empires. Here was Ætion's cedar statue of Æsculapius, much decayed, and Alcon's iron statue of Hercules, lamentably rusted. Here was the statue of Victory, six feet high, which the Jupiter Olympus of Phidias had held in his hand. Here was a forefinger of the Colossus of Rhodes, seven feet in length. Here was the Venus Urania of Phidias, and other images of male and female beauty or grandeur, wrought by sculptors who appear never to have debased their souls by the sight of any meaner forms than those of gods or godlike mortals. But the deep simplicity of these great works was not to be comprehended by a mind excited and disturbed, as

mine was, by the various objects that had recently been presented to it.   I therefore turned away with merely a passing
glance, resolving on some future occasion to brood over each
individual statue and picture until my inmost spirit should
feel their excellence.   In this department, again, I noticed
the tendency to whimsical combinations and ludicrous analogies which seemed to influence many of the arrangements of
the museum.   The wooden statue so well known as the
Palladium of Troy was placed in close apposition with the
wooden head of General Jackson which was stolen a few
years since from the bows of the frigate Constitution.

We had now completed the circuit of the spacious hall,
and found ourselves again near the door.   Feeling somewhat
wearied with the survey of so many novelties and antiqui-
ties, I sat down upon Cowper's sofa, while the virtuoso threw
himself carelessly into Rabelais's easy-chair.   Casting my
eyes upon the opposite wall, I was surprised to perceive the
shadow of a man flickering unsteadily across the wainscot,
and looking as if it were stirred by some breath of air that
found its way through the door or windows.   No substantial
figure was visible from which this shadow might be thrown ;
nor, had there been such, was there any sunshine that would
have caused it to darken upon the wall.

"It is Peter Schlemihl's shadow," observed the virtuoso,
" and one of the most valuable articles in my collection."

" Methinks a shadow would have made a fitting doorkeeper
to such a museum," said I ; " although, indeed, yonder figure
has something strange and fantastic about him, which suits
well enough with many of the impressions which I have
received here.   Pray, who is he ? "

While speaking, I gazed more scrutinizingly than before
at the antiquated presence of the person who had admitted
me, and who still sat on his bench with the same restless
aspect, and dim, confused, questioning anxiety that I had
noticed on my first entrance.   At this moment he looked

eagerly toward us, and, half starting from his seat, addressed me.

"I beseech you, kind sir," said he, in a cracked, melancholy tone, "have pity on the most unfortunate man in the world. For Heaven's sake, answer me a single question! Is this the town of Boston?"

"You have recognized him now," said the virtuoso. "It is Peter Rugg, the missing man. I chanced to meet him the other day still in search of Boston, and conducted him hither; and, as he could not succeed in finding his friends, I have taken him into my service as doorkeeper. He is somewhat too apt to ramble, but otherwise a man of trust and integrity."

"And might I venture to ask," continued I, "to whom am I indebted for this afternoon's gratification?"

The virtuoso, before replying, laid his hand upon an antique dart or javelin, the rusty steel head of which seemed to have been blunted, as if it had encountered the resistance of a tempered shield, or breastplate.

"My name has not been without its distinction in the world for a longer period than that of any other man alive," answered he. "Yet many doubt of my existence; perhaps you will do so to-morrow. This dart which I hold in my hand was once grim Death's own weapon. It served him well for the space of four thousand years; but it fell blunted as you see, when he directed it against my breast."

These words were spoken with the calm and cold courtesy of manner that had characterized this singular personage throughout our interview. I fancied, it is true, that there was a bitterness indefinably mingled with his tone, as of one cut off from natural sympathies and blasted with a doom that had been inflicted on no other human being, and by the results of which he had ceased to be human. Yet, withal, it seemed one of the most terrible consequences of that doom that the victim no longer regarded it as a calamity, but had finally accepted it as the greatest good that could have befallen him.

" You are the Wandering Jew ! " exclaimed I.

The virtuoso bowed, without emotion of any kind, for, by centuries of custom, he had almost lost the sense of strangeness in his fate, and was but imperfectly conscious of the astonishment and awe with which it affected such as are capable of death.

" Your doom is indeed a fearful one ! " said I, with irrepressible feeling and a frankness that afterwards startled me ; " yet perhaps the ethereal spirit is not entirely extinct under all this corrupted or frozen mass of earthly life. Perhaps the immortal spark may yet be rekindled by a breath of heaven. Perhaps you may yet be permitted to die before it is too late to live eternally. You have my prayers for such a consummation. Farewell."

" Your prayers will be in vain," replied he, with a smile of cold triumph. " My destiny is linked with the realities of earth. You are welcome to your visions and shadows of a future state ; but give me what I can see, and touch, and understand, and I ask no more."

" It is indeed too late," thought I. " The soul is dead within him."

Struggling between pity and horror, I extended my hand, to which the virtuoso gave his own, still with the habitual courtesy of a man of the world, but without a single heartthrob of human brotherhood. The touch seemed like ice, yet I know not whether morally or physically. As I departed, he bade me observe that the inner door of the hall was constructed with the ivory leaves of the gateway through which Æneas and the Sibyl had been dismissed from Hades.

DORA.

By ALFRED TENNYSON.

WITH Farmer Allan at the farm abode
William and Dora. William was his son,
And she his niece. He often looked at them,
And often thought, "I'll make them man and wife."
Now Dora felt her uncle's will in all,
And yearned towards William; but the youth, because
He had been always with her in the house,
Thought not of Dora.

           Then there came a day
When Allan called his son, and said, "My son:
I married late, but I would wish to see
My grandchild on my knees before I die:
And I have set my heart upon a match.
Now therefore look to Dora; she is well
To look to; thrifty too beyond her age.
She is my brother's daughter: he and I
Had once hard words, and parted, and he died
In foreign lands; but for his sake I bred
His daughter Dora: take her for your wife;
For I have wished this marriage, night and day,
For many years." But William answered short:
"I cannot marry Dora; by my life,
I will not marry Dora." Then the old man
Was wroth, and doubled up his hands, and said:

“ You will not, boy ! you dare to answer thus !
But in my time a father’s word was law,
And so it shall be now for me.   Look to ’t ;
Consider, William : take a month to think,
And let me have an answer to my wish ;
Or, by the Lord that made me, you shall pack,
And nevermore darken my doors again ! ”
But William answered madly ; bit his lips,
And broke away.   The more he looked at her,
The less he liked her ; and his ways were harsh ;
But Dora bore them meekly.   Then before
The month was out he left his father’s house,
And hired himself to work within the fields ;
And half in love, half spite, he wooed and wed
A laborer’s daughter, Mary Morrison.

Then, when the bells were ringing, Allan called
His niece and said : “ My girl, I love you well ;
But if you speak with him that was my son,
Or change a word with her he calls his wife,
My home is none of yours.   My will is law.”
And Dora promised, being meek.   She thought,
“ It cannot be : my uncle’s mind will change ! ”

And days went on, and there was born a boy
To William ; then distresses came on him ;
And day by day he passed his father’s gate,
Heart-broken, and his father helped him not.
But Dora stored what little she could save,
And sent it them by stealth, nor did they know
Who sent it ; till at last a fever seized
On William, and in harvest-time he died.

Then Dora went to Mary.   Mary sat
And looked with tears upon her boy, and thought

Hard things of Dora.   Dora came and said:
"I have obeyed my uncle until now,
And I have sinned, for it was all through me
This evil came on William at the first.
But, Mary, for the sake of him that's gone,
And for your sake, the woman that he chose,
And for this orphan, I am come to you:
You know there has not been for these five years
So full a harvest: let me take the boy,
And I will set him in my uncle's eye
Among the wheat; that when his heart is glad
Of the full harvest, he may see the boy,
And bless him for the sake of him that's gone.

And Dora took the child, and went her way
Across the wheat, and sat upon a mound
That was unsown; where many poppies grew.
Far off the farmer came into the field,
And spied her not; for none of all his men
Dare tell him Dora waited with the child;
And Dora would have risen and gone to him,
But her heart failed her; and the reapers reaped,
And the sun fell, and all the land was dark.

But when the morrow came, she rose and took
The child once more, and sat upon the mound;
And made a little wreath of all the flowers
That grew about, and tied it round his hat
To make him pleasing in her uncle's eye.
Then when the farmer passed into the field
He spied her, and he left his men at work,
And came and said, " Where were you yesterday?
Whose child is that?   What are you doing here?"
So Dora cast her eyes upon the ground,
And answered softly, "This is William's child!"

" And did I not," said Allan, " did I not
Forbid you, Dora?"   Dora said again :
" Do with me as you will, but take the child,
And bless him for the sake of him that 's gone !"
And Allan said, "I see it is a trick
Got up betwixt you and the woman there.
I must be taught my duty, and by you !
You knew my word was law, and yet you dared
To slight it.   Well — for I will take the boy ;
But go you hence, and never see me more."

So saying, he took the boy, that cried aloud
And struggled hard.   The wreath of flowers fell
At Dora's feet.   She bowed upon her hands,
And the boy's cry came to her from the field,
More and more distant.   She bowed down her head,
Remembering the day when first she came,
And all the things that had been.   She bowed down
And wept in secret ; and the reapers reaped,
And the sun fell, and all the land was dark.

Then Dora went to Mary's house, and stood
Upon the threshold.   Mary saw the boy
Was not with Dora.   She broke out in praise
To God, that helped her in her widowhood.
And Dora said, " My uncle took the boy ;
But, Mary, let me live and work with you :
He says that he will never see me more."
Then answered Mary, " This shall never be,
That thou shouldst take my trouble on thyself :
And, now I think, he shall not have the boy,
For he will teach him hardness, and to slight
His mother ; therefore thou and I will go,
And I will have my boy, and bring him home ;
And I will beg of him to take thee back ; ·

But if he will not take thee back again,
Then thou and I will live within one house,
And work for William's child, until he grows
Of age to help us."

                    So the women kissed
Each other, and set out and reached the farm.
The door was off the latch: they peeped and saw
The boy set up betwixt his grandsire's knees,
Who thrust him in the hollows of his arm,
And clapt him on the hands and on the cheeks,
Like one that loved him; and the lad stretched out
And babbled for the golden seal that hung
From Allan's watch, and sparkled by the fire.
Then they came in; but when the boy beheld
His mother, he cried out to come to her:
And Allan set him down, and Mary said:—

   "O Father!—if you let me call you so—
I never came a-begging for myself,
Or William, or this child; but now I come
For Dora: take her back; she loves you well.
O Sir, when William died, he died at peace
With all men; for I asked him, and he said,
He could not ever rue his marrying me.—
I had been a patient wife: but, Sir, he said
That he was wrong to cross his father thus:
'God bless him!' he said, 'and may he never know
The troubles I have gone through!' Then he turned
His face and passed—unhappy that I am!
But now, Sir, let me have my boy, for you
Will make him hard, and he will learn to slight
His father's memory; and take Dora back,
And let all this be as it was before."

   So Mary said, and Dora hid her face
By Mary. There was silence in the room;

And all at once the old man burst in sobs : —
" I have been to blame — to blame !   I have killed my son !
I have killed him ! — but I loved him — my dear son !
May God forgive me ! — I have been to blame.
Kiss me, my children ! "
                              Then they clung about
The old man's neck, and kissed him many times.
And all the man was broken with remorse,
And all his love came back a hundred-fold;
And for three hours he sobbed o'er William's child,
Thinking of William.
                              So those four abode
Within one house together ; and as years
Went forward, Mary took another mate ;
But Dora lived unmarried till her **death.**

A TALE OF WITCHCRAFT.

By SIR WALTER SCOTT.

MARGARET BARCLAY, wife of Archibald Dein, burgess of Irvine, had been slandered by her sister in-law, Janet Lyal, the spouse of John Dein, brother of Archibald, and by John Dein himself, as guilty of some act of theft. Upon this provocation Margaret Barclay raised an action of slander before the church court, which prosecution, after some procedure, the kirk-session discharged, by directing a reconciliation between the parties. Nevertheless, although the two women shook hands before the court, yet the said Margaret Barclay declared that she gave her hand only in obedience to the kirk-session, but that she still retained her hatred and ill-will against John Dein and his wife Janet Lyal. About this time the bark of John Dein was about to sail for France, and Andrew Train, or Tran, Provost of the burgh of Irvine, who was an owner of the vessel, went with him, to superintend the commercial part of the voyage. Two other merchants of some consequence went in the same vessel, with a sufficient number of mariners. Margaret Barclay, the revengeful person already mentioned, was heard to imprecate curses upon the provost's argosy, praying to God that sea nor salt-water might never bear the ship, and that *partans* (crabs) might eat the crew at the bottom of the sea

When, under these auspices, the ship was absent on her voyage, a vagabond fellow, named John Stewart, pretending to have knowledge of jugglery, and to possess the power of a spaeman, came to the residence of Tran, the provost, and dropped explicit hints that the ship was lost, and that the good woman of the house was a widow. The sad truth was afterward learned on more certain information. Two of the seamen, after a space of doubt and anxiety, arrived with the melancholy tidings that the bark of which John Dein was skipper and Provost Tran part-owner had been wrecked on the coast of England, near Padstow, when all on board had been lost, except the two sailors who brought the notice. Suspicion of sorcery, in those days easily awakened, was fixed on Margaret Barclay, who had imprecated curses on the ship; and on John Stewart, the juggler, who had seemed to know of the evil fate of the voyage before he could have become acquainted with it by natural means.

Stewart, who was first apprehended, acknowledged that Margaret Barclay, the other suspected person, had applied to him to teach her some magic arts, "in order that she might get gear, kye's milk, love of man, her heart's desire on such persons as had done her wrong, and, finally, that she might obtain the fruit of sea and land." Stewart declared that he denied to Margaret that he possessed the said arts himself, or had the power of communicating them. So far was well; but, true or false, he added a string of circumstances, whether voluntarily declared or extracted by torture, which tended to fix the cause of the loss of the bark on Margaret Barclay. He had come, he said, to this woman's house in Irvine, shortly after the ship set sail from harbor. He went to Margaret's house by night, and found her engaged, with other two women, in making clay figures; one of the figures was made handsome, with fair hair, supposed to represent Provost Tran. They then proceeded to mould a figure of a ship in clay, and during this labor the Devil appeared to the company in the shape of a handsome black lapdog, such as ladies use to keep. He added that the whole party left the house together, and went into an empty waste-house nearer the seaport, which house he pointed out to the city magistrates. From this house they went to the seaside, followed by the black lapdog aforesaid, and cast in the figures of clay representing the ship and the men; after which the sea raged roared, and became red like the juice of madder in a dyer's caldron.

This confession having been extorted from the unfortunate juggler, the female acquaintances of Margaret Barclay were next convened, that he might point out her associates in forming the charm, when he pitched upon a woman called Isobel Insh, or Taylor, who resolutely denied having ever seen him before. She was imprisoned, however, in the belfry of the church. An addition to the evidence against the poor old woman Insh was then procured from her own daughter, Margaret Tailzeour, *a child of eight years old*, who lived as servant with Margaret Barclay, the person principally accused. This child, who was keeper of a baby belonging to Margaret Barclay, either from terror, or the innate love of falsehood which we have observed as proper to childhood, declared, that she was present when the fatal models of clay were formed, and that, in plunging them in the sea, Margaret Barclay, her mistress, and her mother, Isobel Insh, were assisted by another woman, and a girl of fourteen years old, who dwelt at the town-head. Legally considered, the evidence of this child was contradictory, and inconsistent with the confession of the juggler, for it assigned other particulars and *dramatis personæ* in many respects different. But all was accounted sufficiently regular, especially since the girl failed not to swear to the presence of the black dog, to whose appearance she also added the additional terrors of that of a black man. The dog also, according to her account, emitted flashes from its jaws and nostrils, to illuminate the witches during the performance of the spell. The child maintained this story even to her mother's face, only alleging that Isobel

Insh remained behind in the waste-house, and was not pres‑
ent when the images were put into the sea. For her own
countenance and presence on the occasion, and to insure her
secrecy, her mistress promised her a pair of new shoes.

John Stewart, being re-examined, and confronted with the
child, was easily compelled to allow that the "little smatch‑
et" was there, and to give that marvellous account of his
correspondence with Elfland, which we have given else‑
where.

The conspiracy thus far, as they conceived, disclosed, the
magistrates and ministers wrought hard with Isobel Insh, to
prevail upon her to tell the truth ; and she at length acknowl‑
edged her presence at the time when the models of the ship
and mariners were destroyed, but endeavored so to modify
her declaration as to deny all personal accession to the guilt.
This poor creature almost admitted the supernatural powers
imputed to her, promising Bailie Dunlop (also a mariner),
by whom she was imprisoned, that if he would dismiss her,
he should never make a bad voyage, but have success in all
his dealings by sea and land. She was finally brought to
promise that she would fully confess the whole that she knew
of the affair on the morrow.

But finding herself in so hard a strait, the unfortunate
woman made use of the darkness to attempt an escape.
With this view she got out by a back window of the belfry,
although, says the report, there were "iron bolts, locks, and
fetters on her" ; and attained the roof of the church, where,
losing her footing, she sustained a severe fall, and was greatly
bruised. Being apprehended, Bailie Dunlop again urged
her to confess ; but the poor woman was determined to ap‑
peal to a more merciful tribunal, and maintained her inno‑
cence to the last minute of her life, denying all that she had
formerly admitted, and dying five days after her fall from
the roof of the church. ·The inhabitants of Irvine attributed
her death to poison.

The scene began to thicken, for a commission was granted for the trial of the two remaining persons accused, namely, Stewart the juggler and Margaret Barclay. The day of trial being arrived, the following singular events took place, which we give as stated in the record.

"My Lord and Earl of Eglintoune (who dwells within the space of one mile to the said burgh), having come to the said burgh at the earnest request of the said Justices, for giving to them of his lordship's countenance, concurrence, and assistance, in trying of the aforesaid devilish practices, conform to the tenor of the foresaid commission, the said John Stewart, for his better preserving to the day of the assize, was put in a sure lockfast booth, where no manner of person might have access to him till the downsitting of the Justice Court, and for avoiding of putting violent hands on himself, he was very strictly guarded, and fettered by the arms, as use is. And upon that same day of the assize, about half an hour before the downsitting of the Justice Court, Mr. David Dickson, minister at Irvine, and Mr. George Dunbar, minister of Air, having gone to him, to exhort him to call on his God for mercy for his by-gone wicked and evil life, and that God would of his infinite mercy loose· him out of the bonds of the Devil, whom he had served these many years bygone, he acquiesced in their prayer and godly exhortation, and uttered these words : ' I am so straitly guarded, that it lies not in my power to get my hand to take off my bonnet, nor to get bread to my mouth.' And immediately after the departing of the two ministers from him, the juggler being sent for at the desire of my Lord of Eglintoune, to be confronted with a woman of the burgh of Air, called Janet Bous, who was apprehended by the magistrates of the burgh of Air for witchcraft, and sent to the burgh of Irvine purposely for that affair, he was found by the burgh officers who went about him, strangled and hanged by the cruik of the door, with a *tait* of hemp, or a string made of hemp, supposed to have been his garter or string of his bonnet, not above the length of two span long, his knees not being from the ground half a span, and was brought out of the house, his life not being totally expelled. But, notwithstanding of whatsoever means used in the contrary for remeid of his life, he revived not, but so ended his life miserably, by the help of the Devil his master.

" And because there was then only in life the said Margaret Barclay, and that the persons summoned to pass upon her assize, and upon the assize of the juggler, who, by the help of the Devil his master, had put violent hands on himself, were all present within the said burgh; therefore, and for eschewing of the like in the person of the said Margaret, our sovereign lord's justices in that part, particularly above-named, constituted by commission, after solemn deliberation and advice of the said noble lord, whose concurrence and advice was chiefly required and taken in this matter, concluded with all possible diligence before the downsitting of the Justice Court, to put the said Margaret in torture; in respect the Devil, by God's permission, had made her associates, who were the lights of the cause, to be their own *burrioes* (slayers). They used the torture underwritten, as being most safe and gentle (as the said noble lord assured the said justices), by putting of her two bare legs in a pair of stocks, and thereafter by onlaying of certain iron gauds (bars), severally, one by one, and then eiking and augmenting the weight by laying on more gauds, and in easing of her by offtaking of the iron gauds one or more, as occasion offered, which iron gauds were but little short gauds, and broke not the skin of her legs, &c.

" After using of the which kind of *gentle torture*, the said Margaret began, according to the increase of the pain, to cry, and crave for God's cause to take off her shins the foresaid irons, and she should declare truly the whole matter

Which being removed, she began at her former denial : and being of new assayed in torture as of befoir, she then uttered these words : ' Take off, take off, and before God I shall show you the whole form ! '

" And the said irons being of new, upon her faithfull promise, removed, she then desired my Lord of Eglintoune, the said four justices, and the said Mr. David Dickson, minister of the burgh, Mr. George Dunbar, minister of Ayr, and Mr. Mitchell Wallace, minister of Kilmarnock, and Mr. John Cunninghame, minister of Dalry, and Hugh Kennedy, provost of Ayr, to come by themselves, and to remove all others, and she should declare truly, as she should answer to God, the whole matter. Whose desire in that being fulfilled, she made her confession in this manner, but (i. e. without) any kind of demand, freely, without interrogation ; God's name by earnest prayer being called upon for opening of her lips, and easing of her heart, that she, by rendering of the truth, might glorify and magnify his holy name, and disappoint the enemy of her salvation." — *Trial of Margaret Barclay, &c.*, 1618.

Margaret Barclay, who was a young and lively person, had hitherto conducted herself like a passionate and high-tempered woman innocently accused, and the only appearance of conviction obtained against her was, that she carried about her rowan-tree and colored thread, to make, as she said, her cow give milk, when it began to fail. But the *gentle torture* — a strange junction of words — recommended us an anodyne by the good Lord Eglinton, — the placing, namely, her legs in the stocks, and loading her bare shins with bars of iron, overcame her resolution : when, at her screams and declarations that she was willing to tell all, the weights were removed. She then told a story of destroying the ship of John Dein, affirming that it was with the purpose of killing only her brother-in-law and Provost Tran, and saving the rest of the crew. She at the same time involved in the guilt Isobel Crawford. This poor woman was also apprehended, and, in great terror, confessed the imputed crime, retorting the principal blame on Margaret Barclay herself. The trial was then appointed to proceed, when Alexander Dean, the husband of Margaret Barclay, appeared in court with a lawyer to act in his wife's behalf. Apparently, the sight of her husband awakened some hope and desire of life, for when the prisoner was asked by the lawyer whether she wished to be defended, she answered, " As you please. But all I have confessed was in agony of torture; and, before God, all I have spoken is false and untrue." To which she pathetically added, " Ye have been too long in coming."

The jury, unmoved by these affecting circumstances, proceeded upon the principle that the confession of the accused could not be considered as made under the influence of torture, since the bars were not actually upon her limbs at the time it was delivered, although they were placed at her elbow, ready to be again laid on her bare shins, if she was less explicit in her declaration than her auditors wished. On this nice distinction, they in one voice found Margaret Barclay guilty. It is singular that she should have again returned to her confession after sentence, and died affirming it;—the explanation of which, however, might be, either that she had really in her ignorance and folly tampered with some idle spells, or that an apparent penitence for her offence, however imaginary, was the only mode in which she could obtain any share of public sympathy at her death, or a portion of the prayers of the clergy and congregation, which, in her circumstances, she might be willing to purchase, even by confession of what all believed respecting her. It is remarkable, that she earnestly entreated the magistrates that no harm should be done to Isobel Crawford, the woman whom she had herself accused. This unfortunate young creature was strangled at the stake, and her body burned to ashes, having died with many expressions of religion and penitence.

It was one fatal consequence of these cruel persecutions, that one pile was usually lighted at the embers of another. Accordingly, in the present case, three victims having already perished by this accusation, the magistrates, incensed at the nature of the crime, so perilous as it seemed to men of a maritime life, and at a loss of several friends of their own, one of whom had been their principal magistrate, did not forbear to insist against Isobel Crawford, inculpated by Margaret Barclay's confession. A new commission was granted for her trial, and after the assistant minister of Irvine, Mr. David Dickson, had made earnest prayers to God for opening her obdurate and closed heart, she was subjected to the torture of iron bars laid upon her bare shins, her feet being in the stocks, as in the case of Margaret Barclay.

She endured this torture with incredible firmness, since she did "admirably, without any kind of din or exclamation, suffer above thirty stone of iron to be laid on her legs, never shrinking thereat . in any sort, but remaining, as it were, steady." But in shifting the situation of the iron bars, and removing them to another part of her shins, her constancy gave way; she broke out into horrible cries (though not more than three bars were then actually on her person) of "Tak aff! tak aff!" On being relieved from the torture, she made the usual confession of all that she was charged with, and of a connection with the Devil which had subsisted for several years. Sentence was given against her accordingly. After this had been denounced, she openly denied all her former confessions, and died without any sign of repentance, offering repeated interruptions to the minister in his prayer, and absolutely refusing to pardon the executioner.

This tragedy happened in the year 1613, and recorded as it is very particularly, and at considerable length, forms the

most detailed specimen I have met with, of a Scottish trial
for witchcraft, — illustrating, in particular, how poor wretches
abandoned, as they conceived, by God and the world, de-
prived of all human sympathy, and exposed to personal tor-
tures of an acute description, became disposed to throw away
the lives that were rendered bitter to them, by a voluntary
confession of guilt, rather than struggle hopelessly against
so many evils. Four persons here lost their lives, merely
because the throwing some clay models into the sea, a fact
told differently by the witnesses who spoke of it, corresponded
with the season, for no day was fixed, in which a particular
vessel was lost. It is scarce possible that, after reading such
a story, a man of sense can listen for an instant to the evidence founded on confessions thus obtained, which has been
almost the sole reason by which a few individuals, even in
modern times, have endeavored to justify a belief in the
existence of witchcraft.

The result of the judicial examination of a criminal, when
extorted by such means, is the most suspicious of all evidence,
and even when voluntarily given, is scarce admissible, without the corroboration of other testimony.

ONE WORD MORE.

TO E. B. B.

By ROBERT BROWNING.

I.

THERE they are, my fifty men and women
   Naming me the fifty poems finished!
Take them, Love, the book * and me together.
Where the heart lies, let the brain lie also.

II.

Rafael made a century of sonnets,
Made and wrote them in a certain volume
Dinted with the silver-pointed pencil
Else he only used to draw Madonnas:
These, the world might view, — but One, the volume.
Who that one, you ask? Your heart instructs you.
Did she live and love it all her lifetime?
Did she drop, his lady of the sonnets,
Die, and let it drop beside her pillow
Where it lay in place of Rafael's glory,
Rafael's cheek so duteous and so loving, —
Cheek, the world was wont to hail a painter's,
Rafael's cheek, her love had turned a poet's?

---

* Referring to his volume of Poems entitled " Men and Women."

III.

You and I would rather read that volume,
(Taken to his beating bosom by it,)
Lean and list the bosom-beats of Rafael,
Would we not? than wonder at Madonnas —
Her, San Sisto names, and Her, Foligno,
Her, that visits Florence in a vision,
Her, that 's left with lilies in the Louvre —
Seen by us and all the world in circle.

IV.

You and I will never read that volume.
Guido Reni, like his own eye's apple
Guarded long the treasure-book and loved it.
Guido Reni dying, all Bologna
Cried, and the world with it, "Ours — the treasure!"
Suddenly, as rare things will, it vanished.

V.

Dante once prepared to paint an angel :
Whom to please?   You whisper, "Beatrice."
While he mused and traced it and retraced it,
(Peradventure with a pen corroded
Still by drops of that hot ink he dipped for,
When, his left-hand i' the hair o' the wicked,
Back he held the brow and pricked its stigma,
Bit into the live man's flesh for parchment,
Loosed him, laughed to see the writing rankle,
Let the wretch go festering through Florence,) —
Dante, who loved well because he hated,
Hated wickedness that hinders loving,
Dante standing, studying his angel, —
In there broke the folk of his Inferno.
Says he, "Certain people of importance"

(Such he gave his daily, dreadful line to)
Entered and would seize, forsooth, the poet.
Says the poet, "Then I stopped my painting."

VI.

You and I would rather see that angel,
Painted by the tenderness of Dante,
Would we not? — than read a fresh Inferno.

VII.

You and I will never see that picture.
While he mused on love and Beatrice,
While he softened o'er his outlined angel,
In they broke, those "people of importance":
We and Bice bear the loss forever.

VIII.

What of Rafael's sonnets, Dante's picture?

IX.

This: no artist lives and loves that longs not
Once, and only once, and for One only,
(Ah, the prize!) to find his love a language
Fit and fair and simple and sufficient —
Using nature that 's an art to others,
Not, this one time, art that 's turned his nature.
Ay, of all the artists living, loving,
None but would forego his proper dowry, —
Does he paint? he fain would write a poem, —
Does he write? he fain would paint a picture,
Put to proof art alien to the artist's,
Once, and only once, and for One only,
So to be the man and leave the artist,
Save the man's joy, miss the artist's sorrow.

x.

Wherefore?   Heaven's gift takes earth's abatement!
He who smites the rock and spreads the water,
Bidding drink and live a crowd beneath him,
Even he, the minute makes immortal,
Proves, perchance, his mortal in the minute,
Desecrates, belike, the deed in doing.
While he smites, how can he but remember,
So he smotè before, in such a peril,
When they stood and mocked, " Shall smiting help us?"
When they drank and sneered, " A stroke is easy!"
When they wiped their mouths and went their journey,
Throwing him for thanks, " But drought was pleasant."
Thus old memories mar the actual triumph;
Thus the doing savors of disrelish;
Thus achievement lacks a gracious somewhat;
O'er-importuned brows becloud the mandate,
Carelessness or consciousness, the gesture.
For he bears an ancient wrong about him,
Sees and knows again those phalanxed faces,
Hears, yet one time more, the 'customed prelude, —
" How should'st thou, of all men, smite, and save us?"
Guesses what is like to prove the sequel, —
" Egypt's flesh-pots, — nay, the drought was better."

xi.

O, the crowd must have emphatic warrant!
Theirs, the Sinai-forehead's cloven brilliance,
Right-arm's rod-sweep, tongue's imperial fiat.
Never dares the man put off the prophet.

xii.

Did he love one face from out the thousands,
(Were she Jethro's daughter, white and wifely,

Were she but the Æthiopian bondslave,)
He would envy yon dumb, patient camel,
Keeping a reserve of scanty water
Meant to save his own life in the desert;
Ready in the desert to deliver
(Kneeling down to let his breast be opened)
Hoard and life together for his mistress.

XIII.

I shall never, in the years remaining,
Paint you pictures, no, nor carve you statues,
Make you music that should all-express me;
So it seems: I stand on my attainment.
This of verse alone, one life allows me;
Verse and nothing else have I to give you.
Other heights in other lives, God willing,—
All the gifts from all the heights, your own, Love!

XIV.

Yet a semblance of resource avails us,—
Shade so finely touched, love's sense must seize it.
Take these lines, look lovingly and nearly,
Lines I write the first time and the last time.
He who works in fresco, steals a hair-brush,
Curbs the liberal hand, subservient proudly,
Cramps his spirit, crowds its all in little,
Makes a strange art of an art familiar,
Fills his lady's missal-marge with flowerets.
He who blows through bronze, may breathe through silver,
Fitly serenade a slumbrous princess.
He who writes, may write for once, as I do.

XV.

Love, you saw me gather men and women,
Live or dead or fashioned by my fancy,

Enter each and all, and use their service,
Speak from every mouth, — the speech, a poem.
Hardly shall I tell my joys and sorrows,
Hopes and fears, belief and disbelieving :
I am mine and yours, — the rest be all men's,
Karshook, Cleon, Norbert and the fifty.
Let me speak this once in my true person,
Not as Lippo, Roland, or Andrea,
Though the fruit of speech be just this sentence, —
Pray you, look on these my men and women,
Take and keep my fifty poems finished ;
Where my heart lies, let my brain lie also !
Poor the speech ; be how I speak, for all things.

XVI.

Not but that you know me !   Lo, the moon's self !
Here in London, yonder late in Florence,
Still we find her face, the thrice-transfigured.
Curving on a sky imbrued with color,
Drifted over Fiesole by twilight,
Came she, our new crescent of a hair's-breadth.
Full she flared it, lamping Samminiato,
Rounder 'twixt the cypresses and rounder,
Perfect till the nightingales applauded.
Now, a piece of her old self, impoverished,
Hard to greet, she traverses the house-roofs,
Hurries with unhandsome thrift of silver,
Goes dispiritedly, — glad to finish.

XVII.

What, there 's nothing in the moon noteworthy ?
Nay, — for if that moon could love a mortal,
Use, to charm him, (so to fit a fancy,)
All her magic, ('t is the old sweet mythos,)
She would turn a new side to her mortal,

Side unseen of herdsman, huntsman, steersman, —
Blank to Zoroaster on his terrace,
Blind to Galileo on his turret,
Dumb to Homer, dumb to Keats, — him, even!
Think, the wonder of the moonstruck mortal, —
When she turns round, comes again in heaven,
Opens out anew for worse or better?
Proves she like some portent of an iceberg
Swimming full upon the ship it founders,
Hungry with huge teeth of splintered crystals?
Proves she as the paved-work of a sapphire
Seen by Moses when he climbed the mountain?
Moses, Aaron, Nadab, and Abihu
Climbed and saw the very God, the Highest,
Stand upon the paved-work of a sapphire.
Like the bodied heaven in his clearness
Shone the stone, the sapphire of that paved-work,
When they ate and drank and saw God also!

XVIII.

What were seen? None knows, none ever shall know.
Only this is sure, — the sight were other,
Not the moon's same side, born late in Florence,
Dying now impoverished here in London.
God be thanked, the meanest of his creatures
Boasts two soul-sides, one to face the world with,
One to show a woman when he loves her.

XIX.

This I say of me, but think of you, Love!
This to you, — yourself my moon of poets!
Ah, but that's the world's side, — there's the wonder —
Thus they see you, praise you, think they know you.
There, in turn I stand with them and praise you,

Out of my own self, I dare to phrase it.
But the best is when I glide from out them,
Cross a step or two of dubious twilight,
Come out on the other side, the novel
Silent silver lights, and darks undreamed of,
Where I hush and bless myself with silence.

XX.

O, their Rafael of the dear Madonnas,
O, their Dante of the dread Inferno,
Wrote one song — and in my brain I sing it,
Drew one angel — borne, see, on my bosom!

IN A SKYE BOTHY.

By ALEXANDER SMITH.

MAN is an ease-loving animal, with a lingering affection for Arcadian dales; under the shadow of whose
trees shepherd boys are piping "as they would never grow
old." Human nature is a vagabond still, maugre the six
thousand years of it, and amuses itself with dreams of societies free and unrestrained. It is this vagabond feeling
in the blood which draws one so strongly to Shakespeare.
That sweet and liberal nature of his blossomed into all
wild human generosities. "As You Like It" is a vagabond play; and, verily, if there waved in any wind that
blows upon the earth a forest, peopled as Arden's was in
Shakespeare's imagination, with an exiled king drawing
the sweetest, humanest, lessons from misfortune, a melancholy Jaques stretched by the river's brink, moralizing on
the bleeding deer, a fair Rosalind chanting her saucy
cuckoo song, fools like Touchstone (not like those of our
acquaintance, reader), and the whole place from centre to
circumference filled with mighty oak-bolls, all carven with
lovers' names; I would, be my worldly prospects what they
may, pack up at once and join that vagabond company. For
there I should find more gallant courtesies, finer sentiments,
completer innocence and happiness, than I am like to discover here, although I search for them from shepherd's cot
to king's palace. Just to think how these people lived

Carelessly as the blossoming trees, happily as the singing birds; time measured only by the acorn's patter on the fruitful soil. A world without debtor or creditor; passing rich, yet with never a doit in its purse; with no sordid cares, no regard for appearances; nothing to occupy the young but love-making; nothing to occupy the old but listening to the "sermons in stones," and perusing the musical wisdom which dwells in "running brooks." Arden forest, alas! is not rooted in the earth: it draws sustenance from a poet's brain; and the light asleep on its leafy billows is that "that yet never was seen on sea or shore." But one cannot help dreaming of such a place, and striving to approach as nearly as possible to its sweet conditions.

I am quite alone here: England may have been invaded and London sacked for aught I know. Several weeks since, a newspaper, accidentally blown to my solitude, informed me that the *Great Eastern* had been got under weigh, and was then swinging at the Nore. There is great joy, I perceive. Human nature stands astonished at itself; felicitates itself on its remarkable talent, and will for months to come purr complacently over its achievement in magazines and reviews. A fine world, messieurs, that will attain to heaven — if in the power of steam. A very fine world; yet for all that, I have withdrawn from it for a time, and would rather not hear of its remarkable exploits. In my present mood I do not value them that coil of vapor on the brow of Blavin, which, as I gaze, smoulders into nothing in the fire of sunrise.

Goethe, in his memorable book, "Truth and Poetry," informs his readers that in his youth he loved to shelter himself in the Scripture narratives, from the marching and counter-marching of armies, the cannonading, retreating, and fighting, that lay everywhere around him. He shut his eyes, as it were, and a whole war-convulsed Europe wheeled away into silence and distance, and in its place, lo! the patriarchs, with their tawny tents, their man-servants and maid-servants, and countless flocks in imperceptible procession whitening the Syrian plains. In this my green solitude, I appreciate the full sweetness of the passage. Everything here is silent as the Bible plains themselves. I am cut off from former scenes and associates as by the sullen Styx and the grim ferrying of Charon's boat. The noise of the world does not touch me. I live too far inland to hear the thunder of the reef. To this place no postman comes, no tax-gatherer. This region never heard the sound of the church-going bell. The land is pagan as when the yellow-haired Norseman landed a thousand years ago. I almost feel a pagan myself. Not using a notched stick, I have lost all count of time, and don't know Saturday from Sunday. Civilization is like a soldier's stock; it makes you carry your head a good deal higher, makes the angels weep a little more at your fantastic tricks, and half suffocates you the while. I have thrown it away, and breathe freely. My bed is the heather, my mirror the stream from the hills, my comb and brush the sea-breeze, my watch the sun, my theatre the sunset, and my evening service — not without a rude natural religion in it — watching the pinnacles of the hills of Cuchullin sharpening in intense purple against the pallid orange of the sky, or listening to the melancholy voices of the sea-birds and the tide; that over, I am asleep till touched by the earliest splendor of the dawn. I am, not without reason, hugely enamored of my vagabond existence.

My bothy is situated on the shores of one of the lochs that intersect Skye. The coast is bare and rocky, hollowed into fantastic chambers: and when the tide is making, every cavern murmurs like a sea-shell. The land, from frequent rain green as emerald, rises into soft pastoral heights, and about a mile inland soars suddenly up into peaks of bastard marble, white as the cloud under which the lark sings at noon, bathed in rosy light at sunset. In front are the Cuchullin hills and the monstrous peak of Blavin; then the green Strath runs narrowing out to sea, and the Island of Rum, with a white cloud upon it, stretches like a gigantic shadow across the entrance of the loch, and completes the scene. Twice every twenty-four hours the Atlantic tide sets in upon hollowed shores; twice is the sea withdrawn, leaving spaces of green sand on which mermaids with golden combs might sleek alluring tresses; and black rocks, heaped with brown dulse and tangle, and lovely ocean blooms of purple and orange; and bare islets, — marked at full of tide by a glimmer of pale-green amid the universal sparkle, — where most the sea-fowl love to congregate. To these islets, on favorable evenings, come the crows, and sit in sable parliament; business despatched, they start into air as at a gun, and stream away through the sunset to their roosting-place in the Armadale woods. The shore supplies for me the place of books and companions. Of course Blavin and Cuchullin hills are the chief attractions, and I never weary watching them. In the morning they wear a great white caftan of mist; but that lifts away before noon, and they stand with all their scars and passionate torrent-lines bare to the blue heavens; with perhaps a solitary shoulder for a moment gleaming wet to the sunlight. After a while a vapor begins to steam up from their abysses, gathering itself into strange shapes, knotting and twisting itself like smoke; while above, the terrible crests are now lost, now revealed, in a stream of flying rack. In an hour a wall of rain, gray as granite, opaque as iron, stands up from the sea to heaven. The loch is roughening before the wind, and the islets, black dots a second ago, are patches of roaring foam. You hear the fierce sound of its coming. The lashing tempest sweeps over you, and looking behind, up the long inland glen, you can see on

the birch woods, and on the sides of the hills, driven on the
wind, the white smoke of the rain. Though fierce as a
charge of Highland bayonets, these squalls are seldom of
long duration, and you bless them when you creep from
your shelter, for out comes the sun, and the birch woods
are twinkling, and more intensely flash the levels of the
sea, and at a stroke the clouds are scattered from the wet
brow of Blavin, and to the whole a new element is added,
the voice of the swollen stream as it rushes over a hundred tiny cataracts, and roars river-broad into the sea, making turbid the azure. Then I have my amusements in
this solitary place. The mountains are of course open, and
this morning at dawn a roe swept past me like the wind,
nose to the dewy ground, "tracking," they call it here.
Above all, I can wander on the ebbed beach. Hogg
speaks of that

> "Undefined and mingled hum,
> Voice of the desert, never dumb."

But far more than the murmuring and insecty air of the
moorland, does the wet *chirk-chirking* of the living shore
give one the idea of crowded and multitudinous life. Did
the reader ever hunt razor-fish? — not sport like tiger-
hunting, I admit; yet it has its pleasures and excitements,
and can kill a forenoon for an idle man agreeably. On the
wet sands yonder the razor-fish are spouting like the fountains at Versailles on a fête day. The sly fellow sinks on
discharging his watery *feu de joie.* If you are quickly
after him through the sand, you catch him, and then comes
the tug of war. Address and dexterity are required. If
you pull vigorously, he slips out of his sheath a "mother-
naked" mollusk, and escapes. If you do your spiriting
gently, you drag him up to light, a long, thin case, with a
white fishy bulb protruding at one end like a root. Rinse
him in sea-water, toss him into your basket, and plunge

after another watery flash. These razor-fish are excellent
eating, the people say; and when used as bait, no fish that
swims the ocean stream, cod. whiting, haddock, flat skate
broad-shouldered, crimson bream, — not the detested dog-
fish himself, this summer swarming in every loch and be-
cursed by every fisherman, — can keep himself off the
hook, and in an hour your boat is laden with glittering
spoil. Then if you take your gun to the low islands, —
and you can go dry-shod at ebb of tide, — you have your
chance of sea-fowl. Gulls of all kinds are there, dookers
and divers of every description; flocks of shy curlews,
and specimens of a hundred tribes, to which my limited
ornithological knowledge cannot furnish a name. The
Solan goose yonder falls from heaven into the water like
a meteor-stone. See the solitary scart, with long, narrow
wing and outstretched neck, shooting toward some distant
promontory! Anon, high overhead, come wheeling a
covey of lovely sea-swallows. You fire; one flutters down
never more to skim the horizon or to dip in the sea
sparkle. Lift it up; is it not beautiful? The wild keen
eye is closed, but you see the delicate slate-color of the
wings, and the long tail-feathers white as the creaming
foam. There is a stain of blood on the breast, hardly
brighter than the scarlet of its beak and feet. Lay it
down, for its companions are dashing round and round,
uttering harsh cries of rage and sorrow; and had you the
heart, you could shoot them one by one. At ebb of tide
wild-looking children, from turf-cabins on the hillside, come
down to hunt shell-fish. Even now a troop is busy; how
their shrill voices go the while! Old Effie, I see, is out
to-day, quite a picturesque object with her white cap and
red shawl. With a tin can in one hand, an old reaping-
hook in the other, she goes poking among the tangle. Let
us see what sport she has had. She turns round at our
salutation, — very old, old almost as the worn rocks around

She might have been the wife of Wordsworth's " Leech-gatherer." Her can is sprawling with brown crabs ; and opening her apron, she exhibits a large black and blue lobster, — a fellow such as she alone can capture. A queer woman is Effie, and an awsome. She is familiar with ghosts and apparitions. She can relate legends that have power over the superstitious blood, and with little coaxing will sing those wild Gaelic songs of hers, — of dead lights on the sea, of fishing-boats going down in squalls, of un-buried bodies tossing day and night upon the gray peaks of the waves, and of girls that pray God to lay them by the sides of their drowned lovers ; although for them should never rise mass nor chant, and although their flesh should be torn asunder by the wild fishes of the sea.

Rain is my enemy here, and at this writing I am suffer-ing siege. For three days this rickety dwelling has stood assault of wind and rain. Yesterday a blast breached the door, and the tenement fluttered for a moment like an um-brella caught in a gust. All seemed lost, but the door was got to again, heavily barred across, and the enemy foiled. An entrance, however, had been effected ; and that por-tion of the attacking column which I had imprisoned by my dexterous manœuvre, maddening itself into whirlwind, rushed up the chimney, scattering my turf fire as it went, and so escaped. Since that time the windy columns have retired to the gorges of the hills, where I hear them howl at intervals ; and the only thing I am exposed to is the musketry of the rain. How viciously the small shot pep-pers the walls ! Here must I wait till the cloudy arma-ment breaks up. One's own mind is a dull companion in these circumstances. Sheridan, — wont with his talk to brighten the table more than the champagne ; whose mind was a phosphorescent sea, dark in its rest, every movement a flash of splendor, — if cooped up here, begirt with this murky atmosphere, would be dull as a Lincoln fen uncnlivened by a single will-o'-the-wisp. Books are the only refuge on a rainy day; but in Skye Bothies books are rare. To me, however, the gods have proved kind, for in my sore need I found on a shelf here two volumes of the old *Monthly Review*, and have sauntered through these dingy literary catacombs with considerable satisfaction. What a strange set of old fogies the writers! To read them is like conversing with the antediluvians. Their opinions have fallen into disuse long ago, and resemble to-day the rusty armor and gimcracks of a curiosity-shop. These essays and criticisms were thought brilliant, I suppose, when they appeared last century, and authors praised therein considered themselves rather handsome flies, preserved in pure critical amber for the inspection of posterity. The volumes were published, I notice, from 1790 to 1792, and exhibit a period of wonderful literary activity. Not to speak of novels, histories, travels, farces, tragedies, upwards of two hundred poems are brought to judgment. Plainly, these Monthly Reviewers worked hard, and on the whole with spirit and deftness. A proper sense of the importance of their craft had these gentlemen; they laid down the law with great gravity, and from critical benches shook their awful wigs on offenders. How it all looks *now!* "Let us indulge ourselves with another extract," quoth one, " and contemplate once more the tear of grief before we are called upon to witness the tear of rapture." *Both* tears dried up long ago, as those that sparkled on a Pharaoh's cheek. Hear this other, stern as Rhadamanthus; behold Duty steeling itself against human weakness! "It grieves us to wound a young man's feelings; but our judgment must not be biassed by any plea whatsoever. Why will men apply for our opinion, when they know that we cannot be silent, and that we will not lie?" Listen to this prophet in Israel, one who has not bent the knee to Baal, and say if there is not a touch of hopeless pathos in him: "Fine

words do not make fine poems. Scarcely a month passes
in which we are not obliged to issue this decree. But in
these days of universal heresy, our decrees are no more
respected than the Bulls of the Bishop of Rome." O that
men would hear, that they would incline their hearts to
wisdom! The ghosts of the dim literary Hades are getting tiresome, and as I look up, lo! the rain has ceased,
from sheer fatigue: great white vapors are rising from the
damp valleys; and, better than all, pleasant as Blucher's
cannon on the evening of Waterloo, the sound of wheels
on the boggy ground; and just when the stanched rain-
clouds are burning into a sullen red at sunset, I have a
visitor in my Bothy, and pleasant human intercourse.

Broadford Fair is a great event in the island. The little
town lies on the margin of a curving bay, and under the
shadow of a somewhat celebrated hill. On the crest of it
is a cairn of stones, the burying-place of an ancient Scandinavian woman, tradition informs me, whose wish it was
to be laid high up there, that she might sleep right in the
pathway of the Norway wind. In a green glen, at its base,
stand the ruins of the House of Corrichatachin, where Boswell had his share of four bowls of punch, and went to bed
at five in the morning, and, awakening at noon with a severe
headache, saw Dr. Johnson burst in upon him with the
exclamation, "What, drunk yet!" "His tone of voice was
not that of severe upbraiding," writes the penitent Bozzy,
"so I was relieved a little." Broadford is a post-town of
about a dozen houses, and is a place of great importance.
If Portree is the London of Skye, Broadford is its Man-
chester. The markets, held every three months or so, take
place on a patch of moorland about a mile from the village.
Not only are cattle sold and cash exchanged for the same,
but there a Skye farmer meets his relations, from the brother
of his blood to his cousin forty times removed. To these
meetings he is drawn, not only by his love of coin, but by

his love of kindred, and — the *Broadford Mail* and the *Portree Advertiser* lying yet in the womb of time — by his love of gossip also. The market is the Skyeman's exchange, his family gathering, and his newspaper. From the deep sea of his solitude he comes up to breathe there, and, refreshed, sinks again. This fair at Broadford I resolved to see. Starting early in the morning, my way for the most part lay through a desolation where Nature seemed deteriorated, and at her worst. Winter could not possibly sadden the region; no spring could quicken it into flowers. The hills wear but for ornament the white streak of the torrent; the rocky soil clothes itself in heather to which the purple never comes. Even man, the miracle-worker, who transforms everything he touches, who has rescued a fertile Holland from the waves, who has reared a marble Venice from out salt lagunes and marshes, is defeated here. A turf hut, with smoke issuing from the roof, and a patch of sickly green around, which will ripen by November, is all that he has won from Nature. Gradually, as I proceeded, the aspect of the country changed, began to exhibit traces of cultivation; and erelong the red hill with the Norwegian woman's cairn a-top rose before me, suggesting Broadford and the close of the journey. The roads were filled with cattle, driven forward with oath and shout. Every now and then, a dog-cart came skirring along, and infinite the confusion, and loud the clamor of tongues, when one or other plunged into a herd of sheep, or skittish "three-year-olds." At the entrance to the fair, the horses were taken out of the vehicles, and left, with a leathern thong tied round their forelegs, to limp about in search of breakfast. As you advance, on either side of the road stand hordes of cattle, the wildest looking creatures, black, white, dun, and cream-colored, with fells of hair hanging over their savage eyes, and graced with horns of preposterous dimensions. Horses neighed from their stakes, the owners looking out for customers. Sheep were there, too, in restless masses, scattering hither and thither like quick-silver, with dogs and men flying along their edges, excited to the verge of insanity. What a hubbub of sound! What lowing and neighing! what bleating and barking! It was a novel sight, that rude, primeval traffic. Down in the hollow ground tents had been knocked up since dawn; there potatoes were being cooked for drovers who had been travelling all night; there, also, liquor could be had. To these places, I observed, contracting parties invariably repaired to solemnize a bargain. Booths ranged along the side of the road were plentifully furnished with confections, ribbons, and cheap jewellery; and as the morning wore on, around these the girls swarmed thickly, as bees round summer flowers. The fair was running its full career of bargain-making and consequent dram-drinking, rude flirtation, and meeting of friend with friend, when up the middle of the road, hustling the passengers, terrifying the cattle, came three misguided young gentlemen — medical students, I opined — engaged in botanical researches in these regions. Evidently they had been "dwellers in tents." One of them, gifted with a comic genius, — his companions were desperately solemn, — at one point of the road, threw back his coat, in emulation of Sambo when he brings down the applauses of the threepenny gallery, and executed a shuffle in front of a bewildered cow. Crummie backed and shied, bent on retreat. *He*, agile as a cork, bobbed up and down in her front, turn whither she would, with shouts and hideous grimaces, his companions standing by the while like mutes at a funeral. That feat accomplished, the trio staggered on, amid the derision and scornful laughter of the Gael. Lifting our eyes up out of the noise and confusion, there were the solitary mountain-tops and the clear mirror of Broadford Bay, the opposite coast sleeping green in it with all its woods; and lo! the steamer from the South sliding

in, with her red funnel, breaking the reflection with a tract
of foam, and disturbing the far-off morning silence with the
thunder of her paddles. By noon, a considerable stroke of
business had been done. Hordes of bellowing cattle were
being driven off toward Broadford, and drovers were rushing about in a wonderful manner, armed with tar-pot and
stick, smearing their peculiar mark upon the shaggy hides
of their purchases. Rough-looking customers enough, these
fellows, yet they want not means. Some of them, I am
told, came here this morning with five hundred pounds in
their pocket-books, and have spent every paper of it, and
this day three months they will return with as large a sum.
By three o'clock in the afternoon the place was deserted
by cattle, and fun and business gathered round the booths
and refreshment tents, the noise increasing every hour, and
towards evening deepening into brawl and general combat.

During the last few weeks I have had opportunity of wit-
nessing something of life as it passes in the Skye wilder-
nesses, and have been struck with its self-containedness, not
less than with its remoteness. A Skye family has everything within itself. The bare mountains yield them mutton,
of a flavor and delicacy unknown in the south. The copses
swarm with rabbits; and if a net is set over night at the
Black Island, there is abundance of fish to breakfast. The
farmer grows his own corn, barley, and potatoes, digs his
own peats, makes his own candles; he tans leather, spins
cloth shaggy as a terrier's pile, and a hunchback artist on
the place transforms the raw materials into boots or shepherd garments. Twice every year a huge hamper arrives
from Glasgow, stuffed with all the little luxuries of housekeeping, — tea, sugar, coffee, and the like. At more frequent intervals comes a ten-gallon cask from Greenock,
whose contents can cunningly draw the icy fangs of a north-
easter, or take the chill out of the clammy mists.

" What want they that a king should have?"

And once a week the *Inverness Courier*, like a window suddenly opened on the roaring sea, brings a murmur of the
outer world, its politics, its business, its crimes, its literature,
its whole multitudinous and unsleeping life, making the
stillness yet more still. To the Isle'sman the dial face of
the year is not artificially divided, as in cities, by parlia-
mentary session and recess, college terms or vacations, short
and long, by the rising and sitting of courts of justice nor
yet, as in more fortunate soils, by imperceptible gradations
of colored light, the green flowery year deepening into the
sunset of the October hollyhock, the slow reddening of burdened orchards, the slow yellowing of wheaten plains.
Not by any of these, but by the higher and more affecting
element of animal life, with its passions and instincts, its
gladness and suffering ; existence like our own, although in
a lower key, and untouched by its solemn issues ; the same
music and wail, although struck on ruder and uncertain
chords. To the Isle'sman, the year rises into interest
when the hills, yet wet with melted snows, are pathetic
with newly-yeaned lambs, and completes itself through the
successive steps of weaning, fleecing, sorting, fattening, sale,
final departure, and cash in pocket. The shepherd life is
. more interesting than the agricultural, inasmuch as it deals
with a higher order of being ; for I suppose — apart from
considerations of profit — a couchant ewe, with her young
one at her side, or a ram, "with wreathed horns superb,"
cropping the herbage, is a more pleasing object to the æs-
thetic sense than a field of mangold-wurzel, flourishing ever
so gloriously. The shepherd inhabits a mountain country,
lives more completely in the open air, and is acquainted
with all phenomena of storm and calm, the thunder-smoke
coiling in the wind, the hawk hanging stationary in the
breathless blue. He knows the faces of the hills, recognizes the voices of the torrents as if they were children of
his own, can unknit their intricate melody, as he lies with

his dog beside him on the warm slope at noon, separating tone from tone, and giving this to iron crag, that to pebbly bottom. From long intercourse, every member of his flock wears to his eye its special individuality, and he recognizes the countenance of a "wether" as he would the countenance of a human acquaintance. Sheep-farming is a picturesque occupation; and I think a cataract of sheep descending a hillside, now gathering into a mighty pool, now emptying itself in a rapid stream, — the dogs, urged more by sagacity than by the shepherd's voice, flying along the edges, turning, guiding, changing the shape of the mass, — one of the prettiest sights in the world. But the most affecting incident of shepherd life is the weaning of the lambs; — affecting, because it reveals passions in the "fleecy fools," the manifestation of which we are accustomed to consider ornamental in ourselves. From all the hills men and dogs drive the flocks down into a fold, or *fank*, as it is called here, consisting of several chambers or compartments. Into these compartments the sheep are huddled, and then the separation takes place. The ewes are returned to the mountains, the lambs are driven away to some spot where the pasture is rich, and where they are watched day and night. Midnight comes with dews and stars; the troop is couched peacefully as the cloudlets of a summer sky. Suddenly they are restless, ill at ease, goaded by some sore unknown want, and evince a disposition to scatter in every direction; but the shepherds are wary, the dogs swift and sure, and after a little while the perturbation is allayed, and they rest again. Walk up now to the fank. The full moon is riding between the hills, filling the glen with lustre and floating mysterious glooms. Listen! You hear it on every side of you, till it dies away in the silence of distance, — the fleecy Rachel weeping for her children. The turf walls of the fank are in shadow, but something seems to be moving there. As you approach, it disappears with a quick, short bleat, and a hurry of tiny hooves. Wonderful mystery of instinct! Affection all the more touching that it is so wrapt in darkness, hardly knowing its own meaning! For nights and nights the creatures will be found haunting about these turfen walls, seeking the young that have been taken away.

But my chief delight here is my friend and neighbor, Mr. MacIan. He was a soldier in his youth: is now very old, — ninety and odd, I should say. He would strike one with a sense of strangeness in a city, and among men of the present generation. Here, however, he creates no surprise; he is a natural product of the region, like the red heather, or the bed of the dried torrent. He is a master of legendary lore. He knows the history of every considerable family in the island; he circulates like sap through every genealogical tree; he is an enthusiast in Gaelic poetry, and is fond of reciting compositions of native bards, his eyes lighted up, and his tongue moving glibly over the rugged clots of consonants. He has a servant cunning upon the pipes, and, dwelling there for a week, I heard Ronald often wandering near the house, solacing himself with their music; now a plaintive love-song, now a coronach for chieftain borne to his grave, now a battle march, the notes of which, melancholy and monotonous at first, would all at once soar into a higher strain, and then hurry and madden as beating time to the footsteps of the charging clan. I am the fool of association; and the tree under which a king has rested, the stone in which a banner was planted on the morning of some victorious or disastrous day, the house in which some great man first saw the light, are to me the sacredest things. This slight, gray, keen-eyed man — the scabbard sorely frayed now, the blade sharp and bright as ever — gives me a thrill like an old coin with its half obliterated effigy, a Druid stone on a moor, a stain of blood on the floor of a palace. He stands before me a living figure, and history groups itself behind by way of background. He sits at the same board with me, and yet he lifted Moore at Corunna, and saw the gallant dying eyes flash up with their last pleasure when the Highlanders charged past. He lay down to sleep in the light of Wellington's watch-fires in the gorges of the piny Pyrenees; around him roared the death thunders of Waterloo. There is a certain awfulness about very old men; they are amongst us, but not of us. They crop out of the living soil and herbage of to-day, like rocky strata bearing marks of the glacier or the wave. Their roots strike deeper than ours, and they draw sustenance from an earlier layer of soil. They are lonely amongst the young; they cannot form new friendships, and are willing to be gone. They feel the " sublime attractions of the grave "; for the soil of churchyards once flashed kind eyes on them, heard with them the chimes at midnight, sang and clashed the brimming goblet with them; and the present Tom and Harry are as nothing to the Tom and Harry that swaggered about and toasted the reigning belles seventy years ago. We are accustomed to lament the shortness of life; but it is wonderful how long it is notwithstanding. Often a single life, like a summer twilight, connects two historic days. Count back four lives, and King Charles is kneeling on the scaffold at Whitehall. To hear MacIan speak, one could not help thinking in this way. In a short run across the mainland with him this summer, we reached Culloden Moor. The old gentleman with a mournful air — for he is a great Jacobite, and wears the Prince's hair in a ring — pointed out the burial-grounds of the clans. Struck with his manner, I inquired how he came to know their red resting-places. As if hurt, he drew himself up, laid his hand on my shoulder, saying, " Those who put them in told me." Heavens, how a century and odd years collapsed,

and the bloody field, — the battle-smoke not yet cleared
away, and where Cumberland's artillery told the clansmen
sleeping in thickest swaths, — unrolled itself from the
horizon down to my very feet! For a whole evening he
will sit and speak of his London life; and I cannot help
contrasting the young officer, who trod Bond Street with
powder in his hair at the end of last century, with the old
man living in the shadow of Blavin now.

Dwellers in cities have occasionally seen a house that
has the reputation of being haunted, and heard a ghost story
told. Most of them have knowledge of the trumpet-blast
that sounds when a member of the Airlie family is about
to die. Some few may have heard of the Irish gentleman
who, seated in the London opera-house on the night his
brother died, heard above the clash of the orchestra and the
passion of the singers, the shrill warning *keen* of the banshee,
— an evil omen always to him and his. City people laugh
when these stories are told, even although the blood should
run chill the while. Here, one is steeped in a ghostly atmosphere: men walk about here gifted with the second
sight. There has been something weird and uncanny about
the island for some centuries. Douglas, on the morning of
Otterbourne, according to the ballad, was shaken unto superstitious fears : —

> " But I hae dreamed a dreary dream,
>   Beyond the Isle of Skye ;
> I saw a dead man win a fight,
>   And I think that man was I."

Then the island is full of strange legends of the Norwegian times and earlier, — legends it might be worth Mr.
Dasent's while to take note of, should he ever visit the rainy
Hebrides. One such legend, concerning Ossian and his
poems, struck me a good deal. Near Mr. MacIan's place
is a ruined castle, a mere hollow shell of a building, Dun-
scaith by name, built in Fingalian days by the chieftain

Cuchullin, and so called in honor of his wife. The pile crumbles over the sea on a rocky headland bearded by gray green lichens. The place is quite desolate, and seldom visited. The only sounds heard there are the sharp whistle of the salt breeze, the bleat of a strayed sheep, the cry of wheeling sea-birds. MacIan and myself sat one summer day on the ruined stair. The sea lay calm and bright beneath, its expanse broken only by a creeping sail. Across the loch rose the great red hill, in the shadow of which Boswell got drunk; on the top of which is perched the Scandinavian woman's cairn. And out of the bare blue heaven, down on the ragged fringe of the Coolin hills, flowed a great white vapor gathering in the sunlight in mighty fleece on fleece. The old gentleman was the narrator, and the legend goes as follows: — The castle was built by Cuchullin and his Fingalians in a single night. The chieftain had many retainers, was a great hunter, and terrible in war. Every night at feast the minstrel Ossian sang his exploits. Ossian, on one occasion, in wandering among the hills, was struck by sweet strains of music that seemed to issue from a green knoll on which the sun shone temptingly. He sat down to listen, and was lulled asleep by the melody. He had no sooner fallen asleep than the knoll opened, and he beheld the under-world of the fairies. That afternoon and the succeeding night he spent in revelry, and in the morning he was allowed to return. Again the music sounded, again the senses of the minstrel were steeped in forgetfulness. And on the sunny knoll he awoke a gray-haired man; for in one short fairy afternoon and evening had been crowded a hundred of our human years. In his absence, the world had entirely changed, the Fingalians were extinct, and the dwarfish race, whom we call men, were possessors of the country. Longing for companionship, Ossian married the daughter of a shepherd, and in process of time a little girl was born to him. Years passed on; his wife died, and his daughter, woman grown now, married a pious man, — for the people were Christianized by this time, — called, from his love of psalmody, Peter of the Psalms. Ossian, blind with age, went to reside with his daughter and her husband. Peter was engaged all day in hunting, and when he came home at evening, and when the lamp was lighted, Ossian, sitting in a warm corner, was wont to recite the wonderful songs of his youth, and to celebrate the mighty battles and hunting feats of the big-boned Fingalians. To these songs Peter of the Psalms gave attentive ear, and being something of a penman, carefully inscribed them in a book. One day Peter had been more than usually successful in the chase, and brought home on his shoulders the carcass of a huge stag. Of this stag a leg was dressed for supper, and when it was picked bare, Peter triumphantly inquired of Ossian, "In the Fingalian days you speak about, killed you ever a stag so large as this?" Ossian balanced the bone in his hand; then, sniffing intense disdain, replied, "This bone, big as you think it, could be dropped into the hollow of a Fingalian blackbird's leg." Peter of the Psalms, enraged at what he conceived an unconceivable *crammer* on the part of his father-in-law, started up, swearing that he would not ruin his soul by preserving any more of his lying songs, and flung the volume in the fire; but his wife darted forward and snatched it up, half-charred, from the embers. At this conduct on the part of Peter, Ossian groaned in spirit, and wished to die, that he might be saved from the envy and stupidities of the little people, whose minds were as stunted as their bodies. When he went to bed he implored his ancient gods — for he was a sad heathen — to resuscitate, if but for one hour, the hounds, the stags, and the blackbirds of his youth, that he might astonish and confound the unbelieving Peter. His prayers done, he fell on slumber, and just before dawn a weight upon his breast awoke him. To his great joy, he found that his prayers were answered, for upon his breast was crouched his favorite hound. He spoke to it, and the faithful creature whimpered and licked his face. Swiftly he called his little grandson, and they went out with the hound. When they came to the top of an eminence, Ossian said, "Put your fingers in your ears, little one, else I will make you deaf for life." The boy put his fingers in his ears, and then Ossian whistled so loud that the whole world rang. He then asked the child if he saw anything. "O, such large deer!" said the child. "But a small herd, by the sound of it," said Ossian; "we will let that herd pass." Presently the child called out, "O, *such* large deer!" Ossian bent his ear to the ground to catch the sound of their coming, and then, as if satisfied, let slip the hound, who speedily tore down seven of the fattest. When the animals were skinned and laid in order, Ossian went towards a large lake, in the centre of which grew a remarkable bunch of rushes. He waded- into the lake, tore up the rushes, and brought to light the great Fingalian kettle, which had lain there for more than a century. Returning to their quarry, a fire was kindled; the kettle containing the seven carcasses was placed thereupon; and soon a most savory smell was spread abroad upon all the winds. When the animals were stewed, after the approved fashion of his ancestors, Ossian sat down to his repast. Now as, since his sojourn with the fairies, he had never enjoyed a sufficient meal, it was his custom to gather up the superfluous folds of his stomach by wooden splints, nine in number. As he now fed and expanded, splint after splint was thrown away, till at last, when the kettle was emptied, he lay down perfectly satisfied, and silent as ocean at the full of tide. Recovering himself, he gathered all the bones together, — set fire to them, till the black smoke which arose darkened the heaven. "Little one," then said Ossian, "go up to the knoll, and tell me if you see anything." "A great bird is flying hither," said the child; and immediately the great Fingalian blackbird alighted at the feet of Ossian, who at once caught and throttled it. The fowl was carried home, and was in the evening dressed for supper. After it was devoured, Ossian called for the stag's thigh-bone which had been the original cause of quarrel, and, before the face of the astonished and convicted Peter of the Psalms, dropped it in the hollow of the blackbird's leg. Ossian died on the night of his triumph, and the only record of his songs is the volume which Peter in his rage threw into the fire, and from which, when half consumed, it was rescued by his wife.

I am to stay with Mr. MacIan to-night. A wedding has taken place up among the hills, and the whole party have been asked to make a night of it. The mighty kitchen has been cleared for the occasion; torches are stuck up ready to be lighted; and I already hear the first mutterings of the bagpipe's storm of sound. The old gentleman wears a look of brightness and hilarity, and vows that he will lead off the first reel with the bride. Everything is prepared; and even now the bridal party are coming down the steep hill road. I must go out to meet them. To-morrow I return to my bothy, to watch the sunny mists congregating on the crests of Blavin in radiant billow on billow, and on which the level heaven seems to lean.

RUINS.

By JAMES GATES PERCIVAL.

EARTH is a waste of ruins; so I deemed,
When the broad sun was sinking in the sea
Of sand that rolled around Palmyra.   Night
Shared with the dying day a lonely sky,
The canopy of regions void of life,
And still as one interminable tomb.
The shadows gathered on the desert, dark
And darker, till alone one purple arch
Marked the far place of setting.   All above
Was purely azure, for no moon in heaven
Walked in her brightness, and with snowy light
Softened the deep intensity, that gave
Such awe unto the blue serenity
Of the high throne of gods, the dwelling-place
Of suns and stars, which are to us as gods,
The fountains of existence and the seat
Of all we dream of glory.   Dim and vast
The ruins stood around me, — temples, fanes,
Where the bright sun was worshipped, — where they gave
Homage to Him who frowns in storms, and rolls
The desert like an ocean, — where they bowed
Unto the queen of beauty, she in heaven
Who gives the night its loveliness, and smiles
Serenely on the drifted waste, and lends

A silver softness to the ridgy wave
Where the dark Arab sojourns, and with tales
Of love and beauty wears the tranquil night
In poetry away, her light the while
Falling upon him, as a spirit falls,
Dove-like or curling down in flame, a star
Sparkling amid his flowing locks, or dews
That melt in gold, and steal into the heart,
Making it one enthusiastic glow,
As if the God were present, and his voice
Spake on the eloquent lips that pour abroad
A gush of inspiration, — bright as waves
Swelling around Aurora's car, intense
With passion as the fire that ever flows
In fountains on the Caspian shore, and full
As the wide-rolling majesty of Nile.

Over these temples of an age of wild
And dark belief, and yet magnificent
In all that strikes the senses, — beautiful
In the fair forms they knelt to, and the domes
And pillars which upreared them, — full of life
In their poetic festivals, when youth
Gave loose to all its energy, in dance,
And song, and every charm the fancy weaves
In the soft twine of cultured speech, attuned
In perfect concord to the full-toned lyre :
When nations gathered to behold the pomp
That issued from the hallowed shrine in choirs
Of youths, who bounded to the minstrelsy
Of tender voices, and all instruments
Of ancient harmony, in solemn trains
Bearing the votive offerings, flowing horns
Of plenty wreathed with flowers, and gushing o'er
With the ripe clusters of the purple vine,

The violet of the fig, the scarlet flush
Of granates peeping from the parted rind,
The citron shining through its glossy leaves
In burnished gold, the carmine veiled in down,
Like mountain snow, on which the living stream
Flowed from Astarte's minion, all that hang
In Eastern gardens blended, — while the sheaf
Nods with its loaded ears, and brimming bowls
Foam with the kindling element, the joy
Of banquet, and the nectar that inspires
Man with the glories of a heightened power
To feel the touch of beauty, and combine
The scattered forms of elegance, till high
Rises a magic vision, blending all
That we have seen of glory, such as drew
Assembled Greece to worship, when the form,
Who gathered all its loveliness, arose
Dewy and blushing from the parent foam,
Than which her tint was fairer, and with hand
That seemed of living marble parted back
Her raven locks, and upward looked to Heaven,
Smiling to see all Nature bright and calm ; —
Over these temples, whose long colonnades
Are parted by the hand of time, and fall
Pillar by pillar, block by block, and strew
The ground in shapeless ruin, night descends
Unmingled, and the many stars shoot through
The gaps of broken walls, and glance between
The shafts of tottering columns, marking out
Obscurely, on the dark blue sky, the form
Of Desolation, who hath made these piles
Her home, and, sitting with her folded wings,
Wraps in her dusty robe the skeletons
Of a once countless multitude, whose toil
Reared palaces and theatres, and brought

All the fair forms of Grecian art to give
Glory unto an island girt with sands
As barren as the ocean, where the grave
And stately Doric marked the solemn fane
Where wisdom dwelt, and on the fairer shrine
Of beauty sprang the light Ionian, wreathed
With a soft volute, whose simplicity
Becomes the deity of loveliness,
Who with her snowy mantle, and her zone
Woven with all attractions, and her locks
Flowing as Nature bade them flow, compels
The sterner Powers to hang upon her smiles.
And there the grand Corinthian lifted high
Its flowery capital, to crown the porch
Where sat the sovereign of their hierarchy,
The monarch armed with terror, whose curled locks
Shaded a brow of thought and firm resolve,
Whose eye, deep sunk, shot out its central fires,
To blast and wither all who dared confront
The gaze of highest power; so sat their kings
Enshrined in palaces, and when they came
Thundering on their triumphal cars, all bright
With diadem of gold, and purple robe
Flashing with gems, before their rushing train
Moving in serried columns fenced in steel,
The herd of slaves obsequious sought the dust,
And gazed not as the mystic pomp rolled by.
Such were thy monarchs, Tadmor! now thy streets
Are silent, and thy walls o'erthrown, no voice
Speaks through the long dim night of years, to tell
These were once peopled dwellings; I could dream
Some sorcerer in his moonlight wanderings reared
These wonders in an hour of sport, to mock
The stranger with the show of life, and send
Thought through the mist of ages, in the search

Of nations who are now no more, who lived
Erst in the pride of empire, ruled and swayed
Millions in their supremacy, and toiled
To pile these monuments of wealth and skill,
That here the wandering tribe might pitch its tents
Securer in their empty courts, and we,
Who have the sense of greatness, low might kneel
To ancient mind, and gather from the torn
And scattered fragments visions of the power,
And splendor, and sublimity of old,
Mocking the grandest canopy of heaven,
And imaging the pomp of gods below.

A REVELATION OF CHILDHOOD.

(FROM A LETTER.)

BY MRS. JAMESON.

I WILL here put together some recollections of my own child-life; not because it was in any respect an exceptional or remarkable existence, but for a reason exactly the reverse, because it was like that of many children; at least I have met with many children who throve or suffered from the same or similar unseen causes even under external conditions and management every way dissimilar. Facts, therefore, which can be relied on, may be generally useful as hints towards a theory of conduct. What I shall say here shall be simply the truth so far as it goes; not something between the false and the true, garnished for effect, — not something half remembered, half imagined, — but plain, absolute, matter of fact.

No; certainly I was not an extraordinary child. I have had something to do with children, and have met with several more remarkable for quickness of talent and precocity of feeling. If anything in particular, I believe I was particularly naughty, — at least so it was said twenty times a day. But looking back now, I do not think I was particular even in this respect; I perpetrated not more than the usual amount of mischief — so called — which every lively, active child perpetrates between five and ten years old. I had the usual desire to know, and the usual dislike to learn; the usual love of fairy-tales, and hatred of French exercises. But not of what I learned, but of what I did *not* learn; not of what they taught me, but of what they could *not* teach me; not of what was open, apparent, manageable, but of the under-current, the hidden, the unmanaged or unmanageable, I have to speak, and you, my friend, to hear and turn to account, if you will, and how you will. As we grow old the experiences of infancy come back upon us with a strange vividness. There is a period when the over-flowing, tumultuous life of our youth rises up between us and those first years; but as the torrent subsides in its bed, we can look across the impassable gulf to that haunted fairy-land which we shall never more approach, and never more forget!

In memory I can go back to a very early age. I perfectly remember being sung to sleep, and can remember even the tune which was sang to me, — blessings on the voice that sang it! I was an affectionate, but not, as I now think, a lovable nor an attractive child. I did not, like the little Mozart, ask of every one around me, " Do you love me ? " The instinctive question was, rather, " Can I love you ? " Yet certainly I was not more than six years old when I suffered from the fear of not being loved where I had attached myself, and from the idea that another was preferred before me, such anguish as had nearly killed me. Whether those around me regarded it as a fit of ill-temper, or a fit of illness, I do not know. I could not then have given a name to the pang that fevered me. I knew not the cause, but never forgot the suffering. It left a deeper impression than childish passions usually do; and the recol-lection was so far salutary, that in after life I guarded myself against the approaches of that hateful, deformed, agonizing thing which men call jealousy, as I would from an attack of cramp or cholera. If such self-knowledge has

not saved me from the pain, at least it has saved me from
the demoralizing effects of the passion, by a wholesome
terror, and even a sort of disgust.

With a good temper, there was the capacity of strong,
deep, silent resentment, and a vindictive spirit of rather a
peculiar kind. I recollect that when one of those set over
me inflicted what then appeared a most horrible injury
and injustice, the thoughts of vengeance haunted my fancy
for months; but it was an inverted sort of vengeance.
I imagined the house of my enemy on fire, and rushed
through the flames to rescue her. She was drowning, and
I leaped into the deep water to draw her forth. She was
pining in prison, and I forced bars and bolts to deliver her.
If this were magnanimity, it was not the less vengeance;
for, observe, I always fancied evil, and shame, and humilia-
tion to my adversary; to myself the *rôle* of superiority and
gratified pride. For several years this sort of burning resentment against wrong done to myself and others, though it
took no mean or cruel form, was a source of intense, untold
suffering. · No one was aware of it. I was left to settle it;
and my mind righted itself I hardly know how; not certainly by religious influences, — they passed over my mind,
and did not at the time sink into it, — and as for earthly
counsel or comfort, I never had either when most needed.
And as it fared with me then, so it has been in after life; so
it has been, *must* be, with all those who, in fighting out alone
the pitched battle between principle and passion, will accept
no intervention between the infinite within them and the
infinite above them; so it has been, *must* be, with all strong
natures. Will it be said, that victory in the struggle brings
increase of strength? It may be so with some who survive
the contest; but then, how many sink! how many are crip-
pled morally for life! how many, strengthened in some particular faculties, suffer in losing the harmony of the character as a whole! This is one of the points in which the

matured mind may help the childish nature at strife with
itself. It is impossible to say how far this sort of vindictive-
ness might have penetrated and hardened into the character, if I had been of a timid or retiring nature. It was
expelled at last by no outer influences, but by a growing
sense of power and self-reliance.

In regard to truth — always such a difficulty in education
— I certainly had, as a child, and like most children, confused ideas about it. I had a more distinct and absolute
idea of honor than of truth, — a mistake into which our
conventional morality leads those who educate and those
who are educated. I knew very well, in a general way,
that to tell a lie was *wicked;* to lie for my own profit or
pleasure, or to the hurt of others, was, according to my
infant code of morals, worse than wicked, — it was *dishonor-
able.* But I had no compunction about telling *fictions;*
inventing scenes and circumstances which I related as real,
and with a keen sense of triumphant enjoyment in seeing
the listener taken in by a most artful and ingenious concate-
nation of impossibilities. In this respect " Ferdinand Men-
dez Pinto, that liar of the first magnitude," was nothing in
comparison to me. I must have been twelve years old
before my conscience was first awakened up to a sense of
the necessity of truth as a principle, as well as its holiness
as a virtue. Afterwards, having to set right the minds of
others cleared my own mind on this and some other important points.

I do not think I was naturally obstinate, but remember
going without food all day, and being sent hungry and
exhausted to bed, because I would not do some trifling
thing required of me. I think it was to recite some lines
I knew by heart. I was punished as wilfully obstinate ;
but what no one knew then, and what I know now as the

fact, was, that after refusing to do what was required, and bearing anger and threats in consequence, I lost the power to do it. I became stone: the *will* was petrified, and I absolutely *could* not comply. They might have hacked me in pieces before my lips could have unclosed to utterance. The obstinacy was not in the mind, but on the nerves; and I am persuaded that what we call obstinacy in children, and grown-up people too, is often something of this kind, and that it may be increased by mismanagement, by persistence, or what is called firmness in the controlling power, into disease, or something near to it.

There was in my childish mind another cause of suffering besides those I have mentioned, less acute, but more permanent, and always unacknowledged. It was fear, — fear of darkness and supernatural influences. As long as I can remember anything, I remember these horrors of my infancy. How they had been awakened I do not know; they were never revealed. I had heard other children ridiculed for such fears, and held my peace. At first these haunting, thrilling, stifling terrors were vague; afterwards the form varied; but one of the most permanent was the ghost in Hamlet. There was a volume of Shakespeare lying about, in which was an engraving I have not seen since, but it remains distinct in my mind as a picture. On one side stood Hamlet with his hair on end, literally "like quills upon the fretful porcupine," and one hand with all the fingers outspread. On the other strided the ghost, encased in armor with nodding plumes; one finger pointing forwards, and all surrounded with a supernatural light. O that spectre! for three years it followed me up and down the dark staircase, or stood by my bed: only the blessed light had power to exorcise it. How it was that I knew, while I trembled and quaked, that it was unreal, never cried out, never expostulated, never confessed, I do not know. The figure of Apollyon looming over Christian, which I had found in an old edition of the " Pilgrim's Progress," was also a great torment. But worse, perhaps, were certain phantasms without shape, — things like the vision in Job, — " *A spirit passed before my face ; it stood still, but I could not discern the form thereof*" : — and if not intelligible voices, there were strange, unaccountable sounds filling the air around with a sort of mysterious life. In daylight I was not only fearless, but audacious, inclined to defy all power and brave all danger, — that is, all danger I could see. I remember volunteering to lead the way through a herd of cattle (among which was a dangerous bull, the terror of the neighborhood) armed only with a little stick ; but first I said the Lord's Prayer fervently. In the ghastly night I never prayed ; terror stifled prayer. These visionary sufferings, in some form or other, pursued me till I was nearly twelve years old. If I had not possessed a strong constitution and a strong understanding, which rejected and contemned my own fears, even while they shook me, I had been destroyed. How much weaker children suffer in this way I have since known, and have known how to bring them help and strength, through sympathy and knowledge, — the sympathy that soothes, and does not encourage, the knowledge that dispels, and does not suggest, the evil.

People, in general, even those who have been much interested in education, are not aware of the sacred duty of *truth*, exact truth in their intercourse with children. Limit what you tell them according to the measure of their faculties ; but let what you say be the truth. Accuracy, not merely as to fact, but well-considered accuracy in the use of words, is essential with children. I have read some wise book on the treatment of the insane, in which absolute veracity and accuracy in speaking is prescribed as a *curative* principle ; and deception for any purpose is deprecated as almost fatal to the health of the patient. Now, it is a good sanitary principle, that what is curative is preventive; and that an unhealthy state of mind, leading to madness, may, in some organizations, be induced by that sort of uncertainty and perplexity which grows up where the mind has not been accustomed to truth in its external relations. It is like breathing for a continuance an impure or confined air.

Of the mischief that may be done to a childish mind by a falsehood uttered in thoughtless gayety, I remember an absurd and yet a painful instance. A visitor was turning over, for a little girl, some prints, one of which represented an Indian widow springing into the fire kindled for the funeral pile of her husband. It was thus explained to the child, who asked, innocently, whether, if her father died her mother would be burned? The person to whom the question was addressed, a lively, amiable woman, was probably much amused by the question, and answered giddily, "O, of course, — certainly!" and was believed implicitly. But thenceforth, for many weary months, the mind of that child was haunted and tortured by the image of her mother springing into the devouring flames, and consumed by fire, with all the accessories of the picture, particularly the drums beating to drown her cries. In a weaker organization, the results might have been permanent and serious. But to proceed.

These terrors I have described had an existence external to myself: I had no power over them to shape them by my will, and their power over me vanished gradually before a more dangerous infatuation, — the propensity to reverie. The shaping spirit of imagination began when I was about eight or nine years old to haunt my *inner* life. I can truly say that, from ten years old to fourteen or fifteen, I lived a double existence; one outward, linking me with the external sensible world, the other inward, creating a world to and for itself, conscious to itself only. I carried on for whole years a series of actions, scenes, and adventures; one springing out of another, and colored and modified by increasing knowledge. This habit grew so upon me, that there were moments — as when I came to some crisis in my imaginary adventures — when I was not more awake to outward things than in sleep, — scarcely took cognizance of the beings around me. When punished for idleness by being placed in solitary confinement (the worst of all punishments for children), the intended penance was nothing less than a delight and an emancipation, giving me up to my dreams. I had a very strict and very accomplished governess, one of the cleverest women I have ever met with in my life; but nothing of this was known or even suspected by her, and I exulted in possessing something which her power could not reach. My reveries were my real life: it was an unhealthy state of things.

Those who are engaged in the training of children will perhaps pause here. It may be said, in the first place, How are we to reach those recesses of the inner life which the God who made us keeps from every eye but his own? As when we walk over the field in spring we are aware of a thousand influences and processes at work of which we have no exact knowledge or clear perception, yet must watch and use according, — so it is with education. And, secondly, it may be asked, if such secret processes be working unconscious mischief, where the remedy? The remedy is in employment. Then the mother or the teacher echoes, with astonishment, "Employment! the child is employed from morning till night; she is learning a dozen sciences and languages; she has masters and lessons for every hour of every day; with her pencil, her piano, her books, her companions, her birds, her flowers, — what can she want more?" An energetic child even at a very early age, and yet further as the physical organization is developed, wants something more and something better; employment which shall bring with it the bond of a higher duty than that which centres in self and self-improvement; employment which shall not merely cultivate the understanding, but strengthen and elevate the conscience; employment for the higher and more generous faculties; employment addressed to the sympathies; employment which has the aim of utility, not pretended, but real, obvious, direct utility. A girl who as a mere child is not always being taught or being amused, whose mind is early restrained by the bond of definite duty, and thrown out of the limit of self, will not in after years be subject to fancies that disturb or to reveries that absorb, and the present and the actual will have that power they ought to have as combined in due degree with desire and anticipation.

The Roman Catholic priesthood understand this well employment, which enlists with the spiritual the sympathetic part of our being, is a means through which they guide both young and adult minds. Physicians who have to manage various states of mental and moral disease understand this well; they speak of the necessity of employment (not mere amusement) as a curative means, but of employment with the direct aim of usefulness, apprehended and appreciated by the patient, else it is nothing. It is the same with children. Such employment, chosen with reference to utility, and in harmony with the faculties, would prove in many cases either preventive or curative. In my own case, as I now think, it would have been both.

There was a time when it was thought essential that women should know something of cookery, something of medicine, something of surgery. If all these things are far better understood now than heretofore, is that a reason why a well-educated woman should be left wholly ignorant of them? A knowledge of what people call " common things," — of the elements of physiology, of the conditions of health, **of the qualities, nutritive or remedial, of** substances commonly **used as food or medicine, and the most** economical **and the most beneficial way of applying both,** — these **should form a part of the system of every girls'** school, — **whether for the higher or the lower classes.   At** present **you shall see a girl studying chemistry, and attend-** ing **Faraday's lectures, who would be puzzled to compound a rice-pudding or a cup of** barley-water: **and a girl who** could **work quickly a complicated sum in the Rule of Three, afterwards** wasting **a fourth of her husband's wages through want of** management.

In my own case, how much of the practical and sympathetic **in my nature was exhausted in airy visions!**

As to the stuff out of which my waking dreams were composed, **I cannot tell you much.   I have a** remembrance **that I was always a princess heroine in the disguise of a knight, a sort of Clorinda or Britomart, going** about to redress the **wrongs of the poor, fight giants and kill** dragons; or founding **a society in some far-off solitude or desolate** island, which **would have rivalled that of Gonsalez,** where there were **to be no tears, no tasks, and no laws,** — **except** those which **I made myself,** — **no caged birds nor tormented** kittens.

Enough of the pains, and mistakes, and vagaries of childhood; **let me tell of some of its pleasures equally un-** guessed **and unexpressed.   A great, an exquisite source of** enjoyment **arose out of an early, instinctive, boundless de-** **light in external beauty.   How this went hand in hand with my terrors and reveries, how it could coexist with them, I cannot tell now** — **it was so; and if this sympathy with the external,** living, **beautiful world had been** properly, **scien-** tifically cultivated, and **directed to useful definite purposes,** it would have been the best **remedy for much that was mor-**

bid; this was not the case, and we were, unhappily for me, too early removed from the country to a town residence. I can remember, however, that in very early years the appearances of nature did truly "haunt me like a passion"; the stars were to me as the gates of heaven; the rolling of the wave to the shore; the graceful weeds and grasses bending before the breeze as they grew by the wayside; the minute and delicate forms of insects; the trembling shadows of boughs and leaves dancing on the ground in the highest noon; — these were to me perfect pleasures, of which the imagery now in my mind is distinct. Wordsworth's poem of "The Daffodils," — the one beginning

> "I wandered lonely as a cloud," —

may appear to some unintelligible or overcharged, but to me it was a vivid truth, a simple fact; and if Wordsworth had been then in my hands, I think I must have loved him. It was this intense sense of beauty which gave the first zest to poetry: I loved it, not because it told me what I did not know, but because it helped me to words in which to clothe my own knowledge and perceptions, and reflected back the pictures unconsciously hoarded up in my mind. This was what made Thomson's "Seasons" a favorite book when I first began to read for my own amusement, and before I could understand one half of it; St. Pierre's "Indian Cottage" ("La Chaumière Indienne") was also charming, either because it reflected my dreams, or gave me new stuff for them in pictures of an external world quite different from that I inhabited, — palm-trees, elephants, tigers, dark-turbaned men with flowing draperies; and the "Arabian Nights" completed my Oriental intoxication, which lasted for a long time.

I have said little of the impressions left by books, and of my first religious notions. A friend of mine had once the wise idea of collecting together a variety of evidence as to

the impressions left by certain books on childish or imma-
ture minds. If carried out, it would have been one of the
most valuable additions to educational experience ever made.
For myself, I did not much care about the books put into
my hands, nor imbibe much information from them. I had
a great taste, I am sorry to say, for forbidden books; yet it
was not the forbidden books that did the mischief, except in
their being read furtively. I remember impressions of vice
and cruelty from some parts of the Old Testament and
Goldsmith's "History of England," which I shudder to recall. Shakespeare was on the forbidden shelf. I had read
him all through between seven and ten years old. He
never did me any moral mischief. He never soiled my
mind with any disordered image. What was exceptionable
and coarse in language I passed by without attaching any
meaning whatever to it. How it might have been if I had
read Shakespeare first when I was fifteen or sixteen, I do
not know; perhaps the occasional coarseness and obscuri-
ties might have shocked the delicacy or puzzled the intelligence of that sensitive and inquiring age. But at nine or
ten I had no comprehension of what was unseemly; what
might be obscure in words to wordy commentators, was to
me lighted up by the idea I found or interpreted for myself,
— right or wrong.

No; I repeat, Shakespeare'— bless him! — never did me
any moral mischief. Though the Witches in Macbeth
troubled me, — though the Ghost in Hamlet terrified me
(the picture, that is, — for the spirit in Shakespeare was solemn and pathetic, not hideous), — though poor little Arthur
cost me an ocean of tears, — yet much that was obscure,
and all that was painful and revolting, was merged on the
whole in the vivid presence of a new, beautiful, vigorous
living world. The plays which I now think the most wonderful produced comparatively little effect on my fancy: Ro-
meo and Juliet, Othello, Macbeth, struck me then less than

the historical plays, and far less than the Midsummer Night's Dream and Cymbeline. It may be thought, perhaps, that Falstaff is not a character to strike a child, or to be understood by a child : — no ; surely not. To me Falstaff was not witty and wicked, — only irresistibly fat and funny ; and I remember lying on the ground rolling with laughter over some of the scenes in Henry the Fourth, — the mock play, and the seven men in buckram. But the Tempest and Cymbeline were the plays I liked best and knew best.

Altogether, I should say that in my early years books were known to me, not as such, not for their general contents, but for some especial image or picture I had picked out of them and assimilated to my own mind and mixed up with my own life. For example, out of Homer's Odyssey (lent to me by the parish clerk) I had the picture of Nasicaa and her maidens going down in their chariots to wash their linen : so that when the first time I went to the Pitti Palace, and could hardly see the pictures through blinding tears, I saw *that* picture of Rubens, which all remember who have been at Florence, and it flashed delight and refreshment through those remembered childish associations. The Sirens and Polypheme left also vivid pictures on my fancy. The Iliad, on the contrary, wearied me, except the parting of Hector and Andromache, in which the child, scared by its father's dazzling helm and nodding crest, remains a vivid image in my mind from that time.

The same parish clerk — a curious fellow in his way — lent me also some religious tracts and stories, by Hannah More. It is most certain that more moral mischief was done to me by some of these than by all Shakespeare's plays together. These so-called pious tracts first introduced me to a knowledge of the vices of vulgar life and the excitements of a vulgar religion, — the fear of being hanged and the fear of hell became coexistent in my mind ; and the teaching

resolved itself into this, — that **it was not by** being naughty,
but by being found out, that **I was to incur** the risk of both.
My fairy world was better !

About religion ; — I was taught religion as children used
to be taught it in my younger days, and are taught it still in
some cases, I believe, — through the medium of creeds and
catechisms. I read the Bible too early, and too indiscrim-
inately, and too irreverently. Even the New Testament
was too early placed in my hands ; too early made a lesson-
book, as the custom then was. The *letter* of the Scriptures
— the words — were familiarized to me by sermonizing and
dogmatizing, long before I could enter into the *spirit*. Meantime, happily, another religion was growing up in my heart,
which, strangely enough, seemed to me quite apart from that
which was taught, — which, indeed, I never in any way
regarded as the same which I was taught when I stood up
wearily on a Sunday to repeat the collect and say the cate-
chism. It was quite another thing. Not only the taught
religion and the sentiment of faith and adoration were never
combined, but it never for years entered into my head to
combine them ; the first remained extraneous, the latter had
gradually taken root in my life, even from the moment my
mother joined my little hands in prayer. The histories out
of the Bible (the Parables especially) were, however, en-
chanting to me, though my interpretation of them was in
some instances the very reverse of correct or orthodox. To
my infant conception our Lord was a being who had come
down from heaven to make people good, and to tell them
beautiful stories. And though no pains were spared to
indoctrinate me, and all my pastors and masters took it for
granted that my ideas were quite satisfactory, nothing could
be more confused and heterodox.

It is a common observation that girls of lively talents are
apt to grow pert and satirical. I fell into this danger when

about ten years old. Sallies at the expense of certain people, ill-looking, or ill-dressed, or ridiculous, or foolish, had
been laughed at and applauded in company, until, without
being naturally malignant, I ran some risk of becoming so
from sheer vanity.

The fables which appeal to our higher moral sympathies
may sometimes do as much for us as the truths of science.
So thought our Saviour when he taught the multitude in
parables.

A good clergyman who lived near us, a famous Persian
scholar, took it into his head to teach me Persian, (I was
then about seven years old,) and I set to work with infinite
delight and earnestness. All I learned was soon forgotten;
but a few years afterwards, happening to stumble on a
volume of Sir William Jones's works, — his Persian grammar, — it revived my Orientalism, and I began to study it
eagerly. Among the exercises given was a Persian fable
or poem, — one of those traditions of our Lord which are
preserved in the East. The beautiful apologue of " St.
Peter and the Chefries," which Goethe has versified or
imitated, is a well-known example. This fable I allude to
was something similar, but I have not met with the original
these forty years, and must give it here from memory.

" Jesus," says the story, " arrived one evening at the
gates of a certain city, and he sent his disciples forward to
prepare supper, while he himself, intent on doing good,
walked through the streets into the market-place.

" And he saw at the corner of the market some people
gathered together looking at an object on the ground ; and
he drew near to see what it might be. It was a dead dog,
with a halter round his neck, by which he appeared to have
been dragged through the dirt ; and a viler, a more abject,
a more unclean thing never met the eyes of man.

" And those who stood by looked on with abhorrence.

"' Faugh!' said one, stopping his nose; 'it pollutes the air.' 'How long,' said another, 'shall this foul beast offend our sight?' 'Look at his torn hide,' said a third; 'one could not even cut a shoe out of it.' 'And his ears,' said a fourth, 'all draggled and bleeding!' 'No doubt,' said a fifth, 'he hath been hanged for thieving!'

" And Jesus heard them, and looking down compassionately on the dead creature, he said, 'Pearls are not equal to the whiteness of his teeth!'

" Then the people turned towards him with amazement, and said among themselves, 'Who is this? this must be Jesus of Nazareth, for only He could find something to pity and approve even in a dead dog'; and being ashamed, they bowed their heads before him, and went each on his way."

I can recall, at this hour, the vivid, yet softening and pathetic impression left on my fancy by this old Eastern story.. It struck me as exquisitely humorous, as well as exquisitely beautiful. It gave me a pain in my conscience, for it seemed thenceforward so easy and so vulgar to say satirical things, and so much nobler to be benign and merciful, and I took the lesson so home, that I was in great danger of falling into the opposite extreme, — of seeking the beautiful even in the midst of the corrupt and the repulsive. Pity, a large element in my composition, might have easily degenerated into weakness, threatening to subvert hatred of evil in trying to find excuses for it; and whether my mind has ever completely righted itself, I am not sure.

Educators are not always aware, I think, how acute are the perceptions, and how permanent the memories of children. I remember experiments tried upon my temper and feelings, and how I was made aware of this, by their being repeated, and, in some instances, spoken of, before me. Music, to which I was early and peculiarly sensitive, was sometimes made the medium of these experiments. Discordant sounds were not only hateful, but made me turn white and cold, and sent the blood backward to my heart; and certain tunes had a curious effect, I cannot now account for: for though, when heard for the first time, they had little effect, they became intolerable by repetition; they turned up some hidden emotion within me too strong to be borne. It could not have been from association, which I believe to be a principal element in the *emotion* excited by music. I was too young for that. What associations could such a baby have had with pleasure or with pain? Or could it be possible that associations with some former state of existence awoke up to sound? That our life "hath elsewhere its beginning, and cometh from afar," is a belief, or at least an instinct, in some minds, which music, and only music, seems to thrill into consciousness. At this time, when I was about five or six years old, Mrs. Arkwright, — she was then Fanny Kemble, — used to come to our house, and used to entrance me with her singing. I had a sort of adoration for her, such as an ecstatic votary might have for a Saint Cecilia. I trembled with pleasure, when I only heard her step. But her voice! — it has charmed hundreds since; whom has it ever moved to a more genuine passion of delight than the little child that crept silent and tremulous to her side? And she was fond of me, — fond of singing to me, and, it must be confessed, fond also of playing these experiments on me. The music of " Paul and Virginia " was then in vogue, and there was one air — a very simple air — in that opera, which, after the first few bars, always made me stop my ears and rush out of the room. I became at last aware that this was sometimes done by particular desire to please my parents, or amuse and interest others by the display of such vehement emotion. My infant conscience became perplexed between the reality of the feeling and the exhibition of it. People are not always aware of the injury done to children by repeating before them things they say, or describing things they do: words and actions, spontaneous and unconscious, become thenceforth artificial and conscious. I can speak of the injury done to myself, between five and eight years old. There was some danger of my becoming a precocious actress, — danger of permanent mischief such as I have seen done to other children, — but I was saved by the recoil of resistance and resentment excited in my mind.

This is enough. All that has been told here refers to a period between five and ten years old.

TO MONTAGUE,

AT THIRTY-THREE.

BY CHARLES SPRAGUE.

O NO, I 'll not forget the day, —
　　It claims, at least, a hallowed hour,
A sparkling cup, an honest lay,
　　Sacred to Friendship's soothing power.

'T is not all ice, this heart of mine, —
　　One throb is warm and youthful still;
That throb, dear MONTAGUE, is thine,
　　Nor age nor grief that throb can chill.

How often sung, and yet how sweet
　　To dwell upon the days of old!
Our guiltless pleasures to repeat,
　　Ere in the world our hearts grew cold!

Fond memory wakes! each pulse beats high;
　　Like some sweet tale past joys come o'er,
The years of ruin backward fly,
　　And I am young and gay once more.

Friend of my soul! in this poor verse
　　Let one untutored tribute live;
Here let my tongue my love rehearse;
　　'T is all, alas! I have to give

O, if from time's wide-yawning grave
    There 's aught of mine that I could free,
One line from dull oblivion save,
    'T would be the line that tells of thee.

Though to the busy world unknown
    Each noble act that shrinks from fame,
Goodness its favorite son shall own,
    And orphan lips shall bless his name.

Thou 'rt the small stream, that silent goes,
    By earth's cold, plodding crowd unseen, —
Yet, all unnoticed though it flows,
    Its banks are clothed in living green.

We met in that bright, sunny time,
    When every scene was fresh around,
And youth's warm hour and manhood's prime
    Have blessed the tie that boyhood bound.

Though oft of valued friends bereft,
    I bend, submissive, to the doom;
For thou, the best, the best, art left,
    To cheer my journey to the tomb.

And now, the dear ones of our race
    Have come to live our pleasures o'er;
A lovely troop, to fill our place,
    And weep for us when we 're no more.

Ever, O ever may they keep
    The holy chain of friendship bright,
Till, rich in all that's good, they sleep
    With us through death's long, dreamless night.

THE MAN-HUNTER.

By BARRY CORNWALL.

IT can scarcely be more than eighteen months ago, that
two Englishmen met together unexpectedly at the little
town or city of Dessau. The elder was a grave person, in
no way remarkable; but the younger forced observation
upon him. He was a tall, gaunt, bony figure, presenting the
relics of a formidable man, but seemingly worn with travel
and oppressed by weighty thoughts. He must once have
been handsome; and he was even now imposing. But poverty and toil are sad enemies to human beauty; and he had
endured both. Nevertheless, the black and ragged elf-locks
which fell about his face could not quite conceal its noble
proportions; and, although his cheek was ghastly and macer-
ated, (perhaps by famine,) there was a wild, deep-seated
splendor glowing in his eye, such as we are apt to ascribe
to the poet when his frenzy is full upon him, or to the
madman when he dreams of vengeance.

The usual salutations of friends passed between them,
and they conversed for a short time on indifferent subjects;
the elder, as he spoke, scrutinizing the condition of his acquaintance, and the other glancing about from time to time,
with restless, watchful eyes, as though he feared some one
might escape his observation, or else might detect himself.
The name of the elder of these men was Denbigh: that
of the younger has not reached me. We will call him

Gordon. It was the curiosity of the first-mentioned that, after a reasonable period, broke out into inquiry. (They were just entering the public room of the Black Eagle at Dessau.)

"But what has brought you here?" said he. "I left you plodding at a merchant's desk, with barely the means of living. Though a friend, you would never let me please myself by lending you money; nor would you be my companion down the Rhine, some three years ago. You professed to hate travelling. Yet I find you here,— a traveller evidently, with few comforts. Come, be plain with me. Tell me,— what has brought you hither? Or rather what has withered and wasted you, and made your hair so gray? You are grown quite an old man."

"Ay," replied Gordon; "I am old, as you say, old enough. Winter is upon me, on my head, on my heart; both are frozen up. Do you wish to know what brought me here? Well, you have a right to know; and you shall be told. You shall hear — a tale."

"A true one?" inquired Denbigh, smilingly.

"True!" echoed the other; "ay, as true as hell, as dark, as damnable,— but peace, peace!" said he, checking himself for a moment, and then proceeding in a hoarse, whispering, vehement voice, — "all that in time. We must begin quietly, — quietly. Come, let us drink some wine, and you shall see presently what a calm historian I am."

Wine, together with some more solid refreshments, were accordingly ordered. Gordon did not taste the latter, but swallowed a draught or two of the bold liquid, which seemed to still his nerves like an opiate. He composed himself, and indeed appeared disposed to forget that there was such a thing as trouble in the world, until the impatience of his friend (which vented itself in the shape of various leading questions) induced him to summon up his recollections. He compressed his lips together for a moment, and drew a short, deep breath, through his inflated nostrils; but otherwise there was no preface or introduction to his story, which commenced nearly, if not precisely, in the following words : —

"About three years ago, a young girl was brought to one of those charitable institutions in the neighborhood of London, where the wretched (the sinful and the destitute) find refuge and consolation. She was, you may believe me, beautiful; *so* beautiful, so delicate, and, as I have said, so young, that she extorted a burst of pity and admiration from people long inured to look upon calamity.

"She was attended by her mother, — a widow. This woman differed from her child; not merely in age or feature. She was, in comparison, masculine; her face was stern; her frame strong and enduring; she looked as though hunger and shame had been busy with her, — as though she had survived the loss of all things, and passed the extreme limits of human woe. Once — for I knew her — she would have disdained to ask even for pity. O, what she must have borne, in body, in mind, before she could have brought herself to become a suppliant there! Yet there she was, — she, and her youngest born in her hand, beggars. She presented her child to the patronesses of the institution; and, with an unbroken voice, prayed them to take her in for refuge.

"The common questions were asked, the who, the whence, the wherefore, &c. Even something more than common curiosity displayed itself in the inquiries, and all was answered with an unflinching spirit. The mother's story was sad enough. Let us hope that such things are rare in England. She was the widow of a military man, an officer of courage and conduct, who died in battle. If we could live upon laurels, his family need not have starved. But the laurel is a poisonous tree. It is gay and shining, and undecaying; but whoso tasteth it dies! No matter now.

The widow and three children were left almost without money. The father had indeed possessed some little property; but it consisted of bonds, or notes, or securities of a transferable nature; and was intrusted (without receipt or acknowledgment) to — a villain. The depositary used it for his own purposes; denied his trust; and, with the coldness of a modern philosopher, saw his victims thrust out of doors, to starve! A good Samaritan gave them bread and employment for a few weeks; but he died suddenly, and they were again at the mercy of fortune.

" It was now that the mother felt that her children looked up to her for life. And she answered the appeal as a mother only can. She toiled to the very utmost of her strength: nothing was too much, nothing too base or menial for her. She worked, and watched, and endured all things, from all persons; and thus it was that she obtained coarse food for her young ones, — sometimes even enough to satisfy their hunger; till at last the eldest boy became useful, and began to earn money also; and *then* they were able almost daily to taste — bread! It is a wonder how they lived, — how they shunned the vices and squalid evils which beset the poor. But they *did* so. They withstood all temptations. They felt no envy nor hatred for the great and fortunate. The sordid errors of their station never fastened on them. They grew up honest, liberal-minded, courageous. They wanted not even for learning, or at least knowledge. For, after a time, a few cheap books were bought or borrowed, and the ambition which the mother taught them to feel served the boys in place of instructors. They read and studied. After working all day, (running on errands, hewing wood, and drawing water,) these children of a noble mother sat down to gather learning; never disobeying, never murmuring to do what she, to whom they owed all things, commanded them to achieve. Yet, little merit is due to *them*. It was *she*, the incomparable mother, who did all; saved, supported, endured all for her children's sake, for her dead husband's sake, and for the disinterested love of virtue!

"I know not what frightful crimes some progenitor might have committed, what curse he might have brought upon this race; but if *none*, in the name of God's mercy, why, (when they had been steeped in baseness and poverty to the lips,) *why* was a curse more horrible than all to come upon them? Poor creatures! had they not endured enough? What is the axe or the gibbet to the daily never-dying pain which a mother feels who sees her children famishing away before her? Sickness, cold, hunger, the contempt of friends, the hate or indifference of all the world besides, the perpetual heart-breaking toil and struggle to live! to get bread, yet often want it! Was not all enough? I suppose not; for a curse greater than all fell upon them.

"A friend, — ha, ha, ha! — let me use common words, — a friend of the elder son (who had, by degrees, risen to be a manufacturer's clerk), visited them at their humble abode. He was rich, he was, moreover, a specious youth, fair and florid, — such as young girls fancy; but as utterly hard and impenetrable to every touch of honor or pity as the stone we tread upon. He — I must make short work of this part of my story — he loved the young sister of his friend, or rather he sought her with the brutal appetite of an animal. He talked, and smiled, and flattered her, — (she was a weak thing, and his mummery pleased her): he brought presents to her mother, and, at last, ruin and shame upon herself. She was *so* young, — not fifteen years of age! But this base and hellish slave had no mercy on her innocent youth, no respect for her desolate condition. He ruined her — O, there were horrid circumstances! — force, and fraud, and cruelty of all kinds, that I will not touch upon. It is sufficient to say that her destruction was achieved, and all her family in his power. The child (herself now about to be a mother) meditated death. She was timid, however, and shrank from the vague and gloomy terrors of the grave. So she lived on, pale and humbled, uttering no complaint, and disclosing no disgrace, until her mother noticed her despondency, and reproached her for it. With a trembling heart — trembling at she knew not what — she inquired solemnly the cause of all this woe. The girl could not stand those piercing looks. The mother whom she had obeyed, not only with love, but in fear also, commanded a disclosure, and the poor victim sunk on her knees before her. She told her sad story with sobs and streaming eyes, and with her figure abased to absolute prostration. Her parent listened (she would rather have listened to her own death-warrant), — looked ghastly at her for a minute, and reproached her no more! Some accident, — some intermission of employment, (I forget what,) made it impossible to support the poor fallen child with proper care. This inability it was, joined to a wish to keep her shame secret, that carried the mother and daughter to the charitable place of which I have spoken. And there the child was deposited, under a feigned name, to undergo the pangs of childbirth.

"But the sons! Do you not ask, where are *they*? Ha, ha! I am coming to that. They knew nothing, — suspected nothing, till all the mother's plans were effected; and then, with a gloomy countenance, and a voice troubled to its depths with many griefs, she told them — ALL."

"How did they bear it? What did they say or do?" inquired Denbigh, breaking silence for the first time since the commencement of the story. Gordon answered : —

"Her communication was, at first, absolutely unintelligible. It was so sudden, and so utterly unsuspected, that it bore the character of a dream or a fable. They stood bewildered. But when the truth, — the real, bad, terrible truth became plain, — when it was repeated with more particulars, and made frightfully distinct, — the eldest son burst into a rage of words. The younger, a youth of more concentrated passions, started up, opened his mouth as though he would utter some curse; but instantly fell dead on the floor."

"Good G—d!" interrupted Denbigh again, "and did he die?"

"No," replied the other, "he but appeared to die. Did I say 'dead'? No; I was wrong. He was not irrecoverably dead. By prompt help he was revived. In the struggle between life and death blood burst from his mouth and from his nose, and he felt easier. Perhaps the oath which he at that moment was prescribing to himself — the fierce, implacable, unalterable determination which his soul was forming — tranquillized his spirit; for he awoke to apparent calmness, and expressed himself resigned. But he was not so to be satisfied. Patience, — resignation, — forgiveness, — these are good words: they are virtues, perhaps; but they were not *his*. He was of a fiery spirit —"

"Like yourself," said Denbigh, trying to smile away the painful impression which the story was producing on his mind.

"Ay, like myself, sir," was the fierce answer. "He thought that vengeance, where punishment was manifestly due, was scarcely the shadow of a crime; and *I* think so too. He swore, silently, but solemnly, (and invoked all Heaven and Hell to attest his oath,) that he would thenceforward have but one object, one ambition; and this was — REVENGE! He swore to take the blood of the betrayer, and — *he did*."

"When? where?" asked Denbigh, quickly.

"Let us take some wine," said Gordon; "I am speaking now," continued he, after he had drunk, "of what *must* be. The future is not yet come. But as sure as I see you be-

fore me, so surely do I see the consummation of this revenge. There is a fate in some things: there is one in this.
Do you remember the story of the Spaniard Aguirra?"

"No!" answered the other.

"Yet, it is well known, — it is true, — it is memorable,
and it deserves to be remembered; for (except in the one
instance of which I now speak) it stands alone in the catalogue of extraordinary events. You shall hear it presently,
if it be only to rescue, by a parallel case, my story from the
character of a fiction. At present, let it suffice to say, that
sure as was Aguirra's vengeance, so sure shall be — MINE!"

"Yours!" exclaimed Denbigh, "do I hear aright?"

"Ay, open your ears wide. I am *the Revenger!* *My*
family it is who owe Fortune so little, — to whom vengeance
owes so much! *My* mother and her famished brood it was
of whose sufferings I have spoken, and whose injuries I am
destined to revenge."

"But the villain —?" inquired Denbigh.

"You do well to bring me back to him. Yet think not
that I for a moment forget him. He fled when he knew, —
nay, *before* he knew, — when he but *surmised* that we had
discovered his villany. He collected money together, and
left his country. But I was soon upon his track. I too had
gathered some hard earnings, and my brother more; and
with these united, I commenced a desperate pursuit. I will
not weary you by recounting the many difficulties of my task;
how many thousand miles I have journeyed barefoot, with
little clothing, with less food (for I was forced to economize
my poor means); how for three years I have been generally
a beggar for my bread, a companion with the unsheltered
dog; how I have been wounded, robbed, and even once imprisoned. *That* fortunately was but for a day, or it might
have overthrown my plans of vengeance. Thanks to the
furies, it did not; I followed him, — over all countries, from
Moscow to Madrid, from the Baltic to the Carpathians. He

fled with a sense, with a knowledge, that I was *forever* on his track. He slept trebly armed, locked in and barred from all access. He has been known to rise at night, and take flight for a distant land. But, with the unerring sense of a bloodhound, I was always after him. I was sure of him. He never escaped me. No disguise, no swiftness of journeying, no digressions from the ordinary path, no doubles, nor turnings, nor common feints, such as the hunted beast resorts to in his despair, availed *him*. Wherever he was — *there was I!* not so soon perhaps, but quite as surely.

"Twenty times I have been near meeting him alone, and consummating my purpose. But one thing or other perpetually intervened. A casual blow, without the certainty of its being fatal, would have been nothing. He might have recovered, — he might have lived to see me proclaimed a malefactor, and have borne evidence against me; and then *he* would have triumphed, and not I. I resolved to make surer work; to *see* that he should die; and for myself, I determined to live, for some time at least, in order to enjoy the remembrance of having accomplished one deed of justice.

"I said that I would not weary you with a narrative of my travels and a repetition of my failures. But one adventure amongst many occurs to me, somewhat differing from the rest, and you shall hear it. One of my transits was across the whole face of Europe; from an obscure town in Flanders to the Porte. I had scarcely reached the Fanar (where I was housed by a Greek, whom I had served in an accidental affray), when I fell sick of a fiery distemper, — some plague or fever begot in those burning regions, which sometimes destroys the native and almost always the luckless stranger. In my extremity, my kind hosts sent for a physician, — a converted Jew. He came and heard my ravings, and let the sickness deal with me as it chose. Some words, however, which I threw out in my delirium (at his second

visit) excited his curiosity; and coming, as they did, from a
Frank, he was induced to communicate them to an Englishman who lodged in his house. This Englishman was — *the
fiend,* the fugitive, whom I had chased so long in vain. A
few words and a lump of gold concluded a bargain; and
the next time the scowling Issachar came to my bedside, he
ordered a cup of coffee for his patient. I had at that time
recovered my senses, and became suddenly and sensitively
awake to everything about me. I saw the renegade take a
powder from his vest, and, after looking round to see that
all was clear, put it, with a peculiar look, into the cup. '*It
is poison,*' I said to myself; and by a sudden effort (while
the Israelite's back was turned), I forced myself upwards,
and sat, like a corpse revived, awaiting his attention. After
he had drugged the draught, he turned round suddenly and
beheld me. There I was, unable to speak indeed, but
ghastly and as white as stone, threatening and grinning, and
chattering unintelligible sounds. He was staggered; but
recovering himself with a smile, he tendered the detestable
potion. I had just strength enough to dash it out of his
hand, and sank on the bed exhausted. When I recovered I
found myself alone; nor did I ever again see my physician.

"I do not complain of this. Life for life is an equal
stake. I knew the game which I was playing. Death for
one or both of us, — that was certain. Quiet for him, at all
events (upon the earth or within it); perhaps revenge for
me. I was not angry at this attempt on my life. I liked it
better, in truth, than hunting day after day, week after week,
a flying, timorous, unresisting wretch. The opposition, the
determination he evinced to strike again, spurred me on.
It afforded a relief to my perpetual disappointment; it
checkered the miserable monotony of my life. Sometimes I
had almost felt compassion for my harassed and terrified
enemy, and generally contempt. But *now* — an adder was
before me. It rose up, and strove to use its fangs, and was

no longer to be trod on without peril. These thoughts, strange as it may seem, contributed to my recovery. I grew tranquil and well apace; and when I was fit to travel, I found that my foe had quitted precipitately the banks of the Bosphorus.

"I had little difficulty in learning his route; for my Greek had his national subtilty, and did not spare money to set me on the track. The Jew doctor (he had a second bribe) said that he had overheard my victim bargaining with a Tartar courier to conduct him to Vienna. Upon this hint, I set off on my dreary journey through the Ottoman Empire and its huge provinces, — Roumelia, Wallachia, Transylvania. I traversed the great uncultivated plains of Turkey; I crossed the Balkan and the muddy Danube; escaped the quarantine of the Crapaks; and finally dismounted at Vienna, just as a carriage was heard thundering along the Presburg road containing a traveller to whom haste was evidently of the last importance. 'T WAS HE! I saw him; and he saw *me*. He saw me, and knew in a moment that all his toilsome journey was once more in vain. I saw him grow pale before me, and I triumphed. Ha! ha! — that night I was joyful. I ate, and drank, and dreamt, as though I had no care or injury upon me. The next morning I looked to see that my dagger was sharp, and my pistols primed, and set out on foot to decoy my foe into a quiet place, fit for the completion of my purpose. But I failed, as I had failed often before. I beset him, I tried to surprise him; I kept him in incessant alarm; but the end was still the same. He was still destined to escape me, and I to remain his pursuer.

" How it was that he retained his senses, that he had still spring of mind to fly and hope to escape pursuit, is a mystery to me. I have often wondered that he did not bare his throat before me, and end his misery; as those who grow dizzy on a precipice, cast themselves from it, and find refuge from their intolerable fears — in death. But no; his love of life, his fear (caused by that love of life), were so great, so insuperable, that they never seemed capable, as in ordinary cases, of sinking into indifference or despair. He had no moral, no intellectual qualities, no courage of any sort. Yet by his *fear* alone, he became at times absolutely terrific. His struggles, his holding on to life, (when nothing was left worth living for,) his sleepless, ceaseless activity in flight, assumed a serious and even awful character. He pursued *his purpose* as steadily and as unflinchingly as I pursued mine. Terror never stopped him; hope never forsook him. From one end of the world to the other he fled — backwards and forwards, this way, and that — he fled, and fled; not dropping from apprehension, like the dove or the wren; but still keeping on his way, like some fierce bird of prey, who, driven from one region, will still seek another, and another, and fight it out to the last extremity. So frightful have been his struggles, so wild and fantastic the character of his fears, that once or twice, I — (his destroyer) — I, who was watching him with an ever-deadly purpose, became absolutely daunted and oppressed. I resumed my strength, however, speedily, as you will suppose; for what his fear was to him, hate or revenge was to me, — the sole stirring principle of life. Oh! this accursed wretch! does he ever dream that I relax? — that toil, and destitution, and danger have any effect upon *me*? He shall live to find himself in error. I am the fate, — the bloodhound that *will* follow, and *must* find him at last. Let me give up the contest at once, and all will be quiet; — no more fear for him, — no more sad labors for me! Of what value is life to either of us? But yes, — to *me*, it is of value; for I have a deed to do, an act of justice to perform on the most reckless and heartless villain that ever disgraced the human name."

"And *his* name. what is that?" asked Denbigh.

"Warne, — Warne, — the brand of hell be on him!"

"Hush! do not speak so loud! Look! there is some one in yonder box who has heard you," said Denbigh again, in a suppressed tone.

"I care not," replied the other. "This devil who walks in human shape, and under the name of Warne, is now in this city. He has eluded me for a short — a very short time — by shifting his course and changing his disguises. But I am here, and shall find him, wherever he lurks. Be sure of it."

At this moment a stranger was seen stealing from a box, where he had been taking refreshment. He appeared by his walk (for the two speakers saw only his back) to be an old man. He said nothing; but, walking up towards the end of the room, where a person attached to the inn was standing, put a piece of money in his hand, (evidently more than sufficient to discharge his bill,) and left the house.

From the first movement of the stranger, the attention of Gordon was upon him: his neck was stretched out, his eyes strained and wide open; he even seemed to listen to his tread.

"What is the matter?" said Denbigh. "There is nothing but an old man there, who is tottering home to bed."

Gordon made no reply, but followed the person alluded to stealthily from the house. After a minute's space, Denbigh saw him again hiding behind the buttress of a building on the opposite side of the street. He was evidently watching the stranger He did not continue long, however, in this situation, but stole forwards cautiously. After proceeding a short distance, he turned, and followed the windings of a street or road that intersected the principal street of the town, and finally disappeared.

Denbigh never saw him again. Three or four days afterwards, the body of an unknown man was found in a copse near the city of Dessau. It was pierced with wounds, and disfigured, and the clothes were much torn, as in a struggle. From one hand (which remained clasped) some fragments of dress, coarser than what belonged to the body, were forced with difficulty; but they did not lead to detection. The stranger was buried, and as much inquiry made respecting him as is usual for persons for whom no one feels an interest. His murderer never was discovered. Denbigh left the place immediately that the inquisition was over. He did not volunteer his evidence upon the occasion. His natural love of justice, and perceptions of right, were per haps obscured by his affection for his friend; besides which, nothing that he could have said upon the occasion would have exceeded a vague suspicion of the fact. At all events, he kept Gordon's secret, until he deemed that it was not dangerous to disclose it.

In regard to Gordon himself— he was never more heard of. A man, indeed, bearing somewhat of his appearance, was afterwards seen in the newly-cleared country near the Ohio; but, excepting the resemblance that he bore to Denbigh's friend, and a certain intelligence beyond his situation (which was that of a common laborer), there was nothing to induce a belief that it was the same person. Whoever he might be, however, even *he* too now has disappeared. He was killed accidentally, while felling one of those enormous hemlock-trees, with which some parts of the great continent abound. A shallow grave was scooped for him; a fellow-laborer's prayer was his only requiem; and, whatever may have been his intellect, whatever his passions or strength of purpose, the frail body which once contained them now merely fertilizes the glade of an American forest, or else has become food for the bear or the jackal.

[The story of Aguirra, referred to in the foregoing narrative, occurs in one of our early periodical works, and is to the following effect: Aguirra was a Spanish soldier, under the command of Esquivel, governor of Lima or Potosi.

For some small cause, or for no cause, (to make an example, or to wreak his spite,) this governor caused Aguirra
to be stripped and flogged. He received some hundred
stripes; his remonstrances (that he was a gentleman, and as
such exempt by law from such disgrace, and that what he
had done was unimportant, and justified by common usage)
being treated with contempt. He endured the punishment
in the presence of a crowd of comrades and strangers, and
swore (with a Spaniard's spirit) never to be satisfied but
with his tyrant's blood. He waited patiently, until Esquivel
was no longer governor; refusing consolation, and declin-
ing, from fancied unworthiness, all honorable employment.
But, when the governor put off his authority, *then* Aguirra
commenced his revenge. He followed his victim from
place to place,— haunted him like a ghost,— and filled
him (though surrounded by friends and servants) with perpetual dread. No place, no distance, could stop him. He
has been known to track his enemy for three, four, five
hundred leagues at a time! He continued pursuing him for
three years and four months; and at last, after a journey
of five hundred leagues, came upon him suddenly at Cuzco;
found him, for the first time, without his guards, and instantly — stabbed him to the heart!

Such is the story of Aguirra. It is believed to be a fact;
and so is the story which I have recounted above. The
circumstances are not only curious as showing a strange
coincidence, but they show also what a powerful effect a
narrative of this kind may produce. For there is little
doubt but that the South American tale, although it may
not absolutely have generated the spirit of vengeance in
Gordon's mind, so shaped and modified it as to stimulate
his flagging animosity; carried him through all impedi-
ments and reverses to the catastrophe; and enabled him
to exhibit a perseverance that is to be paralleled nowhere,
except perhaps in the history of fanatics or martyrs.]

THE NORSEMAN.

By GERALD MASSEY.

A SWARTHY strength with face of light,
As dark sword-iron is beaten bright;
A brave, frank look, with health aglow,
Bonny blue eyes and open brow;
His friend he welcomes, heart-in-hand,
But foot to foot his foe must stand:
A Man who will face, to his last breath,
The sternest facts of life and death:
       This is the brave old Norseman.

The wild wave-motion weird and strange
Rocks in him! seaward he must range;
His life is just a mighty lust
To wear away with use, not rust!
Though bitter wintry cold the storm,
The fire within him keeps him warm:
Kings quiver at his flag unfurled,
The Sea-King's master of the world!
       And conquering rides the Norseman.

He hides at heart of his rough life
A world of sweetness for the Wife:
From his rude breast a Babe may press
Soft milk of human tenderness, —
Make his eyes water, his heart dance,
And sunrise in his countenance:

In merry mood his ale he quaffs
By firelight, and his jolly heart laughs :
      The blithe, great-hearted Norseman.

But when the Battle Trumpet rings,
His soul's a war-horse clad with wings!
He drinks delight in with the breath
Of Battle and the dust of death :
The Axes redden ; spring the sparks
Blood-radiant grow the gray mail-sarks ;
Such blows might batter, as they fell,
Heaven's gates, or burst the booms of hell !
      So fights the fearless Norseman.

The Norseman's king must stand up tall,
If he would be head over all ;
Mainmast of Battle ! when the plain
Is miry red with bloody rain !
And grip his weapon for the fight,
Until his knuckles all grow white ;
Their banner-staff he bears is best
If double handful for the rest :
      When " Follow me ! " cries the Norseman.

Valiant and true, as Sagas tell,
The Norseman hated lies like hell ;
Hardy from cradle to the grave,
'T was their religion to be brave :
Great, silent fighting-men, whose words
Were few, soon said, and out with Swords !
One saw his heart cut from his side
Living, and smiled ; and smiling, died :
      The unconquerable Norseman.

They swam the flood ; they strode in flame ;
Nor quailed when the Valkyrie came

To kiss the chosen, for her charms,
With " Rest my Hero, in mine arms."
Their spirits through a grim wide wound,
The Norse door-way to heaven found ;
And borne upon the battle blast,
Into the hall of Heroes passed :
   And there was crowned the Norseman.

The Norseman wrestled with old Rome,
For Freedom in our Island home ;
He taught us how to ride the sea
With hempen bridle, horse of tree :
The Norseman stood with Robin Hood
By Freedom in the merry green wood,
When William ruled the English land
With cruel heart and bloody hand.
   For Freedom fights the Norseman.

Still in our race the Norse king reigns ;
His best blood beats along our veins ;
With his old glory we can glow,
And surely sail where he could row :
Is danger stirring ? from its sleep
Our War-dog wakes his watch to keep,
Stands with our Banner over him,
True as of old, and stern and grim !
   Come on, you 'll find the Norseman.

When Swords are gleaming you shall see
The Norseman's face flash gloriously,
With look that makes the foeman reel ;
His mirror from of old was steel !
And still he wields, in Battle's hour,
The old Thor's hammer of Norse power,
Strikes with a desperate arm of might,
And at the last tug turns the fight :
   For never yields the Norseman.

THE DRUIDS.

By EDMUND BURKE.

BRITAIN was in the time of Julius Cæsar what it is at this day in climate and natural advantages, temperate and reasonably fertile. But, destitute of all those improvements which in a succession of ages it has received from ingenuity, from commerce, from riches and luxury, it then wore a very rough and savage appearance. The country, forest or marsh; the habitations, cottages; the cities, hiding-places in woods; the people naked, or only covered with skins; their sole employment, pasturage and hunting. They painted their bodies for ornament or terror, by a custom general amongst all savage nations, who, being passionately fond of show and finery, and having no object but their naked bodies on which to exercise this disposition, have in all times painted or cut their skins, according to their ideas of ornament. They shaved the beard on the chin; that on the upper lip was suffered to remain, and grow to an extraordinary length, to favor the martial appearance, in which they placed their glory. They were in their natural temper not unlike the Gauls; impatient, fiery, inconstant, ostentatious, boastful, fond of novelty, and, like all barbarians, fierce, treacherous, and cruel. Their arms were short javelins, small shields of a slight texture, and great cutting swords with a blunt point, after the Gaulish fashion.

Their chiefs went to battle in chariots, not unartfully contrived, nor unskilfully managed. I cannot help thinking it something extraordinary, and not easily to be accounted for, that the Britons should have been so expert in the fabric of those chariots, when they seem utterly ignorant in all other mechanic arts; but thus it is delivered to us. They had also horse, though of no great reputation, in their armies. Their foot was without heavy armor; it was no firm body; nor instructed to preserve their ranks, to make their evolutions, or to obey their commanders; but in tolerating hardships, in dexterity of forming ambuscades (the art military of savages), they are said to have excelled. A natural ferocity and an impetuous onset stood them in the place of discipline.

It is very difficult, at this distance of time, and with so little information, to discern clearly what sort of civil government prevailed among the ancient Britons. In all very uncultivated countries, as society is not close or intricate, nor property very valuable, liberty subsists with few restraints. The natural equality of mankind appears, and is asserted; and therefore there are but obscure lines of any form of government. In every society of this sort the natural connections are the same as in others, though the political ties are weak. Among such barbarians, therefore, though there is little authority in the magistrate, there is often great power lodged, or rather left, in the father; for, as among the Gauls, so among the Britons, he had the power of life and death in his own family, over his children and his servants.

But among freemen and heads of families causes of all sorts seem to have been decided by the Druids: they summoned and dissolved all the public assemblies; they alone had the power of capital punishments, and indeed seem to have had the sole execution and interpretation of whatever laws subsisted among this people. In this respect the

Celtic nations did not greatly differ from others, except that we view them in an earlier stage of society. Justice was in all countries originally administered by the priesthood; nor indeed could laws in their first feeble state have either authority or sanction, so as to compel men to relinquish their natural independence, had they not appeared to come down to them enforced by beings of more than human power. The first openings of civility have been everywhere made by religion. Amongst the Romans, the custody and interpretation of the laws continued solely in the college of the pontiffs for above a century.

The time in which the Druid priesthood was instituted is unknown. It probably rose, like other institutions of that kind, from low and obscure beginnings; and acquired from time, and the labors of able men, a form, by which it extended itself so far, and attained at length so mighty an influence over the minds of a fierce, and otherwise ungovernable, people. Of the place where it arose there is somewhat less doubt. Cæsar mentions it as the common opinion that this institution began in Britain; that there it always remained in the highest perfection, and that from thence it diffused itself into Gaul. I own I find it not easy to assign any tolerable cause why an order of so much authority, and a discipline so exact, should have passed from the more barbarous people to the more civilized; from the younger to the older; from the colony to the mother country; but it is not wonderful that the early extinction of this order, and that general contempt in which the Romans held all the barbarous nations, should have left these matters obscure and full of difficulty.

The Druids were kept entirely distinct from the body of the people; and they were exempted from all the inferior and burdensome offices of society, that they might be at leisure to attend the important duties of their own charge. They were chosen out of the best families, and from the young men of the most promising talents; a regulation which placed and preserved them in a respectable light with the world. None were admitted into this order but after a long and laborious novitiate, which made the character venerable in their own eyes by the time and difficulty of attaining it. They were much devoted to solitude, and thereby acquired that abstracted and thoughtful air which is so imposing upon the vulgar. And when they appeared in public it was seldom, and only on some great occasion; in the sacrifices of the gods, or on the seat of judgment. They prescribed medicine; they formed the youth; they paid the last honors to the dead; they foretold events; they exercised themselves in magic. They were at once the priests, lawgivers, and physicians of their nation, and consequently concentred in themselves all that respect that men have diffusively for those who heal their diseases, protect their property, or reconcile them to the Divinity. What contributed not a little to the stability and power of this order was the extent of its foundation, and the regularity and proportion of its structure. It took in both sexes; and the female Druids were in no less esteem for their knowledge and sanctity than the males. It was divided into several subordinate ranks and classes; and they all depended upon a chief, or Arch-Druid, who was elected to his place with great authority and pre-eminence for life. They were further armed with a power of interdicting from their sacrifices, or excommunicating, any obnoxious persons. This interdiction, so similar to that used by the ancient Athenians, and to that since practised among Christians, was followed by an exclusion from all the benefits of civil community; and it was accordingly the most dreaded of all punishments. This ample authority was in general usefully exerted; by the interposition of the Druids, differences were composed and wars ended; and the minds of the fierce Northern people, being reconciled to each other, under the influence of religion, united with signal effect against their common enemies.

There was a class of the Druids, whom they called Bards, who delivered in songs (their only history) the exploits of their heroes; and who composed those verses which contained the secrets of Druidical discipline, their principles of natural and moral philosophy, their astronomy, and the mystical rites of their religion. These verses in all probability bore a near resemblance to the golden verses of Pythagoras; to those of Phocylides, Orpheus, and other remnants of the most ancient Greek poets. The Druids, even in Gaul, where they were not altogether ignorant of the use of letters, in order to preserve their knowledge in greater respect, committed none of their precepts to writing. The proficiency of their pupils was estimated principally by the number of technical verses which they retained in their memory: a circumstance that shows this discipline rather calculated to preserve with accuracy a few plain maxims of traditionary science, than to improve and extend it. And this is not the sole circumstance which leads us to believe that among them learning had advanced no further than its infancy.

The scholars of the Druids, like those of Pythagoras, were carefully enjoined a long and religious silence; for if barbarians come to acquire any knowledge, it is rather by instruction than examination: they must therefore be silent. Pythagoras, in the rude times of Greece, required silence in his disciples; but Socrates, in the meridian of the Athenian refinement, spoke less than his scholars: everything was disputed in the Academy.

The Druids are said to be very expert in astronomy, in geography, and in all parts of mathematical knowledge. And authors speak, in a very exaggerated strain, of their excellence in these, and in many other sciences. Some elemental knowledge I suppose they had; but I can

scarcely be persuaded that their learning was either deep
or extensive.   In all countries where Druidism was professed, the youth were generally instructed by that order;
and yet was there little, either in the manners of the people, in their way of life, or their works of art, that demon-
strates profound science, or particularly mathematical skill.
Britain, where their discipline was in its highest perfection,
and which was therefore resorted to by the people of Gaul,
as an oracle in Druidical questions, was more barbarous in
all other respects than Gaul itself, or than any other country then known in Europe.   These piles of rude magnificence, Stonehenge and Abury, are in vain produced in
proof of their mathematical abilities.   These vast structures
have nothing which can be admired, but the greatness of
the work; and they are not the only instances of the great
things which the mere labor of many hands united, and
persevering in their purpose, may accomplish with very
little help from mechanics.   This may be evinced by the
immense buildings, and the low state of the sciences, among
the original Peruvians.

The Druids were eminent, above all the philosophic
lawgivers of antiquity, for their care in impressing the
doctrine of the soul's immortality on the minds of their
people, as an operative and leading principle.   This doctrine was inculcated on the scheme of transmigration, which
some imagine them to have derived from Pythagoras.   But
it is by no means necessary to resort to any particular
teacher for an opinion which owes its birth to the weak
struggles of unenlightened reason, and to mistakes natural
to the human mind.   The idea of the soul's immortality is
indeed ancient, universal, and in a manner inherent in our
nature: but it is not easy for a rude people to conceive any
other mode of existence than one similar to what they had
experienced in life; nor any other world as the scene of
such an existence but this we inhabit, beyond the bounds of

which the mind extends itself with great difficulty. Admiration, indeed, was able to exalt to heaven a few selected heroes: it did not seem absurd that those, who in their mortal state had distinguished themselves as superior and overruling spirits, should after death ascend to that sphere which influences and governs everything below; or that the proper abode of beings, at once so illustrious and permanent, should be in that part of nature in which they had always observed the greatest splendor and the least mutation. But on ordinary occasions it was natural some should imagine that the dead retired into a remote country, separated from the living by seas or mountains. It was natural that some should follow their imagination with a simplicity still purer, and pursue the souls of men no further than the sepulchres in which their bodies had been deposited; whilst others of deeper penetration, observing that bodies worn out by age, or destroyed by accidents, still afforded the materials for generating new ones, concluded likewise that a soul being dislodged did not wholly perish, but was destined, by a similar revolution in nature, to act again, and to animate some other body. This last principle gave rise to the doctrine of transmigration; but we must not presume, of course, that where it prevailed it necessarily excluded the other opinions; for it is not remote from the usual procedure of the human mind, blending, in obscure matters, imagination and reasoning together, to unite ideas the most inconsistent. When Homer represents the ghosts of his heroes appearing at the sacrifices of Ulysses, he supposes them endued with life, sensation, and a capacity of moving, but he has joined to these powers of living existence uncomeliness, want of strength, want of distinction, the characteristics of a dead carcass. This is what the mind is apt to do: it is very apt to confound the ideas of the surviving soul and the dead body. The vulgar have always, and still do, confound these very irreconcilable ideas. They lay the

scene of apparitions in churchyards; they habit the ghost
in a shroud, and it appears in all the ghastly paleness of a
corpse. A contradiction of this kind has given rise to a
doubt whether the Druids did in reality hold the doctrine
of transmigration. There is positive testimony that they
did hold it. There is also testimony as positive that they
buried or burned with the dead utensils, arms, slaves, and
whatever might be judged useful to them, as if they were to
be removed into a separate state. They might have held
both these opinions; and we ought not to be surprised to
find error inconsistent.

The objects of the Druid worship were many. In this
respect they did not differ from other heathens; but it must
be owned, that in general their ideas of divine matters were
more exalted than those of the Greeks and Romans, and
that they did not fall into an idolatry so coarse and vulgar.
That their gods should be represented under a human form,
they thought derogatory to beings uncreated and imperisha-
ble. To confine what can endure no limits within walls
and roofs, they judged absurd and impious. In these particulars there was something refined, and suitable enough
to a just idea of the Divinity. But the rest was not equal.
Some notions they had, like the greatest part of mankind, of
a Being eternal and infinite; but they also, like the greatest
part of mankind, paid their worship to inferior objects, from
the nature of ignorance and superstition always tending
downwards.

The first and chief objects of their worship were the elements; and, of the elements, fire, as the most pure, active,
penetrating, and what gives life and energy to all the rest.
Among fires, the preference was given to the sun, as the
most glorious visible being, and the fountain of all life.
Next they venerated the moon and the planets. After fire,
water was held in reverence. This, when pure, and ritually
prepared, was supposed to wash away all sins, and to qual-

ify the priest to approach the altar of the gods with more acceptable prayers ; washing with water being a type natural enough of inward cleansing and purity of mind. They also worshipped fountains, and lakes, and rivers.

Oaks were regarded by this sect with a particular veneration, as by their greatness, their shade, their stability and duration, not ill representing the perfections of the Deity. From the great reverence in which they held this tree, it is thought their name of Druids is derived, the word Deru in the Celtic language signifying an oak. But their reverence was not wholly confined to this tree. All forests were held sacred ; and many particular plants were respected, as endued with a particular holiness. No plant was more revered than the mistletoe, especially if it grew on the oak ; not only because it is rarely found upon that tree, but because the oak was among the Druids peculiarly sacred. Towards the end of the year they searched for this plant, and when it was found great rejoicing ensued : it was approached with reverence ; it was cut with a golden hook ; it was not suffered to fall to the ground, but received with great care and solemnity upon a white garment.

In ancient times, and in all countries, the profession of physic was annexed to the priesthood. Men imagined that all their diseases were inflicted by the immediate displeasure of the Deity, and therefore concluded that the remedy would most probably proceed from those who were particularly employed in his service. Whatever, for the same reason, was found of efficacy to avert or cure distempers was considered as partaking somewhat of the Divinity. Medicine was always joined with magic ; no remedy was administered without mysterious ceremony and incantation. The use of plants and herbs, both in medicinal and magical practices, was early and general. The mistletoe, pointed out by its very peculiar appearance and manner of growth, must have struck powerfully on the imaginations of a superstitious people. Its virtues may have been soon discovered. It has been fully proved, against the opinion of Celsus, that internal remedies were of very early use. Yet if it had not, the practice of the present savage nations supports the probability of that opinion. By some modern authors the mistletoe is said to be of signal service in the cure of certain convulsive distempers, which, by their suddenness, their violence, and their unaccountable symptoms, have been ever considered as supernatural. The epilepsy was by the Romans for that reason called *Morbus Sacer;* and all other nations have regarded it in the same light. The Druids also looked upon vervain, and some other plants, as holy, and probably for a similar reason.

The other objects of the Druid worship were chiefly serpents in the animal world, and rude heaps of stone, or great pillars without polish or sculpture, in the inanimate. The serpent, by his dangerous qualities, is not ill adapted to inspire terror; by his annual renewals, to raise admiration; by his make, easily susceptible of many figures, to serve for a variety of symbols; and by all, to be an object of religious observance: accordingly no object of idolatry has been more universal. And this is so natural, that serpent-veneration seems to be rising again even in the bosom of Mahometanism.

The great stones, it has been supposed, were originally monuments of illustrious men, or the memorials of considerable actions, or they were landmarks for deciding the bounds of fixed property. In time, the memory of the persons or facts which these stones were erected to perpetuate wore away; but the reverence which custom, and probably certain periodical ceremonies, had preserved for those places was not so soon obliterated. The monuments themselves then came to be venerated; and not the less because the reason for venerating them was no longer known. The landmark was in those times held sacred on account of its great uses, and easily passed into an object of worship. Hence the god Terminus amongst the Romans. This religious observance towards rude stones is one of the most ancient and universal of all customs. Traces of it are to be found in almost all, and especially in these Northern nations; and to this day in Lapland, where heathenism is not yet entirely extirpated, their chief divinity, which they call *Stor Junkare*, is nothing more than a rude stone.

Some writers, among the moderns, because the Druids ordinarily made no use of images in their worship, have given in to an opinion, that their religion was founded on the unity of the Godhead. But this is no just consequence. The spirituality of the idea, admitting their idea to have been spiritual, does not infer the unity of the object. All the ancient authors who speak of this order agree, that, besides those great and more distinguishing objects of their worship already mentioned, they had gods answerable to those adored by the Romans. And we know that the Northern nations who overran the Roman Empire had in fact a great plurality of gods, whose attributes, though not their names, bore a close analogy to the idols of the Southern world.

The Druids performed the highest act of religion by sacrifice, agreeably to the custom of all other nations. They not only offered up beasts, but even human victims; a barbarity almost universal in the heathen world, but exercised more uniformly, and with circumstances of peculiar cruelty, amongst those nations where the religion of the Druids prevailed. They held that the life of a man was the only atonement for the life of a man. They frequently enclosed a number of wretches, some captives, some criminals, and, when these were wanting, even innocent victims, in a gigantic statue of wicker-work, to which they set fire, and invoked their deities amidst the horrid cries and shrieks of the sufferers, and the shouts of those who assisted at this tremendous rite.

There were none among the ancients more eminent for all the arts of divination than the Druids. Many of the superstitious practices in use to this day among the country people for discovering their future fortune seem to be remains of Druidism. Futurity is the great concern of mankind. Whilst the wise and learned look back upon experience and history, and reason from things past about events to come, it is natural for the rude and ignorant, who have the same desires without the same reasonable means of satisfaction, to inquire into the secrets of futurity, and to govern their conduct by omens, dreams, and prodigies. The Druids, as well as the Etruscan and Roman priesthood, attended with diligence the flight of birds, the pecking of chickens, and the entrails of their animal sacrifices. It was obvious that no contemptible prognostics of the weather were to be taken from certain motions and appearances in birds and beasts. A people who lived mostly in the open air must have been well skilled in these observations. And as changes in the weather influenced much the fortune of their huntings, or their harvests, which were all their fortunes, it was easy to apply the same prognostics to every event by a transition very natural and common ; and thus probably arose the science of auspices, which formerly guided the deliberations of councils, and the motions of armies, though now they only serve, and scarcely serve, to amuse the vulgar.

The Druid temple is represented to have been nothing more than a consecrated wood. The ancients speak of no other. But monuments remain which show that the Druids were not in this respect wholly confined to groves. They had also a species of building, which in all probability was destined to religious use. This sort of structure was indeed without walls or roof. It was a colonnade, generally circular, of huge rude stones, sometimes single, sometimes double ; sometimes with, often without, an architrave. These open temples were not in all respects peculiar to the Northern nations. Those of the Greeks which were dedicated to the celestial gods, ought in strictness to have had no roof, and were thence called *Hypæthra.*

Many of these monuments remain in the British islands, curious for their antiquity, or astonishing for the greatness of the work; enormous masses of rock, so poised as to be set in motion with the slightest touch, yet not to be pushed from their place by a very great power: vast altars, peculiar and mystical in their structure, thrones, basins, heaps or kearns; and a variety of other works, displaying a wild industry, and a strange mixture of ingenuity and rudeness. But they are all worthy of attention; not only as such monuments often clear up the darkness, and supply the defects, of history, but as they lay open a noble field of speculation for those who study the changes which have happened in the manners, opinions, and sciences of men, and who think them as worthy of regard as the fortune of wars, and the revólutions of kingdoms.

The short account which I have here given does not contain the whole of what is handed down to us by ancient writers, or discovered by modern research, concerning this remarkable order. But I have selected those which appear to me the most striking features, and such as throw the strongest light on the genius and true character of the Druidical institution. In some respects it was undoubtedly very singular; it stood out more from the body of the people than the priesthood of other nations; and their knowledge and policy appeared the more striking by being contrasted with the great simplicity and rudeness of the people over whom they presided. But, notwithstanding some peculiar appearances and practices, it is impossible not to perceive a great conformity between this and the ancient orders which have been established for the purposes

of religion in almost all countries.   For, to say nothing of
the resemblance which many have traced between this and
the Jewish priesthood, the Persian Magi, and the India
Brachmans, it did not so greatly differ from the Roman
priesthood either in the original objects, or in the general
mode of worship, or in the constitution of their hierarchy.
In the original institution, neither of these nations had the
use of images ; the rules of the Salian as well as Druid
discipline were delivered in verse ; both orders were under
an elective head ; and both were for a long time the law-
yers of their country.   So that when the order of Druids
was suppressed by the emperors, it was rather from a dread
of an influence incompatible with the Roman government,
than from any dislike of their religious opinions.

THE WITCH'S DAUGHTER.

By JOHN G. WHITTIER.

IT was the pleasant harvest time,
 When cellar-bins are closely stowed,
 And garrets bend beneath their load,

And the old swallow-haunted barns —
 Brown-gabled, long, and full of seams
 Through which the moted sunlight streams,

And winds blow freshly in, to shake
 The red plumes of the roosted cocks,
 And the loose haymow's scented locks —

Are filled with summer's ripened stores,
 Its odorous grass and barley sheaves,
 From their low scaffolds to their eaves.

On Esek Harden's oaken floor,
 With many an autumn threshing worn,
 Lay the heaped ears of unhusked corn.

And thither came young men and maids,
 Beneath a moon that, large and low,
 Lit that sweet eve of long ago.

They took their places; some by chance,
　And others by a merry voice
　Or sweet smile guided to their choice.

How pleasantly the rising moon,
　Between the shadow of the mows,
　Looked on them through the great elm boughs!—

On sturdy boyhood sun-embrowned,
　On girlhood with its solid curves
　Of healthful strength and painless nerves!

And jests went round, and laughs that made
　The house-dog answer with his howl,
　And kept astir the barn-yard fowl;

And quaint old songs their fathers sung,
　In Derby dales and Yorkshire moors,
　Ere Norman William trod their shores;

And tales, whose merry license shook
　The fat sides of the Saxon thane,
　Forgetful of the hovering Dane!

But still the sweetest voice was mute
　That river-valley ever heard,
　From lip of maid or throat of bird;

For Mabel Martin sat apart,
　And let the haymow's shadow fall
　Upon the loveliest face of all.

She sat apart, as one forbid,
　Who knew that none would condescend
　To own the Witch-wife's child a friend.

The seasons scarce had gone their round,
  Since curious thousands thronged to see
  Her mother on the gallows-tree;

And mocked the palsied limbs of age,
  That faltered on the fatal stairs,
  And wan lip trembling with its prayers!

Few questioned of the sorrowing child,
  Or, when they saw the mother die,
  Dreamed of the daughter's agony.

They went up to their homes that day,
  As men and Christians justified:
  God willed it, and the wretch had died!

Dear God and Father of us all,
  Forgive our faith in cruel lies, —
  Forgive the blindness that denies!

Forgive thy creature when he takes,
  For the all-perfect love thou art,
  Some grim creation of his heart.

Cast down our idols, overturn
  Our bloody altars; let us see
  Thyself in thy humanity!

Poor Mabel from her mother's grave
  Crept to her desolate hearthstone,
  And wrestled with her fate alone;

With love, and anger, and despair,
  The phantoms of disordered sense,
  The awful doubts of Providence!

The school-boys jeered her as they passed
   And, when she sought the house of prayer,
   Her mother's curse pursued her there.

And still o'er many a neighboring door
   She saw the horseshoe's curvéd charm,
   To guard against her mother's harm;—

That mother, poor, and sick, and lame,
   Who daily, by the old arm-chair,
   Folded her withered arms in prayer;—

Who turned, in Salem's dreary jail,
   Her worn old Bible o'er and o'er,
   When her dim eyes could read no more!

Sore tried and pained, the poor girl kept
   Her faith, and trusted that her way,
   So dark, would somewhere meet the day.

And still her weary wheel went round
   Day after day, with no relief:
   Small leisure have the poor for grief.

So in the shadow Mabel sits;
   Untouched by mirth she sees and hears;
   Her smile is sadder than her tears.

But cruel eyes have found her out,
   And cruel lips repeat her name,
   And taunt her with her mother's shame.

She answered not with railing words,
   But drew her apron o'er her face,
   And, sobbing, glided from the place.

And only pausing at the door,
   Her sad eyes met the troubled gaze
   Of one who, in her better days,

Had been her warm and steady friend,
   Ere yet her mother's doom had made
   Even Esek Harden half afraid.

He felt that mute appeal of tears,
   And, starting, with an angry frown
   Hushed all the wicked murmurs down.

" Good neighbors mine," he sternly said,
   " This passes harmless mirth or jest;
   I brook no insult to my guest.

" She is indeed her mother's child;
   But God's sweet pity ministers
   Unto no whiter soul than hers.

" Let Goody Martin rest in peace;
   I never knew her harm a fly,
   And witch or not, God knows — not L

"I know who swore her life away;
   And, as God lives, I 'd not condemn
   An Indian dog on word of them."

The broadest lands in all the town,
   The skill to guide, the power to awe,
   Were Harden's ; and his word was law.

None dared withstand him to his face,
   But one sly maiden spake aside ·
   " The little witch is evil eyed !

" Her mother only killed a cow,
    Or witched a churn or dairy-pan ;
    But she, forsooth, must charm a man !"

Poor Mabel, in her lonely home,
    Sat by the window's narrow pane,
    White in the moonlight's silver rain.

The river, on its pebbled rim,
    Made music such as childhood knew ;
    The door-yard tree was whispered through

By voices such as childhood's ear
    Had heard in moonlights long ago ;
    And through the willow boughs below

She saw the rippled water shine ;
    Beyond, in waves of shade and light,
    The hills rolled off into the night.

Sweet sounds and pictures mocking so
    The sadness of her human lot,
    She saw and heard, but heeded not.

She strove to drown her sense of wrong,
    And, in her old and simple way,
    To teach her bitter heart to pray.

Poor child ! the prayer, begun in faith,
    Grew to a low, despairing cry
    Of utter misery : " Let me die !

" O, take me from the scornful eyes,
    And hide me where the cruel speech
    And mocking finger may not reach !

" I dare not breathe my mother's name :
    A daughter's right I dare not crave
    To weep above her unblest grave !

" Let me not live until my heart,
    With few to pity, and with none
    To love me, hardens into stone.

"O God ! have mercy on thy child,
    Whose faith in thee grows weak and small,
    And take me ere I lose it all !"

A shadow on the moonlight fell,
    And murmuring wind and wave became
    A voice whose burden was her name.

Had then God heard her ?   Had he sent
    His angel down ?   In flesh and blood,
    Before her Esek Harden stood ?

He laid his hand upon her arm :
    " Dear Mabel, this no more shall be ;
    Who scoffs at you, must scoff at me.

" You know rough Esek Harden well ;
    And if he seems no suitor gay,
    And if his hair is touched with gray,

" The maiden grown shall never find
    His heart less warm than when she smiled,
    Upon his knees, a little child !"

Her tears of grief were tears of joy,
    As, folded in his strong embrace,
    She looked in Esek Harden's face.

" O, truest friend of all ! " she said,
      " God bless you for your kindly thought,
      And make me worthy of my lot ! "

He led her through his dewy fields,
      To where the swinging lanterns glowed,
      And through the doors the huskers showed.

" Good friends and neighbors ! " Esek said,
      " I 'm weary of this lonely life ;
      In Mabel see my chosen wife !

" She greets you kindly, one and all ;
      The past is past, and all offence
      Falls harmless from her innocence.

" Henceforth she stands no more alone ;
      You know what Esek Harden is ; —
      He brooks no wrong to him or his."

Now let the merriest tales be told,
      And let the sweetest songs be sung,
      That ever made the old heart young !

For now the lost has found a home ;
      And a lone hearth shall brighter burn,
      As all the household joys return !

O, pleasantly the harvest moon,
      Between the shadow of the mows,
      Looked on them through the great elm boughs !

On Mabel's curls of golden hair
      On Esek's shaggy strength it fell ;
      And the wind whispered, " It is well ! "

THE OLD LADY, AND THE OLD GENTLEMAN

By LEIGH HUNT.

THE OLD LADY.

IF the Old Lady is a widow and lives alone, the manners of her condition and time of life are so much the more apparent. She generally dresses in plain silks, that make a gentle rustling as she moves about the silence of her room; and she wears a nice cap with a lace border, that comes under the chin. In a placket at her side is an old enamelled watch, unless it is locked up in a drawer of her toilet, for fear of accidents. Her waist is rather tight and trim than otherwise, as she had a fine one when young; and she is not sorry if you see a pair of her stockings on a table, that you may be aware of the neatness of her leg and foot. Contented with these and other evident indications of a good shape, and letting her young friends understand that she can afford to obscure it a little, she wears pockets, and uses them well too. In the one is her handkerchief, and any heavier matter that is not likely to come out with it, such as the change of a sixpence; in the other is a miscellaneous assortment, consisting of a pocket-book, a bunch of keys, a needle-case, a spectacle-case, crumbs of biscuit, a nutmeg and grater, a smelling-bottle, and, according to the season, an orange or apple, which after many days she draws out, warm and glossy,

to give to some little child that has well behaved itself.
She generally occupies two rooms, in the neatest condition
possible. In the chamber is a bed with a white coverlet,
built up high and round, to look well, and with curtains
of a pastoral pattern, consisting alternately of large plants,
and shepherds and shepherdesses. On the mantel-piece
are more shepherds and shepherdesses, with dot-eyed sheep
at their feet, all in colored ware: the man, perhaps, in a
pink jacket and knots of ribbons at his knees and shoes,
holding his crook lightly in one hand, and with the other
at his breast, turning his toes out and looking tenderly at
the shepherdess; the woman holding a crook also, and
modestly returning his look, with a gypsy-hat jerked up
behind, a very slender waist, with petticoat and hips to
counteract, and the petticoat pulled up through the pocket-
holes, in order to show the trimness of her ankles. But
these patterns, of course, are various. The toilet is ancient, carved at the edges, and tied about with a snow-
white drapery of muslin. Beside it are various boxes,
mostly japan; and the set of drawers are exquisite things
for a little girl to rummage, if ever little girl be so bold, —
containing ribbons and laces of various kinds; linen smell-
ing of lavender, of the flowers of which there is always
dust in the corners; a heap of pocket-books for a series
of years; and pieces of dress long gone by, such as head-
fronts, stomachers, and flowered satin shoes, with enormous
heels. The stock of letters are under especial lock and
key. So much for the bedroom. In the sitting-room is
rather a spare assortment of shining old mahogany furniture, or carved arm-chairs equally old, with chintz draperies down to the ground; a folding or other screen, with
Chinese figures, their round, little-eyed, meek faces perking
sideways; a stuffed bird, perhaps in a glass case (a living
one is too much for her); a portrait of her husband over
the mantel-piece, in a coat with frog-buttons, and a delicate

frilled hand lightly inserted in the waistcoat; and opposite
him on the wall is a piece of embroidered literature,
framed and glazed, containing some moral distich or maxim,
worked in angular capital letters, with two trees or parrots
below, in their proper colors; the whole concluding with an
A B C and numerals, and the name of the fair industrious,
expressing it to be "her work, Jan. 14, 1762." The rest
of the furniture consists of a looking-glass with carved
edges, perhaps a settee, a hassock for the feet, a mat for
the little dog, and a small set of shelves, in which are
the "Spectator" and "Guardian," the "Turkish Spy," a
Bible and Prayer-Book, "Young's Night Thoughts," with a
piece of lace in it to flatten, "Mrs. Rowe's Devout Exercises of the Heart," "Mrs. Glasse's Cookery," and perhaps
"Sir Charles Grandison," and "Clarissa." "John Buncle"
is in the closet among the pickles and preserves. The
clock is on the landing-place between the two room doors,
where it ticks audibly but quietly; and the landing-place,
as well as the stairs, is carpeted to a nicety. The house
is most in character, and properly coeval, if it is in a
retired suburb, and strongly built, with wainscot rather
than paper inside, and lockers in the windows. Before
the windows should be some quivering poplars. Here the
Old Lady receives a few quiet visitors to tea, and perhaps an early game at cards: or you may see her going
out on the same kind of visit herself, with a light umbrella
running up into a stick and crooked ivory handle, and her
little dog, equally famous for his love to her and captious
antipathy to strangers. Her grandchildren dislike him on
holidays, and the boldest sometimes ventures to give him
a sly kick under the table. When she returns at night,
she appears, if the weather happens to be doubtful, in a
calash; and her servant in pattens, follows half behind and
half at her side, with a lantern.

Her opinions are not many nor new. She thinks the

clergyman a nice man. The Duke of Wellington, in her opinion, is a very great man; but she has a secret preference for the Marquis of Granby. She thinks the young women of the present day too forward, and the men not respectful enough; but hopes her grandchildren will be better; though she differs with her daughter in several points respecting their management. She sets little value on the new accomplishments; is a great though delicate connoisseur in butcher's meat and all sorts of housewifery; and if you mention waltzes, expatiates on the grace and fine breeding of the minuet. She longs to have seen one danced by Sir Charles Grandison, whom she almost considers as a real person. She likes a walk of a summer's evening, but avoids the new streets, canals, &c., and sometimes goes through the churchyard, where her children and her husband lie buried, serious, but not melancholy. She has had three great epochs in her life: her marriage,— her having been at court, to see the King and Queen and Royal Family,—and a compliment on her figure she once received, in passing, from Mr. Wilkes, whom she describes as a sad, loose man, but engaging. His plainness she thinks much exaggerated. If anything takes her at a distance from home, it is still the court; but she seldom stirs, even for that. The last time but one that she went, was to see the Duke of Wurtemberg; and most probably for the last time of all, to see the Princess Charlotte and Prince Leopold. From this beatific vision she returned with the same admiration as ever for the fine, comely appearance of the Duke of York and the rest of the family, and great delight at having had a near view of the Princess, whom she speaks of with smiling pomp and lifted mittens, clasping them as passionately as she can together, and calling her, in a transport of mixed loyalty and self-love, a fine royal young creature, and "Daughter of England."

THE OLD GENTLEMAN.

OUR Old Gentleman, in order to be exclusively him-self, must be either a widower or a bachelor. Suppose the former. We do not mention his precise age, which would be invidious : nor whether he wears his own hair or a wig ; which would be wanting in universality. If a wig, it is a compromise between the more modern scratch and the departed glory of the toupee. If his own hair, it is white, in spite of his favorite grandson, who used to get on the chair behind him, and pull the silver hairs out, ten years ago. If he is bald at top, the hair-dresser, hovering and breathing about him like a second youth, takes care to give the bald place as much powder as the covered ; in order that he may convey to the sensorium within a pleasing indistinctness of idea respecting the exact limits of skin and hair. He is very clean and neat ; and, in warm weather, is proud of opening his waistcoat half-way down, and letting so much of his frill be seen, in order to show his hardiness as well as taste. His watch and shirt-buttons are of the best ; and he does not care if he has two rings on a finger. If his watch ever failed him at the club or coffee-house, he would take a walk every day to the nearest clock of good character, purely to keep it right. He has a cane at home, but seldom uses it, on finding it out of fashion with his elderly juniors. He has a small cocked hat for gala days, which he lifts higher from his head than the round one, when bowed to. In his pockets are two handkerchiefs (one for the neck at night-time), his spectacles, and his pocket-book. The pocket-book, among other things, contains a receipt for a cough, and some verses cut out of an odd sheet of an old magazine, on the lovely Duchess of A., beginning.

" When beauteous Mira walks the plain "

He intends this for a commonplace-book which he keeps, consisting of passages in verse and prose, cut out of newspapers and magazines, and pasted in columns; some of them rather gay. His principal other books are Shakespeare's Plays and Milton's Paradise Lost; the Spectator, the History of England, the Works of Lady M. W. Montague, Pope, and Churchill; Middleton's Geography; the Gentleman's Magazine; Sir John Sinclair on Longevity; several plays with portraits in character; Account of Elizabeth Canning, Memoirs of George Ann Bellamy, Poetica Amusements at Bath-Easton, Blair's Works, Elegant Extracts; Junius as originally published; a few pamphlets on the American War, and Lord George Gordon, &c., and one on the French Revolution. In his sitting-rooms are some engravings from Hogarth and Sir Joshua; an engraved portrait of the Marquis of Granby; ditto of M. le Comte de Grasse surrendering to Admiral Rodney; a humorous piece after Penny; and a portrait of himself, painted by Sir Joshua. His wife's portrait is in his chamber, looking upon his bed. She is a little girl, stepping forward with a smile, and a pointed toe, as if going to dance. He lost her when she was sixty.

The Old Gentleman is an early riser, because he intends to live at least twenty years longer. He continues to take tea for breakfast, in spite of what is said against its nervous effects; having been satisfied on that point some years ago by Dr. Johnson's criticism on Hanway, and a great liking for tea previously. His china cups and saucers have been broken since his wife's death, all but one, which is religiously kept for his use. He passes his morning in walking or riding, looking in at auctions, looking after his India bonds or some such money securities, furthering some subscription set on foot by his excellent friend Sir John, or cheapening a new old print for his portfolio. He also hears of the newspapers; not caring to see them till after dinner at the coffee-house. He may also cheapen a fish or so; the fishmonger soliciting his doubting eye as he passes, with a profound bow of recognition. He eats a pear before dinner.

His dinner at the coffee-house is served up to him at the accustomed hour, in the old accustomed way, and by the accustomed waiter. If William did not bring it, the fish would be sure to be stale, and the flesh new. He eats no tart; or if he ventures on a little, takes cheese with it. You might as soon attempt to persuade him out of his senses as that cheese is not good for digestion. He takes port; and if he has drunk more than usual, and in a more private place, may be induced, by some respectful inquiries respecting the old style of music, to sing a song composed by Mr. Oswald or Mr. Lampe, such as,

> " Chloë, by that borrowed kiss,"

or,

> " Come, gentle god of soft repose,"

or his wife's favorite ballad, beginning,

> "At Upton on the hill,
> There lived a happy pair."

Of course, no such exploit can take place in the coffee-room; but he will canvass the theory of that matter there with you, or discuss the weather, or the markets, or the theatres, or the merits of "my lord North" or "my lord Rockingham"; for he rarely says simply, lord; it is generally "my lord," trippingly and genteelly off the tongue. If alone after dinner, his great delight is the newspaper; which he prepares to read by wiping his spectacles, carefully adjusting them on his eyes, and drawing the candle close to him, so as to stand sideways betwixt his ocular aim and the small type. He then holds the paper at arm's length, and dropping his eyelids half down and his

mouth half open, takes cognizance of the day's information. If he leaves off, it is only when the door is opened
by a new-comer, or when he suspects somebody is over-
anxious to get the paper out of his hand. On these occasions he gives an important hem! or so; and resumes.

In the evening, our Old Gentleman is fond of going to
the theatre, or of having a game of cards. If he enjoys
the latter at his own house or lodgings, he likes to play
with some friends whom he has known for many years;
but an elderly stranger may be introduced, if quiet and
scientific; and the privilege is extended to younger men
of letters; who, if ill players, are good losers. Not that
he is a miser, but to win money at cards is like proving
his victory by getting the baggage; and to win of a
younger man is a substitute for his not being able to beat
him at rackets. He breaks up early, whether at home
or abroad.

At the theatre, he likes a front row in the pit. He
comes early, if he can do so without getting into a squeeze,
and sits patiently waiting for the drawing up of the curtain, with his hands placidly lying one over the other on
the top of his stick. He generously admires some of
the best performers, but thinks them far inferior to Garrick, Woodward, and Clive. During splendid scenes, he
is anxious that the little boy should see.

He has been induced to look in at Vauxhall again, but
likes it still less than he did years back, and cannot bear
it in comparison with Ranelagh. He thinks everything
looks poor, flaring, and jaded. "Ah!" says he, with a
sort of triumphant sigh, "Ranelagh was a noble place!
Such taste, such elegance, such beauty! There was the
Duchess of A., the finest woman in England, sir; and
Mrs. L., a mighty fine creature; and Lady Susan what's
her name, that had that unfortunate affair with Sir Charles.
Sir, they came swimming by you like the swans."

The Old Gentleman is very particular in having his slippers ready for him at the fire, when he comes home. He is also extremely choice in his snuff, and delights to get a fresh box-full in Tavistock Street, in his way to the theatre. His box is a curiosity from India. He calls favorite young ladies by their Christian names, however slightly acquainted with them; and has a privilege of saluting all brides, mothers, and indeed every species of lady, on the least holiday occasion. If the husband, for instance, has met with a piece of luck, he instantly moves forward, and gravely kisses the wife on the cheek. The wife then says, "My niece, sir, from the country"; and he kisses the niece. The niece, seeing her cousin biting her lips at the joke, says, "My cousin Harriet, sir"; and he kisses the cousin. He "never recollects such weather," except during the "Great Frost," or when he rode down with "Jack Skrimshire to Newmarket." He grows young again in his little grandchildren, especially the one which he thinks most like himself; which is the handsomest. Yet he likes best, perhaps, the one most resembling his wife; and will sit with him on his lap, holding his hand in silence, for a quarter of an hour together. He plays most tricks with the former, and makes him sneeze. He asks little boys in general who was the father of Zebedee's children. If his grandsons are at school, he often goes to see them; and makes them blush by telling the master or the upper scholars, that they are fine boys, and of a precocious genius. He is much struck when an old acquaintance dies, but adds that he lived too fast; and that poor Bob was a sad dog in his youth; "a very sad dog, sir; mightily set upon a short life and a merry one."

When he gets very old indeed, he will sit for whole evenings, and say little or nothing; but informs you, that there is Mrs. Jones (the housekeeper) — "*She* 'll talk."

How mute is every feathered breast
   That swelled with melody!
And yet bright bead-like eyes declare
   This hour is ecstasy.

Heart forth! as uncaged bird through air
   And mingle in the tide
Of blessed things, that, lacking care,
   Now full of beauty glide
Around thee, in their angel hues
   Of joy and sinless pride.

Here, on this green bank that o'erviews
   The far-retreating glen,
Beneath the spreading beech-tree muse,
   Of all within thy ken;
For lovelier scene shall never break
   On thy dimmed sight again.

Slow stealing from the tangled brake
   That skirts the distant hill,
With noiseless hoof, two bright fawns make
   For yonder lapsing rill;
Meek children of the forest gloom,
   Drink on, and fear no ill!

And buried in the yellow broom
   That crowns the neighboring height,
Couches a loutish shepherd groom,
   With all his flocks in sight;
Which dot the green braes gloriously
   With spots of living light.

It is a sight that filleth me
   With meditative joy,

To mark these dumb things curiously
  Crowd round their guardian boy;
As if they felt this Sabbath hour
  Of bliss lacked all alloy.

I bend me towards the tiny flower,
  That underneath this tree
Opens its little breast of sweets
  In meekest modesty,
And breathes the eloquence of love
  In muteness, Lord! to thee.

There is no breath of wind to move
  The flag-like leaves, that spread
Their grateful shadow far above
  This turf-supported head;
All sounds are gone,—all murmurings
  With living nature wed.

The babbling of the clear well-springs,
  The whisperings of the trees,
And all the cheerful jargonings
  Of feathered hearts at ease,
That whilom filled the vocal wood,
  Have hushed their minstrelsies.

The silentness of night doth brood
  O'er this bright summer noon;
And Nature, in her holiest mood,
  Doth all things well attune
To joy, in the religious dreams
  Of green and leafy June.

Far down the glen in distance gleams
  The hamlet's tapering spire,

And, glittering in meridial beams,
  Its vane is tongued with fire;
And hark how sweet its silvery bell,—
  And hark the rustic choir!

The holy sounds float up the dell
  To fill my ravished ear,
And now the glorious anthems swell
  Of worshippers sincere,—
Of hearts bowed in the dust, that shed
  Faith's penitential tear.

Dear Lord! thy shadow is forth spread
  On all mine eye can see;
And, filled at the pure fountain-head
  Of deepest piety,
My heart loves all created things,
  And travels home to thee.

Around me while the sunshine flings
  A flood of mocky gold,
My chastened spirit once more sings,
  As it was wont of old,
That lay of gratitude which burst
  From young heart uncontrolled.

When in the midst of nature nursed,
  Sweet influences fell
On chilly hearts that were athirst,
  Like soft dews in the bell
Of tender flowers, that bowed their heads
  And breathed a fresher smell,—

So, even now this hour hath sped
  In rapturous thought o'er me.

Feeling myself with nature wed, —
  A holy mystery, —
A part of earth, a part of heaven,
  A part, Great God! of thee.

Fast fade the cares of life's dull sweven,
  They perish as the weed,
While unto me the power is given,
  A moral deep to read
In every silent throe of mind
  External beauties breed.

THE INCENDIARY.

By MARY RUSSELL MITFORD.

NO one that had the misfortune to reside during the last winter in the disturbed districts of the south of England will ever forget the awful impression of that terrible time. The stilly gatherings of the misguided peasantry amongst the wild hills, partly heath and partly woodland, of which so much of the northern part of Hampshire is composed, — dropping in one by one, and two by two in the gloom of evening, or the dim twilight of a November morning; or the open and noisy meetings of determined men at noontide in the streets and greens of our Berkshire villages, and even sometimes in the very churchyards, sallying forth in small but resolute numbers to collect money or destroy machinery, and compelling or persuading their fellow-laborers to join them at every farm they visited; or the sudden appearance and disappearance of these large bodies, whe sometimes remained together to the amount of several hundreds for many days, and sometimes dispersed, one scarcely knew how, in a few hours; their daylight marches on the high road, regular and orderly as those of an army, or their midnight visits to lonely houses, lawless and terrific as the descent of pirates or the incursions of banditti; — all brought close to us a state of things which we never thought to have witnessed in peaceful and happy England. In the sister island, indeed, we had read of such horrors, but now they were brought home to our very household hearths; wo tasted of fear, the bitterest cup that an imaginative woman can taste, in all its agonizing varieties; and felt, by sad experience, the tremendous difference between that distant report of danger, with which we had so often fancied that we sympathized, and the actual presence of danger itself. Such events are salutary, inasmuch as they show to the human heart its own desperate self-deceit. I could not but smile at the many pretty letters of condolence and fellow-feeling which I received from writers who wrote far too well to feel anything, who most evidently felt nothing; but the smile was a melancholy one, — for I recollected how often, not intending to feign, or suspecting that I was feigning, I myself had written such.

Nor were the preparations for defence, however necessary, less shocking than the apprehensions of attack. The hourly visits of bustling parish officers, bristling with importance (for our village, though in the centre of the insurgents, continued uncontaminated, — "faithful amidst the unfaithful found," — and was, therefore, quite a rallying-point for loyal men and true); the swearing in of whole regiments of petty constables; the stationary watchmen, who every hour, to prove their vigilance, sent in some poor wretch, beggar or match-seller, or rambling child, under the denomination of suspicious persons; the mounted patrol, whose deep "All's well!" which ought to have been consolatory, was about the most alarming of all alarming sounds; the soldiers, transported from place to place in carts the better to catch the rogues, whose local knowledge gave them great advantage in a dispersal; the grave processions of magistrates and gentlemen on horseback; and above all, the nightly collecting of arms and armed men within our own dwelling, kept up a continual sense of nervous inquietude.

Fearful, however, as were the realities, the rumors were a hundred-fold more alarming. Not an hour passed, but, from some quarter or other, reports came pouring in of mobs gathering, mobs assembled, mobs marching upon us. Now the high roads were blockaded by the rioters, travellers murdered, soldiers defeated, and the magistrates, who had gone out to meet and harangue them, themselves surrounded and taken by the desperate multitude. Now the artisans — the commons, so to say, of B. — had risen to join the peasantry, driving out the gentry and tradespeople, while they took possession of their houses and property, and only detaining the mayor and aldermen as hostages. Now that illustrious town held loyal, but was besieged. Now the mob had carried the place ; and artisans, constables, tradespeople, soldiers, and magistrates, the mayor and corporation included, were murdered to a man, to say nothing of women and children ; the market-place running with blood, and the town-hall piled with dead bodies. This last rumor, which was much to the taste of our villagers, actually prevailed for several hours ; terrified maid-servants ran shrieking about the house, and every corner of the village street realized Shakespeare's picture of "a smith swallowing a tailor's news."

So passed the short winter's day. With the approach of night came fresh sorrows ; the red glow of fires gleaming on the horizon, and mounting into the middle sky ; the tolling of bells ; and the rumbling sound of the engines clattering along from place to place, and often, too often, rendered useless by the cutting of the pipes after they had begun to play, — a dreadful aggravation of the calamity, since it proved that among those who assembled, professedly to help, were to be found favorers and abettors of the concealed incendiaries. O the horrors of those fires, — breaking forth night after night, sudden, yet expected, always seeming nearer than they actually were, and always said to have been more mischievous to life and property than they actually had been ! Mischievous enough they were, Heaven

knows! A terrible and unholy abuse of the most beautiful and comfortable of the elements!—a sinful destruction of the bounties of Providence!—an awful crime
against God and man! Shocking it was to behold the
peasantry of England becoming familiarized with this
tremendous power of evil,—this desperate, yet most cow-
ardly sin!

The blow seemed to fall, too, just where it might least have
been looked for,—on the unoffending, the charitable, the
kind; on those who were known only as the laborer's friends;
to impoverish whom was to take succor, assistance and pro-
tection from the poor. One of the objects of attack in our
own immediate neighborhood was a widow lady, between
eighty and ninety, the best of the good, the kindest of the
kind. Occurrences like this were in every way dreadful.
They made us fear (and such fear is a revengeful passion,
and comes near to hate) the larger half of our species
They weakened our faith in human nature.

The revulsion was, however, close at hand. A time came
which changed the current of our feelings,—a time of ret-
ribution. The fires were quenched; the riots were put
down; the chief of the rioters were taken. Examination
and commitment were the order of the day; the crowded
jails groaned with their overload of wretched prisoners; soldiers were posted at every avenue to guard against possible
escape; and every door was watched night and day by
miserable women, the wives, mothers, or daughters of the
culprits, praying for admission to their unfortunate relatives.
The danger was fairly over, and pity had succeeded to
fear.

Then, above all, came the special commission: the judges
in threefold dignity; the array of counsel; the crowded
court; the solemn trial; the awful sentence;—all the more
impressive from the merciful feeling which pervaded the
government, the counsel, and the court. My father, a very

old magistrate, being chairman of the bench, as well as one of the grand jury, and the then high sheriff, with whom it is every way an honor to claim acquaintance, being his intimate friend, I saw and knew more of the proceedings of this stirring time than usually falls to the lot of women, and took a deep interest in proceedings which had in them a thrilling excitement, as far beyond acted tragedy as truth is beyond fiction.

I shall never forget the hushed silence of the auditors, a dense mass of human bodies, the heads only visible, ranged tier over tier to the very ceiling of the lofty hall; the rare and striking importance which that silence and the awfulness of the occasion gave to the mere official forms of a court of justice, generally so hastily slurred over and slightly attended to; the unusual seriousness of the counsel; the watchful gravity of the judges; and, more than all, the appearance of the prisoners themselves, belonging mostly to the younger classes of the peasantry, such men as one is accustomed to see in the fields, on the road, or the cricket-ground, with sunburnt faces, and a total absence of reflection or care, but who now, under the influence of a keen and bitter anxiety, had acquired not only the sallow paleness proper to a prison, but the look of suffering and of thought, the brows contracted and brought low over the eyes, the general sharpness of feature and elongation of countenance, which give an expression of intellect, a certain momentary elevation, even to the commonest and most vacant of human faces. Such is the power of an absorbing passion, a great and engrossing grief. One man only amongst the large number whom I heard arraigned (for they were brought out by tens and by twenties) would, perhaps, under other circumstances, have been accounted handsome; yet a painter would at that moment have found studies in many.

I shall never forget, either, the impression made on my mind by one of the witnesses. Several men had been arraigned together for machine-breaking. All but one of them had employed counsel for their defence, and under their direction had called witnesses to character, the most respectable whom they could find, — the clergy and overseers of their respective parishes, for example, — masters with whom they had lived, neighboring farmers or gentry, or even magistrates, — all that they could muster to grace or credit their cause. One poor man alone had retained no counsel, offered no defence, called no witness, though the evidence against him was by no means so strong as that against his fellow-prisoners; and it was clear that his was exactly the case in which testimony to character would be of much avail. The defences had ended, and the judge was beginning to sum up, when suddenly a tall, gaunt, upright figure, with a calm, thoughtful brow, and a determined but most respectful demeanor, appeared in the witnesses' box. He was dressed in a smock-frock, and was clean and respectable in appearance, but evidently poor. The judge interrupted himself in his charge to inquire the man's business; and hearing that he was a voluntary witness for the undefended prisoner, proceeded to question him, when the following dialogue took place. The witness's replies, which seemed to me then, and still do so, very striking from their directness and manliness, were delivered with the same humble boldness of tone and manner that characterized the words.

Judge. "You are a witness for the prisoner, an unsummoned witness?"

"I am, my lord. I heard that he was to be tried to-day, and have walked twenty miles to speak the truth of him, as one poor man may do of another."

"What is your situation in life?"

"A laborer, my lord; nothing but a day-laborer."

"How long have you known the prisoner?"

"As long as I have known anything. We were playmates together, went to the same school, have lived in the same parish. I have known him all my life."

"And what character has he borne?"

"As good a character, my lord, as a man need work under."

It is pleasant to add, that this poor man's humble testimony was read from the judge's notes, and mentioned in the judge's charge, with full as much respect, perhaps a little more, than the evidence of clergymen and magistrates for the rest of the accused; and that, principally from this direct and simple tribute to his character, the prisoner in question was acquitted.

To return, however, from my evil habit of digressing (if I may use an Irish phrase) before I begin, and making my introduction longer than my story, a simple sin to which in many instances, and especially in this, I am fain to plead guilty;—to come back to my title and my subject,—I must inform my courteous readers, that the case of arson which attracted most attention and excited most interest in this part of the country, was the conflagration of certain ricks, barns, and farm-buildings, in the occupation of Richard Mayne; and that, not so much from the value of the property consumed (though that value was considerable), as on account of the character and situation of the prisoner, whom, after a long examination, the magistrates found themselves compelled to commit for the offence. I did not hear this trial, the affair having occurred in the neighboring county, and do not, therefore, vouch for "the truth, the whole truth, and nothing but the truth," as one does when an ear-witness; but the general outline of the story will suffice for our purpose.

Richard Mayne was a wealthy yeoman of the old school, sturdy, boisterous, bold, and kind, always generous, and generally good-natured, but cross-grained and obstinate by fits, and sometimes purse-proud,—after the fashion of men who

have made money by their own industry and shrewdness.
He had married late in life, and above him in station, and
had now been for two or three years a widower, with one
only daughter, a girl of nineteen, of whom he was almost as
fond as of his greyhound Mayfly, and for pretty much the
same reason, — that both were beautiful and gentle, and his
own, and both admired and coveted by others, — that May
fly had won three cups, and that Lucy had refused four
offers.

A sweet and graceful creature was Lucy Mayne. Her
mother, a refined and cultivated woman, the daughter of an
unbeneficed clergyman, had communicated, perhaps unconsciously, much of her own taste to her daughter. It is true,
that most young ladies, even of her own station, would have
looked with great contempt on Lucy's acquirements, who
neither played nor drew, and was wholly, in the phrase of
the day, unaccomplished; but then she read Shakespeare
and Milton, and the poets and prose-writers of the Jameses'
and Charleses' times, with a perception and relish of their
beauty very uncommon in a damsel under twenty; and
when her father boasted of his Lucy as the cleverest as well
as the prettiest lass within ten miles, he was not so far
wrong as many of his hearers were apt to think him.

After all, the person to whom Lucy's education owed
most was a relation of her mother's, a poor relation, who,
being left a widow with two children almost totally destitute,
was permitted by Richard Mayne to occupy one end of a
small farm-house, about a mile from the old substantial
manorial residence which he himself inhabited, whilst he
farmed the land belonging to both. Nothing could ex-
ceed his kindness to the widow and her family; and Mrs.
Owen, a delicate and broken-spirited woman, who had known
better days, and was now left with a sickly daughter and a
promising son dependent on the precarious charity of relatives and friends, found in the free-handed and open-hearted

farmer and his charming little girl her only comfort. He
even restored to her the blessing of her son's society, who
had hitherto earned his living by writing for an attorney in
the neighboring town, but whom her wealthy kinsman now
brought home to her, and established as the present assistant and future successor of the master of a well-endowed
grammar-school in the parish, Farmer Mayne being one
of the trustees, and all-powerful with the other function-
aries joined in the trust, and the then schoolmaster in so
wretched a state of health as almost to insure a speedy
vacancy.

In most instances, such an exertion of an assumed rather
than a legitimate authority, would have occasioned no small
prejudice against the party protected; but Philip Owen was
not to be made unpopular, even by the unpopularity of his
patron. Gentle, amiable, true, and kind, — kind, both in
word and deed, — it was found absolutely impossible to dislike him. He was clever, too, very clever, with a remarkable aptitude for teaching, as both parents and boys soon
found to their mutual satisfaction; for the progress of one
half-year of his instruction equalled that made in a twelve-
month under the old *régime*. He must also, one should
think, have been fond of teaching, for, after a hard day's
fagging at Latin and English, and writing, and accounts,
and all the drudgery of a boys' school, he would make a
circuit of a mile and a half home in order to give Lucy
Mayne a lesson in French or Italian. For a certainty, Philip Owen must have had a strong natural turn for
playing the pedagogue, or he never would have gone so far
out of his way just to read Fénelon and Alfieri with Lucy
Mayne.

So for two happy years matters continued. At the expi-
ration of that time, just as the old schoolmaster, who declared that nothing but Philip's attention had kept him alive
so long, was evidently on his death-bed, Farmer Mayne sud-

denly turned Mrs. Owen, her son, and her sick daughter out
of the house, which, by his permission, they had hitherto
occupied; and declared publicly, that whilst he held an
acre of land in the parish, Philip Owen should never be
elected master of the grammar-school, — a threat which
there was no doubt of his being able to carry into effect.
The young man, however, stood his ground; and sending
off his mother and sister to an uncle in Wales, who had
lately written kindly to them, hired a room at a cottage in
the village, determined to try the event of an election, which
the languishing state of the incumbent rendered inevitable.

The cause of Farmer Mayne's inveterate dislike to one
whom he had so warmly protected, and whose conduct, manners, and temper had procured him friends wherever he was
known, nobody could assign with any certainty. Perhaps
he had unwittingly trodden on Mayfly's foot, or had opposed
some prejudice of her master's, — but his general careful-
ness not to hurt anything, or offend anybody, rendered either
of these conjectures equally improbable; — perhaps he had
been found only too amiable by the farmer's other pet, —
those lessons in languages were dangerous things! — and
when Lucy was seen at church with a pale face and red
eyes, and when his landlord Squire Hawkins's blood-hunter
was seen every day at Farmer Mayne's door, it became cur-
rently reported and confidently believed, that the cause of
the quarrel was a love affair between the cousins, which the
farmer was determined to break off, in order to bestow his
daughter on the young lord of the manor.

Affairs had been in this posture for about a fortnight, and
the old schoolmaster was just dead, when a fire broke out in
the rick-yard of Farley Court, and Philip Owen was apprehended and committed as the incendiary! The astonishment of the neighborhood was excessive; the rector and
half the farmers of the place offered to become bail; but the
offence was not bailable; and the only consolation left for

the friends of the unhappy young man, was the knowledge
that the trial would speedily come on, and their internal
conviction that an acquittal was certain.

As time wore on, however, their confidence diminished.
The evidence against him was terribly strong. He had been
observed lurking about the rick-yard with a lantern, in
which a light was burning, by a lad in the employ of
Farmer Mayne, who had gone thither for hay to fodder his
cattle, about an hour before the fire broke out. At eleven
o'clock the haystack was on fire, and at ten Robert Doyle
had mentioned to James White, another boy in Farmer
Mayne's service, that he had seen Mr. Philip Owen behind
the great rick. Farmer Mayne himself had met him at
half past ten (as he was returning from B. market) in the
lane leading from the rick-yard towards the village, and had
observed him throw something he held in his hand into the
ditch. Humphry Harris, a constable employed to seek for
evidence, had found the next morning a lantern, answering
to that described by Robert Doyle, in the part of the ditch
indicated by Farmer Mayne, which Thomas Brown, the village shopkeeper, in whose house Owen slept, identified as
having lent to his lodger in the early part of the evening.
A silver pencil, given to Owen by the mother of one of his
pupils, and bearing his full name on the seal at the end, was
found close to where the fire was discovered; and, to crown
all, the curate of the village, with whom the young man's
talents and character had rendered him a deserved favorite,
had unwillingly deposed that he had said "it might be in his
power to take a great revenge on Farmer Mayne," or words
to that effect; whilst a letter was produced from the accused
to the farmer himself, intimating that one day he would be
sorry for the oppression which he had exercised towards
him and his. These two last facts were much relied upon
as evincing malice, and implying a purpose of revenge from
the accused towards the prosecutor; yet there were many

who thought that the previous circumstances might well account for them without reference to the present occurrence, and that the conflagration of the ricks and farm-buildings might, under the spirit of the time (for fires were raging every night in the surrounding villages), be merely a remarkable coincidence.　The young man himself simply denied the fact of setting fire to any part of the property or premises ; inquired earnestly whether any lives had been lost, and still more earnestly after the health of Miss Lucy ; and on finding that she had been confined to her bed by fever and delirium, occasioned, as was supposed, by the fright, ever since that unhappy occurrence, relapsed into a gloomy silence, and seemed to feel no concern or interest in the issue of the trial.

His friends, nevertheless, took kind and zealous measures for his defence, — engaged counsel, sifted testimony, and used every possible means, in the assurance of his innocence, to trace out the true incendiary.　Nothing, however, could be discovered to weaken the strong chain of circumstantial evidence, or to impeach the credit of the witnesses, who, with the exception of the farmer himself, seemed all friendly to the accused, and most distressed at being obliged to bear testimony against him.　On the eve of the trial, the most zealous of his friends could find no ground of hope, except in the chances of the day ; Lucy, for whom alone the prisoner asked, being still confined by severe illness.

The judges arrived, — the whole terrible array of the special commission ; the introductory ceremonies were gone through ; the cause was called on, and the case proceeded with little or no deviation from the evidence already cited. When called upon for his defence, the prisoner again asked if Lucy Mayne were in court? and hearing that she was ill in her father's house, declined entering into any defence whatsoever.　Witnesses to character, however, pressed forward, — his old master, the attorney, the rector and curate

of the parish, half the farmers of the village, everybody, in
short, who ever had an opportunity of knowing him, even
his reputed rival, Mr. Hawkins, who, speaking, he said, on
the authority of one who knew him well, professed himself
confident that he could not be guilty of a bad action, — a
piece of testimony that seemed to strike and affect the prisoner more than anything that had passed; — evidence to
character crowded into court; — but all was of no avail
against the strong chain of concurrent facts; and the judge
was preparing to sum up, and the jury looking as if they
had already condemned, when suddenly a piercing shriek
was heard in the hall, and pale, tottering, dishevelled,
Lucy Mayne rushed into her father's arms, and cried
out, with a shrill, despairing voice, that "she was the only
guilty; that she had set fire to the rick; and that if they
killed Philip Owen for her crime, they would be guilty of
murder."

The general consternation may be imagined, especially
that of the farmer, who had left his daughter almost insen-
sible with illness, and still thought her light-headed. Medical assistance, however, was immediately summoned, and it
then appeared that what she said was most true; that the
lovers, for such they were, had been accustomed to deposit
letters in one corner of that unlucky hay-rick; that having
seen from her chamber-window Philip Owen leaving the
yard, she had flown with a taper in her hand to secure the
expected letter, and, alarmed at her father's voice, had ran
away so hastily, that she had, as she now remembered, left
the lighted taper amidst the hay; that then the fire came,
and all was a blank to her, until, recovering that morning
from the stupor succeeding to delirium, she had heard that
Philip Owen was to be tried for his life from the effect of
her carelessness, and had flown to save him she knew not
how !

The sequel may be guessed; Philip was, of course, ac-

quitted; everybody, even the very judge, pleaded for the
lovers; the young landlord and generous rival added his
good word; and the schoolmaster of Farley and his pretty
wife are at this moment one of the best and happiest couples
in his Majesty's dominions.

WISHING.

By JOHN G. SAXE.

OF all amusements for the mind,
  From logic down to fishing,
There is n't one that you can find
  So very cheap as "wishing."
A very choice diversion too,
  If we but rightly use it,
And not, as ye are apt to do,
  Pervert it, and abuse it.

I wish — a common wish indeed —
  My purse were somewhat fatter,
That I might cheer the child of need,
  And not my pride to flatter ;
That I might make Oppression reel,
  As only gold can make it,
And break the Tyrant's rod of steel,
  As only gold can break it.

I wish — that Sympathy and Love,
  And every human passion
That has its origin above,
  Would come and keep in fashion ;
That Scorn, and Jealousy, and Hate,
  And every base emotion,
Were buried fifty fathom deep
  Beneath the waves of Ocean !

I wish — that friends were always true,
   And motives always pure ;
I wish the good were not so few,
   I wish the bad were fewer ;
I wish that parsons ne'er forgot
   To heed their pious teaching ;
I wish that practising was not
   So different from preaching !

I wish — that modest worth might be
   Appraised with truth and candor ;
I wish that innocence were free
   From treachery and slander ;
I wish that men their vows would mind ;
   That women ne'er were rovers ;
I wish that wives were always kind,
   And husbands always lovers !

I wish — in fine — that Joy and Mirth,
   And every good Ideal,
May come erewhile, throughout the earth,
   To be the glorious Real ;
Till God shall every creature bless
   With his supremest blessing,
And Hope be lost in Happiness,
   And Wishing in Possessing !

THE GREAT PORTRAIT-PAINTERS

By CHARLES ROBERT LESLIE.

THERE has never existed a great painter of History or Poetry who has not been great in portrait. Even Michael Angelo is no exception. There may not remain any *painted* portraits of known persons by his hand, but there are sculptured portraits by him, and it is impossible to look even at the *engravings* of the Prophets and Sibyls, without seeing that they are from a hand practised in portrait, a hand, too, that had acquired its power by the practice of literal exactness. "Fuseli distinguishes the styles, epic, dramatic, and historic, beautifully," says Mr. Haydon. But I think, as I do of such distinctions generally, that these are entirely imaginary; and that the style of Michael Angelo is distinguished, as are all others, by the peculiar mind of the artist *only*. Haydon adds that, "the same instruments are used in all styles, men and women; and no two men or women were ever the same in form, feature, or proportion. After Fuseli has said, 'the detail of character is not consistent with the epic,' he goes on to show the great difference of character between each Prophet, as decided as any character chosen by Raphael in any of his more essentially dramatic works. 'Nor are the Sibyls,' continues Fuseli, 'those female oracles, less expressive or less individually marked.'" Thus, though Haydon was unwilling to abandon the classifications of

Fuseli, the contradiction involved in them did not escape him.

There cannot be a doubt that Michael Angelo, had he devoted himself to portrait only, would have been a superlative portrait-painter; for in his works we find everything in perfection that portrait requires, — dignity, the expression of character, the highest perception of beauty, in man, woman, and child; and not only in the unfinished marble that adorns our Academy library, but in the smaller compartments of the Sistine ceiling, the most natural and familiar domestic incidents treated in the most graceful manner. It is right this should be remembered, because painters (as they fancy themselves) of High Art, who really have not the talents portrait requires, must not be allowed to class themselves with Michael Angelo, as long as they *cannot do* what he, in perfection, *could do*.

Conspicuous as he stands among great portrait-painters, Vandyke is not first of the first. The attitudes of his single figures are often formal and unmeaning; and his groups, however finely connected by composition, are seldom connected by sentiment. Fathers, mothers, sons, and daughters, stand or sit beside each other, as they stood or sat in his room, for the mere purpose of being painted; and it is therefore the nicely discriminated individual character of every head, the freshness and delicacy of his color, and the fine treatment of his masses, that have placed him high among portrait-painters. The Countess of Bedford, at Petworth, his Snyders at Castle Howard, his whole lengths at Warwick and at Windsor, the noble equestrian picture at Blenheim, of Charles I., with its magnificent landscape background, and the whole length of Charles in the Louvre, are among the masterpieces of Vandyke; but he has nowhere shown such dramatic powers as are displayed by Velasquez, in his portrait picture of "The Surrender of Breda."

The Governor of the town is presenting its keys to the Marquis Spinola, who (hat in hand) neither takes them, nor allows his late antagonist to kneel. But, laying his hand gently on his shoulder, he seems to say, " Fortune has favored me, but our cases might have been reversed." To paint such an act of generous courtesy was worthy of a contemporary of Cervantes. It is not, however, in the choice of the subject, but in the manner in which he has brought the scene before our eyes, that the genius and mind of Velasquez are shown. The cordial, unaffected bearing of the conqueror could only have been represented by as thorough a gentleman as himself. I know this picture but from copies. Mr. Ford says of the original, " Never were knights, soldiers, or national character better painted, or the heavy Fleming, the intellectual Italian, and the proud Spaniard more nicely marked, even to their boots and breeches ; the lances of the guards actually vibrate. Observe the contrast of the light-blue, delicate page, with the dark, iron-clad General, Spinola, who, the model of a high-bred, generous warrior, is consoling a gallant but vanquished enemy."

Another great portrait picture, the conception of which is equally dramatic and original, is at Windsor Castle. The Archduke Ferdinand of Austria and the Prince of Spain, mounted on chargers, are directing an assault in the battle of Nortlingen. The conventional manner, sanctioned indeed by great painters, of representing commanders of armies, whether mounted or on foot, quietly looking out of the picture, while the battle rages behind them, is here set aside. The generals are riding into the scene of action ; and yet their attitudes are so contrived as sufficiently to show their features. Nearer to the spectator are half-length figures, the end of a long line of steel-clad infantry, diminishing in perspective up a hill to the fortress they are storming. All is action ; and though we are only shown

the generals and the common soldiers, yet, as the horses
of the former are in profile, and have just come into the
picture, we may imagine a train of attendant officers about
to appear; and though portrait was the first object of
Rubens, the picture is a noble representation of a battle.
The conception, as regards the foot-soldiers, has been imitated, though differently applied, by Opie; and probably
Raphael's composition in the Vatican, representing David
gazing at Bathsheba, while the troops of Uriah pass below
him, suggested it to Rubens.

The pendant to this picture is the group of Sir Balthasar
Gerbier, his wife, and children; which Dr. Waagen inclines
to attribute to Vandyke. But the arrangement and dramatic connection of the figures is entirely free from the
formality of Vandyke; and a comparison of this fine composition with Vandyke's "Children of Charles I." at
Windsor, his "Pembroke Family" at Wilton, his "Earl
and Countess of Derby" belonging to Lord Clarendon,
or "The Nassau Family" at Penshanger, will show that
it is by Rubens.

Perhaps the noblest group of portraits ever painted, for
it is considered the greatest work of its class by Titian, is
that of the male part of the family of Luigi Cornaro. The
fine old man, whose life by an extraordinary system of
temperance was protracted to a hundred years, kneels before an altar in the open air, followed by his son-in-law
and grandchildren, except the three youngest, who are
sitting on the steps of the altar playing with a little dog,
an incident like some I have noticed in the works of Raphael. The characteristic arrangement of the figures, the
noble simplicity of the lines, and the truth and power of
the color, unite in placing this picture on the summit of
Art. There is no apparent sacrifice of detail, no trick, that
we can discover, to give supremacy to the heads, which
yet rivet our attention at the first glance, and to which we

return again and again, impressed by the thought and mind in the countenances of the elder personages, and charmed with the youthful innocence of the boys. I have seen people, ignorant of the principles of Art, and caring little about pictures, stand before this one in astonishment, and I have heard them express themselves in a way which proved that little of its excellence was lost on them. Fortunately for England, it belongs to his Grace the Duke of Northumberland.

There was a time when kings, warriors, and other eminent persons were painted, almost as a matter of course, in devotional attitudes. It was, in fact, a fashion, and was continued to a later date than the close of Titian's life. But is not so much what the individual painted may be doing, as its consistency with his whole life, and the look and manner given him by the painter, which interests or offends us. The piety of a kneeling hero may be ostentatious; or we might happen to know that devotion was all the religion he practised, and that he was lifting to Heaven hands that had been steeped, and were again to be steeped, in innocent blood. Sir Thomas More was several times painted by Holbein, yet never, that I recollect, in an attitude of devotion, or accompanied by any symbol of that religion which was the rule of his life; and what would the memory of More, or the genius of Holbein, have gained had he so painted him? Raphael flattered Leo the Tenth, as he was directed, by introducing him, in the "Attila," as Leo the First. But when he was to paint a more characteristic portrait of the Pope, he represented only the sovereign and the dilettante. Leo is examining with a glass a splendidly-illuminated manuscript. He sits in a chair of state, attended, not by saints, but by two princes of the church; and the portrait is, as all portraits should be, biographical. Even in copies (from which only I know it), I fancy I see faint indications of a love of fun, so characteristic of a Pontiff who delighted in a practical joke.

The admirers of devotional portrait object to the more modern custom of indicating the deeds of the person represented, as savoring of vanity; forgetting that acts of devotion are deeds, and, as far as attitude and expression have to do with devotion, the easiest of all deeds; and when consisting in these alone, the most criminal of all vanities. The only portrait of that admirable woman Margaret Tudor, represents her in a religious habit, with her hands joined in prayer, and she could not have been so characteristically handed down to us in any other dress or attitude. Neither could Sir Joshua's portrait of General Eliott be more happily conceived than it is. The key of the fortress he is defending is held firmly in his hand. But commanding as are the air and attitude, they have nothing of the vanity of bravado; indeed, if what is most honorable to the man should not be painted, the world would not have possessed the noble conception of Velasquez that has been described.

What may be called masquerading or fancy-ball portrait is seldom happy; and though we do not object to Sir Joshua's "Kitty Fisher as Cleopatra," or "Emily Bertie as Thais," yet, as in such cases, let us be sure the assumed character accords with the real one. Sir Thomas Lawrence made a sketch of George the Fourth in the armor of the Black Prince, but had the good sense not to carry the matter further than a sketch.

Are portrait-painters, it may be asked, to paint the vices of their sitters? Assuredly, if these vices exhibit themselves in the countenance. And Fuseli praises Titian for expressing some of the most odious individual characteristics, in portraits that he selects as works of the highest order.

Allan Cunningham accuses Reynolds of flattery, and I apprehend Sir Joshua was just as much of a flatterer as Titian. With a vulgar head before him, he would not, or rather *could* not, make a vulgar picture. But I do not believe that he would have given to Colonel Charteris "an aspect worthy a President of the Society for the Suppression of Vice," unless, which is not impossible, he had such an aspect. In his whole length of the Duke of Orleans, the debauchee was as apparent as the Prince.

No man can be a good portrait-painter who is not a good physiognomist. I do not mean that he should know Lavater by heart, or that he must believe in all that phrenology assumes. But he must be, what all of us are, in some degree, a judge of character by the signs exhibited in the face. A few of the broad distinctions of physiognomy depend on the forms of the features, but all its nicer shades have far more to do with expression; and in this, indeed, the real character is often seen where the conformation of the features seems to contradict it. Socrates had the face and figure of a Silenus, but the great mind of the philosopher must have been visible, through the disguise, to all who could read expression. There are some general and well-known rules for the determination of physiognomical character, as far as it has to do with the shapes of the features; the aquiline nose and eye, for instance, belong to the heroic class, thick lips to the sensual, and thin to the selfish; yet all these may be liable to many exceptions; the first certainly are; for Nelson, Wolfe, Turenne, and many other heroes, will occur to our recollection who had nothing of the eagle physiognomy. It is natural to associate beauty with goodness, and ugliness with wickedness; and children generally do this. But an acquaintance with the world soon shows us that bad and selfish hearts may be concealed under the handsomest features, and the highest virtues hidden under the homeliest; and that goodness may even consist with conformations of face absolutely ugly. We then begin to look for the character in the expression rather than in the forms of the features, and to distinguish assumed expressions from natural ones; and so we go on, and, as we grow older, become better physiognomists, though

we never arrive at that certainty of judgment which seems
not to be intended we ever should.

The best portrait-painters, though they may not have
penetrated through the mask to *all* beneath it, have, by the
fidelity of their Art, given resemblances that sometimes
correct and sometimes confirm the verdicts of historians.
Who can look at Vandyke's three heads, painted to enable
Bernini to make a bust, and believe all that has been said
against Charles I.? Or who can look at Holbein's portraits of Henry VIII., and doubt the worst that has been
said of his selfish cruelty?

Among the many excellences of Holbein, his treatment
of the hands is not the least; and it is evident that in his
whole-lengths of Henry, they are portraits, and so are the
legs, and that the king stood for the entire figure in that
characteristic, but by no means graceful attitude, in which
he set the fashion to his courtiers. We feel that we could
swear to the truth, the whole truth, and nothing but the
truth, of such portraits.

Among the pictures at Hampton Court attributed to
Holbein, few can be relied on as genuine. I cannot believe that those historical curiosities, "The Embarkation of
Henry VIII. from Dover," "The Field of the Cloth of
Gold," "The Meeting of Henry and Maximilian," or "The
Battle of the Spurs," are his works; neither do I believe
he painted the picture that includes Henry, Jane Seymour,
Prince Edward, Mary, and Elizabeth, nor the life-sized
whole-length of "The Earl of Surry." According to the
general custom of attributing the portraits of every age
to the greatest master of that age, Holbein is made answerable for these, and many others, greatly inferior to the
picture, certainly by him, belonging to the Surgeon Barbers'
Company; a work rivalling Titian in its color, and in the
finely-marked individual character of the heads. It is
remarkable that, although it has hung in the very heart of

London for more than three hundred years, it has not in the least suffered from smoke; and if it has ever been cleaned, it has sustained no injury from the process. Dr. Waagen urges the importance of so fine a picture being removed to the National Gallery, and thinks an arrangement might be made to that purpose, between the Government and the company that possesses it; "a consummation devoutly to be wished." There is not a Holbein in the National Gallery.

While speaking of this great painter, I must not omit to notice the interest given to his picture of the family of Sir Thomas More, by making the background an exact representation of an apartment in More's house. This example might effect a great improvement in portrait, and it would often be found easier to the painter (as well as far more agreeable) to copy realities, than to weary himself with ineffectual attempts to make the eternal pillar and curtain, or the conventional sky and tree, look as well as they do in the backgrounds of Reynolds and Gainsborough.

The question relating to the degree in which personal defects are to be marked must, in every case, be settled by the taste of the painter. Reynolds has not only shown that Baretti was near-sighted, but he has made that defect as much the subject of the picture as the sitter himself, and Baretti's absorption in his book strongly marks the literary man. But near-sightedness is not a deformity, and there can be no doubt that Reynolds abated whatever of malformation he might not for the sake of individuality think it right to exclude, and that he also invariably softened harshness of feature or expression, and diminished positive ugliness, as far as he could do so without losing character. Chantrey did the same; but Lawrence softened harshness so much as often to lose character. The portraits of neither of the three could ever be called ridiculously like, an expression sometimes used in the way of compliment, but in reality pointing exactly to what a portrait should not be; and Wilkie felt this so much that he went to the other extreme, and even deviated into unlikeness in his portraits, from the dread of that un-ideal mode of representation which excites us to laugh.

We undervalue that which costs us least effort, and West, while engaged on a small picture of his own family, little thought how much it would surpass in interest many of his more ambitious works. Its subject is the first visit of his father and elder brother to his young wife, after the birth of her second child. They are Quakers; and the venerable old man and his eldest son wear their hats, according to the custom of their sect. Nothing can be more beautifully conceived than the mother bending over the babe, sleeping in her lap. She is wrapped in a white dressing-gown, and her other son, a boy of six years old, is leaning on the arm of her chair. West stands behind his father, with his palette and brushes in his hand, and the silence that reigns over the whole is that of religious meditation, which will probably end, according to the Quaker custom, in a prayer from the patriarch of the family. The picture is a very small one, the engraving from it being of the same size. It has no excellence of color, but the masses of light and shadow are impressive and simple, and I know not a more original illustration of the often-painted subject, the ages of man. Infancy, childhood, youth, middle life, and extreme age, are beautifully brought together in the quiet chamber of the painter's wife. Had he been employed to paint these five ages, he would perhaps have given himself a great deal of trouble to produce a work that would have been classical, but, compared with this, commonplace; while he has here succeeded in making a picture which, being intended only for himself, is for that reason a picture for the whole world; and if painters could always thus put their hearts into their work, how much would the general interest of the Art be increased!

Among the many great lessons in portrait composition, by Rembrandt, are "The Night Watch," at Amsterdam, "The Group of Surgeons assembled round a Corpse," in the Musée at the Hague, and the picture which Mr. Smith, in his "Catalogue Raisonné," calls "Ranier Hanslo and his Mother." A sight of the two first is well worth a journey to Holland. The last is sometimes described as "a woman consulting a Baptist minister," and at others, "a woman consulting an eminent lawyer, or an eminent physician." As there are large books on a table and in the background, and the expressions of the heads are earnest and serious, the subject might be either of these. I saw the picture (which belongs to the Earl of Ashburnham) many years ago, and have ever since been haunted with the wish to see it again. Indeed, I was about to make a day's journey for that sole purpose, when it was sent to London for sale. The persons it represents are unknown, the heads of neither are remarkable for beauty, or any other interest than that marked individuality that carries with it a certainty of likeness; and yet it is a picture that throws down every barrier that would exclude it from the highest class of Art; nor do I know anything from the hand of Rembrandt in which he appears greater than in this simple and unpretending work. I remember being surprised to hear Sir Thomas Lawrence object to its treatment, that though the man turns towards the woman, and is speaking earnestly, while she is listening with great attention, yet they do not look in each other's faces. I was surprised that he should not have noticed how frequently this happens, in conversations on the most important subjects, and oftenest, indeed, in such conversations. Rembrandt has repeated these attitudes and expressions, in the two principal personages in "The Night Watch," with the difference only, that the

figures are walking as they converse. There is an engraving of the "Hanslo and his Mother" by Josiah Boydell,
which, however, fails in giving the breadth of light on the
female head, the color of which is as near to perfection as
Art ever approached.

The hands in Rembrandt's portraits, as in those of Holbein, do everything required of them in the most natural
and expressive way. But very different are the hands
of Vandyke, which have an affected grace, adopted from
Rubens, though carried further from Nature, and which may
be traced from Rubens to Coreggio. The hands in Vandyke's portraits are always of one type, thin and elegant,
with long, tapered fingers. He was followed in these particulars by Lely with still more of affectation, who carried
a corresponding mannerism into his faces, losing nearly all
individuality in that one style of beauty that was in fashion.

A nobleman said to Lely, " How is it that you have so
great a reputation, when you know, as well as I do, that
you are no painter? "   " True, but I am the best you have,"
was the answer. And so it is ; the best artist of the age
will generally, while living, have a reputation equal to the
greatest that have preceded him. Lely, however, *was* a
painter, and of very great merit. His color, always pearly
and refined, is often very charming. He understood well
the treatment of landscape as background, and there are
some of his pictures which I prefer to some pictures by
Vandyke.

Sir Joshua Reynolds remarks that in general the greatest
portrait-painters have not copied closely the dresses of their
time. Holbein, however, took no liberties with the doublets,
hose, or mantles of the gentlemen he painted, nor with the
head-gear or kirtles of the ladies ; neither did Velasquez ;
and their portraits are, therefore, curious records of fashions,
picturesque, and sometimes fantastic in the extreme, yet
always treated with admirable Art ; and I confess I prefer

those of Sir Joshua's portraits in which he has faithfully adhered to the dress of the sitter; which is always characteristic, and often highly so. The manner in which Queen Elizabeth covered herself with jewels, and the splendor with which Raleigh decorated his person, pertain to biography.

In some of Vandyke's portraits, no change is made in the dress, while in many (I believe the most), that which is stiff and formal is loosened, and alterations are introduced that we are only aware of when we compare his pictures with exact representations, by other artists, of the costume of the time. Such deviations from matter of fact were carried much further by Lely and Kneller, particularly in their portraits of ladies; and the first adopted an elegant, but impossible, undress, that assists the voluptuous expression which he aimed at, either to please a dissolute Court, or because it pleased himself; possibly for both reasons.

With Kneller, however, the ideal style of the dress does not affect the prevailing character he gave to the beauties he painted, who seem a higher order of beings than the ladies of Lely. Among the attractions of the latter the expression of strict virtue is by no means conspicuous, while it would seem profane to doubt the purity of the high-born dames of Kneller. Though, as a painter, not to be compared to Lely, his women seem secured from moral degradation by an ever-present consciousness of noble birth, which sits well on them; and though their demeanor is as studied as the grace of a minuet, it does not offend like vulgar affectation. Fielding, the natural Fielding, greatly admired the stately beauties of Kneller, at Hampton Court, and compared Sophia Western to one of them. Conscious that, " when unadorned, adorned the most," they reject the aid of jewellery, and are content with only so much assistance from Art as they receive from well-arranged draperies.

The great fault of Lely is the family likeness, closer than

that of sisters, which forbids our relying on his pictures
as portraits; and this unpardonable fault is carried even
further by Kneller, whose ladies are all cast in one mould
of feature and form, and all alike tall to a degree rare in
nature.

Reynolds adopted something from both which he used
to advantage; but he did far more, — he recovered portrait from all the mannerism that had accumulated on it,
from the death of Vandyke to his own time, and restored
it to truth.

When we compare his style with that of his master,
Hudson, we are struck with its vast superiority, its wide
difference, not merely in degree, but in kind; and in this
it would appear to form an exception to what has generally
been the case, namely, that the style of every extraordinary
genius is but a great improvement on that of the school in
which he was reared. But it was not from Hudson, nor
from his visit to Italy, that the Art of Reynolds was formed.
The seed that was to produce fruit, so excellent and abun-
dant, was sown before he quitted Devonshire. He there
saw, and probably among the first pictures he ever saw,
the works of a painter wholly unknown in the metropolis.
"This painter," Northcote tells us, "was William Gandy, of
Exeter, whom," he says, "I cannot but consider as an early
master of Reynolds. He told me himself that he had seen
portraits by Gandy equal to those of Rembrandt; one in
particular of an alderman of Exeter, which is placed in a
public building in that city. I have also heard him repeat
some observations of Gandy's which had been mentioned
to him, and that he approved of; one, in particular was,
that a picture ought to have a richness in its texture, as
if the colors had been composed of cream or cheese, and the
reverse of a hard and husky or dry manner." Now a
single precept like this, falling into an ear fitted to receive
it, is sufficient to create a style; while, upon the inapt, all
the best instruction that can be given is wasted.

I have seen a portrait by Gandy, which I should have mistaken for an early work of Reynolds; and this, with what Northcote tells us, is enough to establish, in my mind, Gandy's claim to the honor of being the first instructor of a great genius whom he never saw. Gandy's father was a pupil of Vandyke; and being patronized by the Duke of Ormond, and retained in his service in Ireland, his works were as little known in London as those of his son, who practised only in Devonshire. Thus, while the style of Vandyke degenerated through the hands of his successors in the Capital, till it was totally lost in the beginning of the eighteenth century, some of its best qualities were preserved in remote parts of the kingdom, to lead to a splendid revival of portraiture; so true it is that, however obscured from sight, at times, some of the links in the chain of Art may be, still it is a chain never wholly broken.

Nothing can be further from my intention than to lessen the fame of Reynolds. What I have stated merely shows what indeed we might be certain of without a knowledge of the facts, namely, that the birth of his Art was not miraculous. Praise enough is still left for him; for that which he derived from Gandy was but the medium of his own fascinating conceptions of Nature. "There is a charm," says Northcote, "in his portraits, a mingled softness and force, a grasping at the end, with nothing harsh or unpleasant in the means, that you will find nowhere else. He may go out of fashion for a time, but you must come back to him again, while a thousand imitators and academic triflers are forgotten."

In looking over prints from his works, we are astonished at the many attitudes and incidents we find new to Art, and yet often such as from their very familiarity in life have been overloked by other painters. The three Ladies Waldegrave, one winding silk from the hands of another, while the third is bending over a drawing, Mrs. Abington leaning on the back of her chair, and Lady Fenoulhet with her hands in a muff, for instance; and then the many exquisitely natural groupings of mothers and children, and of children with children; how greatly superior in interest are such conceptions, fresh from Nature, to some of his inventions, — as of ladies sacrificing to the Graces, or decorating a statue of Hymen, of which indeed he made fine pictures (for that he could not help), but pictures the impression of which is comparatively languid.

In the collected works of no other portrait-painter do we find so great a diversity of individual character illustrated by so great a variety of natural incident, or aided by such various and well-chosen effects of light and shadow; many entirely new to Art, as, for instance, the partial shadows thrown by branches of trees over whole-length figures. Indeed, by no other painter, except Gainsborough, has landscape been so beautifully or effectively brought in aid of portrait. Vandyke generally subdues its brightness to give supremacy to the head, and Lely and Kneller did this still more; but Reynolds, without lessening its power, always contrived it so as to relieve the face most effectively.

We may learn nearly everything relating to portrait from Reynolds. Those deviations from the exact correspondence of the sides of the face which are so common in Nature are never corrected by him, as they sometimes are by inferior artists under the notion of improving the drawing. He felt that a marked difference in the lines surrounding the eyes often greatly aids the expression of the face. He took advantage of this in painting the fixed despair of Ugolino, no doubt finding it in the model; and in a very different head, his front face of Garrick, he has, by observing the difference of the eyes, given great archness of expression, and assisted its intelligence without making the face less handsome.

It has been said, and I believe it, that no painter can

put more sense into a head than he possesses himself, and it must have been rare for Reynolds to meet with an in tellect superior to his own. Had we no other evidence, that of Goldsmith, who knew him well, was a close observer, and no flatterer, would be conclusive : —

> " Here Reynolds is laid, and to tell you my mind,
> He has not left a wiser or better behind."

But his portraits were not always so satisfactory to his sitters as the works of inferior painters. The truth is, sitters are no judges of their own likenesses, and in their immediate family circle the best judges are not always to be found. Lord Thurlow said, "There are two factions, the Reynolds faction and the Romney faction. I am of the Romney faction." Now in Romney's whole-length the Chancellor appeared a more handsome man than in the half-length of Reynolds. Romney avoided all indication of the suppressed temper that was so apt to explode in violent paroxysms, and this rendered his picture more acceptable to the original. But he missed what Reynolds alone could give, — that extraordinary sapience which made Charles Fox say, " No man could be so wise as Lord Thurlow looked."

That the portraits of Reynolds were the best of all likenesses, I have no manner of doubt. I know several of his pictures of children, the originals of whom I have seen in middle and old age, and in every instance I could discover much likeness. He painted Lord Melbourne when a boy, and with that genuine laugh that was so characteristic of the future Prime Minister at every period of his life ; and no likeness between a child and a man of sixty (an age at which I remember Lord Melbourne) was ever more striking. Lord Melbourne recollected that Sir Joshua bribed him to sit, by giving him a ride on his foot, and said, " If you behave well, you shall have another ride."

His fondness of children is recorded on all his canvases in which they appear. A matchless picture of Miss Bowls, a beautiful laughing child caressing a dog, was sold a few years ago at auction, and cheaply, at a thousand guineas. The father and mother of the little girl intended she should sit to Romney, who at one time more than divided the town with Reynolds. Sir George Beaumont, however, advised them to employ Sir Joshua. "But his pictures fade." "No matter, take the chance; even a faded picture by Reynolds will be the finest thing you can have. Ask him to dine with you; and let him become acquainted with her." The advice was taken; the little girl was placed beside Sir Joshua at the table, where he amused her so much with tricks and stories that she thought him the most charming man in the world, and the next day was delighted to be taken to his house, where she sat down with a face full of glee, the expression of which he caught at once and never lost; and the affair turned out every way happily, for the picture did not fade, and has till now escaped alike the inflictions of time or of the ignorant among cleaners.

Doubts have been expressed of the sincerity of Sir Joshua's great admiration of Michael Angelo. Had he, on his return from Italy, undertaken to decorate a church (supposing an opportunity) with imitations of the Sistine ceiling, I should doubt his appreciation of the great works that cover it. But a painter may sincerely admire Art very different from his own; and I rest my belief of his full appreciation of Michael Angelo less on his "Tragic Muse" (Mrs. Siddons) or his "Ugolino," both of which we may in some degree trace among the conceptions in the Sistine Chapel, than to that general greatness and grace of style stamped on all his works. "Reynolds," says Sterne, "great and graceful as he paints"; nor could his Art be so well characterized by any other two words.

It has been more than once intimated that Reynolds cared for no other artist's success. But if this were the case, why did he take the trouble to write and deliver his discourses? in which he did not fail to give all the instruction he could convey, by words, in his own branch of the Art, as well as in those which he considered higher. He was daily accessible to all young artists who sought his advice, and readily lent them the finest of his own works; but in doing this he always said to the portrait-painter, "It will be better for you to study Vandyke." It is clear, that, though he felt his own superiority among his contemporaries, he had a belief that British Art was advancing, and that he should be surpassed by future painters; like the belief in which Shakespeare supposes an ideal mistress to say of himself, —

"But since he died, and poets better prove,"

for Reynolds, like all men of the loftiest minds, was modest. Mrs. Bray, in her "Life of Stothard," says, with great truth, of the modesty of such men, that it "is not at all inconsistent with that strong internal conviction, which every man of real merit possesses, respecting his own order of capacity. He feels that Nature has given him a stand on higher ground than most of his contemporaries; but he does not look down on them, but above himself. What he does is great, but he still feels that greatness has a spirit which is ever mounting, — that rests on no summit within mortal view, but soars again and again in search of an ideal height on which to pause and fold its wings."

Gainsborough was the most formidable rival of Reynolds. Whether he felt it hopeless to make use of Sir Joshua's weapons, or whether his peculiar taste led him to the choice of other means; he adopted a system of chiaroscuro, of more frequent occurrence in Nature than those extremes of light and dark which Reynolds managed with

such consummate judgment. His range in portrait was
more limited, but within that range he is at times so delightful that we should not feel inclined to exchange a head
by him for a head of the same person by Sir Joshua. His
men are as thoroughly gentlemen, and his women as entirely ladies, nor had Reynolds a truer feeling of the charms
of infancy. Indeed his cottage children are more interesting because more natural than the "Robinettas" and "Mus-
cipulas" of his illustrious rival, the only class of pictures
by Reynolds in which mannerism in expression and attitude
obtrudes itself in the place of what is natural. Gainsborough's barefoot child on her way to the well, with her
little dog under her arm, is unequalled by anything of the
kind in the world. I recollect it at the British Gallery,
forming part of a very noble assemblage of pictures, and
I could scarcely look at or think of anything else in the
rooms. This inimitable work is a portrait, and not of a
peasant child, but of a young lady, who appears also in his
picture of the girl and pigs, which Sir Joshua purchased.

That Reynolds and Gainsborough were not on terms of
friendship seems to have been the fault of the latter, who,
with all his excellent qualities, had not so equable a temper
as Sir Joshua. Reynolds did not, as Allan Cunningham
intimates, wait till the death of Gainsborough to do justice
to his genius. The brief allusion to their last interview in
his fourteenth discourse, which is as modest as it is touching,
proves that he had not done so; and it seems clear that Sir
Joshua would have told much more, had it not been to his
own honor, and that he has only said what he felt necessary
for the removal of any charge of injustice on his part.

The powers of Gainsborough, in portrait, may be well
estimated by that charming picture in the Dulwich Gallery,
of "Mrs. Sheridan and Mrs. Tickell"; and the whole-
lengths at Hampton Court, of "Colonel St. Leger," and
"Fisher the Composer."

A painter may have great ability, and yet be inferior to those of whom I have spoken. Sir Thomas Lawrence was perhaps hindered from rising to the highest rank as a colorist by his early and first practice of making portraits in colorless chalk only. His wish to please the sitter made him yield more than his English predecessors had done to the foolish desire of most people to be painted with a smile: though he was far from extending this indulgence to that extreme of a self-satisfied simper that the French painters of the age preceding his had introduced to portrait. Of indefatigable industry, Lawrence's habit of undertaking too many pictures at the same time was a serious drawback, in many cases, to their excellence. He began the portraits of children which he did not finish till they were grown up, and of gentlemen and ladies while their hair was of its first color, but which remained incomplete in his rooms till the originals were gray. The most beautiful of his female heads, and beautiful it is, is the one he painted of Lady Elizabeth Leveson Gower (afterwards Marchioness of Westminster). This was begun and finished off-hand; and so was the best male head he ever painted, his first portrait of Mr. West, not the whole-length in the National Gallery, in which he has much exaggerated the stature of the original. He took especial delight in painting the venerable and amiable President, who offered a remarkable instance of what I have described elsewhere, the increase of beauty in old age, and of whom this portrait is a work of great excellence.

Without any of those peculiar blandishments of manner, either as a painter or a man, that contributed to make Lawrence the most popular portrait-painter of his time, Jackson was more of an artist, much truer in color, and, indeed, in this respect approaching to Reynolds, whose pictures he sometimes copied so closely as to deceive even Northcote. When his sitters were ordinary people, his

portraits were often ordinary works; but when they were
notable persons, he exerted all his powers. The portrait he
painted of Canova, for Chantrey, is in all respects superior
to that which Lawrence painted of the great sculptor;
more natural, more manly, and much finer in effect. His
heads of Sir John Franklin (painted for Mr. Murray), of
Flaxman, of Stothard, and of Liston, are all admirably
characteristic, and among the finest portraits of the British
school; and I remember seeing at Castle Howard his half-
length of Northcote, hanging in company with Vandyke's
half-length of Snyders, and a magnificent head of a Jew
Rabbi by Rembrandt, and well sustaining so trying a
position. Perfectly amiable in his nature, nothing pleased
Jackson more than opportunities of recommending young
painters of merit to patronage; and he introduced Wilkie
and Haydon to Lord Mulgrave and Sir George Beaumont. With strong natural sense, playful in his manner,
and with a true relish of humor, Jackson was a great
favorite with all who had the happiness to know him, and
his loss, by an early death, was irreparable to his friends,
and a very great one to Art.

The many advantages in many ways resulting from
Photography are yet but imperfectly appreciated; for 'its
improvements have followed each other so rapidly, that we
cannot but expect many more, and are quite in the dark
as to what may be its next wonder. In its present state it
confirms what has always been felt by the best artists and the
best critics, that fac-simile is not that species of resemblance
to Nature, even in a portrait, that is most agreeable: for
while the best calotypes remind us of mezzotint engravings
from Velasquez, Rembrandt, or Reynolds, they are still
inferior in general effect to such engravings: and they thus
help to show that the ideal is equally a principle of por-
trait-painting as of all other Art: and that not only does
this consist in the best view of the face, the best light and

shadow, and the most characteristic attitude of the figure, for all these may be selected for a photographic picture, but that the ideal of a portrait, like the ideal of all Art, depends on something which can only be communicated by the mind, through the hand and eye, and without any other mechanical intervention than that of the pencil. Photography may tend to relax the industry of inferior painters, but it may be hoped and reasonably expected that it will stimulate the exertions of the best; for much may be learnt from it if used as a means of becoming better acquainted with the beauties of Nature, but nothing if resorted to only as a substitute for labor.

TO AGE.

By WALTER SAVAGE LANDOR.

WELCOME, old friend! These many years
   Have we lived door by door;
The Fates have laid aside their shears
   Perhaps for some few more.

I was indocile at an age
   When better boys were taught,
But thou at length hast made me sage,
   If I am sage in aught.

Little I know from other men,
   Too little they from me,
But thou hast pointed well the pen
   That writes these lines to thee.

Thanks for expelling Fear and Hope,
   One vile, the other vain;
One's scourge, the other's telescope,
   I shall not see again;

Rather what lies before my feet
   My notice shall engage:
He who hath braved Youth's dizzy heat
   Dreads not the frost of Age.

THE YOUTH OF MAN.

By MATTHEW ARNOLD.

WE, O Nature, depart:
    Thou survivest us: this,
This, I know, is the law.
Yes, but more than this,
Thou who seest us die
Seest us change while we live;
Seest our dreams one by one,
Seest our errors depart:
   Watchest us, Nature, throughout,
Mild and inscrutably calm.

   Well for us that we change!
Well for us that the Power
Which in our morning prime
Saw the mistakes of our youth,
Sweet and forgiving and good,
Sees the contrition of age!

   Behold, O Nature, this pair!
See them to-night where they stand,
Not with the halo of youth
Crowning their brows with its light,
Not with the sunshine of hope,
Not with the rapture of spring,

Which they had of old, when they stood
Years ago at my side
In this selfsame garden, and said:
"We are young, and the world is ours,
For man is the king of the world.
Fools that these mystics are
Who prate of Nature! but she
Has neither beauty, nor warmth,
Nor life, nor emotion, nor power.
But Man has a thousand gifts,
And the generous dreamer invests
The senseless world with them all.
    Nature is nothing! her charm
Lives in our eyes which can paint,
Lives in our hearts which can feel!"

    Thou, O Nature, wert mute,—
Mute as of old: days flew,
Days and years; and Time
With the ceaseless stroke of his wings
Brushed off the bloom from their soul.
Clouded and dim grew their eye;
Languid their heart; for Youth .
Quickened its pulses no more.
Slowly within the walls
Of an ever-narrowing world
They drooped, they grew blind, they grew old.
Thee and their Youth in thee,
Nature, they saw no more.

    Murmur of living!
Stir of existence!
Soul of the world!
Make, O make yourselves felt
To the dying spirit of Youth.

Come, like the breath of spring.
Leave not a human soul
To grow old in darkness and pain.
　Only the living can feel you :
But leave us not while we live.

　Here they stand to-night, —
Here, where this gray balustrade
Crowns the still valley : behind
Is the castled house with its woods
Which sheltered their childhood, the sun
On its ivied windows : a scent
From the gray-walled gardens, a breath
Of the fragrant stock and the pink,
Perfumes the evening air.
Their children play on the lawns.
They stand and listen : they hear
The children's shouts, and, at times,
Faintly, the bark of a dog
From a distant farm in the hills :—
Nothing besides : in front
The wide, wide valley outspreads
To the dim horizon, reposed
In the twilight, and bathed in dew,
　Cornfield and hamlet and copse
Darkening fast ; but a light,
Far off, a glory of day,
Still plays on the city spires :
And there in the dusk by the walls,
With the gray mist marking its course
Through the silent flowery land,
　On, to the plains, to the sea,
Floats the Imperial Stream.

　Well I know what they feel.
They gaze, and the evening wind

Plays on their faces: they gaze;
Airs from the Eden of Youth
Awake and stir in their soul:
The Past returns; they feel
What they are, alas! what they were.
    They, not Nature, are changed.
Well I know what they feel.

    Hush! for tears
Begin to steal to their eyes.
Hush! for fruit
Grows from such sorrow as theirs.

    And they remember
With piercing, untold anguish
The proud boasting of their youth.
    And they feel how Nature was fair.
And the mists of delusion,
And the scales of habit,
Fall away from their eyes.
And they see, for a moment,
Stretching out, like the Desert
In its weary, unprofitable length,
Their faded, ignoble lives

    While the locks are yet brown on thy head,
While the soul still looks through thine eyes,
While the heart still pours
The mantling blood to thy cheek,
    Sink, O Youth, in thy soul!
Yearn to the greatness of Nature!
Rally the good in the depths of thyself!

HANNIBAL'S MARCH INTO ITALY.

By DR. ARNOLD.

TWICE in history has there been witnessed the struggle of the highest individual genius against the resources and institutions of a great nation; and in both cases the nation has been victorious. For seventeen years Hannibal strove against Rome; for sixteen years Napoleon Bonaparte strove against England: the efforts of the first ended in Zama, those of the second in Waterloo.

True it is, as Polybius has said, that Hannibal was supported by the zealous exertions of Carthage; and the strength of the opposition to his policy has been very possibly exaggerated by the Roman writers. But the zeal of his country in the contest, as Polybius himself remarks in another place, was itself the work of his family. Never did great men more show themselves the living spirit of a nation than Hamilcar, and Hasdrubal, and Hannibal, during a period of nearly fifty years, approved themselves to be to Carthage. It is not, then, merely through our ignorance of the internal state of Carthage that Hannibal stands so prominent in all our conceptions of the second Punic war; he was really its moving and directing power, and the energy of his country was but a light reflected from his own. History therefore gathers itself into his single person: in that vast tempest which, from north and south, from the west and the east, broke upon Italy, we see nothing but Hannibal.

But if Hannibal's genius may be likened to the Homeric god, who in his hatred of the Trojans rises from the deep to rally the fainting Greeks, and to lead them against the enemy, so the calm courage with which Hector met his more than human adversary in his country's cause is no unworthy image of the unyielding magnanimity displayed by the aristocracy of Rome. As Hannibal utterly eclipses Carthage, so on the contrary Fabius, Marcellus, Claudius, Nero, even Scipio himself, are as nothing when compared to the spirit and wisdom and power of Rome. The senate which voted its thanks to its political enemy, Varro, after his disastrous defeat, "because he had not despaired of the Commonwealth," and which disdained either to solicit or to reprove, or to threaten, or in any way to notice the twelve colonies which had refused their accustomed supplies of men for the army, is far more to be honored than the conqueror of Zama. This we should the more carefully bear in mind, because our tendency is to admire individual greatness far more than national; and as no single Roman will bear comparison with Hannibal, we are apt to murmur at the event of the contest, and to think that the victory was awarded to the least worthy of the combatants. On the contrary, never was the wisdom of God's providence more manifest than in the issue of the struggle between Rome and Carthage. It was clearly for the good of mankind that Hannibal should be conquered; his triumph would have stopped the progress of the world. For great men can only act permanently by forming great nations; and no one man, even though it were Hannibal himself, can in one generation effect such a work. But where the nation has been merely enkindled for a while by a great man's spirit, the light passes away with him who communicated it; and the nation, when he is gone, is like a dead body, to which magic power had for a moment given an unnatural life: when the charm has ceased, the body is cold and stiff as before. He who grieves over the battle of Zama should carry on his thoughts to a period thirty years later, when Hannibal must, in the course of nature, have been dead, and consider how the isolated Phœnician city of Carthage was fitted to receive and to consolidate the civilization of Greece, or by its laws and institutions to bind together barbarians of every race and language into an organized empire, and prepare them for becoming, when that empire was dissolved, the free members of the commonwealth of Christian Europe.

Hannibal was twenty-six years of age when he was appointed commander-in-chief of the Carthaginian armies in Spain, upon the sudden death of Hasdrubal. Two years, we have seen, had been employed in expeditions against the native Spaniards; the third year was devoted to the siege of Saguntum. Hannibal's pretext for attacking it was, that the Saguntines had oppressed one of the Spanish tribes in alliance with Carthage; but no caution in the Saguntine government could have avoided a quarrel, which their enemy was determined to provoke. Saguntum, although not a city of native Spaniards, resisted as obstinately as if the very air of Spain had breathed into foreign settlers on its soil the spirit so often, in many different ages, displayed by the Spanish people. Saguntum was defended like Numantia and Gerona: the siege lasted eight months; and when all hope was gone, several of the chiefs kindled a fire in the market-place, and after having thrown in their most precious effects, leapt into it themselves, and perished. Still the spoil found in the place was very considerable; there was a large treasure of money, which Hannibal kept for his war expenses; there were numerous captives, whom he distributed amongst his soldiers as their share of the plunder; and there was much costly furniture from the public and private buildings, which he sent home to decorate the temples and palaces of Carthage.

It must have been towards the close of the year, but

apparently before the consuls were returned from Illyria, that the news of the fall of Saguntum reached Rome. Immediately ambassadors were sent to Carthage; M. Fabius Buteo, who had been consul seven-and-twenty years before, C. Licinius Varus, and Q. Bæbius Tamphilus. Their orders were simply to demand that Hannibal and his principal officers should be given up for their attack upon the allies of Rome, in breach of the treaty, and, if this were refused, to declare war. The Carthaginians tried to discuss the previous question, whether the attack on Saguntum was a breach of the treaty; but to this the Romans would not listen. At length M. Fabius gathered up his toga, as if he was wrapping up something in it, and holding it out thus folded together, he said, "Behold, here are peace and war; take which you choose!" The Carthaginian suffete, or judge, answered, "Give whichever thou wilt." Hereupon Fabius shook out the folds of his toga, saying, "Then here we give you war"; to which several members of the council shouted in answer, "With all our hearts we welcome it." Thus the Roman ambassadors left Carthage, and returned straight to Rome.

But before the result of this embassy could be known in Spain, Hannibal had been making preparations for his intended expedition, in a manner which showed, not only that he was sure of the support of his government, but that he was able to dispose at his pleasure of all the military resources of Carthage. At his suggestion fresh troops from Africa were sent over to Spain to secure it during his absence, and to be commanded by his own brother, Hasdrubal; and their place was to be supplied by other troops raised in Spain; so that Africa was to be defended by Spaniards, and Spain by Africans, the soldiers of each nation, when quartered amongst foreigners, being cut off from all temptation or opportunity to revolt. So completely was he allowed to direct every military measure, that he is said to have sent Spanish and Numidian troops to garrison Carthage itself; in other words, this was a part of his general plan, and was adopted accordingly by the government. Meanwhile he had sent ambassadors into Gaul, and even across the Alps, to the Gauls who had so lately been at war with the Romans, both to obtain information as to the country through which his march lay, and to secure the assistance and guidance of the Gauls in his passage of the Alps, and their co-operation in arms when he should arrive in Italy. His Spanish troops he had dismissed to their several homes at the end of the last campaign, that they might carry their spoils with them, and tell of their exploits to their countrymen, and enjoy, during the winter, that almost listless ease which is the barbarian's relief from war and plunder. At length he received the news of the Roman embassy to Carthage, and the actual declaration of war; his officers also had returned from Cisalpine Gaul. "The natural difficulties of the passage of the Alps were great," they said, "but by no means insuperable; while the disposition of the Gauls was most friendly, and they were eagerly expecting his arrival." Then Hannibal called his soldiers together, and told them openly that he was going to lead them into Italy. "The Romans," he said, have demanded that I and my principal officers should be delivered up to them as malefactors. Soldiers, will you suffer such an indignity? The Gauls are holding out their arms to us, inviting us to come to them, and to assist them in revenging their manifold injuries. And the country which we shall invade, so rich in corn and wine and oil, so full of flocks and herds, so covered with flourishing cities, will be the richest prize that could be offered by the gods to reward your valor." One common shout from the soldiers assured him of their readiness to follow him. He thanked them, fixed the day on which they were to be ready to march, and then dismissed them.

In this interval, and now on the very eve of commencing his appointed work, to which for eighteen years he had been solemnly devoted, and to which he had so long been looking forward with almost sickening hope, he left the head-quarters of his army to visit Gades, and there, in the temple of the supreme god of Tyre, and all the colonies of Tyre, to offer his prayers and vows for the success of his enterprise. He was attended only by those immediately attached to his person; and amongst these was a Sicilian Greek, Silenus, who followed him throughout his Italian expedition, and lived at his table. When the sacrifice was over, Hannibal returned to his army at New Carthage; and, everything being ready, and the season sufficiently advanced, for it was now late in May, he set out on his march for the Iberus.

And here the fulness of his mind, and his strong sense of being the devoted instrument of his country's gods to destroy their enemies, haunted him by night as they possessed him by day. In his sleep, so he told Silenus, he fancied that the supreme god of his fathers had called him into the presence of all the gods of Carthage, who were sitting on their thrones in council. There he received a solemn charge to invade Italy; and one of the heavenly council went with him and with his army, to guide him on his way. He went on, and his divine guide commanded him, " See that thou look not behind thee." But after a while, impatient of the restraint, he turned to look back; and there he beheld a huge and monstrous form, thick-set all over with serpents; wherever it moved orchards and woods and houses fell crushing before it. He asked his guide in wonder what that monster form was? The god answered, " Thou seest the desolation of Italy; go on thy way, straight forward, and cast no look behind." Thus, with no divided heart, and with an entire resignation of all personal and domestic enjoyments forever, Hannibal went forth, at the age of twenty-seven, to do the work of his country's gods, and to redeem his early vow.

The consuls at Rome came into office at this period on the fifteenth of March; it was possible, therefore, for a consular army to arrive on the scene of action in time to dispute with Hannibal, not only the passage of the Rhone, but that of the Pyrenees. But the Romans exaggerated the difficulties of his march, and seem to have expected that the resistance of the Spanish tribes between the Iberus and the Pyrenees, and of the Gauls between the Pyrenees and the Rhone, would so delay him that he would not reach the Rhone till the end of the season. They therefore made their preparations leisurely.

Of the consuls for this year, the year of Rome 536, and 218 before the Christian era, one was P. Cornelius Scipio, the son of L. Scipio, who had been consul in the sixth year of the first Punic war, and the grandson of L. Scipio Barbatus, whose services in the third Samnite war are recorded in his famous epitaph. The other was Ti. Sempronius Longus, probably, but not certainly, the son of that C. Sempronius Blæsus who had been consul in the year 501. The consul's provinces were to be Spain and Sicily; Scipio, with two Roman legions, and 15,600 of the Italian allies, and with a fleet of sixty quinqueremes, was to command in Spain; Sempronius, with a somewhat larger army, and a fleet of 160 quinqueremes, was to cross over to Lilybæum, and from thence, if circumstances favored, to make a descent on Africa. A third army, consisting also of two Roman legions, and 11,000 of the allies, was stationed in Cisalpine Gaul, under the prætor, L. Manlius Vulso. The Romans suspected that the Gauls would rise in arms erelong; and they hastened to send out the colonists of two colonies, which had been resolved on before, but not actually founded, to occupy the important stations of Placentia and Cremona on the opposite banks of the Po.

The colonists sent to each of these places were no fewer than six thcusand; and they received notice to be at their colonies in thirty days. Three commissioners, one of them C. Lutatius Catulus, being of consular rank, were sent out as usual, to superintend the allotment of lands to the settlers; and these 12,000 men, together with the prætor's army, were supposed to be capable of keeping the Gauls quiet.

It is a curious fact, that the danger on the side of Spain was considered to be so much the less urgent, that Scipio's army was raised the last, after those of his colleague and of the prætor, L. Manlius. Indeed, Scipio was still at Rome, when tidings came that the Boians and Insubrians had revolted, had dispersed the new settlers at Placentia and Cremona, and driven them to take refuge at Mutina, had treacherously seized the three commissioners at a conference, and had defeated the prætor, L. Manlius, and obliged him also to take shelter in one of the towns of Cisalpine Gaul, where they were blockading him. One of Scipio's legions, with five thousand of the allies, was immediately sent off into Gaul under another prætor, C. Atilius Serranus; and Scipio waited till his own army should again be completed by new levies. Thus, he cannot have left Rome till late in the summer; and when he arrived with his fleet and army at the mouth of the eastern branch of the Rhone, he found that Hannibal had crossed the Pyrenees; but he still hoped to impede his passage of the river.

Hannibal, meanwhile, having set out from New Carthage with an army of 90,000 foot and 12,000 horse, crossed the Iberus; and from thenceforward the hostile operations of his march began. He might, probably, have marched through the country between the Iberus and the Pyrenees, had that been his sole object, as easily as he made his way from the Pyrenees to the Rhone; a few presents and civilities would easily have induced the Spanish chiefs to allow

him a free passage. But some of the tribes northward of
the Iberus were friendly to Rome : on the coast were the
Greek cities of Rhoda and Emporiæ, Massaliot colonies,
and thus attached to the Romans as the old allies of their
mother city : if this part of Spain were left unconquered,
the Romans would immediately make use of it as the base
of their operations, and proceed from thence to attack the
whole Carthaginian dominion. Accordingly, Hannibal employed his army in subduing the whole country, which he
effected with no great loss of time, but at a heavy expense
of men, as he was obliged to carry the enemy's strongholds
by assault, rather than incur the delay of besieging them.
He left Hanno with eleven thousand men to retain possession of the newly-conquered country; and he further diminished his army by sending home as many more of his
Spanish soldiers, próbably those who had most distinguished
themselves, as an earnest to the rest, that they too, if they
did their duty well, might expect a similar release, and
might look forward to return erelong to their homes full of
spoil and of glory. These detachments, together with the
heavy loss sustained in the field, reduced the force with
which Hannibal entered Gaul to no more than 50,000 foot
and 9,000 horse.

From the Pyrenees to the Rhone his progress was easy.
Here he had no wish to make regular conquests ; and presents to the chiefs mostly succeeded in conciliating their
friendship, so that he was allowed to pass freely. But on
the left bank of the Rhone the influence of the Massaliots
with the Gaulish tribes had disposed them to resist the in-
vader ; and the passage of the Rhone was not to be effected
without a contest.

Scipio, by this time, had landed his army near the eastern mouth of the Rhone ; and his information of Hannibal's
movements was vague and imperfect. His men had suffered from sea-sickness on their voyage from Pisa to the

Rhone; and he wished to give them a short time to recover
their strength and spirits, before he led them against the
enemy. He still felt confident that Hannibal's advance
from the Pyrenees must be slow, supposing that he would
be obliged to fight his way; so that he never doubted that
he should have ample time to oppose his passage of the
Rhone.   Meanwhile he sent out 300 horse, with some
Gauls, who were in the service of the Massaliots, ordering
them to ascend the left bank of the Rhone, and discover, if
possible, the situation of the enemy. He seems to have
been unwilling to place the river on his rear, and therefore
never to have thought of conducting his operations on the
right bank, or even of sending out reconnoitring parties
in this direction.

The resolution which Scipio formed a few days afterwards, of sending his army to Spain, when he himself returned to Italy, was deserving of such high praise, that we
must hesitate to· accuse him of over caution or needless
delay at this critical moment. Yet he was sitting idle at
the mouth of the Rhone, while the Gauls were vainly
endeavoring to oppose Hannibal's passage of the river.
We must understand that Hannibal kept his army as far
away from the sea as possible, in order to conceal his movements from the Romans; therefore he came upon the
Rhone, not on the line of the later Roman road from Spain
to Italy, which crossed the river at Tarasco, between Avig-
non and Arles, but at a point much higher up, above its
confluence with the Durance, and nearly half-way, if we
can trust Polybius's reckoning, from the sea to its confluence
with the Isere. Here he obtained from the natives on the
right bank, by paying a fixed price, all their boats and vessels of every description with which they were accustomed
to traffic down the river: they allowed him also to cut tim-
ber for the construction of others; and thus in two days he
was provided with the means of transporting his army.

But finding that the Gauls were assembled on the eastern bank to oppose his passage, he sent off a detachment of his army by night with native guides, to ascend the right bank, for about two-and-twenty miles, and there to cross as they could, where there was no enemy to stop them. The woods, which then lined the river, supplied this detachment with the means of constructing barks and rafts enough for the passage ; they took advantage of one of the many islands in this part of the Rhone, to cross where the stream was divided ; and thus they all reached the left bank in safety. There they took up a strong position, probably one of those strange masses of rock which rise here and there with steep cliffy sides like islands out of the vast plain, and rested for four-and-twenty hours after their exertions in the march and the passage of the river.

Hannibal allowed eight-and-forty hours to pass from the time when the detachment left his camp ; and then, on the morning of the fifth day after his arrival on the Rhone, he made his preparations for the passage of his main army. The mighty stream of the river, fed by the snows of the high Alps, is swelled rather than diminished by the heats of summer ; so that, although the season was that when the southern rivers are generally at their lowest, it was rolling the vast mass of its waters along with a startling fulness and rapidity. The heaviest vessels were therefore placed on the left, highest up the stream, to form something of a break-water for the smaller craft crossing below ; the small boats held the flower of the light-armed foot, while the cavalry were in the larger vessels ; most of the horses being towed astern swimming, and a single soldier holding three or four together by their bridles. Everything was ready, and the Gauls on the opposite side had poured out of their camp, and lined the bank in scattered groups at the most accessible points, thinking that their task of stopping the enemy's landing would be easily accomplished. At length Hannibal's eye observed a column of smoke rising on the farther shore, above or on the right of the barbarians. This was the concerted signal which assured him of the arrival of his detachment; and he instantly ordered his men to embark, and to push across with all possible speed. They pulled vigorously against the rapid stream, cheering each other to the work; while behind them were their friends, cheering them also from the bank; and before them were the Gauls singing their war-songs, and calling them to come on with tones and gestures of defiance. But on a sudden a mass of fire was seen on the rear of the barbarians; the Gauls on the bank looked behind, and began to turn away from the river; and presently the bright arms and white linen coats of the African and Spanish soldiers appeared above the bank, breaking in upon the disorderly line of the Gauls. Hannibal himself, who was with the party crossing the river, leaped on shore amongst the first, and forming his men as fast as they landed, led them instantly to the charge. But the Gauls, confused and bewildered, made little resistance; they fled in utter rout; whilst Hannibal, not losing a moment, sent back his vessels and boats for a fresh detachment of his army; and before night his whole force, with the exception of his elephants, was safely established on the eastern side of the Rhone.

As the river was no longer between him and the enemy, Hannibal early on the next morning sent out a party of Numidian cavalry to discover the position and number of Scipio's forces, and then called his army together, to see and hear the communications of some chiefs of the Cisalpine Gauls, who were just arrived from the other side of the Alps. Their words were explained to the Africans and Spaniards in the army by interpreters; but the very sight of the chiefs was itself an encouragement; for it told the soldiers that the communication with Cisalpine Gaul was not impracticable, and that the Gauls had undertaken so

long a journey for the purpose of obtaining the aid of the
Carthaginian army, against their old enemies, the Romans.
Besides, the interpreters explained to the soldiers that the
chiefs undertook to guide them into Italy by a short and
safe route, on which they would be able to find provisions;
and spoke strongly of the great extent and richness of Italy,
when they did arrive there, and how zealously the Gauls
would aid them. Hannibal then came forward himself and
addressed his army: their work, he said, was more than half
accomplished by the passage of the Rhone; their own eyes
and ears had witnessed the zeal of their Gaulish allies in
their cause; for the rest, their business was to do their duty,
and obey his orders implicitly, leaving everything else to
him. The cheers and shouts of the soldiers again satisfied
him how fully he might depend upon them; and he then
addressed his prayers and vows to the gods of Carthage,
imploring them to watch over the army, and to prosper its
work to the end, as they had prospered its beginning. The
soldiers were now dismissed, with orders to prepare for
their march on the morrow.

Scarcely was the assembly broken up, when some of the
Numidians who had been sent out in the morning were
seen riding for their lives to the camp, manifestly in flight
from a victorious enemy. Not half of the original party
returned; for they had fallen in with Scipio's detachment of
Roman and Gaulish horse, and, after an obstinate conflict,
had been completely beaten. Presently after, the Roman
horsemen appeared in pursuit; but when they observed the
Carthaginian camp, they wheeled about and rode off, to
carry back word to their general. Then at last Scipio put
his army in motion, and ascended the left bank of the river
to find and engage the enemy. But when he arrived at the
spot where his cavalry had seen the Carthaginian camp, he
found it deserted, and was told that Hannibal had been gone
three days, having marched northwards, ascending the left

bank of the river. To follow him seemed desperate: it was plunging into a country wholly unknown to the Romans, where they had neither allies nor guides, nor resources of any kind; and where the natives, over and above the common jealousy felt by all barbarians towards a foreign army, were likely, as Gauls, to regard the Romans with peculiar hostility. But if Hannibal could not be followed now, he might easily be met on his first arrival in Italy; from the mouth of the Rhone to Pisa was the chord of a circle, while Hannibal was going to make a long circuit; and the Romans had an army already in Cisalpine Gaul; while the enemy would reach the scene of action exhausted with the fatigues and privations of his march across the Alps. Accordingly, Scipio descended the Rhone again, embarked his army and sent it on to Spain under the command of his brother, Cnæus Scipio, as his lieutenant; while he himself in his own ship, sailed for Pisa, and immediately crossed the Apennines to take the command of the forces of the two prætors, Manlius and Atilius, who, as we have seen, had an army of about 25,000 men, over and above the colonists of Placentia and Cremona, still disposable in Cisalpine Gaul.

This resolution of Scipio to send his own army on to Spain, and to meet Hannibal with the army of the two prætors, appears to show that he possessed the highest qualities of a general, which involve the wisdom of a statesman no less than of a soldier. As a mere military question, his calculation, though baffled by the event, was sound; but if we view it in a higher light, the importance to the Romans of retaining their hold on Spain would have justified a far greater hazard; for if the Carthaginians were suffered to consolidate their dominion in Spain, and to avail themselves of its immense resources, not in money only, but in men, the hardiest and steadiest of barbarians, and, under the training of such generals as Hannibal and his brother, equal to the best soldiers in the world, the Romans would hardly have been able to maintain the contest. Had not P. Scipio then despatched his army to Spain at this critical moment, instead of carrying it home to Italy, his son in all probability would never have won the battle of Zama.

Meanwhile Hannibal, on the day after the skirmish with Scipio's horse, had sent forward his infantry, keeping the cavalry to cover his operations, as he still expected the Romans to pursue him; while he himself waited to superintend the passage of the elephants. These were thirty-seven in number; and their dread of the water made their transport a very difficult operation. It was effected by fastening to the bank large rafts of 200 feet in length, covered carefully with earth: to the end of these smaller rafts were attached, covered with earth in the same manner, and with towing lines extended to a number of the largest barks, which were to tow them over the stream. The elephants, two females leading the way, were brought upon the rafts by their drivers without difficulty; and as soon as they came upon the smaller rafts, these were cut loose at once from the larger, and towed out into the middle of the river. Some of the elephants, in their terror, leaped overboard, and drowned their drivers; but they themselves, it is said, held their huge trunks above water, and struggled to the shore; so that the whole thirty-seven were landed in safety. Then Hannibal called in his cavalry, and covering his march with them and with the elephants, set forward up the left bank of the Rhone to overtake the infantry.

In four days they reached the spot where the Isere, coming down from the main Alps, brings to the Rhone a stream hardly less full or mighty than his own. In the plains above the confluence two Gaulish brothers were contending which should be chief of their tribe; and the elder called in the stranger general to support his cause. Hannibal readily complied, established him firmly on the throne, and received important aid from him in return. He supplied

the Carthaginian army plentifully with provisions, furnished
them with new arms, gave them new clothing, especially
shoes, which were found very useful in the subsequent
march, and accompanied them to the first entrance on the
mountain country, to secure them from attacks on the part
of his countrymen.

The attentive reader, who is acquainted with the geography of the Alps and their neighborhood, will perceive that
this account of Hannibal's march is vague. It does not
appear whether the Carthaginians ascended the left bank of
the Isere or the right bank; or whether they continued to
ascend the Rhone for a time, and, leaving it only so far as to
avoid the great angle which it makes at Lyons, rejoined it
again just before they entered the mountain country, a little
to the left of the present road from Lyons to Chamberri.
But these uncertainties cannot now be removed, because
Polybius neither possessed a sufficient knowledge of the
bearings of the country, nor sufficient liveliness as a painter,
to describe the line of the march so as to be clearly recognized. I believe, however, that Hannibal crossed the Isere,
and continued to ascend the Rhone; and that afterwards,
striking off to the right across the plains of Dauphiné, he
reached what Polybius calls the first ascent of the Alps, at
the northern extremity of that ridge of limestone mountains, which, rising abruptly from the plain to the height of
4,000 or 5,000 feet, and filling up the whole space between
the Rhone at Belley and the Isere below Grenoble, first
introduces the traveller coming from Lyons to the remarkable features of Alpine scenery.

At the end of the lowland country, the Gaulish chief, who
had accompanied Hannibal thus far, took leave of him: his
influence probably did not extend to the Alpine valleys;
and the mountaineers, far from respecting his safe-conduct, ·
might be in the habit of making plundering inroads on his
own territory. Here then Hannibal was left to himself;

and he found that the natives were prepared to beset his
passage. They occupied all such points as commanded the
road; which, as usual, was a sort of terrace cut in the
mountain-side, overhanging the valley whereby it penetrated to the central ridge. But as the mountain line is of
no great breadth here, the natives guarded the defile only
by day, and withdrew when night came on to their own
homes, in a town or village among the mountains, and lying
in the valley behind them. Hannibal, having learnt this
from some of his Gaulish guides whom he sent among them,
encamped in their sight just below the entrance of the defile; and as soon as it was dusk, he set out with a detachment of light troops, made his way through the pass, and
occupied the positions which the barbarians, after their usual
practice, had abandoned at the approach of night.

Day dawned; the main army broke up from its camp,
and began to enter the defile; while the natives, finding
their positions occupied by the enemy, at first looked on quietly, and offered no disturbance to the march. But when
they saw the long narrow line of the Carthaginian army
winding along the steep mountain-side, and the cavalry and
baggage-cattle struggling at every step with the difficulties
of the road, the temptation to plunder was too strong to be
resisted; and from many points of the mountain above the
road they rushed down upon the Carthaginians. The confusion was terrible: for the road or track was so narrow,
that the least crowd or disorder pushed the heavily loaded
baggage-cattle down the steep below; and the horses,
wounded by the barbarians' missiles, and plunging about
wildly in their pain and terror, increased the mischief. At
last Hannibal was obliged to charge down from his position,
which commanded the whole scene of confusion, and to
drive the barbarians off. This he effected; yet the conflict
of so many men on the narrow road made the disorder
worse for a time; and he unavoidably occasioned the de-

struction of many of his own men. At last, the barbarians
being quite beaten off, the army wound its way out of the
defile in safety, and rested in the wide and rich valley which
extends from the lake of Bourget, with scarcely a perceptible change of level, to the Isere at Montmeillan. Hannibal meanwhile attacked and stormed the town, which was
the barbarians' principal stronghold; and here he not only
recovered a great many of his own men, horses, and baggage-cattle, but also found a large supply of corn and cattle
belonging to the barbarians, which he immediately made
use of for the consumption of his soldiers.

In the plain which he had now reached, he halted for a
whole day, and then, resuming his march, proceeded for
three days up the valley of the Isere on the right bank,
without encountering any difficulty. Then the natives met
him with branches of trees in their hands, and wreaths on
their heads, in token of peace: they spoke fairly, offered
hostages, and wished, they said, neither to do the Carthaginians any injury, nor to receive any from them. Hannibal mistrusted them, yet did not wish to offend them; he
accepted their terms, received their hostages, and obtained
large supplies of cattle; and their whole behavior seemed
so trustworthy, that at last he accepted their guidance, it is
said, through a difficult part of the country, which he was
now approaching. For all the Alpine valleys become nar-
rower, as they draw nearer to the central chain; and the
mountains often come so close to the stream, that the roads
in old times were often obliged to leave the valley and
ascend the hills by any accessible point, to descend again
when the gorge became wider, and follow the stream as
before. If this is not done, and the track is carried nearer
the river, it passes often through defiles of the most formidable character, being no more than a narrow ledge above a
furious torrent, with cliffs rising above it absolutely precip-
itous, and coming down on the other side of the torrent

abruptly to the water, leaving no passage by which man or even goat could make its way.

It appears that the barbarians persuaded Hannibal to pass through one of these defiles, instead of going round it; and while his army was involved in it, they suddenly, and without provocation, as we are told, attacked him. Making their way along the mountain-sides above the defile, they rolled down masses of rock on the Carthaginians below, or even threw stones upon them from their hands, stones and rocks being equally fatal against an enemy so entangled. It was well for Hannibal, that, still doubting the barbarians' faith, he had sent forward his cavalry and baggage, and covered the march with his infantry, who thus had to sustain the brunt of the attack. Foot-soldiers on such ground were able to move where horses would be quite helpless; and thus at last Hannibal, with his infantry, forced his way to the summit of one of the bare cliffs overhanging the defile, and remained there during the night, whilst the cavalry and baggage slowly struggled out of the defile. Thus again baffled, the barbarians made no more general attacks on the army; some partial annoyance was occasioned at intervals, and some baggage was carried off; but it was observed that wherever the elephants were the line of march was secure; for the barbarians beheld those huge creatures with terror, having never had the slightest knowledge of them, and not daring to approach when they saw them.

Without any further recorded difficulty, the army on the ninth day after they had left the plains of Dauphiné arrived at the summit of the central ridge of the Alps. Here there is always a plain of some extent, immediately overhung by the snowy summits of the high mountains, but itself in summer presenting in many parts a carpet of the freshest grass, with the chalets of the shepherds scattered over it, and gay with a thousand flowers. But far different is its aspect through the greatest part of the year: then it is one unvaried waste of snow; and the little lakes, which on many of the passes enliven the summer landscape, are now frozen over and covered with snow, so as to be no longer distinguishable. Hannibal was on the summit of the Alps about the end of October: the first winter snows had already fallen; but two hundred years before the Christian era, when all Germany was one vast forest, the climate of the Alps was far colder than at present, and the snow lay on the passes all through the year. Thus the soldiers were in dreary quarters; they remained two days on the summit, resting from their fatigues, and giving opportunity to many of the stragglers, and of the horses and cattle, to rejoin them by following their track; but they were cold, and worn, and disheartened; and mountains still rose before them, through which, as they knew too well, even their descent might be perilous and painful.

But their great general, who felt that he now stood victorious on the ramparts of Italy, and that the torrent which rolled before him was carrying its waters to the rich plains of Cisalpine Gaul, endeavored to kindle his soldiers with his own spirit of hope. He called them together; he pointed out the valley beneath, to which the descent seemed the work of a moment. "That valley," he said, "is Italy; it leads us to the country of our friends the Gauls; and yonder is our way to Rome." His eyes were eagerly fixed on that point of the horizon; and as he gazed, the distance between seemed to vanish, till he could almost fancy that he was crossing the Tiber, and assailing the capitol.

After the two days' rest the descent began. Hannibal experienced no more open hostility from the barbarians, only some petty attempts here and there to plunder; a fact strange in itself, but doubly so, if he was really descending the valley of the Doria Baltea, through the country of the Salassians, the most untamable robbers of all the Alpine barbarians. It is possible that the influence of the Insubrians may partly have restrained the mountaineers; and partly also may they have been deterred by the ill success of all former attacks, and may by this time have regarded the strange army and its monstrous beasts with something of superstitious terror. But the natural difficulties of the ground on the descent were greater than ever. The snow covered the track so that the men often lost it, and fell down the steep below: at last they came to a place where an avalanche had carried it away altogether for about three hundred yards, leaving the mountain-side a mere wreck of scattered rocks and snow. To go round was impossible; for the depth of the snow on the heights above rendered it hopeless to scale them; nothing therefore was left but to repair the road. A summit of some extent was found, and cleared of the snow; and here the army was obliged to encamp, whilst the work went on. There was no want of hands; and every man was laboring for his life; the road therefore was restored, and supported with solid substructions below; and in a single day it was made practicable for the cavalry and baggage-cattle, which were immediately sent forward, and reached the lower valley in safety, where they were turned out to pasture. A harder labor was required to make a passage for the elephants: the way for them must be wide and solid; and the work could not be accomplished in less than three days. The poor animals suffered severely in the interval from hunger; for no forage was to be found in that wilderness of snow, nor any trees whose leaves might supply the place of other herbage. At last they too were able to proceed with safety; Hannibal overtook his cavalry and baggage; and in three days more the whole army had got clear of the Alpine valleys, and entered the country of their friends, the Insubrians, on the wide plain of Northern Italy.

Hannibal was arrived in Italy, but with a force so weakened by its losses in men and horses, and by the exhausted state of the survivors, that he might seem to have accomplished his great march in vain. According to his own statement, which there is no reason to doubt, he brought out of the Alpine valleys no more than 12,000 African and 8,000 Spanish infantry, with 6,000 cavalry; so that his march from the Pyrenees to the plains of Northern Italy must have cost him 33,000 men; an enormous loss, which proves how severely the army must have suffered from the privations of the march and the severity of the Alpine climate; for not half of these 33,000 men can have fallen in battle. With his army in this condition, some period of repose was absolutely necessary; accordingly, Hannibal remained in the country of the Insubrians till rest, and a more temperate climate, and wholesome food, with which the Gauls plentifully supplied him, restored the bodies and spirits of his soldiers, and made them again ready for action. His first movement was against the Taurinians, a Ligurian people, who were constant enemies of the Insubrians, and therefore would not listen to Hannibal, when he invited them to join his cause. He therefore attacked and stormed their principal town, put the garrison to the sword, and struck such terror into the neighboring tribes, that they submitted immediately, and became his allies. This was his first accession of strength in Italy, the first-fruits, as he hoped, of a long succession of defections among the allies of Rome, so that the swords of the Italians might effect for him the conquest of Italy.

THE MONK FELIX.

By HENRY W. LONGFELLOW.

ONE morning, all alone,
  Out of his convent of gray stone,
Into the forest, older, darker, grayer,
His lips moving as if in prayer,
His head sunken upon his breast
As in a dream of rest,
Walked the Monk Felix.   All about
The broad, sweet sunshine lay without,
Filling the summer air ;
And within the woodlands as he trod
The twilight was like the Truce of God
With worldly woe and care ;
Under him lay the golden moss ;
And above him the boughs of hemlock-trees
Waved, and made the sign of the cross,
And whispered their Benedicites ;
And from the ground
Rose an odor sweet and fragrant
Of the wild-flowers and the vagrant
Vines that wandered,
Seeking the sunshine, round and round.

These he heeded not, but pondered
On the volume in his hand,

A volume of Saint Augustine,
Wherein he read of the unseen
Splendors of God's great town
In the unknown land,
And, with his eyes cast down
In humility, he said :
" I believe, O God,
What herein I have read,
But alas ! I do not understand !"

And lo ! he heard
The sudden singing of a bird,
A snow-white bird, that from a cloud
Dropped down,
And among the branches brown
Sat singing
So sweet, and clear, and loud,
It seemed a thousand harp-strings ringing.
And the Monk Felix closed his book,
And long, long,
With rapturous look,
He listened to the song,
And hardly breathed or stirred,
Until he saw, as in a vision,
The land Elysian,
And in the heavenly city heard
Angelic feet
Fall on the golden flagging of the street.
And he would fain
Have caught the wondrous bird,
But strove in vain ;
For it flew away, away,
Far over hill and dell,
And instead of its sweet singing
He heard the convent bell
Suddenly in the silence ringing

For the service of noonday.
And he retraced
His pathway homeward sadly and in haste.

In the convent was a change!
He looked for each well-known face,
But the faces were new and strange;
New figures sat in the oaken stalls,
New voices chanted in the choir;
Yet the place was the same place,
The same dusky walls
Of cold, gray stone,
The same cloisters and belfry and spire.

A stranger and alone
Among that brotherhood
The Monk Felix stood.
"Forty years," said a Friar,
"Have I been Prior
Of this convent in the wood,
But for that space
Never have I beheld thy face!"

The heart of the Monk Felix fell:
And he answered, with submissive tone,
"This morning, after the hour of Prime
I left my cell,
And wandered forth alone,
Listening all the time
To the melodious singing
Of a beautiful white bird,
Until I heard
The bells of the convent ringing
Noon from their noisy towers.
It was as if I dreamed;

For what to me had seemed
Moments only, had been hours!"

"Years!" said a voice close by.
It was an aged monk who spoke,
From a bench of oak
Fastened against the wall;—
He was the oldest monk of all.
For a whole century
Had he been there,
Serving God in prayer,
The meekest and humblest of his creatures.
He remembered well the features
Of Felix, and he said,
Speaking distinct and slow:
"One hundred years ago,
When I was a novice in this place,
There was here a monk, full of God's grace,
Who bore the name
Of Felix, and this man must be the same."

And straightway
They brought forth to the light of day
A volume old and brown,
A huge tome, bound
In brass and wild-boar's hide,
Wherein were written down
The names of all who had died
In the convent, since it was edified.
And there they found,
Just as the old monk said,
That on a certain day and date,
One hundred years before,
Had gone forth from the convent gate
The Monk Felix, and never more
Had entered that sacred door.

He had been counted among the dead!
And they knew, at last,
That, such had been the power
Of that celestial and immortal song,
A hundred years had passed,
And had not seemed so long
As a single hour!

A MOUNTAIN CATASTROPHE.

By THOMAS DE QUINCEY.

THE little valley of Easedale is one of the most impressive solitudes among the mountains of the lake district; and I must pause to describe it. Easedale is impressive, *first, as* a solitude; for the depth of the seclusion is brought out and forced more pointedly upon the feelings by the thin scattering of houses over its sides, and the surface of what may be called its floor. These are not above five or six at the most; and one, the remotest of the whole, was untenanted for all the thirty years of my acquaintance with the place. *Secondly,* it is impressive from the excessive loveliness which adorns its little area. This is broken up into small fields and miniature meadows, separated not — as too often happens, with sad injury to the beauty of the lake country — by stone-walls, but sometimes by little hedge-rows, sometimes by little sparkling, pebbly "beck," lustrous to the very bottom, and not too broad for a child's flying leap; and sometimes by wild self-sown woodlands of birch, alder, holly, mountain-ash, and hazel, that meander through the valley, intervening the different estates with natural sylvan marches, and giving cheerfulness in winter, by the bright scarlet of their barrier. It is the character of all the northern English valleys, as I have already remarked, — and it is a character first noticed by Wordsworth, — that they assume, in their bottom areas, the level, floor-like shape,

making everywhere a direct angle with the surrounding
hills, and definitely marking out the margin of their outlines; whereas the Welsh valleys have too often the glar-
ing imperfection of the basin shape, which allows no sense
of any absolute valley surface; the hills are already commencing at the very centre of what is called the level area.
The little valley of Easedale is, in this respect, as highly
finished as in every other; and in the Westmoreland spring,
which may be considered May and the earlier half of June,
whilst the grass in the meadows is yet short from the
habit of keeping the sheep on it until a much later period
than elsewhere, (viz. until the mountains are so far cleared
of snow and the probability of storms as to make it safe
to send them out on their summer migration,) the little
fields of Easedale have the most lawny appearance, and,
from the humidity of the Westmoreland climate, the most
verdant that it is possible to imagine; and on a gentle
vernal day — when vegetation has been far enough advanced to bring out the leaves, an April sun gleaming
coyly through the clouds, and genial April rain gently
penciling the light spray of the wood with tiny pearl-
drops — I have often thought, whilst looking with silent
admiration upon this exquisite composition of landscape,
with its miniature fields running up like forest glades into
miniature woods; its little columns of smoke, breathing up
like incense to the household gods, from the hearths of two
or three picturesque cottages, — abodes of simple, primi-
tive manners, and what, from personal knowledge, I will
call humble virtue, — whilst my eyes rested on this charming combination of lawns and shrubberies, I have thought
that if a scene on this earth could deserve to be sealed up,
like the valley of Rasselas, against the intrusion of the
world, — if there were one to which a man would willingly
surrender himself a prisoner for the years of a long life,
— that it is this Easedale, — which would justify the

choice, and recompense the sacrifice. But there is a third
advantage possessed by this Easedale, above other rival
valleys, in the sublimity of its mountain barriers. In one
of its many rocky recesses is seen a "force" (such is the
local name for a cataract), white with foam, descending at
all seasons with respectable strength, and after the melting
of snows with an Alpine violence. Follow the leading of
this "force" for three quarters of a mile, and you come to
a little mountain lake, locally termed a "tarn," the very
finest and most gloomy sublime of its class. From this
tarn it was, I doubt not, though applying it to another,
that Wordsworth drew the circumstances of his general
description : —

> " Thither the rainbow comes, the cloud,
>   And mists that spread the flying shroud;
> '   And winds
>   That, if they could, would hurry past :
>   But that enormous barrier binds them fast.
>   &c.   &c.   &c.
>   The rocks repeat the raven's croak,
>   In symphony austere."

And far beyond this "enormous barrier," that thus impris-
ons the very winds, tower upwards the aspiring heads
(usually enveloped in cloud and mist) of Glaramara, Bow
Fell, and the other fells of Langdale Head and Borrowdale. Finally, superadded to the other circumstances of
solitude, arising out of the rarity of human life, and of the
signs which mark the goings on of human life, — two other
accidents there are of Easedale which sequester it from
the world, and intensify its depth of solitude beyond what
could well be looked for or thought possible in any vale
within a district so beaten by modern tourists. One is,
that it is a chamber within a chamber, or rather a closet
within a chamber, — a chapel within a cathedral, — a little
private oratory within a chapel. For Easedale is, in fact,
a dependency of Grasmere, — a little recess lying within

the same general basin of mountains, but partitioned off by a screen of rock and swelling uplands, so inconsiderable in height, that, when surveyed from the commanding summits of Fairfield or Seat Sandal, they seem to subside into the level area, and melt into the general surface. But, viewed from below, these petty heights form a sufficient partition; which is pierced, however, in two points,— once by the little murmuring brook threading its silvery line onwards to the lake of Grasmere, and again by a little rough lane, barely capable (and I think not capable in all points) of receiving a postchaise. This little lane keeps ascending amongst wooded steeps for a quarter of a mile; and then, by a downward course of a hundred yards or so, brings you to a point at which the little valley suddenly bursts upon you with as full a revelation of its tiny proportions as the traversing of the wooded backgrounds will permit. The lane carries you at last to a little wooden bridge, practicable for pedestrians; but for carriages, even the doubtful road already mentioned ceases altogether: and this fact, coupled with the difficulty of suspecting such a lurking paradise from the high road through Grasmere, at every point of which the little hilly partition crowds up into one mass with the capital barriers in the rear, seeming, in fact, not so much to blend with them as to be a part of them, may account for the fortunate neglect of Easedale in the tourist's route; and also because there is no one separate object, such as a lake or a splendid cataract, to bribe the interest of those who are hunting after sights; for the "force" is comparatively small, and the tarn is beyond the limits of the vale, as well as difficult of approach.

One other circumstance there is about Easedale, which completes its demarcation, and makes it as entirely a landlocked little park, within a ring-fence of mountains, as ever human art, if rendered capable of dealing with moun-

tains and their arrangement, could have contrived. The
sole approach, as I have mentioned, is from Grasmere;
and some *one* outlet there must inevitably be in every vale
that can be interesting to a human occupant, since without
water it would not be habitable; and running water must
force an exit for itself, and, consequently, an inlet for the
world; but, properly speaking, there is no other. For,
when you explore the remoter end of the vale, at which
you suspect some communication with the world outside,
you find before you a most formidable amount of climbing,
the extent of which can hardly be measured where there
is no solitary object of human workmanship or vestige of
animal life, not a sheep-track even, not a shepherd's hovel,
but rock and heath, heath and rock, tossed about in monotonous confusion. And, after the ascent is mastered, you
descend into a second vale, — long, narrow, sterile, known
by the name of "Far Easedale," — from which point, if
you could drive a tunnel below the everlasting hills, perhaps six or seven miles might bring you to the nearest
habitation of man, in Borrowdale; but, crossing the moun
tains, the road cannot be less than twelve or fourteen, and,
in point of fatigue, at the least twenty. This long valley,
which is really terrific at noonday, from its utter loneli-
ness and desolation, completes the defences of little sylvan
Easedale. There is one door into it from the Grasmere
side; but that door is hidden; and on every other quarter
there is no door at all, nor any, the roughest, access, but
what would demand a day's walking.

Such is the solitude — so deep, so seventimes guarded,
and so rich in miniature beauty — of Easedale; and in
this solitude it was that George and Sarah Green, two
poor and hard-working peasants, dwelt, with a numerous
family of small children. Poor as they were, they had
won the general respect of the neighborhood, from the
uncomplaining firmness with which they bore the hard-

ships of their lot, and from the decent attire in which the
good mother of the family contrived to send out her children to the Grasmere school. It is a custom, and a very
ancient one, in Westmoreland, — and I have seen the same
usage prevailing in Southern Scotland, — that any sale
by auction, whether of cattle, of farming-produce, farming-
stock, wood, or household furniture, — and seldom a fortnight passes without something of the sort, — forms an excuse for the good women, throughout the whole circumference of perhaps a dozen valleys, to assemble at the place
of sale, with the nominal purpose of aiding the sale, or of
buying something they may happen to want. No doubt
the real business of the sale attracts numbers; although of
late years, — that is, for the last twenty-five years, through
which so many sales of furniture the most expensive (hastily made by casual settlers, on the wing for some fresher
novelty), — have made this particular article almost a
drug in the country; and the interest in such sales has
greatly declined. But, in 1807, this fever of founding vil-
las or cottages *ornées* was yet only beginning; and a sale,
except it were of the sort exclusively interesting to farming-
men, was a kind of general intimation to the country, from
the owner of the property, that he would, on that afternoon,
be "at home" for all comers, and hoped to see as large
an attendance as possible. Accordingly, it was the almost
invariable custom — and often, too, when the parties were
far too poor for such an effort of hospitality — to make
ample provision, not of eatables, but of liquor, for all who
came. Even a gentleman, who should happen to present
himself on such a festal occasion, by way of seeing the
"humors" of the scene, was certain of meeting the most
cordial welcome. The good woman of the house more
particularly testified her sense of the honor done to her
house, and was sure to seek out some cherished and solitary article of china, — a wreck from a century back, —

in order that he, being a porcelain man amongst so many delf men and women, might have a porcelain cup to drink from.

The main secret of attraction at these sales—many a score of which I have attended—was the social rendezvous thus effected between parties so remote from each other (either by real distance, or by the virtual distance which results from a separation by difficult tracts of hilly country), that, in fact, without some such common object and oftentimes something like a bisection of the interval between them, they would not be likely to hear of each other for months, or actually to meet for years. This principal charm of the "gathering," seasoned, doubtless, to many by the certain anticipation that the whole budget of rural scandal would then and there be opened, was not assuredly diminished to the men by the anticipation of excellent ale (usually brewed six or seven weeks before, in preparation for the event), and possibly of still more excellent *pow-sowdy* (a combination of ale, spirits, and spices); nor to the women by some prospect, not so inevitably fulfilled, but pretty certain in a liberal house, of communicating their news over excellent tea. Even the auctioneer was always "part and parcel" of the mirth: he was always a rustic old humorist, a "character," and a jovial drunkard, privileged in certain good-humored liberties and jokes with all bidders, gentle or simple, and furnished with an ancient inheritance of jests appropriate to the articles offered for sale,—jests that had, doubtless, done their office from Elizabeth's golden days; but no more, on that account, failed of their expected effect, with either man or woman of this nineteenth century, than the sun fails to gladden the heart because it is that same old obsolete sun that has gladdened it for thousands of years.

One thing, however, in mere justice to the poor indigenous Dalesmen of Westmoreland and Cumberland, I am bound, in this place, to record, that, often as I have been at these sales, and through many a year before even a scattering of gentry began to attend, yet so true to the natural standard of politeness was the decorum uniformly maintained, even the old buffoon (as sometimes he was) of an auctioneer never forgot himself so far as to found upon any article of furniture a jest that could have called up a painful blush in any woman's face. He might, perhaps, go so far as to awaken a little rosy confusion upon some young bride's countenance, when pressing a cradle upon her attention : but never did I hear him utter, nor would he have been tolerated in uttering, a scurrilous or disgusting jest, such as might easily have been suggested by something offered at a household sale. Such jests as these I heard for the first time at a sale in Grasmere in 1814, and, I am ashamed to say it, from some "gentlemen" of a great city. And it grieved me to see the effect, as it expressed itself upon the manly faces of the grave Dalesmen, — a sense of insult offered to their women, who met in confiding reliance upon the forbearance of the men, and upon their regard for the dignity of the female sex, this feeling struggling with the habitual respect they are inclined to show towards what they suppose gentle blood and superior education. Taken generally, however, these were the most picturesque and festal meetings which the manners of the country produced. There you saw all ages and both sexes assembled; there you saw old men whose heads would have been studies for Guido; there you saw the most colossal and stately figures amongst the young men that England has to show; there the most beautiful young women. There it was that sometimes I saw a lovelier face than ever I shall see again : there it was that local peculiarities of usage or of language were best to be studied; there — at least in the earlier years of my residence in that district — that the social benevolence, the grave wisdom, the innocent mirth, and the neighborly kindness of the people, most delightfully expanded, and expressed themselves with the least reserve.

To such a scene it was, to a sale of domestic furniture at the house of some proprietor on the point of giving up housekeeping, perhaps in order to live with a married son or daughter, that George and Sarah Green set forward in the forenoon of a day fated to be their last on earth. The sale was to take place in Langdale Head; to which, from their own cottage in Easedale, it was possible in daylight, and supposing no mist upon the hills, to find out a short cut of not more than eight miles. By this route they went; and notwithstanding the snow lay on the ground, they reached their destination in safety. The attendance at the sale must have been diminished by the rigorous state of the weather; but still the scene was a gay one as usual. Sarah Green, though a good and worthy woman in her maturer years, had been imprudent,— and, as the tender consideration of the country is apt to express it,— "unfortunate" in her youth. She had an elder daughter, and I believe the father of this girl was dead. The girl herself was grown up; and the peculiar solicitude of poor Sarah's maternal heart was at this time called forth on *her* behalf: she wished to see her placed in a very respectable house, where the mistress was distinguished for her notable qualities and her success in forming good servants. This object — so important to Sarah Green in the narrow range of her cares, as in a more exalted family it might be to obtain a ship for a lieutenant that had passed as master and commander, or to get him "posted" — occupied her almost throughout the sale. A doubtful answer had been given to her application; and Sarah was going about the crowd, and weaving her person in and out in order to lay hold of this or that intercessor who might have, or might seem to have, some weight with the principal person concerned.

This was the last occupation which is known to have stirred the pulses of her heart. An illegitimate child is everywhere, even in the indulgent society of Westmoreland Dalesmen, under some shade of discountenance; so that Sarah Green might consider her duty to be the stronger toward the child of her "misfortune." And she probably had another reason for her anxiety — as some words dropped by her on this evening led people to presume — in her conscientious desire to introduce her daughter into a situation less perilous than that which had compassed her own youthful steps with snares. If so, it is painful to know that the virtuous wish, whose

> "vital warmth
> Gave the last human motion to the heart,"

should not have been fulfilled. She was a woman of ardent and affectionate spirit, of which Miss Wordsworth's memoir, or else her subsequent memorials in conversation, (I forget which,) gave some circumstantial and affecting instances, which I cannot now recall with accuracy. This ardor it was, and her impassioned manner, that drew attention to what she did; for, otherwise, she was too poor a person to be important in the estimation of strangers, and, of all possible situations, to be important at a sale, where the public attention was naturally fixed upon the chief purchasers, and the attention of the purchasers upon the chief competitors. Hence it happened that, after she ceased to challenge notice by the emphasis of her solicitations for her daughter, she ceased to be noticed at all; and nothing was recollected of her subsequent behavior until the time arrived for general separation. This time was considerably after sunset; and the final recollections of the crowd with respect to George and Sarah Green were, that, upon their intention being understood to retrace their morning path, and to attempt the perilous task of dropping down into Easedale from the mountains above Langdale Head, a sound of remonstrance arose from many quarters. However, at a moment when everybody was in the hurry of departure, — and, to persons of their mature age, the opposition could not be very obstinate, — party after party rode off; the meeting melted away, or, as the Northern phrase is, *scaled;* and at length nobody was left of any weight that could pretend to influence the decision of elderly people. They quitted the scene, professing to obey some advice or other upon the choice of roads; but, at as early a point as they could do so unobserved, began to ascend the hills, everywhere open from the rude carriage-way. After this, they were seen no more. They had disappeared into the cloud of death. Voices were heard, some hours afterwards, from the mountains, — voices, as some thought, of alarm; others said, no, — that it was only the voices of jovial people, carried by the wind into uncertain regions. The result was, that no attention was paid to the sounds.

That night, in little peaceful Easedale, six children sat by a peat fire, expecting the return of their parents, upon whom they depended for their daily bread. Let a day pass, and they were starved. Every sound was heard with anxiety; for all this was reported many a hundred times to Miss Wordsworth, and those who, like myself, were never wearied of hearing the details. Every sound, every echo amongst the hills was listened to for five hours, — from seven to twelve. At length, the eldest girl of the family — about nine years old — told her little brothers and sisters to go to bed. They had been taught obedience; and all of them, at the voice of their eldest sister, went off fearfully to their beds. What could be *their* fears, it is difficult to say! they had no knowledge to instruct them in the dangers of the hills; but the eldest sister always averred that they had a deep solicitude, as she herself had, about their parents. Doubtless she had communicated her fears to *them*. Some time in the course of the evening, — but it was late and

after midnight, — the moon arose, and shed a torrent of light
upon the Langdale fells, which had already, long hours before, witnessed in darkness the death of their parents. It
may be well here to cite Mr. Wordsworth's stanzas : —

> "Who weeps for strangers ?   Many wept
>   For George and Sarah Green ;
>   Wept for that pair's unhappy fate,
>   Whose graves may here be seen.
>
> "By night, upon these stormy fells,
>   Did wife and husband roam ;
>   Six little ones at home had left,
>   And could not find that home.
>
> "For *any* dwelling-place of man
>   As vainly did they seek.
>   He perished ; and a voice was heard —
>   The widow's lonely shriek.
>
> "Not many steps, and she was left
>   A body without life, —
>   A few short steps were the chain that bound
>   The husband to the wife.
>
> "Now do these sternly-featured hills,
>   Look gently on this grave ;
>   And quiet now are the depths of air,
>   As a sea without a wave.
>
> "But deeper lies the heart of peace
>   In quiet more profound ;
>   The heart of quietness is here
>   Within this churchyard bound.
>
> "And from all agony of mind
>   It keeps them safe, and far
>   From fear and grief, and from all need
>   Of sun or guiding star.
>
> "O darkness of the grave ! how deep,
>   After that living night, —
>   That last and dreary living one
>   Of sorrow and affright !

> " O sacred marriage-bed of death,
>   That keeps them side by side
> In bond of peace, in bond of love,
>   That may not be untied ! "

That night, and the following morning, came a further
and a heavier fall of snow; in consequence of which the
poor children were completely imprisoned, and cut off from
all possibility of communicating with their next neighbors.
The brook was too much for them to leap; and the little
crazy wooden bridge could not be crossed, or even approached with safety, from the drifting of the snow having
made it impossible to ascertain the exact situation of some
treacherous hole in its timbers, which, if trod upon, would
have let a small child drop through into the rapid waters.
Their parents did not return. For some hours of the morning the children clung to the hope that the extreme severity
of the night had tempted them to sleep in Langdale; but
this hope forsook them as the day wore away. Their father,
George Green, had served as a soldier, and was an active
man, of ready resources, who would not, under any circumstances, have failed to force a road back to his family,
had he been still living; and this reflection, or rather semi-
conscious feeling, which the awfulness of their situation
forced upon the minds of all but the mere infants, taught
them to feel the extremity of their danger. Wonderful it is
to see the effect of sudden misery, sudden grief, or sudden
fear, (where they do not utterly upset the faculties,) in
sharpening the intellectual perceptions. Instances must
have fallen in the way of most of us. And I have noticed
frequently that even sudden and intense bodily pain is part
of the machinery employed by nature for quickening the
development of the mind. The perceptions of infants are
not, in fact, excited *gradatim* and continuously, but *per
saltum*, and by unequal starts. At least, in the case of my
own children, one and all, I have remarked, that, after any

very severe fit of those peculiar pains to which the delicate
digestive organs of most infants are liable, there always
become apparent on the following day a very considerable
increase of vital energy and of vivacious attention to the objects around them. The poor desolate children of Blentarn
Ghyll, hourly becoming more ruefully convinced that they
were orphans, gave many evidences of this awaking power,
as lodged by a providential arrangement, in situations of
trial that most require it. They huddled together, in the
evening, round their hearth-fire of peats, and held their little
councils upon what was to be done towards any chance —
if chance remained — of yet giving aid to their parents ;
for a slender hope had sprung up that some hovel or sheep-
fold might have furnished them a screen (or, in Westmoreland phrase, a *bield*) against the weather-quarter of the
storm, in which hovel they might be lying disabled or
snowed up ; and secondly, as regarded themselves, in what
way they were to make known their situation, in case the
snow should continue or increase ; for starvation stared them
in the face, if they should be confined for many days to their
house.

Meantime, the eldest sister, little Agnes, though sadly
alarmed, and feeling the sensation of *eariness* as twilight
came on, and she looked out from the cottage door to the
dreadful fells, on which, too probably, her parents were
lying corpses, (and possibly not many hundred yards from
their own threshold,) yet exerted herself to take all the
measures which their own prospects made prudent. And
she told Miss Wordsworth, that, in the midst of the oppression on her little spirit, from vague ghostly terrors, she did
not fail, however, to draw some comfort from the consideration, that the very same causes which produced their danger
in one direction, sheltered them from danger of another
kind, — such dangers as she knew, from books that she had
read, would have threatened a little desolate flock of children

in other parts of England ; that, if they could not get out
into Grasmere, on the other hand, bad men, and wild seafar-
ing foreigners, who sometimes passed along the high road
in that vale, could not get to them ; and that, as to their
neighbors, so far from having anything to fear in that
quarter, their greatest apprehension was lest they might not
be able to acquaint them with their situation ; but that, if
that could be accomplished, the very sternest amongst them
were kind-hearted people, that would contend with each
other for the privilege of assisting them. Somewhat cheered
with these thoughts, and having caused all her brothers and
sisters — except the two little things, not yet of a fit age —
to kneel down and say the prayers which they had been
taught, this admirable little maiden turned herself to every
household task that could have proved useful to them in a
long captivity. First of all, upon some recollection that the
clock was nearly going down, she wound it up. Next, she
took all the milk which remained from what her mother had
provided for the children's consumption during her absence,
and for the breakfast of the following morning, — this luck-
ily was still in sufficient plenty for two days' consumption,
(skimmed or "blue" milk being only one half-penny a quart,
and the quart a most redundant one, in Grasmere,) — this
she took and scalded, so as to save it from turning sour.
That done, she next examined the meal-chest ; made the
common oatmeal porridge of the country (the burgoo of the
royal navy) ; but put all of the children, except the two
youngest, on short allowance ; and, by way of reconciling
them in some measure to this stinted meal, she found out a
little hoard of flour, part of which she baked for them upon
the hearth into little cakes ; and this unusual delicacy persuaded them to think that they had been celebrating a feast.
Next, before night coming on should make it too trying to
her own feelings, or before fresh snow coming on might make
it impossible, she issued out of doors. There her first task

was, with the assistance of two younger brothers, to carry
in from the peat-stack as many peats as might serve them for
a week's consumption. That done, in the second place, she
examined the potatoes, buried in "brackens" (that is, withered fern) : these were not many ; and she thought it better
to leave them where they were, excepting as many as would
make a single meal, under a fear that the heat of their cottage would spoil them, if removed.

Having thus made all the provision in her power for
supporting their own lives, she turned her attention to the
cow. Her she milked ; but, unfortunately the milk she
gave, either from being badly fed, or from some other cause,
was too trifling to be of much consideration towards the
wants of a large family. Here, however, her chief anxiety
was to get down the hay for the cow's food from a loft above
the outhouse ; and in this she succeeded but imperfectly,
from want of strength ánd size to cope with the difficulties
of the case ; besides that the increasing darkness by this
time, together with the gloom of the place, made it a matter
of great self-conquest for her to work at all ; and, as respected one night at any rate, she placed the cow in a situation of luxurious warmth and comfort. Then retreating
into the warm house, and " barring " the door, she sat down
to undress the two youngest of the children ; them she laid
carefully and cosily in their little nests up-stairs, and sang
them to sleep. The rest she kept up to bear her company
until the clock should tell them it was midnight ; up to
which time she had still a lingering hope that some welcome
shout from the hills above, which they were all to strain
their ears to catch, might yet assure them that they were
not wholly orphans, even though one parent should have
perished. No shout, it may be supposed, was ever heard ;
nor could a shout, in any case, have been heard, for the
night was one of tumultuous wind. And though, amidst its
ravings, sometimes they fancied a sound of voices, still, in

the dead lulls that now and then succeeded, they heard
nothing to confirm their hopes. As last services to what she
might now have called her own little family, Agnes took
precautions against the drifting of the snow within the door
and the imperfect window which had caused them some dis-
comfort on the preceding day; and, finally, she adopted the
most systematic and elaborate plans for preventing the possibility of their fire being extinguished, which, in the event
of their being thrown upon the ultimate resource of their
potatoes, would be absolutely (and in any event nearly) in-
dispensable to their existence.

The night slipped away, and another morning came,
bringing with it no better hopes of any kind. Change there
had been none but for the worse. The snow had greatly
increased in quantity; and the drifts seemed far more formidable. A second day passed like the first; little Agnes
still keeping her little flock quiet, and tolerably comfortable;
and still calling on all the elders in succession to say their
prayers, morning and night.

A third day came; and whether it was on that or on
the fourth, I do not now recollect; but on one or other there
came a welcome gleam of hope. The arrangement of the
snow-drifts had shifted during the night; and though the
wooden bridge was still impracticable, a low wall had been
exposed, over which, by a very considerable circuit, and
crossing the low shoulder of a hill, it seemed possible that a
road might be found into Grasmere. In some walls it was
necessary to force gaps; but this was effected without much
difficulty, even by children, for the Westmoreland walls are
always " open," that is, uncemented with mortar, and the
push of a stick will readily detach so much from the upper
part of an old crazy field wall, as to lower it sufficiently for
female or for childish steps to pass. The little boys accompanied their sister until she came to the other side of the
hill, which, lying more sheltered from the weather, and to

windward, offered a path onwards comparatively easy. Here they parted; and little Agnes pursued her solitary mission to the nearest house she could find accessible in Grasmere.

No house could have proved a wrong one in such a case. Miss Wordsworth and I often heard the description renewed of the horror which, in an instant, displaced the smile of hospitable greeting, when little weeping Agnes told her sad tale. No tongue can express the fervid sympathy which travelled through the vale, like the fire in an American forest, when it was learned that neither George nor Sarah Green had been seen by their children since the day of the Langdale sale. Within half an hour, or little more, from the remotest parts of the valley, — some of them distant nearly two miles from the point of rendezvous, — all the men of Grasmere had assembled at the little cluster of cottages called " Kirktown," from their adjacency to the venerable parish church of St. Oswald. There were at the time I settled in Grasmere (viz. in the spring of 1809, and, therefore, I suppose at this time, fifteen months previously) about sixty-three households in the vale, and the total number of souls was about two hundred and sixty-five; so that the number of fighting men would be about sixty or sixty-six, according to the common way of computing the proportion; and the majority were so athletic and powerfully built, that, at the village games of wrestling and leaping, Professor Wilson, and some visitors of his and mine, scarcely one of whom was under five feet eleven in height, with proportionable breadth, seem but middle-sized men amongst the towering forms of the Dalesmen. Sixty at least, after a short consultation as to the plan of operations, and for arranging the kind of signals by which they were to communicate from great distances, and in the perilous events of mists or snow-storms, set off, with the speed of Alpine hunters, to the hills. The dangers of the undertaking were considerable, under the uneasy and agitated state of the weather; and all the women of the vale were in the greatest anxiety, until night brought them back, in a body, unsuccessful. Three days at the least, and I rather think five, the search was ineffectual; which arose partly from the great extent of the ground to be examined, and partly from the natural mistake made of ranging almost exclusively on the earlier days on that part of the hills over which the path of Easedale might be presumed to have been selected under any reasonable latitude of circuitousness. But the fact is, when the fatal accident (for such it has often proved) of a permanent mist surprises a man on the hills, if he turns and loses his direction, he is a lost man; and without doing this so as to lose the power of *s'orienter* in one instant, it is well known how difficult it is to avoid losing it insensibly and by degrees. Baffling snow-showers are the worst kind of mists. And the poor Greens had, under that kind of confusion, wandered many a mile out of their proper track.

The zeal of the people, meantime, was not in the least abated, but rather quickened, by the wearisome disappointments; every hour of daylight was turned to account; no man of the valley ever came home to dinner; and the reply of a young shoemaker, on the fourth night's return, speaks sufficiently for the unabated spirit of the vale. Miss Wordsworth asked what he would do on the next morning. " Go up again, of course," was his answer. But what if to-morrow also should turn out like all the rest ? " Why, go up in stronger force on the next day." Yet this man was sacrificing his own daily earnings without a chance of recompense. At length sagacious dogs were taken up; and, about noonday, a shout from an aerial height, amongst thick volumes of cloudy vapor, propagated through repeating bands of men from a distance of many miles, conveyed as by telegraph the news that the bodies were found. George Green was found lying at the bottom of a precipice, from which he had fallen. Sarah Green was found on the summit of the precipice; and, by laying together all the indications of what had passed, the sad hieroglyphics of their last agonies, it was conjectured that the husband had desired his wife to pause for a few minutes, wrapping her, meantime, in his own great-coat, whilst he should go forward and reconnoitre the ground, in order to catch a sight of some object (rocky peak, or tarn, or peat-field) which might ascertain their real situation. Either the snow above, already lying in drifts, or the blinding snow-storms driving into his eyes, must have misled him as to the nature of the circumjacent ground; for the precipice over which he had fallen was but a few yards from the spot in which he had quitted his wife. The depth of the descent, and the fury of the wind (almost always violent on these cloudy altitudes), would prevent any distinct communication between the dying husband below and his despairing wife above; but it was believed by the shepherds best acquainted with the ground and the range of sound as regarded the capacities of the human ear, under the probable circumstances of the storm, that Sarah might have caught, at intervals, the groans of her unhappy partner, supposing that his death were at all a lingering one. Others, on the contrary, supposed her to have gathered this catastrophe rather from the want of any sounds, and from his continued absence, than from any one distinct or positive expression of it; both because the smooth and unruffled surface of the snow where he lay seemed to argue that he had died without a struggle, perhaps without a groan, and because that tremendous sound of "hurtling" in the upper chambers of the air, which often accompanies a snow-storm, when combined with heavy gales of wind, would utterly oppress and stifle (as they conceived) any sounds so feeble as those from a dying man. In any case, and by whatever sad language of sounds or signs, positive or negative, she might have learned or guessed her loss, it was generally agreed that the wild shrieks heard towards midnight in

Langdale Head announced the agonizing moment which brought to her now widowed heart the conviction of utter desolation and of final abandonment to her own fast-fleeting energies. It seemed probable that the sudden disappearance of her husband from her pursuing eyes would teach her to understand his fate, and that the consequent indefinite apprehension of instant death lying all around the point on which she sat had kept her stationary to the very attitude in which her husband left her, until her failing powers and the increasing bitterness of the cold, to one no longer in motion, would soon make those changes of place impossible, which, at any rate, had appeared too dangerous. The footsteps in some places, wherever drifting had not obliterated them, yet traceable as to the outline, though partially filled up with later falls of snow, satisfactorily showed that, however much they might have rambled, after crossing and doubling upon their own paths, and many a mile astray from their right track, still they must have kept together to the very plateau or shelf of rock at which their wanderings had terminated; for there were evidently no steps from this plateau in the retrograde order.

By the time they had reached this final stage of their erroneous course, all possibility of escape must have been long over for both alike; because their exhaustion must have been excessive before they could have reached a point so remote and high; and, unfortunately, the direct result of all this exhaustion had been to throw them farther off their home, or from " *any* dwelling-place of man," than they were at starting. Here, therefore, at this rocky pinnacle, hope was extinct for either party. But it was the impression of the vale, that, perhaps within half an hour before reaching this fatal point, George Green might, had his conscience or his heart allowed him in so base a desertion, have saved himself singly, without any very great difficulty. It is to be hoped, however, — and, for my part, I think too well of

human nature to hesitate in believing,—that not many,
even amongst the meaner-minded and the least generous of
men, could have reconciled themselves to the abandonment
of a poor fainting female companion in such circumstances.
Still, though not more than a most imperative duty, it was
one (I repeat) which most of his associates believed to have
cost him (perhaps consciously) his life. For his wife not
only must have disabled him greatly by clinging to his arm
for support ; but it was known, from her peculiar character
and manner, that she would be likely to rob him of his
coolness and presence of mind by too painfully fixing his
thoughts, where her own would be busiest, upon their helpless little family. " *Stung* with the thoughts of home," — to
borrow the fine expression of Thomson in describing a similar case, — alternately thinking of the blessedness of that
warm fireside at Blentarn Ghyll, which was not again to
spread its genial glow through her freezing limbs, and of
those darling little faces which, in this world, she was to see
no more ; unintentionally, and without being aware even of
that result, she would rob the brave man (for such he was)
of his fortitude, and the strong man of his *animal* resources.
And yet, — (such in the very opposite direction, was equally
the impression universally through Grasmere,) — had Sarah
Green foreseen, could her affectionate heart have guessed
even the tenth part of that love and neighborly respect for
herself which soon afterwards expressed themselves in showers of bounty to her children ; could she have looked behind
the curtain of destiny sufficiently to learn that the very desolation of these poor children which wrung her maternal
heart, and doubtless constituted to her the sting of death,
would prove the signal and the pledge of such anxious
guardianship as not many rich men's children receive, and
that this overflowing offering to her own memory would not
be a hasty or decaying tribute of the first sorrowing sensi-
bilities, but would pursue her children steadily until their

hopeful settlement in life, — or anything approaching this, to have known or have guessed, would have caused her (as all said who knew her) to welcome the bitter end by which such privileges were to be purchased.

The funeral of the ill-fated Greens was, it may be supposed, attended by all the vale ; it took place about eight days after they were found ; and the day happened to be in the most perfect contrast to the sort of weather which prevailed at the time of their misfortune : some snow still remained here and there upon the ground ; but the azure of the sky was unstained by a cloud, and a golden sunlight seemed to sleep, so balmy and tranquil was the season, upon the very hills where they had wandered, — then a howling wilderness, but now a green pastoral lawn, in its lower ranges, and a glittering expanse, smooth, apparently, and not difficult to the footing, of virgin snow, in its higher. George Green had, I believe, an elder family by a former wife ; and it was for some of these children, who lived at a distance, and who wished to give their attendance at the grave, that the funeral was delayed. After this solemn ceremony was over, — at which, by the way, I then heard Miss Wordsworth say that the grief of Sarah's illegitimate daughter was the most overwhelming she had ever witnessed, — a regular distribution of the children was made amongst the wealthier families of the vale. There had already, and before the funeral, been a perfect struggle to obtain one of the children, amongst all who had any facilities for discharging the duties of such a trust ; and even the poorest had put in their claim to bear some part in the expenses of the case. But it was judiciously decided that none of the children should be intrusted to any persons who seemed likely, either from old age or from slender means, or from nearer and more personal responsibilities, to be under the necessity of devolving the trust, sooner or later, upon strangers, who might have none of that interest in the chil-

dren which attached, in their minds, the Grasmere people to
the circumstances that made them orphans. Two twins,
who had naturally played together and slept together from
their birth, passed into the same family: the others were
dispersed ; but into such kind-hearted and intelligent families, with continued opportunities of meeting each other on
errands, or at church, or at sales, that it was hard to say
which had the happier fate. And thus in so brief a period
as one fortnight, a household that, by health and strength,
by the humility of poverty, and by innocence of life, seemed
sheltered from all attacks but those of time, came to be
utterly broken up. George and Sarah Green slept in Grasmere churchyard, never more to know the want of " sun or
guiding star." Their children were scattered over wealthier
houses than those of their poor parents, through the vales of
Grasmere or Rydal ; and Blentarn Ghyll, after being shut
up for a season, and ceasing for months to send up its little
slender column of smoke at morning and evening, finally
passed into the hands of a stranger.

THRENODY.

By RALPH WALDO EMERSON.

THE South-wind brings
  Life, sunshine, and desire,
And on every mount and meadow
Breathes aromatic fire;
But over the dead he has no power,
The lost, the lost, he cannot restore;
And, looking over the hills, I mourn
The darling who shall not return.

I see my empty house,
I see my trees repair their boughs;
And he, the wondrous child,
Whose silver warble wild
Outvalued every pulsing sound
Within the air's cerulean round,—
The hyacinthine boy, for whom
Morn well might break and April bloom,—
The gracious boy, who did adorn
The world whereinto he was born,
And by his countenance repay
The favor of the loving Day,—
Has disappeared from the Day's eye;
Far and wide she cannot find him;
My hopes pursue, they cannot bind him.

Returned this day, the South-wind searches,
And finds young pines and budding birches;
But finds not the budding man;
Nature, who lost, cannot remake him;
Fate let him fall, Fate can't retake him;
Nature, Fate, men, him seek in vain.

And whither now, my truant wise and sweet,
O, whither tend thy feet?
I had the right, few days ago,
Thy steps to watch, thy place to know;
How have I forfeited the right?
Hast thou forgot me in a new delight?
I hearken for thy household cheer,
O eloquent child!
Whose voice, an equal messenger,
Conveyed thy meaning mild.
What though the pains and joys
Whereof it spoke were toys
Fitting his age and ken,
Yet fairest dames and bearded men,
Who heard the sweet request,
So gentle, wise, and grave,
Bended with joy to his behest,
And let the world's affairs go by,
Awhile to share his cordial game,
Or mend his wicker wagon-frame,
Still plotting how their hungry ear
That winsome voice again might hear;
For his lips could well pronounce
Words that were persuasions.

Gentlest guardians marked serene
His early hope, his liberal mien;

Took counsel from his guiding eyes
To make this wisdom earthly wise.
Ah, vainly do these eyes recall
The school-march, each day's festival,
When every morn my bosom glowed
To watch the convoy on the road;
The babe in willow wagon closed,
With rolling eyes and face composed;
With children forward and behind,
Like Cupids studiously inclined;
And he the chieftain paced beside,
The centre of the troop allied,
With sunny face of sweet repose,
To guard the babe from fancied foes.
The little captain innocent
Took the eye with him as he went;
Each village senior paused to scan
And speak the lovely caravan.
From the window I look out
To mark thy beautiful parade,
Stately marching in cap and coat
To some tune by fairies played; —
A music heard by thee alone
To works as noble led thee on.

Now Love and Pride, alas! in vain,
Up and down their glances strain.
The painted sled stands where it stood;
The kennel by the corded wood;
The gathered sticks to stanch the wall
Of the snow-tower, when snow should fall;
The ominous hole he dug in the sand,
And childhood's castles built or planned;
His daily haunts I well discern, —
The poultry-yard, the shed, the barn, —

And every inch of garden ground
Paced by the blessed feet around,
From the roadside to the brook
Whereinto he loved to look.
Step the meek birds where erst they ranged;
The wintry garden lies unchanged;
The brook into the stream runs on;
But the deep-eyed boy is gone.
On that shaded day,
Dark with more clouds than tempests are,
When thou didst yield thy innocent breath
In bird-like heavings unto death,
Night came, and Nature had not thee;
I said, "We are mates in misery."
The morrow dawned with needless glow;
Each snow-bird chirped, each fowl must crow;
Each tramper started; but the feet
Of the most beautiful and sweet
Of human youth had left the hill
And garden, — they were bound and still.
There's not a sparrow or a wren,
There's not a blade of autumn grain,
Which the four seasons do not tend,
And tides of life and increase lend;
And every chick of every bird,
And weed and rock-moss is preferred.
O ostrich-like forgetfulness!
O loss of larger in the less!
Was there no star that could be sent,
No watcher in the firmament,
No angel from the countless host
That loiters round the crystal coast,
Could stoop to heal that only child,
Nature's sweet marvel undefiled,
And keep the blossom of the earth,
Which all her harvests were not worth?

Not mine, — I never call thee mine.
But Nature's heir, — if I repine,
And seeing rashly torn and moved
Not what I made, but what I loved,
Grow early old with grief that thou
Must to the wastes of Nature go, —
'T is because a general hope
Was quenched, and all must doubt and grope.
For flattering planets seemed to say
This child should ills of ages stay,
By wondrous tongue, and guided pen,
Bring the flown Muses back to men.
Perchance not he but Nature ailed,
The world and not the infant failed.
It was not ripe yet to sustain
A genius of so fine a strain,
Who gazed upon the sun and moon
As if he came unto his own,
And, pregnant with his grander thought,
Brought the old order into doubt.
His beauty once their beauty tried;
They could not feed him, and he died,
And wandered backward as in scorn,
To wait an æon to be born.
Ill day which made this beauty waste,
Plight broken, this high face defaced!
Some went and came about the dead;
And some in books of solace read;
Some to their friends the tidings say;
Some went to write, some went to pray
One tarried here, there hurried one;
But their heart abode with none.
Covetous death bereaved us all,
To aggrandize one funeral.
The eager fate which carried thee
Took the largest part of me:

For this losing is true dying;
This is lordly man's down-lying,
This his slow but sure reclining,
Star by star his world resigning.

O child of paradise,
Boy who made dear his father's home,
In whose deep eyes
Men read the welfare of the times to come,
I am too much bereft.
The world dishonored thou hast left.
O truth's and nature's costly lie!
O trusted broken prophecy!
O richest fortune sourly crossed!
Born for the future, to the future lost!

THE deep Heart answered, "Weepest thou?
Worthier cause for passion wild
If I had not taken the child.
And deemest thou as those who pore,
With aged eyes, short way before, —
Think'st Beauty vanished from the coast
Of matter, and thy darling lost?
Taught he not thee — the man of eld,
Whose eyes within his eyes beheld
Heaven's numerous hierarchy span
The mystic gulf from God to man?
To be alone wilt thou begin
When worlds of lovers hem thee in?
To-morrow, when the masks shall fall
That dizen Nature's carnival,
The pure shall see by their own will,
Which overflowing Love shall fill,
'T is not within the force of fate
The fate-conjoined to separate.

But thou, my votary, weepest thou?
I gave thee sight — where is it now?
I taught thy heart beyond the reach
Of ritual, bible, or of speech;
Wrote in thy mind's transparent table,
As far as the incommunicable;
Taught thee each private sign to raise,
Lit by the supersolar blaze.
Past utterance, and past belief,
And past the blasphemy of grief,
The mysteries of Nature's heart;
And though no Muse can these impart,
Throb thine with Nature's throbbing breast,
And all is clear from east to west.

" I came to thee as to a friend;
Dearest, to thee I did not send
Tutors, but a joyful eye,
Innocence that matched the sky,
Lovely locks, a form of wonder,
Laughter rich as woodland thunder,
That thou might'st entertain apart
The richest flowering of all art:
And as the great all-loving Day
Through smallest chambers takes its way,
That thou might'st break thy daily bread
With prophet, saviour, and head;
That thou might'st cherish for thine own
The riches of sweet Mary's Son,
Boy-Rabbi, Israel's paragon.
And thoughtest thou such guest
Would in thy hall take up his rest?
Would rushing life forget her laws,
Fate's glowing revolution pause?
High omens ask diviner guess;
Not to be conned to tediousness.

And know my higher gifts unbind
The zone that girds the incarnate mind.
When the scanty shores are full
With Thought's perilous, whirling pool;
When frail Nature, can no more,
Then the Spirit strikes the hour:
My servant Death, with solving rite,
Pours finite into infinite.

" Wilt thou freeze love's tidal flow,
Whose streams through nature circling go?
Nail the wild star to its track
On the half-climbed zodiac?
Light is light which radiates,
Blood is blood which circulates,
Life is life which generates,
And many-seeming life is one, —
Wilt thou transfix and make it none?
Its onward force too starkly pent
In figure, bone, and lineament?
Wilt thou, uncalled, interrogate,
Talker! the unreplying Fate?
Nor see the genius of the whole
Ascendant in the private soul,
Beckon it when to go and come,
Self-announced its hour of doom?
Fair the soul's recess and shrine,
Magic-built to last a season;
Masterpiece of love benign;
Fairer than expansive reason
Whose omen 't is, and sign.
Wilt thou not ope thy heart to know
What rainbows teach, and sunsets show?
Verdict which accumulates
From lengthening scroll of human fates,

Voice of earth to earth returned,
Prayers of saints that inly burned,—
Saying, *What is excellent,*
As God lives, is permanent;
Hearts are dust, hearts' loves remain;
Heart's love will meet thee again.
Revere the Maker; fetch thine eye
Up to his style, and manners of the sky.
Not of adamant and gold
Built he heaven stark and cold;
No, but a nest of bending reeds,
Flowering grass, and scented weeds;
Or like a traveller's fleeing tent,
Or bow above the tempest bent;
Built of tears and sacred flames,
And virtue reaching to its aims;
Built of furtherance and pursuing,
Not of spent deeds, but of doing.
Silent rushes the swift Lord
Through ruined systems still restored,
Broadsowing, bleak and void to bless,
Plants with worlds the wilderness;
Waters with tears of ancient sorrow
Apples of Eden ripe to-morrow.
House and tenant go to ground,
Lost in God, in Godhead found."

LAST DAYS OF SIR WALTER SCOTT.

By JOHN G. LOCKHART.

THE last jotting of Sir Walter's Diary — perhaps the last specimen of his handwriting — records his starting from Naples on the 16th of April, 1832. After the 11th of May the story can hardly be told too briefly.

The irritation of impatience, which had for a moment been suspended by the aspect and society of Rome, returned the moment he found himself on the road, and seemed to increase hourly. His companions could with difficulty prevail on him to see even the Falls of Terni, or the Church of Santa Croce, at Florence. On the 17th, a cold and dreary day, they passed the Apennines, and dined on the top of the mountains. The snow and the pines recalled Scotland, and he expressed pleasure at the sight of them. That night they reached Bologna, and he would see none of the interesting objects there, — and next day, hurrying in like manner through Ferrara, he proceeded as far as Monselice. On the 19th he arrived at Venice; and he remained there till the 23d; but showed no curiosity about anything except the Bridge of Sighs and the adjoining dungeons, — down into which he would scramble, though the exertion was exceeding painful to him. On the other historical features of that place — one so sure in other days to have inexhaustible attractions for him — he would not even look; and it was the same with all that he came within reach of—even with the fondly anticipated chapel at Inspruck—as they proceeded through the Tyrol, and so onwards, by Munich, Ulm, and Heidelberg, to Frankfort. Here (June 5) he entered a bookseller's shop; and the people seeing an English party, brought out among the first things a lithographed print of Abbotsford. He said, "I know that already, sir," and hastened back to the inn without being recognized. Though in some parts of the journey they had very severe weather, he repeatedly wished to travel all the night as well as all the day; and the symptoms of an approaching fit were so obvious, that he was more than once bled, ere they reached Mayence, by the hand of his affectionate domestic.

At this town they embarked on the 8th June in the Rhine steamboat; and while they descended the famous river through its most picturesque region, he seemed to enjoy, though he said nothing, the perhaps unrivalled scenery it presented to him. His eye was fixed on the successive crags and castles, and ruined monasteries, each of which had been celebrated in some German ballad familiar to his ear, and all of them blended in the immortal panorama of Childe Harold. But so soon as he resumed his carriage at Cologne, and nothing but flat shores, and here and there a grove of poplars and a village spire were offered to the vision, the weight of misery sunk down again upon him. It was near Nimeguen, on the evening of the 9th, that he sustained another serious attack of apoplexy, combined with paralysis. Nicolson's lancet restored, after the lapse of some minutes, the signs of animation; but this was the crowning blow. Next day he insisted on resuming his journey, and on the 11th was lifted from the carriage into a steamboat at Rotterdam.

He reached London about six o'clock on the evening of Wednesday the 13th of June. Owing to the unexpected rapidity of the journey his eldest daughter had had no notice when to expect him; and fearful of finding her either out of town, or unprepared to receive him and his attendants under her roof, Charles Scott drove to the St. James's hotel, in Jermyn Street, and established his quarters there before he set out in quest of his sister and myself. When we reached the hotel, he recognized us with every mark of tenderness, but signified that he was totally exhausted; so no attempt was made to remove him further, and he was put to bed immediately. Dr. Ferguson saw him the same night, and next day Sir Henry Halford and Dr. Holland saw him also; and during the next three weeks the two former visited him daily, while Ferguson was scarcely absent from his pillow. The Major was soon on the spot. To his children, all assembled once more about him, he repeatedly gave his blessing in a very solemn manner, as if expecting immediate death, but he was never in a condition for conversation, and sunk either into sleep or delirious stupor upon the slightest effort.

Mrs. Thomas Scott came to town as soon as she heard of his arrival, and remained to help us. She was more than once recognized and thanked. Mr. Cadell, too, arrived from Edinburgh, to render any assistance in his power. I think Sir Walter saw no other of his friends except Mr. John Richardson, and him only once. As usual, he woke up at the sound of a familiar voice, and made an attempt to put forth his hand, but it dropped powerless, and he said, with a smile, "Excuse my hand." Richardson made a struggle to suppress his emotion, and after a moment, got out something about Abbotsford and the woods which he had happened to see shortly before. The eye brightened, and he said, "How does Kirklands get on?" Mr. Richardson had lately purchased the estate so called on the Teviot, and Sir Walter had left him busied with plans of building. His friend told him that his new house was begun, and that the Marquis of Lothian had very

kindly lent him one of his own, meantime, in its vicinity.
"Ay, Lord Lothian is a good man," said Sir Walter; "he
is a man from whom one may receive a favor, and that's
saying a good deal for any man in these days." The stupor then sank back upon him, and Richardson never heard
his voice again. This state of things continued till the
beginning of July.

During those melancholy weeks great interest and sympathy were manifested. Allan Cunningham mentions that,
walking home late one night, he found several working-
men standing together at the corner of Jermyn Street, and
one of them asked him, as if there was but one death-bed
in London, "Do you know, sir, if this is the street where
he is lying?" The inquiries both at the hotel and at my
house were incessant; and I think there was hardly a member of the Royal family who did not send every day. The
newspapers teemed with paragraphs about Sir Walter; and
one of these, it appears, threw out a suggestion that his
travels had exhausted his pecuniary resources, and that if
he were capable of reflection at all, cares of that sort might
probably harass his pillow. This paragraph came from a
very ill-informed, but, I dare say, a well-meaning quarter.
It caught the attention of some members of the then government; and, in consequence, I received a private communication to the effect that, if the case were as stated, Sir
Walter's family had only to say what sum would relieve
him from embarrassment, and it would be immediately
advanced by the Treasury. The then Paymaster of the
Forces, Lord John Russell, had the delicacy to convey this
message through a lady with whose friendship he knew us
to be honored. We expressed our grateful sense of his
politeness, and of the liberality of the government, and I
now beg leave to do so once more; but his Lordship was
of course informed that Sir Walter Scott was not situated
as the journalist had represented.

Dr. Ferguson's memorandum on Jermyn Street will be acceptable to the reader. He says:—

"When I saw Sir Walter he was lying in the second floor back-room of the St. James's Hotel, in Jermyn Street, in a state of stupor, from which, however, he could be roused for a moment by being addressed, and then he recognized those about him, but immediately relapsed. I think I never saw anything more magnificent than the symmetry of his colossal bust, as he lay on the pillow with his chest and neck exposed. During the time he was in Jermyn Street he was calm, but never collected, and in general either in absolute stupor or in a waking dream. He never seemed to know where he was, but imagined himself to be still in the steamboat. The rattling of carriages, and the noises of the street sometimes disturbed this illusion, and then he fancied himself at the polling-booth of Jedburgh, where he had been insulted and stoned.

"During the whole of this period of apparent helplessness, the great features of his character could not be mistaken. He always exhibited great self-possession, and acted his part with wonderful power whenever visited, though he relapsed the next moment into the stupor from which strange voices had roused him. A gentleman stumbled over a chair in his dark room;—he immediately started up, and though unconscious that it was a friend, expressed as much concern and feeling as if he had never been laboring under the irritability of disease. It was impossible even for those who most constantly saw and waited on him in his then deplorable condition to relax from the habitual deference which he had always inspired. He expressed his will as determinedly as ever, and enforced it with the same apt and good-natured irony as he was wont to use.

"At length his constant yearning to return to Abbotsford induced his physicians to consent to his removal, and the moment this was notified to him, it seemed to infuse new vigor into his frame. It was on a calm, clear afternoon of the 7th July, that every preparation was made for his embarkation on board the steamboat. He was placed on a chair by his faithful servant, Nicolson, half dressed, and loosely wrapped in a quilted dressing-gown. He requested Lockhart and myself to wheel him towards the light of the open window, and we both remarked the vigorous lustre of his eye. He sat there silently gazing on space for more than half an hour, apparently wholly occupied with his own thoughts, and having no distinct perception of where he was or how he came there. He suffered himself to be lifted into his carriage, which was surrounded by a crowd among whom were many gentlemen on horseback, who had loitered about to gaze on the scene.

"His children were deeply affected, and Mrs. Lockhart trembled from head to foot and wept bitterly. Thus surrounded by those nearest to him, he alone was unconscious of the cause or the depth of their grief, and while yet alive seemed to be carried to his grave."

On this his last journey, Sir Walter was attended by his two daughters, Mr. Cadell, and myself, and also by Dr. James Watson, who (it being impossible for Dr. Ferguson to leave town at that moment) kindly undertook to see him safe at Abbotsford. We embarked in the James Watt steamboat, the master of which (Captain John Jamieson), as well as the agent of the proprietors, made every arrangement in their power for the convenience of the invalid. The Captain gave up for Sir Walter's use his own private cabin, which was a separate erection, a sort of cottage, on the deck; and he seemed unconscious, after laid in bed there, that any new removal had occurred. On arriving at Newhaven, late on the 9th, we found careful preparations made for his landing by the manager of the Shipping Company (Mr. Hamilton); and Sir Walter, prostrate in his

carriage, was slung on shore, and conveyed from thence to
Douglas's hotel, in St. Andrew's Square, in the same com-
plete apparent unconsciousness.   Mrs. Douglas had in
former days been the Duke of Buccleuch's housekeeper
at Bowhill, and she and her husband had also made the
most suitable provision.   At a very early hour on the
morning of Wednesday, the 11th, we again placed him in
his carriage, and he lay in the same torpid state during the
first two stages on the road to Tweedside.   But as we descended the vale of the Gala he began to gaze about him,
and by degrees it was obvious that he was recognizing the
features of that familiar landscape.   Presently he mur-
mured a name or two, — Gala Water, surely, — Buck-
holm, — Torwoodlee."   As we rounded the hill at Ladhope,
and the outline of the Eildons burst on him, he became
greatly excited, and when turning himself on the couch his
eye caught at length his own towers, at the distance of a
mile, he sprang up with a cry of delight.   The river being
in flood, we had to go round a few miles by Melrose bridge,
and during the time this occupied, his woods and house
being within prospect, it required occasionally both Dr.
Watson's strength and mine, in addition to Nicolson's, to
keep him in the carriage.   After passing the bridge, the
road for a couple of miles loses sight of Abbotsford, and he
relapsed into his stupor; but on gaining the bank immediately above it, his excitement became again ungovernable.

Mr. Laidlaw was waiting at the porch, and assisted us
in lifting him into the dining-room, where his bed had been
prepared.   He sat bewildered for a few moments, and then
resting his eye on Laidlaw, said, " Ha! Willie Laidlaw!
O man, how often have I thought of you!"   By this time
his dogs had assembled about his chair, — they began to
fawn upon him and lick his hands, and he alternately
sobbed and smiled over them, until sleep oppressed him.

Dr. Watson having consulted on all things with Mr Clarkson and his father, resigned the patient to them, and returned to London. None of them could have any hope, but that of soothing irritation. Recovery was no longer to be thought of; but there might be *Euthanasia*.

And yet something like a ray of hope did break in upon us next morning. Sir Walter awoke perfectly conscious where he was, and expressed an ardent wish to be carried out into his garden. We procured a Bath-chair from Huntly-Burn, and Laidlaw and I wheeled him out before his door, and up and down for some time on the turf, and among the rose-beds, then in full bloom. The grandchildren admired the new vehicle, and would be helping in their way to push it about. He sat in silence, smiling placidly on them, and the dogs their companions, and now and then admiring the house, the screen of the garden, and the flowers and trees. By and by he conversed a little, very composedly, with us,—said he was happy to be at home, --that he felt better than he had ever done since he left it, and would perhaps disappoint the doctors after all.

He then desired to be wheeled through his rooms, and we moved him leisurely for an hour or more up and down the hall and the great library. "I have seen much," he kept saying, "but nothing like my ain house,—give me one turn more!" He was gentle as an infant, and allowed himself to be put to bed again, the moment we told him that we thought he had had enough for one day.

Next morning he was still better; after again enjoying the Bath-chair for perhaps a couple of hours out of doors, he desired to be drawn into the library, and placed by the central window, that he might look down upon the Tweed.

Here he expressed a wish that I should read to him, and when I asked from what book, he said, "Need you ask? There is but one." I chose the 14th chapter of St. John's Gospel; he listened with mild devotion, and said when I had done, " Well, this is a great comfort, — I have followed you distinctly, and I feel as if I were yet to be myself again." In this placid frame he was again put to bed, and had many hours of soft slumber.

On the third day Mr. Laidlaw and I again wheeled him about the small piece of lawn and shrubbery in front of the house for some time, and the weather being delightful, and all the richness of summer around him, he seemed to taste fully the balmy influences of nature. The sun getting very strong, we halted the chair in a shady corner, just within the verge of his verdant arcade around the court-wall; and breathing the coolness of the spot, he said, " Read me some amusing thing, — read me a bit of Crabbe." I brought out the first volume of his old favorite that I could lay hand on, and turned to what I remembered as one of his most favorite passages in it, — the description of the arrival of the players in the Borough. He listened with great interest, and also, as I soon perceived, with great curiosity. Every now and then he exclaimed, " Capital — excellent — very good — Crabbe has lost nothing," — and we were too well satisfied that he considered himself as hearing a new production, when, chuckling over one couplet, he said, " Better and better — but how will poor Terry endure these cuts?" I went on with the poet's terrible sarcasms upon the theatrical life, and he listened eagerly, muttering, " Honest Dan!" — " Dan won't like this." At length I reached those lines,

> " Sad happy race ! soon raised and soon depressed,
> Your days all passed in jeopardy and jest :
> Poor without prudence, with afflictions vain,
> Not warned by misery, nor enriched by gain."

" Shut the book," said Sir Walter, — " I can't stand more of this, — it will touch Terry to the very quick."

On the morning of Sunday, the 15th, he was again taken out into the little *pleasaunce,* and got as far as his favorite

terrace-walk between the garden and the river, from which
he seemed to survey the valley and the hills with much
satisfaction. On re-entering the house, he desired me to
read to him from the New Testament, and after that, he
again called for a little of Crabbe; but whatever I selected from that poet seemed to be listened to as if it made
part of some new volume published while he was in Italy.
He attended with this sense of novelty, even to the tale of
Phœbe Dawson, which, not many months before, he could
have repeated every line of, and which I chose for one of
these readings, because, as is known to every one, it had
formed the last solace of Mr. Fox's death-bed. On the contrary, his recollection of whatever I read from the Bible
appeared to be lively; and in the afternoon, when we made
his grandson, a child of six years, repeat some of Dr.
Watts's hymns by his chair, he seemed also to remember
them perfectly. That evening he heard the Church service, and when I was about to close the book, said, "Why
do you omit the visitation for the sick?"— which I added
accordingly.

On Monday he remained in bed and seemed extremely
feeble; but after breakfast on Tuesday, the 17th, he appeared revived somewhat, and was again wheeled about
on the turf. Presently he fell asleep in his chair, and after
dozing for perhaps half an hour, started awake, and shak-
ing the plaids we had put about him from off his shoulders, said: "This is sad idleness. I shall forget what I have
been thinking of, if I don't set it down now. Take me into
my own room, and fetch the keys of my desk." He repeated this so earnestly that we could not refuse; his
daughters went into his study, opened his writing-desk, and
laid paper and pens in the usual order, and I then moved
him through the hall and into the spot where he had always been accustomed to work. When the chair was
placed at the desk, and he found himself in the old posi-

tion, he smiled and thanked us, and said, "Now give me my pen, and leave me for a little to myself." Sophia put the pen into his hand, and he endeavored to close his fingers upon it, but they refused their office, — it dropped on the paper. He sank back among his pillows, silent tears rolling down his cheeks; but composing himself by and by, motioned to me to wheel him out of doors again. Laidlaw met us at the porch, and took his turn of the chair. Sir Walter, after a little while, again dropped into slumber. When he awakened, Laidlaw said to me, "Sir Walter has had a little repose." "No, Willie," said he, "no repose for Sir Walter but in the grave." The tears again rushed from his eyes. "Friends," said he, "don't let me expose myself — get me to bed, — that's the only place."

With this scene ended our glimpse of daylight. Sir Walter never, I think, left his room afterwards, and hardly his bed, except for an hour or two in the middle of the day; and after another week he was unable even for this. During a few days he was in a state of painful irritation, — and I saw realized all that he had himself prefigured in his description of the meeting between Crystal Croftangry and his paralytic friend. Dr. Ross came out from Edinburgh, bringing with him his wife, one of the dearest *nieces* of the Clerk's Table. Sir Walter with some difficulty recognized the Doctor, — but, on hearing Mrs. Ross's voice, exclaimed at once, "Is n't that Kate Hume?" These kind friends remained for two or three days with us. Clarkson's lancet was pronounced necessary, and the relief it afforded was, I am happy to say, very effectual.

After this he declined daily, but still there was great strength to be wasted, and the process was long. He seemed, however, to suffer no bodily pain, and his mind, though hopelessly obscured, appeared, when there was any symptom of consciousness, to be dwelling, with rare exceptions, on serious and solemn things; the accent of the voice

grave, sometimes awful, but never querulous, and very
seldom indicative of any angry or resentful thoughts. Now
and then he imagined himself to be administering justice
as Sheriff; and once or twice he seemed to be ordering
Tom Purdie about trees. A few times also, I am sorry to
say, we could perceive that his fancy was at Jedburgh, —
and *Burk Sir Walter* escaped him in a melancholy tone.
But commonly whatever we could follow him in was a
fragment of the Bible (especially the Prophecies of Isaiah
and the Book of Job) — of some petition in the litany —
or a verse of some psalm (in the old Scotch metrical ver-
sion) — or of some of the magnificent hymns of the Romish ritual in which he had always delighted, but which
probably hung on his memory now in connection with the
church services he had attended while in Italy. We very
often heard distinctly the cadence of the *Dies Iræ;* and I
think that the very last *stanza* that we could make out was
the first of a still greater favorite : —

> " Stabat Mater dolorosa,
> Juxta crucem lachrymosa,
> Dum pendebat Filius."

All this time he continued to recognize his daughters,
Laidlaw, and myself, whenever we spoke to him, — and
received every attention with a most touching thankfulness.
Mr. Clarkson, too, was always saluted with the old courtesy, though the cloud opened but a moment for him to
do so. Most truly might it be said that the gentleman survived the genius.

After two or three weeks had passed in this way, I was
obliged to leave Sir Walter for a single day, and go into
Edinburgh, to transact business on his account, with Mr.
Henry Cockburn (now Lord Cockburn), then Solicitor-
General for Scotland. The Scotch Reform Bill threw a
great burden of new duties and responsibilities upon the
Sheriffs ; and Scott's Sheriff-substitute, the Laird of Rae-

burn, not having been regularly educated for the law, found himself incompetent to encounter these novelties, especially as regarded the registration of voters, and other details connected with the recent enlargement of the electoral franchise. Under such circumstances, as no one but the Sheriff could appoint another Substitute, it became necessary for Sir Walter's family to communicate the state he was in in a formal manner to the Law Officers of the Crown; and the Lord Advocate (Mr. Jeffrey), in consequence, introduced and carried through Parliament a short bill (2 and 3 William IV. cap. 101), authorizing the government to appoint a new Sheriff of Selkirkshire, " during the incapacity or non-resignation of Sir Walter Scott." It was on this bill that the Solicitor-General had expressed a wish to converse with me; but there was little to be said, as the temporary nature of the new appointment gave no occasion for any pecuniary question; and, if that had been otherwise, the circumstances of the case would have rendered Sir Walter's family entirely indifferent upon such a subject. There can be no doubt that, if he had recovered in so far as to be capable of executing a resignation, the government would have considered it just to reward thirty-two years' faithful services by a retired allowance equivalent to his salary, — and as little that the government would have had sincere satisfaction in settling that matter in the shape most acceptable to himself. And perhaps (though I feel that it is scarcely worth while) I may as well here express my regret that a statement highly unjust and injurious should have found its way into the pages of some of Sir Walter's preceding biographers. These writers have thought fit to insinuate that there was a want of courtesy and respect on the part of the Lord Advocate, and the other official persons connected with this arrangement. On the contrary, nothing could be more handsome and delicate than the whole of their conduct in it; Mr

Cockburn could not have entered into the case with greater feeling and tenderness, had it concerned a brother of his own ; and when Mr. Jeffrey introduced his bill in the House of Commons, he used language so graceful and touching, that both Sir Robert Peel and Mr. Croker went across the House to thank him cordially for it.

Perceiving, towards the close of August, that the end was near, and thinking it very likely that Abbotsford might soon undergo many changes, and myself, at all events, never see it again, I felt a desire to have some image preserved of the interior apartments as occupied by their founder, and invited from Edinburgh for that purpose Sir Walter's dear friend, William Allan, — whose presence, I well knew, would, even under the circumstances of that time, be nowise troublesome to any of the family, but the contrary in all respects. Mr. Allan willingly complied, and executed a series of beautiful drawings, which may probably be engraved hereafter. He also shared our watchings, and witnessed all but the last moments. Sir Walter's cousins, the ladies of Ashestiel, came down frequently, for a day or two at a time, and did whatever sisterly affection could prompt, both for the sufferer and his daughters. Miss Barbara Scott (daughter of his Uncle Thomas) and Mrs. Scott of Harden did the like.

As I was dressing on the morning of Monday the 17th of September, Nicolson came into my room, and told me that his master had awoke in a state of composure and consciousness, and wished to see me immediately. I found him entirely himself, though in the last extreme of feebleness. His eye was clear and calm — every trace of the wild fire of delirium extinguished. "Lockhart," he said, " I may have but a minute to speak to you. My dear, be a good man — be virtuous — be religious — be a good man. Nothing else will give you any comfort when you come to lie here." He paused, and I said, " Shall I send for Sophia and Anne?" "No," said he, "don t disturb them. Poor souls! I know they were up all night — God bless you all." With this he sunk into a very tranquil sleep, and, indeed, he scarcely afterwards gave any sign of consciousness, except for an instant on the arrival of his sons. They, on learning that the scene was about to close, obtained a new leave of absence from their posts, and both reached Abbotsford on the 19th. About half past one P. M., on the 21st of September, Sir Walter breathed his last, in the presence of all his children. It was a beautiful day, — so warm that every window was wide open, — and so perfectly still that the sound of all others most delicious to his ear, the gentle ripple of the Tweed over its pebbles, was distinctly audible as we knelt around the bed, and his eldest son kissed and closed his eyes.

No sculptor ever modelled a more majestic image of repose.

His funeral was conducted in an unostentatious manner, but the attendance was very great. Few of his old friends then in Scotland were absent, and many, both friends and strangers, came from a great distance. His old domestics and foresters made it their petition that no hireling hand might assist in carrying his remains. They themselves bore the coffin to the hearse, and from the hearse to the grave. The pall-bearers were his sons, his son-in-law, and his little grandson; his cousins, Charles Scott of Nesbitt, James Scott of Jedburgh, (sons to his Uncle Thomas,) William Scott of Raeburn, Robert Rutherford, Clerk to the Signet, Colonel (now Sir James) Russell of Ashestiel, William Keith (brother to Sir Alexander Keith of Ravelstone), and the chief of his family, Hugh Scott of Harden, now Lord Polwarth.

When the company were assembled, according to the usual Scotch fashion, prayers were offered up by the very Reverend Dr. Baird, Principal of the University of Edin

burgh, and by the Rev. Dr. David Dickson, minister of St
Cuthbert's, who both expatiated in a very striking manner
on the virtuous example of the deceased.

The court-yard and all the precincts of Abbotsford were
crowded with uncovered spectators as the procession was
arranged; and as it advanced through Darnick and Melrose, and the adjacent villages, the whole population appeared at their doors in like manner, almost all in black.
The train of carriages extended, I understand, over more
than a mile, — the Yeomanry followed in great numbers
on horseback — and it was late in the day ere we reached
Dryburgh. Some accident, it was observed, had caused
the hearse to halt for several minutes on the summit of the
hill at Bemerside — exactly where a prospect of remarkable richness opens, and where Sir Walter always had been
accustomed to rein up his horse. The day was dark and
lowering, and the wind high.

The wide enclosure at the abbey of Dryburgh was
thronged with old and young; and when the coffin was
taken from the hearse, and again laid on the shoulders of
the afflicted serving-men, one deep sob burst from a thousand
lips. Mr. Archdeacon Williams read the Burial Service of
the Church of England; and thus, about half past five
o'clock, in the evening of Wednesday, the 26th September,
1832, the remains of Sir Walter Scott were laid by the
side of his wife, in the sepulchre of his ancestors, — "*in
sure and certain hope of the resurrection to eternal life,
through our Lord Jesus Christ; who shall change our vile
body that it may be like unto his glorious body, according to
the mighty working, whereby he is able to subdue all things
to himself.*"

THE NEW EDEN.

(WRITTEN FOR A HORTICULTURAL FESTIVAL.)

By OLIVER WENDELL HOLMES.

SCARCE could the parting ocean close,
   Seamed by the Mayflower's cleaving bow,
When o'er the rugged desert rose
   The waves that tracked the Pilgrim's plough.

Then sprang from many a rock-strewn field
   The rippling grass, the nodding grain,
Such growths as English meadows yield
   To scanty sun and frequent rain.

But when the fiery days were done,
   And Autumn brought his purple haze,
Then, kindling in the slanted sun,
   The hillsides gleamed with golden maize.

Nor treat his homely gift with scorn
   Whose fading memory scarce can save
The hillocks where he sowed his corn,
   The mounds that mark his nameless grave.

The food was scant, the fruits were few :
   A red-streak glistened here and there ;
Perchance in statelier precincts grew
   Some stern old Puritanic pear.

Austere in taste, and tough at core
Its unrelenting bulk was shed,
To ripen in the Pilgrim's store
When all the summer sweets were fled.

Such was his lot, to front the storm
With iron heart and marble brow,
Nor ripen till his earthly form
Was cast from life's autumnal bough.

But ever on the bleakest rock
We bid the brightest beacon glow,
And still upon the thorniest stock
The sweetest roses love to blow.

So on our rude and wintry soil
We feed the kindling flame of art,
And steal the tropic's blushing spoil
To bloom on Nature's icy heart.

See how the softening Mother's breast
Warms to her children's patient wiles, —
Her lips by loving Labor pressed
Break in a thousand dimpling smiles,

From when the flushing bud of June
Dawns with its first auroral hue,
Till shines the rounded harvest-moon,
And velvet dahlias drink the dew.

Nor these the only gifts she brings ;
Look where the laboring orchard groans,
And yields its beryl-threaded strings
For chestnut burs and hemlock cones.

Dear though the shadowy maple be,
  And dearer still the whispering pine,
Dearest yon russet-laden tree
  Browned by the heavy rubbing kine !

There childhood flung its venturous stone,
  And boyhood tried its daring climb,
And though our summer birds have flown
  It blooms as in the olden time.

Nor be the Fleming's pride forgot,
  With swinging drops and drooping bells,
Freckled and splashed with streak and spot,
  On the warm-breasted, sloping swells;

Nor Persia's painted garden-queen, —
  Frail Houri 'of the trellised wall, —
Her deep-cleft bosom scarfed with green, —
  Fairest to see, and first to fall.

———

When man provoked his mortal doom,
  And Eden trembled as he fell,
When blossoms sighed their last perfume,
  And branches waved their long farewell.

One sucker crept beneath the gate,
  One seed was wafted o'er the wall,
One bough sustained his trembling weight;
  These left the garden, — these were all.

And far o'er many a distant zone
  These wrecks of Eden still are flung;
The fruits that Paradise hath known
  Are still in earthly gardens hung.

Yes, by our own unstoried stream
  The pink-white apple-blossoms burst
That saw the young Euphrates gleam, —
  That Gihon's circling waters nursed.

For us the ambrosial pear displays
  The wealth its arching branches hold,
Bathed by a hundred summery days
  In floods of mingling fire and gold.

And here, where beauty's cheek of flame
  With morning's earliest beam is fed,
The sunset-painted peach may claim
  To rival its celestial red.

———

What though in some unmoistened vale
  The summer leaf grow brown and sere,
Say, shall our star of promise fail
  That circles half the rolling sphere,

From beaches salt with bitter spray,
  O'er prairies green with softest rain,
And ridges bright with evening's ray,
  To rocks that shade the stormless main ?

If by our slender-threaded streams
  The blade and leaf and blossom die,
If, drained by noontide's parching beams,
  The milky veins of Nature dry,

See, with her swelling bosom bare,
  Yon wild-eyed Sister in the West, —
The ring of Empire round her hair, —
  The Indian's wampum on her breast!

We saw the August sun descend,
    Day after day, with blood-red stain,
And the blue mountains dimly blend
    With smoke-wreaths from the burning plain;

Beneath the hot Sirocco's wings
    We sat and told the withering hours,
Till Heaven unsealed its azure springs,
    And bade them leap in flashing showers.

Yet in our Ishmael's thirst we knew
    The mercy of the Sovereign hand
Would pour the fountain's quickening dew
    To feed some harvest of the land.

No flaming swords of wrath surround
    Our second Garden of the Blest;
It spreads beyond its rocky bound,
    It climbs Nevada's glittering crest.

God keep the tempter from its gate!
    God shield the children, lest they fall
From their stern fathers' free estate,
    Till Ocean is its only wall!

CAMBRIDGE WORTHIES—THIRTY YEARS AGO.

By JAMES RUSSELL LOWELL.

CAMBRIDGE has long had its port, but the greater part of its maritime trade was, thirty years ago, intrusted to a single Argo, the sloop Harvard, which belonged to the College, and made annual voyages to that vague Orient, known as Down East, bringing back the wood that in those days gave to winter life at Harvard a crackle and a cheerfulness, for the loss of which the greater warmth of anthracite hardly compensates. New England life, to be genuine, must have in it some sentiment of the sea, — it was this instinct that printed the device of the pine-tree on the old money and the old flag, and these periodic ventures of the sloop Harvard made the old Viking fibre vibrate in the hearts of all the village boys. What a vista of mystery and adventure did her sailing open to us ! With what pride did we hail her return ! She was our scholiast upon Robinson Crusoe and the Mutiny of the Bounty. Her captain still lords it over our memories, the greatest sailor that ever sailed the seas, and we should not look at Sir John Franklin himself with such admiring interest as that with which we enhaloed some larger boy who had made a voyage in her, and had come back without braces to his trousers (*gallowses* we called them) and squirting ostentatiously the juice of that weed which still gave him little private returns of something very like sea-

sickness. All our shingle vessels were shaped and rigged by her, who was our glass of naval fashion and our mould of aquatic form. We had a secret and wild delight in believing that she carried a gun, and imagined her sending grape and canister among the treacherous savages of Old-town. Inspired by her were those first essays at navigation on the Winthrop duck-pond of the plucky boy who was afterward to serve two famous years before the mast.

The greater part of what is now Cambridgeport was then (in the native dialect) a *huckleberry pastur.* Woods were . not wanting on its outskirts, of pine, and oak, and maple, and the rarer tupelo with downward limbs. Its veins did not draw their blood from the quiet old heart of the village, but it had a distinct being of its own, and was rather a great caravansary than a suburb. The chief feature of the place was its inns, of which there were five, with vast barns and court-yards, which the railroad was to make as silent and deserted as the palaces of Nimroud. Great white-topped wagons, each drawn by double files of six or eight horses, with its dusty bucket swinging from the hinder axle, and its grim bull-dog trotting silent underneath, or in midsummer panting on the lofty perch beside the driver (how elevated thither baffled conjecture), brought all the wares and products of the country to their mart and seaport in Boston. These filled the inn-yards, or were ranged side by side under broad-roofed sheds, and far into the night the mirth of their lusty drivers clamored from the red-curtained bar-room, while the single lantern swaying to and fro in the black cavern of the stables made a Rembrandt of the group of hostlers and horses below. There were, beside the taverns, some huge square stores where groceries were sold, some houses, by whom or why inhabited was to us boys a problem, and, on the edge of the marsh, a currier's shop, where, at high tide, on a floating platform, men were always beating skins in a way to remind

one of Don Quixote's fulling-mills. Nor did these make
all the Port.   As there is always a Coming Man who never
comes, so there is a man who always comes (it may be
only a quarter of an hour) too early.   This man, as far as
the Port is concerned, was Rufus Davenport. Looking at
the marshy flats of Cambridge, and considering their near-
ness to Boston, he resolved that there should grow up a
suburban Venice.   Accordingly, the marshes were bought,
canals were dug, ample for the commerce of both Indies,
and four or five rows of brick houses were built to meet
the first wants of the wading settlers who were expected
to rush in — WHENCE?   This singular question had never
occurred to the enthusiastic projector.   There are laws
which govern human migrations quite beyond the control
of the speculator, as many a man with desirable building-
lots has discovered to his cost.   Why mortal men will pay
more for a chess-board square in that swamp than for an
acre on the breezy upland close by, who shall say?   And
again, why, having shown such a passion for *your* swamp,
they are so coy of *mine*, who shall say?   Not certainly any
one who, like Davenport, had got up too early for his generation.   If we could only carry that slow, imperturbable
old clock of Opportunity, that never strikes a second too
soon or too late, in our fobs, and push the hands forward
as we can those of our watches!   With a foreseeing economy of space which now seems ludicrous, the roofs of this
forlorn hope of houses were made flat that the swarming
population might have where to dry their clothes.   But
A. U. C. 30 showed the same view as A. U. C. 1, — only
that the brick blocks looked as if they had been struck by a
malaria.   The dull weed upholstered the decaying wharves,
and the only freight that heaped them was the kelp and
eelgrass left by higher floods.   Instead of a Venice, behold
a Torzelo!   The unfortunate projector took to the last
refuge of the unhappy, — bookmaking, — and bored the

reluctant public with what he called a Rightaim Testament,
prefaced by a recommendation from General Jackson, who
perhaps, from its title, took it for some treatise on ball-
practice.

But even Cambridgeport, my dear Storg, did not want
associations poetic and venerable. The stranger who took
the "Hourly" at Old Cambridge, if he were a physiognomist and student of character might perhaps have had
his curiosity excited by a person who mounted the coach
at the Port. So refined was his whole appearance, so
fastidiously neat his apparel, — but with a neatness that
seemed less the result of care and plan than a something
as proper to the man as whiteness to the lily, — that you
would have at once classed him with those individuals,
rarer than great captains and almost as rare as great poets,
whom nature sends into the world to fill the arduous office
of Gentleman. Were you ever emperor of that Barataria
which under your peaceful sceptre would present, of course,
a model of government, this remarkable person should be
Duke of Bienséance and Master of Ceremonies. There
are some men whom destiny has endowed with the faculty
of external neatness, whose clothes are repellant of dust
and mud, whose unwithering white neckcloths persevere
to the day's end, unappeasably seeing the sun go down
upon their starch, and whose linen makes you fancy them
heirs in the maternal line to the instincts of all the wash-
erwomen from Eve downward. There are others whose
inward natures possess this fatal cleanness, incapable of
moral dirt-spot. You are not long in discovering that the
stranger combines in himself both these properties. A
nimbus of hair, fine as an infant's, and early white, showing refinement of organization and the predominance of
the spiritual over the physical, undulated and floated around
a face that seemed like pale flame, and over which the flitting shades of expression chased each other, fugitive and

gleaming as waves upon a field of rye. It was a countenance that, without any beauty of feature, was very beautiful. I have said that it looked like pale flame, and can
find no other words for the impression it gave. Here was
a man all soul, whose body seemed only a lamp of finest
clay, whose service was to feed with magic oils, rare and
fragrant, that wavering fire which hovered over it. You,
who are an adept in such matters, would have detected
in the eyes that artist-look which seems to see pictures ever
in the air, and which, if it fall on you, makes you feel as
if all the world were a gallery, and yourself the rather
indifferent Portrait of a Gentleman hung therein. As the
stranger brushes by you in alighting, you detect a single
incongruity, — a smell of dead tobacco-smoke. You ask
his name, and the answer is, Mr. Allston.

"Mr. Allston!" and you resolve to note down at once
in your diary every look, every gesture, every word of the
great painter? Not in the least. You have the true An-
glo-Norman indifference, and most likely never think of
him again till you hear that one of his pictures has sold
for a great price, and then contrive to let your grandchildren know twice a week that you met him once in a
coach, and that he said, "Excuse me, sir," in a very Titian-
esque manner when he stumbled over your toes in getting
out. Hitherto Boswell is quite as unique as Shakespeare.
The country-gentleman, journeying up to London, inquires
of Mistress Davenant at the Oxford inn the name of his
pleasant companion of the night before. "Master Shakespeare, an 't please your worship," and the Justice, not without a sense of unbending, says, "Truly, a merry and
conceited gentleman!" It is lucky for the peace of great
men that the world seldom finds out contemporaneously
who its great men are, or, perhaps, that each man esteems
himself the fortunate he who shall draw the lot of memory from the helmet of the future. Had the eyes of some

Stratford burgess been achromatic telescopes capable of a perspective of two hundred years! But, even then, would not his record have been fuller of *says-Is* than of *says-hes?* Nevertheless, it is curious to consider from what infinitely varied points of view we might form our estimate of a great man's character, when we remember that he had his points of contact with the butcher, the baker, and the candle-stick-maker, as well as with the ingenious A, the sublime B, and the Right Honorable C. If it be true that no man ever clean forgets everything, and that the act of drowning (as is asserted) forthwith brightens up all those o'er-rusted impressions, would it not be a curious experiment, if, after a remarkable person's death, the public, eager for minutest particulars, should gather together all who had ever been brought into relations with him, and, submerging them to the hair's-breadth hitherward of the drowning-point, subject them to strict cross-examination by the Humane Society, as soon as they became conscious between the resuscitating blankets? All of us probably have brushed against destiny in the street, have shaken hands with it, fallen asleep with it in railway carriages, and knocked heads with it in some one or other of its yet unrecognized incarnations.

Will it seem like presenting a tract to a *colporteur*, my dear Storg, if I say a word or two about an artist to you over there in Italy? Be patient, and leave your button in my grasp yet a little longer. A person whose opinion is worth having once said to me, that, however one's opinions might be modified by going to Europe, one always came back with a higher esteem for Allston. Certainly he is thus far the greatest English painter of historical subjects. And only consider how strong must have been the artistic bias in him to have made him a painter at all under the circumstances. There were no traditions of art, so necessary for guidance and inspiration. Blackburn, Smibert, Copley, Trumbull, Stuart, — it was, after all, but a Brentford scep-

tre which their heirs could aspire to, and theirs were not
names to conjure with, like those through which Fame, as
through a silver trumpet, had blown for three centuries.
Copley and Stuart were both remarkable men, but the one
painted like an inspired silk-mercer, and the other seems to
have mixed his colors with the claret of which he and his
generation were so fond. And what could a successful
artist hope for at that time beyond the mere wages of his
work? His pictures would hang in cramped back-parlors,
between deadly cross-fires of lights, sure of the garret or
the auction-room erelong, in a country where the nomad
population carry no household gods with them but their five
wits and their ten fingers. As a race, we care nothing
about Art, but the Puritan and the Quaker are the only
Anglo-Saxons who have had pluck enough to confess it. If
it were surprising that Allston should have become a painter
at all, how almost miraculous that he should have been a
great and original one. We call him original deliberately,
because, though his school is essentially Italian, it is of less
consequence where a man buys his tools, than what use he
makes of them. Enough English artists went to Italy and
came back painting history in a very Anglo-Saxon manner,
and creating a school as melodramatic as the French, without its perfection in technicalities. But Allston carried
thither a nature open on the Southern side, and brought
it back so steeped in rich Italian sunshine that the east
winds (whether physical or intellectual) of Boston and the
dusts of Cambridgeport assailed it in vain. To that bare
wooden studio one might go to breathe Venetian air, and
better yet, the very spirit wherein the elder brothers of Art
labored, etherealized by metaphysical speculation, and sub-
limed by religious fervor. The beautiful old man! Here
was genius with no volcanic explosions (the mechanic result
of vulgar gunpowder often), but lovely as a Lapland night:
here was fame, not sought after nor worn in any cheap

French fashion as a ribbon at the button-hole, but so gentle, so retiring, that it seemed no more than an assured and emboldened modesty; here was ambition, undebased by rivalry and incapable of the downward look; and all these massed and harmonized together into a purity and depth of character, into a *tone*, which made the daily life of the man the greatest masterpiece of the artist.

But let us go to the Old Town. Thirty years since, the Muster and the Cornwallis allowed some vent to those natural instincts which Puritanism scotched, but not killed. The Cornwallis had entered upon the estates of the old Guy Fawkes procession, confiscated by the Revolution. It was a masquerade, in which that grave and suppressed humor of which the Yankees are fuller than other people, burst through all restraints, and disported itself in all the wildest vagaries of fun. It' is a curious commentary on the artificiality of our lives, that men must be disguised and masked before they will venture into the obscurer corners of their individuality, and display the true features of their nature. One remarked it in the Carnival, and one especially noted it here among a race naturally self-restrained; for Silas, and Ezra, and Jonas were not only disguised as Redcoats, Continentals, and Indians, but not unfrequently disguised in drink also. It is a question whether the Lyceum, where the public is obliged to comprehend all vagrom men, supplies the place of the old popular amusements. A hundred and fifty years ago, Cotton Mather bewails the carnal attractions of the tavern and the training-field, and tells of an old Indian, who imperfectly understood the English tongue, but desperately mastered enough of it (when under sentence of death) to express a desire for instant hemp rather than listen to any more ghostly consolations. Puritanism — I am perfectly aware how great a debt we owe it — tried over again the old experiment of driving out nature with a pitchfork, and had the usual success. It was like a ship inwardly on fire, whose hatches must be kept hermetically battened down, for the admittance of an ounce of heaven's own natural air would explode it utterly. Morals can never be safely embodied in the constable. Polished, cultivated, fascinating Mephistophiles! it is for the ungovernable breakings-away of the soul from unnatural compressions that thou waitest with a patient smile. Then it is that thou offerest thy gentlemanly arm to unguarded youth for a pleasant stroll through the City of Destruction, and, as a special favor, introducest him to the bewitching Miss Circe, and to that model of the hospitable old English gentleman, Mr. Comus!

But the Muster and the Cornwallis were not peculiar to Cambridge. Commencement Day was. Saint Pedagogus was a worthy whose feast could be celebrated by men who quarrelled with minced-pies and blasphemed custard through the nose. The holiday preserved all the features of an English fair. Stations were marked out beforehand by the town constables, and distinguished by numbered stakes. These were assigned to the different vendors of small wares, and exhibitors of rarities, whose canvas booths, beginning at the market-place, sometimes half encircled the common with their jovial embrace. Now, all the Jehoiada-boxes in town were forced to give up all their rattling deposits of specie, if not through the legitimate orifice, then to the brute force of the hammer. For hither were come all the wonders of the world, making the Arabian Nights seem possible, and which we beheld for half price, not without mingled emotions, — pleasure at the economy, and shame at not paying the more manly fee. Here the mummy unveiled her withered charms, a more marvellous Ninon, still attractive in her three thousandth year. Here were the Siamese Twins — ah, if all such enforced and unnatural unions were made a show of! Here were the flying-horses (their supernatural effect injured — like that of some poems — by the visibility of the man who turned the crank), on which, as we tilted at the ring, we felt our shoulders tingle with the *accolade*, and heard the clink of golden spurs at our heels.   Are the realities of life ever worth half so much as its cheats? and are there any feasts half so filling at the price as those Barmecide ones spread for us by Imagination?   Hither came the Canadian giant, surreptitiously seen, without price, as he alighted, in broad day (giants were always foolish), at the tavern.   Hither came the great horse Columbus, with shoes two inches thick, and more wisely introduced by night.   In the trough of the town-pump might be seen the mermaid, its poor monkey's head carefully sustained above water for fear of drowning. There were dwarfs, also, who danced and sang, and many a proprietor regretted the transaudient properties of canvas, which allowed the frugal public to share in the melody without entering the booth.   Is it a slander of J. II., who reports that he once saw a deacon, eminent for psalmody, lingering near one of these vocal tents, and, with an assumed air of abstraction, furtively drinking in, with unhabitual ears, a song, not secular merely, but with a dash of libertinism! The New England proverb says, " All deacons are good, but — there's a difference in deacons."   On these days Snow became super-terranean, and had a stand in the square, and Lewis temperately contended with the stronger fascinations of egg-pop.   But space would fail me to make a catalogue of everything.   No doubt, Wisdom also, as usual, had her quiet booth at the corner of some street, without entrance-fee, and, even at that rate, got never a customer the whole day long.   For the bankrupt afternoon there were peep-shows, at a cent each.

But all these shows and their showers are as clean gone now as those of Cæsar and Timour and Napoleon, for which the world paid dearer.   They are utterly gone out, not leaving so much as a snuff behind, — as little thought of

now as that John Robins, who was once so considerable
a phenomenon as to be esteemed the last great Antichrist
and son of perdition by the entire sect of Muggletonians.
Were Commencement what it used to be, I should be
tempted to take a booth myself, and try an experiment
recommended by a satirist of some merit, whose works
were long ago dead and (I fear) deeded to boot : —

> " Menenius, thou who fain wouldst know how calmly men can pass
> Those biting portraits of themselves, disguised as fox or ass, —
> Go, borrow coin enough to buy a full-length psyche-glass,
> Engage a rather darkish room in some well-sought position,
> And let the town break out with bills, so much per head admission, —
> GREAT NATURAL CURIOSITY !! THE BIGGEST LIVING FOOL !!!
> Arrange your mirror cleverly, before it set a stool,
> Admit the public one by one, place each upon the seat,
> Draw up the curtain, let him look his fill, and then retreat :
> Smith mounts and takes a thorough view, then comes serenely down,
> Goes home and tells his wife the thing is curiously like Brown ;
> Brown goes and stares, and tells his wife the wonder's core and pith
> Is that 't is just the counterpart of that conceited Smith :
> Life calls us all to such a show ; Menenius, trust in me,
> While thou to see thy neighbor smil'st, he does the same for thee ! "

My dear Storg, would you come to my show, and, instead
of looking in my glass, insist on taking your money's worth
in staring at the exhibitor ?

Not least among the curiosities which the day brought
together, were some of the graduates, posthumous men, as
it were disentombed from country parishes and district
schools, but perennial also, in whom freshly survived all
the college jokes, and who had no intelligence later than
their Senior year. These had gathered to eat the college
dinner, and to get the Triennial Catalogue (their Libro d'oro)
referred to oftener than any volume but the Concordance.
Aspiring men they were, certainly, but in a right, unworldly
way ; this scholastic festival opening a peaceful path to the
ambition which might else have devasted mankind with
Prolusions on the Pentateuch, or Genealogies of the Dor-

mouse Family. For, since in the Academic processions the classes are ranked in the order of their graduation, and he has the best chance at the dinner who has the fewest teeth to eat it with, so by degrees there springs up a competition in longevity, the prize contended for being the oldest surviving graduateship. This is an office, it is true, without emolument, but having certain advantages, nevertheless. The incumbent, if he come to Commencement, is a prodigious lion, and commonly gets a paragraph in the newspapers once a year with the (fiftieth) last survivor of Washington's Life Guard. If a clergyman, he is expected to ask a blessing and return thanks at the dinner, a function which he performs with centenarian longanimity, as if he reckoned the ordinary life of man to be fivescore years, and that a grace must be long to reach so very far away as heaven. Accordingly, this silent race is watched, on the course of the catalogue, with an interest worthy of Newmarket; and, as star after star rises in that galaxy of death,* till one name is left alone, an oasis of life in the Stellar desert, it grows solemn. The natural feeling is reversed, and it is the solitary life that becomes sad and monitory, the Stylites, there, on the lonely top of his century-pillar, who has heard the passing-bell of youth, love, friendship, hope, — of everything but immitigable eld.

Dr. K. was President of the University then, a man of genius, but of genius that evaded utilization, a great water-power, but without rapids, and flowing with too smooth and gentle a current to be set turning wheels and whirling spindles. His was not that restless genius, of which the man seems to be merely the representative, and which wreaks itself in literature or politics, but of that milder sort, quite as genuine, and perhaps of more contemporaneous value, which *is* the man, permeating a whole life with placid force, and giving to word, look, and gesture a meaning only justifiable by our belief in a reserved power

of latent reinforcement. The man of talents possesses
them like so many tools, does his job with them, and there
an end ; but the man of genius is possessed by it, and it
makes him into a book or a life according to its whim.
Talent takes the existing moulds and makes its castings,
better or worse, of richer or baser metal, according to knack
and opportunity ; but genius is always shaping new ones
and runs the man in them, so that there is always that
human feel in its results which gives us a kindred thrill.
What it will make we can only conjecture, contented always
with knowing the infinite balance of possibility against
which it can draw at pleasure. Have you ever seen a
man whose check would be honored for a million pay his
toll of one cent, and has not that bit of copper, no bigger
than your own and piled with it by the careless tollman,
given you a tingling vision of what golden bridges *he* could
pass, into what Elysian regions of taste and enjoyment and
culture, barred to the rest of us ? Something like it is the
impression made by such characters as K.'s on those who
come in contact with them.

There was that in the soft and rounded (I had almost
said melting) outlines of his face which reminded one of
Chaucer. The head had a placid yet dignified droop like
his. He was an anachronism, fitter to have been Abbot of
Fountains or Bishop Golias, courtier and priest, humorist
and lord spiritual, all in one, than for the mastership of a
provincial college which combined with its purely scholastic
functions those of accountant and chief of police. For
keeping books he was incompetent, (unless it were those he
borrowed,) and the only discipline he exercised was by the
unobtrusive pressure of a gentlemanliness which rendered
insubordination to *him* impossible. But the world always
judges a man (and rightly enough, too) by his little faults
which he shows a hundred times a day, rather than by his
great virtues which he discloses perhaps but once in a life-

time and to a single person, nay, in proportion as they are rarer, and as he is nobler, is shier of letting their existence be known at all. He was one of those misplaced persons whose misfortune it is that their lives overlap two distinct eras, and are already so impregnated with one, that they can never be in healthy sympathy with the other. Born when the New England clergy were still an establishment and an aristocracy, and when office was almost always for life and often hereditary, he lived to be thrown upon a time when avocations of all colors might be shuffled together in the life of one man like a pack of cards, so that you could not prophesy that he who was ordained to-day might not accept a colonelcy of filibusters to-morrow. Such temperaments as his attach themselves like barnacles to what seems permanent, but presently the good ship Progress weighs anchor and whirls them away from drowsy tropic inlets to arctic waters of unnatural ice. To such crustaceous natures, created to cling upon the immemorial rock amid softest mosses, comes the bustling Nineteenth Century, and says, " Come, come, bestir yourself to be practical : get out of that old shell of yours forthwith ! "   Alas, to get out of the shell is to die !

One of the old travellers in South America tells of fishes that built their nests in trees (*piscium et summa hæsit genus ulmo*), and gives a print of the mother fish upon her nest, while her mate mounts perpendicularly to her without aid of legs or wings. Life shows plenty of such incongruities between a man's place and his nature, (not so easily got over as by the traveller's undoubting engraver,) and one cannot help fancying that K. was an instance in point. He never encountered, one would say, the attraction proper to draw out his native force. Certainly few men who impressed others so strongly, and of whom so many good things are remembered, left less behind them to justify contemporary estimates. He printed nothing, and was, perhaps, one of those the electric sparkles of whose brains, discharged naturally and healthily in conversation, refuse to pass through the non-conducting medium of the inkstand. His *ana* would make a delightful collection. One or two of his official ones will be in place here. Hearing that Porter's flip (which was exemplary) had too great an attraction for the collegians, he resolved to investigate the matter himself. Accordingly, entering the old inn one day, he called for a mug of it, and, having drunk it, said, " And so, Mr. Porter, the young gentlemen come to drink your flip, do they ? "

" Yes sir — sometimes."

" Ah, well, I should think they would. Good day, Mr. Porter," and departed, saying nothing more, for he always wisely allowed for the existence of a certain amount of human nature in ingenuous youth. At another time the " Harvard Washington " asked leave to go into Boston to a collation which had been offered them. " Certainly, young gentlemen," said the President, " but have you engaged any one to bring out your muskets ? " — the College being responsible for these weapons, which belonged to the State. Again, when a student came with a physician's certificate, and asked leave of absence, K. granted it at once, and then added, " By the way, Mr. ——, persons interested in the relation which exists between states of the atmosphere and health, have noticed a curious fact in regard to the climate of Cambridge, especially within the College limits, — the very small number of deaths in proportion to the cases of dangerous illness." This is told of Judge W., himself a wit, and capable of enjoying the humorous delicacy of the reproof.

Shall I take Brahmin Alcott's favorite word, and call him a dæmonic man ? No, the Latin *genius* is quite old-fashioned enough for me, means the same thing, and its derivative *geniality* expresses, moreover, the base of K.'s being.

How he suggested cloistered repose and quadrangles mossy with centurial associations! How easy he was, and how without creak was every movement of his mind! This life was good enough for him, and the next not too good. The gentlemanlike pervaded even his prayers. His were not the manners of a man of the world, nor of a man of the other world either, but both met in him to balance each other in a beautiful equilibrium. Praying, he leaned forward upon the pulpit-cushion as for conversation, and seemed to feel himself (without irreverence) on terms of friendly but courteous familiarity with Heaven. The expression of his face was that of tranquil contentment, and he appeared less to be supplicating expected mercies than thankful for those already found, as if he were saying the *gratias* in the refectory of the Abbey of Theleme. Under him flourished the Harvard Washington Corps, whose gyrating banner, inscribed *Tam Marti 'quam Mercurio* (*atqui magis Lyæo* should have been added), on the evening of training-days, was an accurate dynamometer of Willard's punch or Porter's flip. It was they who, after being royally entertained by a maiden lady of the town, entered in their orderly book a vote that Miss Blank was a gentleman. I see them now, returning from the imminent deadly breach of the law of Rechab, unable to form other than the serpentine line of beauty, while their officers, brotherly rather than imperious, instead of reprimanding, tearfully embraced the more eccentric wanderers from military precision. Under him the Med. Facs. took their equal place among the learned societies of Europe, numbering among their grateful honorary members Alexander, Emperor of all the Russias, who (if College legends may be trusted) sent them, in return for their diploma, a gift of medals, confiscated by the authorities. Under him the College fire-engine was vigilant and active in suppressing any tendency to spontaneous combustion among the Freshmen, or rushed wildly to imaginary

conflagrations, generally in a direction where punch was
to be had.. All these useful conductors for the natural
electricity of youth, dispersing it or turning it harmlessly
into the earth, are taken away now, wisely or not, is ques-
tionable.

An academic town, in whose atmosphere there is always
something antiseptic, seems naturally to draw to itself certain varieties and to preserve certain humors (in the Ben
Jonsonian sense) of character, — men who come not to study
so much as to be studied.   At the head-quarters of Washington once, and now of the Muses, lived C——, but before
the date of these recollections.   Here for seven years (as
the law was then) he made his house his castle, sunning
himself in his elbow-chair at the front-door, on that seventh
day, secure from every arrest but that of Death.   Here
long survived him his turbaned widow, studious only of Spi-
noza, and refusing to molest the canker-worms that annually
disleaved her elms, because we were all vermicular alike.
She had been a famous beauty once, but the canker years
had left her leafless too, and I used to wonder, as I saw her
sitting always alone at her accustomed window, whether she
were ever visited by the reproachful shade of him who (in
spite of Rosalind) died broken-hearted for her in her radiant youth.

And this reminds me of J. F., who, also crossed in love,
allowed no mortal eye to behold his face for many years.
The eremitic instinct is not peculiar to the Thebais, as many
a New England village can testify, and it is worthy of consideration that the Romish Church has not forgotten this
among her other points of intimate contact with human
nature.   F. became purely vespertinal, never stirring abroad
till after dark.   He occupied two rooms, migrating from one
to the other as the necessities of housewifery demanded,
and when it was requisite that he should put his signature
to any legal instrument, (for he was an anchorite of ample

means,) he wrapped himself in a blanket, allowing nothing to be seen but the hand which acted as scribe. What impressed us boys more than anything was the rumor that he had suffered his beard to grow, such an anti-Sheffieldism being almost unheard of in those days, and the peculiar ornament of man being associated in our minds with nothing more recent than the patriarchs and apostles, whose effigies we were obliged to solace ourselves with weekly in the Family Bible. He came out of his oysterhood at last, and I knew him well, a kind-hearted man, who gave annual sleigh-rides to the town paupers, and supplied the poorer children with school-books. His favorite topic of conversation was Eternity, and, like many other worthy persons, he used to fancy that meaning was an affair of aggregation, and that he doubled the intensity of what he said by the sole aid of the multiplication-table. "Eternity!" he used to say, "it is not a day; it is not a year; it is not a hundred years; it is not a thousand years; it is not a million years; no, sir" (the *sir* being thrown in to recall wandering attention), "it is not ten million years!" and so on, his enthusiasm becoming a mere frenzy when he got among his sextillions, till I sometimes wished he had continued in retirement. He used to sit at the open window during thunder-storms, and had a Grecian feeling about death by lightning. In a certain sense he had his desire, for he died suddenly, — not by fire from heaven, but by the red flash of apoplexy, leaving his whole estate to charitable uses.

If K. were out of place as president, that was not P. as Greek professor. Who that ever saw him can forget him, in his old age, like a lusty winter, frosty but kindly, with great silver spectacles of the heroic period, such as scarce twelve noses of these degenerate days could bear? He was a natural celibate, not dwelling "like the fly in the heart of the apple," but like a lonely bee, rather, absconding himself in Hymettian flowers, incapable of matrimony as a solitary palm-tree. There was not even a tradition of youthful disappointment. I fancy him arranging his scrupulous toilet, not for Amaryllis or Neæra, but, like Machiavelli, for the society of his beloved classics. His ears had needed no prophylactic wax to pass the Sirens' isle, nay, he would have kept them the wider open, studious of the dialect in which they sang, and perhaps triumphantly detecting the Æolic digamma in their lay. A thoroughly single man, single-minded, single-hearted, buttoning over his single heart a single-breasted surtout, and wearing always a hat of a single fashion, — did he in secret regard the dual number of his favorite language as a weakness? The son of an officer of distinction in the Revolutionary War, he mounted the pulpit with the erect port of a soldier, and carried his cane more in the fashion of a weapon than a staff, but with the point lowered in token of surrender to the peaceful proprieties of his calling. Yet sometimes the martial instincts would burst the cerements of black coat and clerical neckcloth, as once when the students had got into a fight upon the training-field, and the licentious soldiery, furious with rum, had driven them at point of bayonet to the College gates, and even threatened to lift their arms against the Muses' bower. Then, like Major Goffe at Deerfield, suddenly appeared the gray-haired P., all his father resurgent in him, and shouted, "Now, my lads, stand your ground; you're in the right now! don't let one of them get inside the College grounds!" Thus he allowed arms to get the better of the *toga*, but raised it, like the Prophet's breeches, into a banner, and carefully ushered resistance with a preamble of infringed right. Fidelity was his strong characteristic, and burned equally in him through a life of eighty-three years. He drilled himself till inflexible habit stood sentinel before all those postern-weaknesses which temperament leaves unbolted to temptation. A lover of the scholar's herb, yet loving freedom more, and knowing that the

animal appetites ever hold one hand behind them for Satan
to drop a bribe in, he would never have two cigars in his
house at once, but walked every day to the shop to fetch his
single diurnal solace.   Nor would he trust himself with two
on Saturdays, preferring (since he could not violate the Sabbath even by that infinitesimal traffic) to depend on Providential ravens, which were seldom wanting in the shape of
some black-coated friend who knew his need and honored
the scruple that occasioned it.   He was faithful also to his
old hats, in which appeared the constant service of the antique world, and which he preserved forever, piled like a
black pagoda under his dressing-table.   No scarecrow was
ever the residuary legatee of *his* beavers, though one of
them in any of the neighboring peach-orchards would have
been sovran against an attack of Freshmen.   He wore them
all in turn, getting through all in the course of the year, like
the sun through the 'signs of the Zodiac, modulating them
according to seasons and celestial phenomena, so that never
was spider-web or chickweed so sensitive a weather-gauge
as they.   Nor did his political party find him less loyal.
Taking all the tickets, he would seat himself apart, and carefully compare them with the list of regular nominations as
printed in his Daily Advertiser before he dropped his ballot
in the box.   In less ambitious moments, it almost seems to
me that I would rather have had that slow, conscientious
vote of P.'s alone, than have been chosen alderman of the
ward !

If you had walked to what was then Sweet Auburn, by
the pleasant Old Road, on some June morning thirty years
ago, you would, very likely, have met two other characteristic persons, both phantasmagoric now and belonging to the
Past.   Fifty years earlier, the scarlet-coated, rapiered figures of Vassall, Oliver, and Brattle creaked up and down
there on red-heeled shoes, lifting the ceremonious three-
cornered hat and offering the fugacious hospitalities of the

snuff-box. They are all shadowy alike now, not one of your Etruscan Lucumos or Roman consuls more so, my dear Storg. First is W., his *queue* slender and tapering like the tail of a violet crab, held out horizontally, by the high collar of his shepherd's-gray overcoat, whose style was of the latest when he studied at Leyden in his hot youth. The age of cheap clothes sees no more of those faithful old garments, as proper to their wearers, and as distinctive as the barks of trees, and by long use interpenetrated with their very nature. Nor do we see so many humors (still in the old sense) now that every man's soul belongs to the Public, as when social distinctions were more marked, and men felt that their personalities were their castles, in which they could entrench themselves against the world. Now-a-days men are shy of letting their true selves be seen, as if in some former life they had committed a crime, and were all the time afraid of discovery and arrest in this. Formerly they used to insist on your giving the wall to their peculiarities, and you may still find examples of it in the parson or the doctor of retired villages. One of W.'s oddities was touching. A little brook used to run across the street, and the sidewalk was carried over it by a broad stone. Of course, there is no brook now. What use did that little glimpse of ripple serve, where the children used to launch their chip fleets? W., in going over this stone, which gave a hollow resonance to the tread, used to strike upon it three times with his cane, and mutter Tom! Tom! Tom! I used to think he was only mimicking with his voice the sound of the blows, and possibly it was that sound which suggested his thought, — for he was remembering a favorite nephew prematurely dead. Perhaps Tom had sailed his boats there; perhaps the reverberation under the old man's foot hinted at the hollowness of life; perhaps the fleeting eddies of the water brought to mind the *fugaces annos*. W., like P., wore amazing spectacles, fit to transmit no smaller image than the page of mightiest folios of Dioscorides or Hercules de Saxoniâ, and rising full-disked upon the beholder like those prodigies of two moons at once, portending change to monarchs. The great collar disallowing any independent rotation of the head, I remember he used to turn his whole person in order to bring their *foci* to bear upon an object. One can fancy that terrified nature would have yielded up her secrets at once, without cross-examination, at their first glare. Through them he had gazed fondly into the great mare's-nest of Junius, publishing his observations upon the eggs found therein in a tall octavo. It was he who introduced vaccination to this Western World. He used to stop and say good morning kindly, and pat the shoulder of the blushing school-boy who now, with the fierce snow-storm wildering without, sits and remembers sadly those old meetings and partings in the June sunshine.

Then there was S., whose resounding "Haw! haw! haw! by George!" positively enlarged the income of every dweller in Cambridge. In downright, honest good cheer and good neighborhood, it was worth five hundred a year to every one of us. Its jovial thunders cleared the mental air of every sulky cloud. Perpetual childhood dwelt in him, the childhood of his native Southern France, and its fixed air was all the time bubbling up and sparkling and winking in his eyes. It seemed as if his placid old face were only a mask behind which a merry Cupid had ambushed himself, peeping out all the while, and ready to drop it when the play grew tiresome. Every word he uttered seemed to bo hilarious, no matter what the occasion. If he were sick and you visited him, if he had met with a misfortune (and there are few men so wise that they can look even at the back of a retiring sorrow with composure), it was all one; his great laugh went off as if it were set like an alarum-clock, to run down, whether he would or no, at a certain nick. Even after an ordinary *good-morning!* (especially if to an old pupil, and in French,) the wonderful *Haw! haw! haw! by George!* would burst upon you unexpectedly, like a salute of artillery on some holiday which you had forgotten. Everything was a joke to him, — that the oath of allegiance had been administered to him by your grandfather, — that he had taught Prescott his first Spanish (of which he was proud), — no matter what. Everything came to him marked by nature — *right side up, with care,* and he kept it so. The world to him, as to all of us, was like a medal, on the obverse of which is stamped the image of Joy, and on the reverse that of Care. S. never took the foolish pains to look at that other side, even if he knew its existence; much less would it have occurred to him to turn it into view and insist that his friends should look at it with him. Nor was this a mere outside good-humor; its source was deeper in a true Christian kindliness and amenity. Once when he had been knocked down by a tipsily-driven sleigh, and was urged to prosecute the offenders, — "No, no," he said, his wounds still fresh, "young blood! young blood! it must have its way; I was young myself." *Was!* few men come into life so young as S. went out. He landed in Boston (then the front-door of America) in '93, and, in honor of the ceremony, had his head powdered afresh and put on a suit of court-mourning before he set foot on the wharf. My fancy always dressed him in that violet silk, and his soul certainly wore a full court-suit. What was there ever like his bow? It was as if you had received a decoration, and could write yourself gentleman from that day forth. His hat rose, re-greeting your own, and having sailed through the stately curve of the old *régime,* sank gently back over that placid brain which harbored no thought less white than the powder which covered it. I have sometimes imagined that there was a graduated arc over his head, invisible to other eyes than his, by which he meted out to each his rightful share of castorial consideration. I carry in my memory three exemplary bows. The first is that of an old beggar, who already carrying in his hand a white hat, the gift of benevolence, took off the black one from his head also, and profoundly saluted me with both at once, giving me, in return for my alms, a dual benediction, puzzling as a nod from Janus Bifrons. The second I received from an old Cardinal who was taking his walk just outside the Porta San Giovanni at Rome. I paid him the courtesy due to his age and rank. Forthwith rose — first *the* Hat; second, the hat of his confessor; third, that of another priest who attended him; fourth, the fringed cocked-hat of his coachman; fifth and sixth, the ditto, ditto, of his two footmen. Here was an investment, indeed; six hundred per cent interest on a single bow! The third bow, worthy to be noted in one's almanac among the other *mirabilia*, was that of S. in which courtesy had mounted to the last round of her ladder, — and tried to draw it up after her.

But the genial veteran is gone even while I am writing this, and I will play Old Mortality no longer. Wandering among these recent graves, my dear friend, we may chance to —— but no, I will not end my sentence. I bid you heartily farewell!

BEETHOVEN.

A LETTER TO GOETHE.

By BETTINA VON ARNIM

IT is Beethoven of whom I will now speak to you, and with whom I have forgotten the world and you: true, I am not ripe for speaking, but I am nevertheless not mistaken when I say (what no one understands and believes) that he far surpasses all in mind, and whether we shall ever overtake him?—I doubt it! may he only live till that mighty and sublime enigma which lies within his spirit be matured to its highest perfection! Yes, may he reach his highest aim, then will he surely leave a key to heavenly knowledge in our hands which will bring us one step nearer to true happiness.

To you I may confess, that I believe in a divine magic, which is the element of mental nature; this magic does Beethoven exercise in his art; all relating to it which he can teach you is pure magic; each combination is the organization of a higher existence: and thus, too, does Beethoven feel himself to be the founder of a new sensual basis in spiritual life. You will understand what I mean to say by this, and what is true. Who could replace this spirit? from whom could we expect an equivalent? The whole business of mankind passes to and fro before him like clock-work; he alone produces freely from out himself the unforeseen, the uncreated. What is intercourse with

the world to him who ere the sunrise is already at his sacred work, and who after sunset scarcely looks around him, — who forgets to nourish his body, and is borne in his flight on the stream of inspiration far beyond the shores of that every-day life? He says himself: "When I open my eyes, I cannot but sigh, for what I see is against my religion, and I am compelled to despise the world, which has no presentiment that music is a higher revelation than all their wisdom and philosophy. Music is the wine which inspires new creations; and I am the Bacchus who presses out this noble wine for mankind, and makes them spirit-drunk; and then, when they are sober again, what have they not fished up to bring with them to dry land? I have no friend; I must live with myself alone; but I well know that God is nearer to me in my art than to others. I commune with him without dread; I have ever acknowledged and understood him; neither have I any fear for my music; it can meet no evil fate. He to whom it makes itself intelligible must become freed from all the wretchedness which others drag about with them." All this did Beethoven say to me the first time I saw him. A feeling of reverence penetrated me, as, with such friendly openness, he uttered his mind to me, who could have been only very unimportant to him. I was surprised, too, because I had been told he was very shy, and conversed with no one.

They were afraid to introduce me to him, and I was forced to find him out alone. He has three dwellings, in which he alternately secretes himself; one in the country, one in the town, and the third upon the bulwarks. Here I found him upon the third floor; unannounced, I entered, — he was seated at the piano; I mentioned my name: he was very friendly, and asked if I would hear a song that he had just composed; then he sung, shrill and piercing, so that the plaintiveness reacted upon the hearer, "Know'st thou the land." "It 's beautiful, is it not?" said he in

spired, "most beautiful! I will sing it again." He was
delighted at my cheerful praise. "Most men," said he, are
touched by something good, but they are no *artist-natures;*
artists are ardent, they do not weep." Then he sung another of your songs, to which he had a few days ago composed music, "Dry not the tears of eternal love." He
accompanied me home, and it was upon the way that he
said so many beautiful things upon art; withal he spoke so
loud, stood still so often upon the street, that some courage
was necessary to listen; he spoke passionately and much
too startlingly for me not also to forget that we were in the
street. They were much surprised to see me enter, with
him, in a large company assembled to dine with us. After
dinner, he placed himself, unasked, at the instrument, and
played long and wonderfully: his pride and genius were
both in ferment; under such excitement his spirit creates
the inconceivable, and his fingers perform the impossible.
Since this he comes every day, or I go to him. For this
I neglect parties, picture-galleries, theatres, and even St.
Stephen's tower itself. Beethoven says, "Ah! what should
you see there? I will fetch you, and towards evening we
will go through the Schönbrunn alley." Yesterday, I
walked with him in a splendid garden, in full blossom, all
the hot-houses open; the scent was overpowering. Beethoven stood still in the burning sun, and said, "Goethe's
poems maintain a powerful sway over me, not only by their
matter, but also their rhythm; I am disposed and excited
to compose by this language, which ever forms itself, as
through spirits, to more exalted order, already carrying
within itself the mystery of harmonies. Then, from the
focus of inspiration, I feel myself compelled to let the melody stream forth on all sides. I follow it,—passionately
overtake it again; I see it escape me, vanish amidst the
crowd of varied excitements,—soon I seize upon it again
with renewed passion; I cannot part from it,—with quick

rapture I multiply it, in every form of modulation, — and at the last moment, I triumph over the first musical thought, — see now, — that 's a symphony; — yes, music is indeed the mediator between the spiritual and sensual life. I should like to speak with Goethe upon this, if he would understand me. Melody is the sensual life of poetry. Do not the spiritual contents of a poem become sensual feeling through melody? Do we not in Mignon's song perceive its entire sensual frame of mind through melody? and does not this perception excite again to new productions? There, the spirit extends itself to unbounded universality, where all in all forms itself into a bed for the stream of feelings which take their rise in the simple musical thought, and which else would die unperceived away; *this* is harmony, this is expressed in my symphonies; the blending of various forms rolls on as in a bed to its goal. Then one feels that an Eternal, an Infinite, never quite to be embraced, lies in all that is spiritual; and although in my works I have always a feeling of success, yet I have an eternal hunger, — that what seemed exhausted with the last stroke of the drum with which I drive my enjoyment, my musical convictions, into the hearers, — to begin again like a child. Speak to Goethe of me, tell him he should hear my symphonies; he would then allow me to be right in saying that music is the only unembodied entrance into a higher sphere of knowledge which possesses man, but he will never be able to possess it. One must have rhythm in the mind to comprehend music in its essential being; music gives presentiment, inspiration of heavenly knowledge; and that which the spirit feels sensual in it is the embodying of spiritual knowledge. Although the spirits live upon music, as one lives upon air, yet it is something else spiritually to understand it; but the more the soul draws out of it its sensual nourishment, the more ripe does the spirit become for a happy intelligence with it. But few attain to this; for,

as thousands engage themselves for love's sake, and among
these thousands love does not once reveal itself, although
they all occupy **themselves of love, in** like **manner do**
thousands hold communion **with** music, and do not possess
its revelation: signs of **an elevated moral sense** form, too,
the groundwork **of** music, **as of every art. All** genuine
invention is **a** moral progress. To subject **one's** self to
music's unsearchable laws; by virtue of these laws **to curb**
and guide the spirit, so that it pours forth these revelations,
this is the isolating principle of art; **to be** dissolved in its
revelations, this is abandonment to genius, which tranquilly
exercises its authority **over the** delirium **of unbridled powers; and** thus **grants to fancy the** highest efficacy. **Thus
does art** ever represent divinity, **and that** which **stands in**
human relation to it is religion; what **we acquire through**
art is from God, a divine suggestion, **which sets up a goal**
for human capacities, **which the spirit** attains.

" **We do not** know **what grants us** knowledge; **the firmly**
enclosed seed needs the **moist,** warm, **electric soil to grow,**
think, express itself. **Music is the electric soil** in which the
spirit lives, thinks, **invents. Philosophy is the** precipitation
of its electric spirit; **and its** necessity, **which will ground**
everything upon a first principle, **is supplied by** music;
and although the **spirit be not** master **of that** which **it**
creates through music, yet is **it blessed in this creation;**
in this manner, **too, is** every **creation of art independent;**
mightier **than the artist himself, and returns by its appearance back to the divine; and is only connected with men,
in so much as it bears witness to the divine mediation
in** him.

" Music **gives to the spirit relation to harmony. A**
thought **abstracted has still the feeling of communion, of**
affinity, **in the spirit; thus each thought in music is in the**
most intimate, **inseparable affinity with the communion of
harmony, which is unity.**

"The electric excites the spirit to musical, fluent, streaming production.

"I am of electric nature. I must break off with my unwitnessed wisdom, else I shall miss the rehearsal; write to Goethe about me, if you understand me; but I can answer nothing, and I will willingly let myself be instructed by him." I promised him to write to you all, as well as I could understand it. He took me to a grand rehearsal, with full orchestra, — there I sat in the wide, unlighted space, in a box quite alone; single gleams stole through the crevices and knot-holes, in which a stream of bright sparks were dancing, like so many streets of light, peopled by happy spirits.

There, then, I saw this mighty spirit exercise his rule. O Goethe! no emperor and no king feels such entire consciousness of his power, and that all power proceeds from him, as this Beethoven, who just now, in the garden, in vain sought out the source from which he receives it all; did I understand him as I feel him, then I should know everything. There he stood so firmly resolved, — his gestures, his countenance, expressed the completion of his creation; he prevented each error, each misconception; not a breath was voluntary; all, by the genial presence of his spirit, set in the most regulated activity. One could prophesy that such a spirit, in its later perfection, would step forth again as ruler of the earth.

A SONG FROM THE ARCADIA.

By SIR PHILIP SIDNEY.

SINCE Nature's works be good, and death doth serve
    As Nature's work : why should we fear to die ?
Since fear is vain but when it may preserve :
Why should we fear that which we cannot fly ?

Fear is more pain than is the pain it fears,
Disarming human minds of native might :
While each conceit an ugly figure bears,
Which were not ill, well viewed in reason's light.

Our only eyes, which dimmed with passions be,
And scarce discern the dawn of coming day,
Let them be cleared, and now begin to see,
Our life is but a step in dusty way.

Then let us hold the bliss of peaceful mind,
Since this we feel, great loss we cannot find.

Cambridge : Stereotyped and Printed by Welch, Bigelow, & Co.

A SABBATH SUMMER NOON.

By WILLIAM MOTHERWELL.

THE calmness of this noontide hour,
  The shadow of this wood,
The fragrance of each wilding flower,
  Are marvellously good ;
O, here crazed spirits breathe the balm
  Of Nature's solitude !

It is a most delicious calm
  That resteth everywhere,—
The holiness of soul-sung psalm,
  Of felt but voiceless prayer !
With hearts too full to speak their bliss,
  God's creatures silent are.

They silent are ; but not the less
  In this most tranquil hour
Of deep, unbroken dreaminess,
  They own that Love and Power
Which, like the softest sunshine, rests
  On every leaf and flower.

How silent are the song-filled nests
  That crowd this drowsy tree,—

www.ingramcontent.com/pod-product-compliance
Lightning Source LLC
Chambersburg PA
CBHW051126120726
47905CB00005B/1444